TRAITOR'S GATE;

OR,

The Headsman of the Old Tower.

BEAUTIFULLY ILLUSTRATED.

COMPLETE.

LONDON:
"BOYS OF ENGLAND" OFFICE, 173, FLEET STREET, E.C.,
AND ALL BOOKSELLERS.

"THE MAN LEAPT FORWARD AND DRAGGED BARCALLY FROM THE SADDLE."

TRAITOR'S GATE;

OR,

THE HEADSMAN OF THE OLD TOWER.

"Ye Towers of Julius, London's lasting shame,
With many a foul and midnight murder fed."—*Gray.*

By the Author of "The Captain of the Guard," "Dark Deeds of Old London," &c., &c. &c.

CHAPTER I.

INTRODUCES THE HEADSMAN AND QUICKSILVER—OF THE DREADFUL DEED COMMITTED AT THE TRAITOR'S GATE, AND OF THE STORY TOLD BY THE HEADSMAN.

It was close upon the hour of ten, on the night of the 24th of August, 1585, and, so far as the City of London proper was concerned, it was a night of intense darkness and silence.

Not a star peeped from the black, lowering clouds, that for hours had foretold a storm, which, when it burst, would prove of no common order.

No lights of any kind lit up the deserted streets, nor were the twinkling rays of a single lantern reflected in the black waters of the Thames.

The gloomy walls of the Tower of London looked more gloomy and forbidding than ever on this particular night.

It seemed as if the sentinels had forgotten to continue their usual monotonous pacing, for they stood leaning on their arms against the hoary walls, and ever and anon they cast anxious glances upward, as if wondering whether the threatened storm would burst before they could be relieved.

Just after the hour of ten had struck, the forerunners of the storm appeared.

As it seemed to the sentinels, a mass of black clouds immediately above the old bridge was suddenly riven asunder, and there darted through it several flashes of forked lightning, which, rushing along the black sky, finally plunged into the bosom of the Thames.

These flashes were followed by a peal of thunder which was perfectly deafening.

Again the brilliant zigzag lightning lit up the inky sky, and again did heaven's artillery thunder forth.

It was followed by something which made even the grim sentinels start.

That was a wild burst of laughter.

Again it rang out, until the whole fortress resounded with it.

At this moment Barcally, one of the chief warders, passed along the path beneath the Bell Tower, and he observed several men looking upward.

"What is this?" he asked. "Who dares to laugh at such a storm?"

Before the men could reply, another laugh rang out. Then a shriek followed.

"Ah! I should know that howl," said Barcally, pointing upward. "Behold—there—just on the left-hand side of the top of the tower!"

The men looked, and simultaneously each cried—

"Quicksilver!"

And then they held their breath in astonishment and horror.

Far up on the sloping roof of the Bell Tower, and balancing himself on the very edge, sat a remarkable figure.

So very small was it, that a stranger might have taken it for a goodly-sized monkey.

This little creature was the companion of the grim, gloomy headsman, Jerome Lomew, but more generally known by the significant title of "Black Lomew," of whom more anon.

"I said it would come!" cried Quicksilver, with another burst of laughter; "I said it would come! Look, look! Mark well the fierce flashes. Ah! I believe one of the houses on the bridge has been struck!"

"Fool!" thundered Barcally, "if you do not instantly come down, I will report you to the lieutenant. Come down, thou hideous little imp! Do you want to be struck by the lightning? Come down, instantly!"

But Quicksilver paid no heed to the command.

He appeared to be intensely amused at the flashes of lightning and the peals of thunder.

"The question is," said one of the soldiers, "how did he get up there?"

Hearing the noise, several other soldiers collected, some to laugh at the antics of the strange little creature, others to advise him to come down, if he valued his life.

But in defiance of all he remained where he was for some few minutes longer, when the overcharged clouds sent forth torrents of rain.

Quicksilver had the greatest horror of getting wet, and so, turning, he dexterously seized one of the rain pipes, and scrambled hand-under-hand down.

Barcally was about to seize him, when he was interrupted by the sudden appearance of a tall, black figure.

So noiselessly had it approached that no one noticed it.

It was Lomew, the headsman.

Reaching out his powerful hand, he seized upon Quicksilver, and treated him to such a violent shaking that the little imp fairly yelled for mercy.

"I heard you were perched up aloft," growled Lomew, "and that instead of doing my bidding. I warrant me you have not delivered my message at all. Have you?"

"No—no. I—I was about to."

"What message did you charge him with?" asked Barcally.

"One to you. It was that I expected a visitor, and that I had the lieutenant's permission to bring him to my chamber."

"Very well, Master Lomew, I doubt not your word. And pray, which way, think you, your friend will arrive?"

"Traitor's Gate."

"What!" cried Barcally, in astonishment. "Traitor's Gate? Impossible! The gate cannot be opened for such a purpose. Do you say that the lieutenant gave you permission to introduce a friend into the Tower by way of Traitor's Gate?"

"I say nothing of the sort. I never said which way my friend would come, nor was the lieutenant curious enough to ask me. I simply sent Quicksilver with a message to you, so that in the event of my friend's boat being observed, you would know that all was right."

All further conversation was interrupted by the rain, which came down in tremendous sheets.

Lomew took Quicksilver in his arms and carried him below.

He quickly reached his apartments, three small vaulted chambers communicating with each other, and used as a sleeping room, a sitting room, and a general room respectively.

If anything, the "general room" was the largest, and contained a collection of extraordinary objects.

The walls were covered with hideous instruments of torture, and so arranged were they that one might have mistaken the place for a kind of museum.

Ponderous chains, rings, and bolts depended from the wall, as well as several rusty weapons.

But the principal objects which struck the eye immediately on passing through the low, narrow doorway, were half-a-dozen axes arranged in a row, and exactly at the head of a large treadle grindstone.

As bright and glittering as steel could be brought, were these dreadful axes, and the edges were as keen as those of razors.

In these terrible implements Lomew took a strange delight, and he was never tired of toying with them; and, when it so suited him, he could perform many a strange trick with them.

Into the sitting room (why it should be so called, heaven only knows, for it was as unlike a sitting room as anything could possibly be, for, like the "general room," it was filled with an extraordinary collection of articles) the headsman took Quicksilver, and having placed him on a stool, he seated himself on a huge log immediately opposite him.

A most remarkable contrast these two presented.

Lomew was at least six feet in height, and though not stout—as stoutness was considered in those days—he was possessed of a broad, powerful chest and enormous limbs, which denoted tremendous strength.

His head was small, but of a somewhat peculiar shape.

No beard or moustache had this man, and his hair was kept closely cropped to his head.

His eyes were large and black, but somewhat sunken in their sockets; his complexion was intensely dark (hence his nickname), and the expression which always rested upon his face was that of the most profound melancholy.

In every respect this huge, grim, herculean headsman of the Tower of London was a most remarkable man.

It was said that that broad chest held a terrible secret—a secret over which Lomew was ever brooding.

However, the Black Headsman was never heard to utter a sentence respecting his family or his antecedents.

To some extent we have already described Quicksilver.

Surely he was about the smallest specimen of humanity that man ever clapped eyes on.

When he stood perfectly upright he by no means reached the buckle of the belt which encircled the waist of the headsman.

But because he was so small a specimen of mankind—and he had passed his twenty-fifth birthday—it must not be supposed that he was deficient in personal attractions.

On the contrary, he was what the ladies regarded as a very "pretty little fellow."

The unfortunate prisoners within this gloomy fortress, many of whom would leave it but to halt for ever on Tower Green, passed many a pleasant hour with tiny Quicksilver, whose little head contained volumes of entertaining dialogue.

He was as daring as a soldier, and as active as a sailor.

Lomew had brought him from abroad—at least, so he said—when he was but an infant, and it was his rapid movements which had caused him to receive the name of Quicksilver.

Quicksilver he called himself, but on State, or any other uncommon occasion, he was

Sir Quicksilver.

"Quicksilver," said Lomew, "you know the state of mind in which I am at this present moment, and yet you must needs go and make yourself a fool instead of doing my bidding."

"I crave your pardon, worshipful Jerome," replied Quicksilver. "Upon my word of honour as a gentleman, and a supposed descendant of the blood royal, your message should have been delivered in but a few more moments. The fact is, that while searching for surly Barcally, the long-threatened storm thought fit to burst, and as you know I am a great lover of a downright good storm, why your message momentarily slipped my memory, and I ascended to the Bell Tower to have a good look over the Thames."

"And amuse yourself and alarm the inmates of the Tower by your unearthly shrieks of laughter. Remember, Quicksilver, no more of this, or you will bring upon yourself my displeasure. But now listen to me— Ha! what is that?"

"Thunder, and 'tis louder than ever. Phew! this *is* a storm with a vengeance. I take it that he will not come."

"But he *must* come. Now look you, Quicksilver. You know the little circular window above the steps?"

"At Traitor's Gate? Yes."

"Well, if I place you up at the window, you can watch and tell me when you see a skiff approach."

"I can see that you are more anxious than you would care to say."

"You are right; I *am* anxious. I know that he is certain to come by way of the Thames. But a little while back, and the river was almost as calm as the water in a ditch; now it rushes onward to the great ocean with resistless fury. A boat passing through either one of the arches of the bridge stands a good chance of being smashed into splinters."

"You are indeed right. Well, assist me to the window, and I will keep a sharp look-out. But would it not be far better if you waited on the steps?"

"It would; but then I should not like the lieutenant to *know* that I waited there."

"I understand. Come, then, I am ready."

Lomew rose, and taking Quicksilver in his arms, placed him on his shoulder, and left the chamber.

The ordinary passages it was not necessary to traverse, as both the headsman and Quicksilver were familiar with the secret ones, and several of these were used to reach the little ante-room, the high circular window in which overlooked the water-gate.

Lomew placed Quicksilver high over his head, and thus enabled him to scramble on to the little ledge of stone.

"Are you safe?" queried Lomew. "Can you see well?"

"Not very well, for the Traitor's Gate casts such a deep shadow. Still the Thames is every now and then brilliantly illuminated, for the lightning is playing on it more vividly than ever."

At that moment a fearful peal of thunder burst forth, which seemed to make the very tower tremble.

"Where will you wait!" asked Quicksilver.

"I will wait here, close by the door, ready to open the gate."

Half-an-hour passed, and the terrible storm still raged.

Presently, what seemed to be the sound of a shot rang out.

It was followed by another, and yet another; and Quicksilver made out that those shots must have been fired close by Traitor's Gate.

Then a loud voice cried out—

"In heaven's name, I pray you, help! Help!"

Instantly Quicksilver's shrill voice rang out, and Jerome dashed to the steps and placed his hand on the huge lever which drew back the massive water-gate.

As he did so, the brilliant flash of a pistol lit up the gloomy archway, and showed the headsman that there were two skiffs without the gate.

Before he could pull the lever, the loud clash of steel mingled with the roll of the thunder.

The flashing of the blades, wielded by determined hands, was as swift as the flashes of lightning which every instant illuminated the black river.

It was easy to see that the occupant of the first skiff had been pursued.

And whereas there was but one person in the first boat, in the other there were three.

The headsman, who was not perceived by the combatants, quickly pulled the gate open, and, without hesitation, plunged into the water.

Just as he did so, another cry—a wild, despairing cry of mortal agony—fell upon his ears, and the occupant of the first skiff fell from the boat with a loud splash into the water.

The headsman snatched his dagger from its sheath and plunged forward.

"Push out!" cried the man who had struck the blow with his sword. "Push out—quick!"

But it was too late.

The mighty hands of the headsman seized the prow of the boat, and exerting all his strength, he overturned it and hurled the occupants into the water.

Instantly a struggle for life was commenced.

One of the men managed to clutch the woodwork of the gate, but he had scarcely succeeded in this before the headsman seized him by the throat.

"Villain!" he hissed, "it was you who struck the blow—you! No mercy shall be shown to the assassin—none! Thus do I avenge your victim's death."

The dagger was upraised and instantly buried in the man's heart.

The fearful cry which left his lips was distinctly heard by the sentinels about St. Thomas' Tower, and at once the call to arms was given.

It was the first they had unmistakably heard of what had been transpiring, for the thunder had, to their ears, deadened all previous sounds.

In the meantime the two other men, by exerting all their strength, had righted the boat and scrambled in.

Guiding themselves by the wall, they had managed to push out some distance from Traitor's Gate—too far for the headsman to follow, even if he had felt inclined.

But he was not.

The man who had fallen from the first skiff commanded his attention.

He found him feebly clutching at a piece of iron chain fastened in the wall.

He was so exhausted that he was unable to utter even a moan.

The headsman took him in his arms, and carrying him to the steps, laid him tenderly down on the top, as a number of the soldiers, carrying links and lanterns, and with their arms ready in case of necessity, came upon the scene.

Another few seconds, and loud cries of "Stand back! Stand back!" rang out.

The soldiers opened in the centre, and allowed the lieutenant, Sir Edward Warner, to approach.

"In heaven's name!" he said, "what is this? What dreadful deed has been committed?"

The headsman, who was kneeling on the wet steps, looked up as this question was asked, and those around him were startled to behold tears glistening in his eyes.

"This," he said, in low tones, which quivered with emotion—"this is murder."

"Murder!" gasped the lieutenant, starting back a pace. "Murder! A murder committed here, within the very shadow of Traitor's Gate?"

"Even so. The blow was struck ere I could prevent it; but it was immediately avenged, for I plunged my dagger into the heart of the villain who committed the foul crime."

"All this is a mystery to me, Master Lomew. I counsel you to repair with all speed to my apartments, so that you may make me acquainted with the meaning of all. By whose authority was Traitor's Gate opened?"

"I had your permission for the visit of a friend," replied Lomew; "but I took it upon myself to admit him by way of Traitor's Gate, thinking that he would thus be entirely unobserved."

"But why did you wish to conceal your friend's identity?"

"I have a very excellent reason, Sir Edward," replied the headsman, in gloomy tones, as he bent over and looked earnestly into his friend's face.

"Think you that he is dead?"

"Yes, dead—dead!" replied the headsman, bitterly. "He has just breathed his last."

"Your friend is richly attired," continued Sir Edward, as he caught the glitter of gold lace.

"He is," replied the headsman, as he hastily drew the heavy but wet cloak over the murdered youth. "But I will wait upon you, Sir Edward, and will give you particulars; and, at the same time, I will crave your pardon for the liberty I took in opening Traitor's Gate without your permission."

"As to that, I freely give you my pardon. But I wish all of you to understand that these gates must never, under any circumstances, be opened except for State purposes. There is an old saying, Master Lomew—a warning with which I should have thought you were familiar. It is—

"'Unless a prisoner of the State,
Try not to pass this gloomy gate;
Or, be it early, be it late,
Thou'lt not escape a tragic fate.'"

"Familiar enough was I with the warning," answered the headsman; "but I remembered it not at the time. Had I done so, however, I should not have paid heed to it."

By this time he had lifted the victim of this sudden attack, and without another word he proceeded towards his own apartments, being joined on the way by Quicksilver.

The lieutenant stood for some few seconds on the top of the steps, looking down into the black water.

He was evidently lost in reflection.

Barcally approached him, and respectfully touching his hat, he said—

"Sir Edward, yonder is the body of the man stricken dead by the hand of the headsman."

"Take the body to the headsman's chamber," replied Sir Edward. "I intend to fully investigate this matter."

The headsman carried his friend to his bedchamber, and laid him carefully down.

Then tenderly he removed the cloak, and handed it to Quicksilver.

"Search it carefully," he said.

He then secured the door.

But he had no sooner shot the bolt than a knock came upon the portal.

"Who knocks?" asked Lomew.

"'Tis I—the lieutenant," was the reply.

At once the headsman reopened the door.

"I am come to converse with you upon this matter," said the lieutenant, gravely.

"Oh, Sir Edward!" replied the headsman, "surely you will not deign to honour my poor apartment with your presence?"

"I have not come to gaze upon the contents of your apartment, but to investigate this mysterious affair. Reclose the door, so that we shall be entirely free from interruption."

Lomew did so.

The lieutenant, who was a compassionate man, slowly approached the bed.

But as his eyes rested upon the face of the dead, he gave utterance to a loud, startled cry.

"Gracious Providence!" he exclaimed. "What is this? Surely mine eyes deceive me. Surely this is—"

"Hush! I conjure you!" interrupted the headsman, hastily; "utter not his name. Sir Edward, I see that you recognise this poor youth, but if you utter his name let it be in a whisper."

"You say well, Lomew. I will be cautious. But listen," and he pointed to the lifeless form. "Is this a portion of the mystery which I have always thought surrounded you?"

"It is," replied the headsman. "Heaven help me—it is!"

"I have searched the cloak," said Quicksilver; "but nothing is there."

"As I expected," said the headsman, bitterly. "And I have no doubt nothing will be found on his person."

The lieutenant was about to speak, when a knocking was heard.

"They have brought the body of the man you slew," said Sir Edward; "you had better bring it in. Perchance something of importance may be found upon it."

Lomew opened the door, and three or four soldiers, headed by Barcally, entered.

The latter cast a hasty glance towards the bed, as if anxious to look upon the features of the person lying thereon.

But Quicksilver had thoughtfully thrown the cloak over the body, and thus effectually hid all, with the exception of the shoes, from sight.

After the body of the assassin had been placed upon the floor, the soldiers lingered; but the lieutenant, suddenly turning towards them, sternly pointed to the door, and they were quickly on the other side of it, and it was again locked.

Quicksilver, by Lomew's orders, now carefully searched the body of the assassin, but nothing whatever was found in the shape of papers.

"Sir Edward," said the headsman, "there is a gulf between our positions —a gulf so wide that it could never be bridged. Therefore I fear to speak as I would like to."

"Fear nothing. Speak out, and if I can advise you I will, most freely."

"Sir Edward," continued the headsman, after a moments reflection, during which his eyes were fixed upon the pale, but strikingly handsome face of the youth lying still in death upon the bed, "you at once recognised that youth as the son of Lord Fitzwilliam Herbert, the son of that martyred lord whose head was severed by the axe wielded by this right arm."

Sir Edward nodded.

"But," continued Lomew, "which of the sons is it?"

Sir Edward, as these words were uttered, instantly changed colour, and, rising to his feet, surveyed the gloomy dark face of the headsman for some few moments in astonishment.

Then dropping into his seat, he said—

"Which son? In heaven's name, what mean you? Lord Herbert had but one son."

"Not so, Sir Edward; you are wrong. Lord Herbert had two sons —twins. But this fact has been known only to the nurse, the physician, and myself. Let me tell you the dark story, Sir Edward. But, first, I will say this: Master Marcus Montague, directly he hears of the death of this poor youth, will think that all obstacles to his inheritance are now removed; but, Sir Edward, this youth, Walter, is the younger of the two; the elder one lives."

"Master Montague, as I well know, is a desperate and evil man," replied the lieutenant; "and there can be no doubt that he will dispute the matter."

"Assuredly he will. And, unless I am mistaken, there will be terrible work to be done, Sir Edward, for the elder son of Lord Herbert is a youth of fierce determination. But the story, Sir Edward. You, like others, are acquainted with only a portion of it. Quicksilver, come hither."

Quicksilver approached, and Bartholomew, placing his lips to his ear, whispered—

"Go to the door, swifty turn the key, and look without."

Quicksilver did as he was desired. He opened the door and plunged outside as if bent upon some hasty errand.

Quickly returning, he said—

"No one is about."

"There had better not be," said the lieutenant. "But who did you suspect was spying?"

"Barcally."

"Is he your enemy?"

"I am not certain. But I like him not."

"Proceed," said the lieutenant. "I am anxious to hear the whole of the story."

The headsman little knew that there was one who, though he could see not, could yet overhear all that was said, and that person was Barcally.

He had climbed up into one of the recesses which was exactly opposite the open ventilator in the headsman's apartment.

Though the headsman spoke in tones little above a whisper, he was enabled distinctly to overhear all.

"Sir Edward," said Jerome Lomew, "some twenty-six years ago I was possessed of great wealth. I am the only son of a man who met his death for a crime which I afterwards proved he never committed. The name under which for so many years I have been known, is not my own. My father was in the habit of travelling in various parts of the world, and I accompanied him. It was in one of these expeditions that, amid the wild rocky mountains off the coast of Labrador, I met with the poor girl who gave birth to this companion of mine, Quicksilver!"

"Ah!" gasped Quicksilver; "at last I learn the secret of my birth."

"Silence!" said the headsman, sternly.

"The name of this girl was Mary Mansell. Her young husband had just been murdered by a number of savages. And she died soon after giving birth to a son, who received the name of Quicksilver.

"On my father's death, I was reduced to beggary, but there was one who took compassion on me. That person was Lord Fitzwilliam Herbert.

"I became his secretary.

"Lord Herbert married the beautiful daughter of the wealthy George Arden, and she gave birth to twins—both boys. Now, Lady Herbert, some time previously, had consulted a fortune-teller as to her future destiny, and among other things the fortune-teller had said that she was to be blessed with two boys at a birth. But if Lady Herbert wished both to live, she was to separate them. If allowed to live together, one would meet with a terrible death.

"This so alarmed Lady Herbert, that I sought out the hag who had thus frightened her.

"I said to her, 'Mean you that one of the sons will meet with his death on Tower Hill?' Well do I remember the reply. It was:

"'Though the son may pass the Gate,
He ne'er shall meet a Traitor's fate!'"

"Heavens!" cried the lieutenant, "and yet you actually made the appointment with the youth to enter the Tower by Traitor's Gate."

"Alas! I did. But when the appointment was made the prophecy had completely slipped my memory."

"Foolish man!" cried the lieutenant, who was himself strongly inclined to be superstitious, "know you not that many who have forced an entrance into the Tower by way of Traitor's Gate have met with terrible deaths? But continue."

"The elder child," continued Lomew, "was taken away to a distant part of the country by myself, and was placed in charge of a gentleman—where he remains to this very day—in total ignorance of his noble birth. A few years after the birth of the twins, Lord Herbert was arrested on a charge of high treason. The principal witness against him was his wife's cousin, Marcus Montague. I need not tell you the details of that long trial, nor of the result.

"I had been headsman then for some years, and it fell to my lot to behead the man who for so long had been my friend. It was a strange freak of fortune! But at the last I proved his best friend, Sir Edward (for even you remarked that the unhappy prisoner could not have endured a moment's agony), for at a single stroke I severed the noble head from the trunk."

"I well remember it," sighed the lieutenant. "And now what of Marcus Montague? You would have me believe that he will now seek this youth's property?"

"Exactly."

"But now, what is easier for the mother than to acknowledge her first-born?"

"Listen! The surgeon who was present at the birth, and the nurse, are dead; and the youth who lives was not registered."

"Great heaven! what an omission. If this Marcus Montague gets to know the story you have told me, depend upon it he will leave no stone unturned to slay the elder son. It appears evident to me that Marcus Montague was instrumental in bringing about the death of this poor youth."

"Yes; as to that, there is not the slightest doubt in the world. The three men who attacked him—of whom this man on the floor is one—were bravos hired by him. They watched and followed him to his death."

"It was indeed a cruel murder," said Sir Edward, "and it would be better did you yourself proceed to the other son and break the news to him."

"I thank you, Sir Edward, most sincerely. On the morrow, then, with your permission, I will set out."

"Do so; and in the meantime, make all arrangements for the removal of this poor murdered lad."

"I pray you, good Lomew," pleaded Quicksilver, "take me with you, for I cannot remain in the Tower without you."

"Fear not," answered the headsman, "you shall go with me."

"As regards this man — this assassin," said the lieutenant, rising, "you can quickly find him a burial-place. And let that be done at once. Before you depart, you will pay me a visit."

The headsman bowed as he opened the door, and allowed the lieutenant to pass out.

Then reclosing the door, he approached the murdered youth, and looked long and earnestly into the noble face.

His huge rough hand smoothed back the rich brown hair from the brow.

Then, indeed, his long pent-up emotion burst its bonds, and falling upon his knees, he laid his face in his hands.

"Grieve not so, dear Lomew," cried Quicksilver; "think of revenge. The elder son is left; let him be the one to avenge his brother's death; and with your assistance, and the assistance I can give, he will be enabled to do it. Have you not said that the first-born is a youth of fierce determination?"

"I have. Every atom of his father's fearless bravery has he inherited."

"You have no fear for his safety?"

"No. Since Marcus Montague knows not of his existence."

"But will you tell me, has not Lady Herbert looked upon her first-born since he was taken away?"

"Yes; she has often visited the house in which he was placed. But when she looked upon this one she looked upon the other. In features they are exactly alike; but their figures are different. The other, Dudley, has a frame of iron. But prepare writing materials, Quicksilver, and pen a few words to the poor lady, his mother, saying that—that—"

"Leave it to me," said Quicksilver.

CHAPTER II.

OF WHAT PASSED BETWEEN BARCALLY AND MASTER MARCUS MONTAGUE, AND OF THE STRANGE AND TERRIBLE TRAGEDY AT MONTAGUE MANOR.

In order that the reader may be the better able to understand the exciting events which will crowd our history, it is necessary that he be at once transported from the gloomy Tower to beautiful Windsor.

It is the third day after the assassination at Traitor's Gate.

The host of the "Royal Arms," at Windsor, Henry Holland, was seated at his doorway talking to a few customers, when a traveller came in sight.

Halting before the hostelry, the traveller ordered a tankard of ale.

While drinking it, he narrowly scrutinised the countenances of the assembled customers, and then inquired of the host the way to Montague Manor.

"Can you tell me, good host," he added, "whether the master is at home?"

"Why, no, sir traveller," replied the host. "Master Montague is like the Will-o'-the-wisp—ever on the move. You have never before been to the Manor, perhaps?"

"Never."

"Well, master, I venture to say that you will not feel any great inclination to go there a second time."

"Indeed! And why?"

"Oh, the reasons are many. But, perhaps," he quickly added, "you are a person of distinction?"

"Which is doubtful," muttered a man close against the traveller.

Barcally (for he was the horseman) turned with a savage growl and asked—

"And how know you that I am not a person of distinction?"

"As to that," was the reply; "the roughness of your voice, which sounds like the voice of a Tower warder."

"Well, sirrah, what you are I know not," cried Barcally; "but your hangdog face requires washing, and thus I do my best towards the cleansing."

So saying, Barcally raised the tankard and flung the contents full into the other's face. Instantly, with a fierce cry, the man prepared to spring upon the villain.

In a moment the man had leapt forward, snatched the tankard from Barcally's hand, then seized him by the waist, and dragged him from the saddle into the roadway.

The host interfered.

"You have brought it on yourself," he said to Barcally; "and now take my advice and get you gone, lest you and the horse-trough come into close acquaintanceship."

Muttering fierce threats as to what he would do anon, Barcally was quickly in the saddle again, and soon some distance past the hostelry, but for some time he was not out of earshot of the derisive laughter of the host and his customers.

The delay had been considerable, and so when Barcally reached the manor it was almost dark.

Montague Manor was one of the most extraordinary mansions to be met with in any part of England.

Very ambitious was Marcus Montague—as ambitious as he was cunning.

The massive gates were open, and so Barcally rode on up the avenue.

He was observed by the porter, who at once came forth.

"Your business, sir?" he queried.

"To see your master—Master Montague."

"Did Master Montague make an appointment with you?"

"He did not."

"Well, I am afraid, sir, that you cannot see him."

"Is he engaged?"

"He is always engaged."

"Well, I will wait."

"Will the secretary do?"

"Who is the secretary?"

"John Barber."

"At your service, whoever you are," said a peculiar voice from within.

In another moment there advanced to the threshold one who will play a conspicuous part in this romance, Marcus Montague's "secretary," as he was called.

He was a young man of twenty, somewhat short, though thick-set, and apparently very muscular.

"Ah! here is Master Barber," said the porter.

"And who are you, my friend?" asked Barber, eyeing the visitor with great curiosity.

"My name is Barcally."

"Well?"

"I am from London."

"Well?"

"I wish to see Master Montague."

"On what business?"

"It is a private matter. But if you are his secretary I will whisper my business to you."

Barber approached, and Barcally whispered a few words in his ear.

The effect was electrical, and, looking at the warder for a moment, the secretary said—

"Follow me."

Straight through the hall went Barber, and ascending a flight of stone stairs at the extreme end, soon reached a small landing hung with heavy curtains.

"Wait here," he said.

Another moment and he had disappeared.

He was not absent long.

When he reappeared, he again told Barcally to follow him, and in another few moments the warder stood in the presence of the master of the house—Marcus Montague.

Barcally had seen many a fine handsome man in his time, but it struck him, as soon as he saw Montague, that he had never before beheld a more handsome one.

Montague was somewhat tall, and his figure was extremely graceful, while his presence was commanding, though decidedly haughty and stern.

As regards age, he did not look more than forty.

"So," he said, "I understand you are one of the chief warders of the Tower. By my faith! your presence is exceedingly welcome, if what you hinted be correct. But be seated. Proceed, and name your reward."

"A hundred crowns."

"That sum shall be yours."

Barcally then proceeded with his story.

Montague was thrown into a state of excitement, and when Barcally had concluded, he cried—

"Twins! Holy Mary! can this be really possible! I will at once repair to Lady Herbert and force her to confess as to whether this is true or false. But no. That would be unnecessary. It must be true.

"I well know Lomew, the headsman, and though I hate him with all my soul, I know he would not speak falsely. Then, after all, I am to be foiled! This great wealth, which, added to what I now hold, and what I shall add when the deed is done, and when I lead a certain lady to the altar, will enable me to live up to the title I fondly believe the blind fool Elizabeth will confer upon me; after all, I say, this is to be wrested from me. Saints of heaven! my very blood chills at the idea! It must not be. Rather than it should be, I would steep my very soul in crime!"

For some few moments, Montague paced the richly carpeted floor, lost in profound reflection.

After some time Barcally said—

"I am most anxious to return to London."

"You have earned the hundred crowns," said Montague, abruptly pausing, and opening a drawer in the table. "But ere I pay over the sum, will you swear that not to a living soul will you mention the fact of this visit?"

"I swear it!"

"Well, here are the hundred crowns. Take them and depart, and pause not until you are well on the road to London."

As soon as he had taken his departure, Montague turned to Barber.

"Listen," he said; "there must be no delay in this matter. The blow must be struck at once. If this son be publicly recognised by his mother, you can guess what will follow. Not only shall I not become the possessor of a fortune, but you and I will be compelled to part."

"You need have no fear," said the secretary. "Find the son, and leave the rest to me and my dagger."

"Now draw yourself to the table. First, however, hand the wine here. Talking, as you often remark, is dry work."

So the pair seated themselves at the table, and after Montague had consumed a couple of tumblers of wine, he said—

"I told you, John, that the time had come for you to strike the blow."

Barber nodded.

"You see," continued Montague, cooly, "my wife is, I verily believe, suspicious that I shall do her some harm. I fancy that she is suspicious of poison."

Barber grinned as he replied.

"I well know that she carefully examines everything she has."

"But," continued Montague, "she must not die by poison. That is the very thing to raise suspicions. I will tell you the plan I have formed. I will at once give out that we are about to make a journey to London. While I am with my wife, you will see that all preparations for setting out are made, and be careful that every servant shall know it.

"All being in readiness, we depart. But at an early hour in the morning, when it is certain that my wife is asleep, you return. I will give you the key of the secret door at the back, and you can easily make your way unobserved to the bedroom.

"Outside, you will proceed carefully so as not to make sufficient noise to attract her attention, and you can then touch the secret spring I spoke about. Do you understand?"

"Yes—quite."

"Of the result there can be no doubt in the world. That over, you will rejoin me at a spot I shall presently name. The Rose of Windsor removed," he sneered, "I shall be free to marry the beauteous Margaret."

"And thus become the possessor of yet another fortune," added Barber.

"Yes, which you shall share with me. Fear not; your reward shall be ample."

"Well," replied Barber; "perhaps you may assist me in obtaining the girl of my choice. You well know to whom I refer."

Montague laughed sardonically.

"Your choice is none of the worst, John," he said; "and perhaps my influence may help to dull the young lady's eyes to some of your imperfections. And now let us set about our plans without delay."

The two at once parted, Barber descending the stairs to give instructions to the grooms, while Montague made his way to his wife's apartments.

Rose Montague — once Rose Sharon—was at one time one of the ladies-in-waiting to the queen.

It was well known that she was a wealthy heiress, and it was for this reason she was wooed by Marcus Montague.

The signing of the deed which placed her property in Montague's hands, was the signal for the commencement of a course of treatment which can only be described as fiendish.

Her gaoler was Barber, and a more brutal gaoler could not have been found.

Not a soul was she permitted to associate with, except her maid.

There was, however, a soldier of the name of Garvel, who, as far as he dared, watched the proceedings of Montague and his precious factotum.

He had watched the arrival of Barcally, and, though he was unable to overhear what passed, he yet managed to place himself in such a position that he was enabled to overhear part of the plot between Montague and Barber as to the murder of his mistress.

But vainly did he endeavour to discover what was meant by "touching the spring."

What spring was there on the landing? And with what did the spring communicate?

However, he determined, as soon as it was possible, to make an examination of the landing.

In the meantime, Montague entered his wife's sitting-room.

As soon as he appeared, the maid departed.

Mistress Montague was reclining on a low couch close against the window. But her husband no sooner entered than she was quickly on her feet.

Standing erect, she fixed her eyes upon her husband's face with a look of bitter scorn and loathing.

"Always the same welcome," he said.

"Yes," was the reply, in low tones, "and it will be always the same welcome until death parts us. But what seek you now? Tell me quickly and depart, for every moment I gaze upon your hateful face is an age of agony."

"Oh, I will soon relieve you of my presence. I am come to tell you that I am about to set out upon a long journey."

"Well, and of what interest can that be to me?"

"Listen to me," replied Montague, after a moment's pause; "it is time this estrangement came to a close. I am most anxious to bring about a reconciliation."

As he spoke, he advanced towards his wife.

But she quickly retreated.

Raising her white hand she said, still in low, but firm tones.

"Beware, Marcus Montague! I have told you what you may expect if you venture to approach too close to me. Think you that I believe one word of what you have just said? No. You are a vile impostor. Nay, you are more, for I know you to be a murderer!"

Montague started.

He had been leaning gracefully against the massive oaken table, but as his wife denounced him as a murderer, his attitude changed.

He instantly became erect, and his face changed to an ashen hue.

"Yes," continued Mistress Montague, now speaking angrily, "I know, Marcus Montague, that you planned the murder of Walter Herbert."

"It is false!" replied Marcus, hoarsely. "He is dead, to be sure, but it is known that he fell a victim to a number of 'river rats,' as the Thames robbers are called. They killed him for what he had about him."

"Then," asked Mistress Montague, "how comes it that what he had about him came into your possession?"

"My possession! What foolery is this? Nothing of his have I."

"Nothing?"

"Nothing, I repeat."

"Then what of these?"

So saying, Mistress Montague snatched from his breast a small roll of papers, and held them aloft.

With a fearful oath, Montague rushed forward to snatch the papers from her.

But, as swift as a flash of lightning, she placed her right hand in the folds of her dress, and Montague halted, for he saw that she held a long, gleaming dagger.

"Attempt to take these from me," she said, "and I plunge this blade deep into your black heart. Yes, you know that my threat is no idle one. Marcus Montague, these papers were in the possession of Walter Herbert. I say that they came into yours through the villains you hired to do your murderous work. There were three of them, and one (the chief) was John Barber. That red deed was done within the shadow of Traitor's Gate."

"Certainly you are giving me some interesting particulars," sneered Marcus, who was controlling himself with the greatest difficulty.

"Ah, you are only too well aware of them," replied Mistress Montague; "but beware, vile murderer! You well know that poor Lady Herbert has one friend on whom she can rely. Well do you know that I mean Jerome Lomew. He will call you to account."

"Indeed, I know nothing of the murder of the youth. And now the next thing is—how came those papers into your possession? I tell you this, madam, that had I observed you looking at those papers, I would have strangled you on the spot."

"Ah, there, Master Montague, you do indeed show your true character! By heaven! what would proud Elizabeth think, did she overhear that remark from one of her petted favourites? But the time will come when her eyes will be opened, as mine have been. And then, Marcus Montague—then your doom will be sealed."

"Your doom is already sealed," muttered Montague.

Aloud he said—

"And so you refuse to hand those papers over to me?"

"Assuredly do I. But you may depend upon it they will find their way into Lady Herbert's hands."

"Well, do as you think proper," replied Marcus," assuming an indifference he by no means felt. "As I but just now said, I am about to set off upon a journey. When I return I will bring you to reason."

So saying, he turned to the door, passed through it, and violently slammed and bolted it.

Half-an-hour passed, and then a gentle knock came upon the door.

Mistress Montague, thinking it was her maid, desired her to enter.

The door opened, and in walked the faithful Garvel.

"Pardon this intrusion, madam," he said.

"To be sure, Garvel," replied Mistress Montague. "Tell me quickly what you require."

"Madam, I hardly know how to commence; but I feel sure that you are not safe here."

"You are, indeed, correct, Garvel. I am not safe. Had it not been for you, I am certain that I should long ago have been poisoned. But have you learned anything fresh? Be quick, or you will be interrupted."

"That is not likely, because Master Montague and Barber have gone. Madam, know you aught of a secret spring on the landing without this room?"

"I know of none."

"Can I have been mistaken?" thought Garvel. Aloud he said—

"I would not alarm you, madam, but I would respectfully caution you to be well on your guard at night."

"I will not forget, Garvel. But, look you—you see those papers? Will you do me a favour?"

"A hundred, madam."

"Take them to the Lady Herbert, and say that by using great daring, they came into my possession; that I send her them with my love. You will tell her," faltered the unhappy lady, the tears now fast falling down the beautiful face—"you will tell her how deeply I sympathise with her in her new bereavement. You will tell her that though I have not seen poor Walter for so long, his handsome face is still engraven on my broken heart. And you will tell her, Garvel, that I am still a prisoner."

"Madam!" faltered Garvel, "I will say all you wish!"

"You will add, Garvel, that I shall not be allowed to live much longer. Tell her that the blow will, I feel, soon be struck; but whence it will come, who will strike it, and how it will be struck, I know not. But you will assure her that my husband will be the instigator of my death."

"All this I will say. But bear in mind the distance, madam. I fear me that I should not return until the morning."

"No, I do not think that would be likely. But you must plead some excuse. And when you are a mile or two on the road, no doubt you will be able to procure a horse. Here," she added, drawing a diamond bracelet from her wrist, "on this you will be able to raise sufficient in London to defray your expenses."

"No, no, madam," replied Garvel, firmly. "I have a little by me—sufficient to defray my few expenses."

"Well, then, since you will not take this, accept this ring. I present it to you, Garvel, as a keepsake."

"In that case, madam, I accept it—thankfully. And now I will at once arrange to set out."

"You will guard well the papers, for they are of the utmost importance to Lady Herbert."

"I will guard them with my life, madam."

Once again warning Mistress Montague to be on her guard, he left the room to communicate to the maid (the only one who could be trusted) his suspicion that all was not right.

But not satisfied with his mistress's assurance that there was no secret spring, he cautiously returned to the landing and made a thorough search.

He found nothing whatever.

There was no sign of a secret spring, and the flooring everywhere appeared to be solid.

* * * *

The hour of two struck.

It was a splendid morning.

The bright moon, sailing high in the sky, undimmed by a single cloud, threw her glorious rays over the lovely country, and brought out the beauty of the scenery to perfection.

If a traveller paused on the road to listen, the only sound which he would catch was the rustling of the leaves which were gently moved by the softest breezes, the rippling of the restless brook, and occasionally the melancholy hoot of the owl.

It was the rarest of things for a traveller to pass through Windsor at such an early hour.

But on this particular morning, one was wending his way, not along the high road, but along the most unfrequented paths towards Montague Manor.

That he was familiar with the paths he was traversing was evident, from the deliberate fashion in which he proceeded.

He was a strange-looking man, his costume being that usually worn by the very humblest of labourers.

His skin was intensely dark, while his beard was long and shaggy.

The person we have thus described was John Barber.

He quickly reached the manor, and proceeding to the back, he fell upon his hands and knees, crawled through the shrubbery, and was presently before a small and exceedingly narrow door set deep back in the wall.

"'FOOL!' HISSED MONTAGUE. 'WHAT WOULD YOU DO?'"

It was supposed by the servants that this door was never used; but it was very frequently used by Montague, and it led to his study—a fact unknown even to Mistress Montague.

For some few moments Barber listened intently, but no sound fell upon his ears.

Satisfied that no one was about, he placed a small key in the rusty lock, and the door was quickly opened.

Passing through the doorway, he again listened.

All was silent. So he closed the door, and proceeded on his way.

This secret staircase communicated with many parts of the house, but the principal was, as we have said, the study.

So many times had Barber been through this place, that he was able to proceed without a light.

Opening the door of the study with a key, he was quickly on the landing, and in another moment stood without Mistress Montague's bedroom.

Here again he paused, and intently listened.

Not the least movement did he hear.

Satisfied that all within the house were fast asleep, he approached the corner of the landing, and placed his hand upon the head of a small bronze statuette.

He turned the head, and the result was, that a portion of the wainscotting close beside it moved upwards, but without the least noise.

Into this aperture went Barber, and stooping, he placed his hand upon the floor.

It came in contact with a steel button.

"All is now ready," muttered the wretch. "And now for it—now to send her to her death!"

* * * *

Mistress Montague, yielding to the solicitations of her maid, who had been greatly alarmed by the warning given her by Garvel, had allowed her to sleep with her.

As long as they were able the pair kept awake, but at last sleep began to steal upon them, and both retired.

Mistress Montague was the first to drop off, and presently the maid, feeling much easier as she noticed that the hands of the clock pointed to the hour of two, also fell sound asleep.

For what length of time Mistress Montague had slept she could not tell, for the taper had become extinguished by the draught from the window; but on awaking she distinctly caught the sound as of a hand being lightly passed over the door.

A feeling of uneasiness at once seized upon her.

She felt inclined to awake the girl at her side.

But, controlling herself by a great effort, she cautiously slipped from the bed to the floor.

She went to the window, and drew aside the massive curtains.

The bright moonlight, pouring into the sumptuously furnished apartment, fell full upon her beauteous figure, and played softly about the pretty head of the maid who slept on calmly and soundly.

Was she mistaken? she asked herself.

Had she dreamed that she had heard the sound of a hand being passed over her door?

No, she was not mistaken, for as she stood the sound was repeated.

With cautious but uneven tread, she advanced to the door and listened.

Again she heard sounds—not of a hand being passed over the door this time, but as of a person cautiously descending the stairs.

Her agony and fear were great.

More than once she turned towards the bed to rouse her maid, but each time she paused.

She stood by the door for the space of a few minutes, and then she turned and silently fell upon her knees.

She raised her clasped hands appealingly to heaven for strength, and murmured a prayer for safety.

Then she arose, feeling stronger and calmer.

With steady footsteps, but making no noise whatever, she approached the table beside the bed, raised a book, and took up what lay beneath it

That was a long, naked dagger—a weapon she always had near her.

"I feel that Montague has yet again deceived me," she thought; "I feel that what he said with reference to his journey, was false. I feel that he is close here, and that it is by his hand I shall fall! Do I fear death? No; heaven knows I do not, for my life is a burthen to me."

Once more she advanced to the door and listened, and this time she heard plainer than ever the sound as of a person on the stairs; but whether that person was ascending or descending she could not tell.

She turned the key in the lock, and pulled the door open.

The moonlight streamed through on to the landing in front of her, and fell upon the upper part of the stairs.

But the side of the landing remained buried in darkness.

"Who is there?" she asked. "Speak."

No answer.

"Is anyone on the stairs?" queried Mistress Montague, her voice trembling in spite of herself.

"Mistress—mistress!" murmured a voice within the chamber; "what is this? Speak, I conjure you!"

"Hush, Jane—hush!" replied Mistress Montague, turning and motioning to her maid not to get off the bed. "Wait but a moment. I fancied I heard sounds as of a person moving. Remain where you are; I will descend the stairs; I can easily see my way."

"Oh, madam," gasped Jane, "you have a dagger in your hand!"

"True, my girl; and I well know how to use it!"

Mistress Montague advanced; she took four steps only.

Then a low, dull thud was heard, and it was instantly followed by a wild, piercing shriek of terror; it was a scream which penetrated to every corner of that mansion.

But, as quickly as it was uttered, it was stifled.

Jane, echoing again and again the terrible shriek which had left the lips of her doomed mistress, dashed from the bed to the door, and narrowly escaped sharing the fate of the hapless lady.

On the threshold she halted to disengage a portion of her night-dress which had caught in the door.

And, as she stooped, she saw before her a yawning chasm!

The whole of the landing, with the exception of the four corners, had disappeared!

Fascinated, as it were, with the sight, she remained where she was.

Suddenly, the dull thud was again heard, and simultaneously the flooring ascended from the black aperture, and resumed its previous position.

At the same moment, a dark figure rose before her.

Again the terrified maid shrieked, but she did not start back and shut the door.

No! She plunged forward with outstretched arms, and seized upon the figure before her.

"Thou murderer!" she shrieked; "I have you! Help, help!"

As she spoke, she fastened her hands upon the throat of John Barber, though she little dreamed who he was.

With all her strength did she clutch the villain, shrieking the while for help.

The mansion now resounded with startled cries.

Women's voices were crying, while men's voices were shouting for lights.

In the meantime, John Barber, well knowing what would follow discovery, struggled to release himself.

"Unhand me, wench!" he said; "unhand me, or I will kill you!"

"Almighty Providence!" cried Jane. "Can I mistake that voice? It belongs to John Barber!"

"By the Holy Virgin, you are correct!" replied Barber, seizing the maid by her slender throat, and forcing her backward to such an extent that she was not only unable to again cry out, but was also compelled to release her hold. "And that knowledge has cost you your life!"

"No, no!" gasped the girl; "Do

not slay me—do not slay me! Mercy—mercy!"

Still farther back Barber forced her, until the centre of the bedroom was reached.

Here the maid, now utterly exhausted, fell upon her knees.

She tried once more to cry for mercy, but that cry was never uttered.

Barber's dagger flashed in the moon's rays, and was buried deep in the maid's heart!

But one word left the poor girl's lips.

It was the simple word—

"Mother!"

Another few moments, and the servants, men and women, led by the butler, swarmed into the room.

A tremendous cry escaped their lips, as they beheld the terrible scene before them.

"Great heaven!" exclaimed the butler. "Who in the name of the Virgin has done this? Quick—quick! let the house be searched from top to bottom! and run, one of you, and ring the alarm-bell! Murder! Yes, it's murder! And Master Montague not in the house! Holy Mary! what shall we do?"

"Where is Mistress Montague?" asked one of the men.

"Yes," cried all; "where is Mistress Montague?"

At once a hush fell upon all present.

Here was a remarkable mystery!

"Perhaps she has fled into another room," said the butler; "it seems to me as if the house has been entered by thieves—but yet no doors have been found open; and here, you see, the windows are securely fastened. Heaven's mercy protect us! A curse is upon the house! But let us not delay—let us search the mansion."

This was at once done, but nothing came of it.

Not a single room was found to have been disturbed, and every door and every window was securely fastened.

The ringing of the alarm-bell was not without effect.

The echoes of its ponderous tongue, rolled away over meadow and stream; and were heard on the opposite side of the Thames, calling the sentinels pacing the battlements of Windsor Castle to attention.

They mounted as high as was possible, and looked away over the trees expecting to see the reflection of some conflagration.

Before long several soldiers, headed by a captain, made their way to the manor, and they were quickly followed by a crowd of persons, the most striking figure among them all being Harry Holland, the portly host of "The Royal Arms."

Finding the doors open, they crowded in, and at once the place became a scene of the wildest disorder.

Holland listened attentively to the story told him by the butler, and then he said—

"Then you haven't searched the cellars?"

"Cellars!" replied the butler, in tones of astonishment. "Certainly not. What would Mistress Montague be doing in a cellar?"

"She may have hidden herself."

"Pshaw!"

"Well, look you; give me a lantern, and I will search the cellars. Who will go with me?"

Some of the soldiers at once volunteered to accompany him below.

The vaults were quickly reached.

Suddenly the host paused.

Pointing to a dark recess, he said—

"What door is that?"

"A door!" replied the butler, opening wide his eyes in astonishment. "Well, I have been into these cellars many's the time, but never before did I notice this door."

"No!" cried Captain Greenaway, the officer who had accompanied the soldiers. "My friends, there's a mystery in all this, and depend upon it, a discovery of some kind will be made. Look here, master butler, see you not this, covered with a tarpaulin? Don't you see that it is a pile of bricks and stones? Can't you see that it has not long been removed from there—there, before that door?"

"I do," replied the bewildered butler; "let us pass through."

But the door was found to be locked.

After a brief consultation, it was decided to burst it open.

For this purpose, a huge beam of wood was procured and used as a ram.

With tremendous force it was brought upon the little nail-studded oaken door; but it did not so much as quiver.

Again and again was the beam used, and at last the door was sent flying backward.

The landlord held the lantern within the doorway.

"Look!" he exclaimed. "Here are another lot of vaults."

"Well — quick!" said Captain Greenaway; "let us descend into them."

In a few moments nearly the whole party had descended, and they found themselves in a perfect wilderness of a place.

Vaults upon vaults were there, massively constructed, the flooring, walls, and vaulted roofs, supported by ponderous dwarf columns, all being of stone.

"Secret vaults?" said Captain Greenaway.

Very cautiously the party traversed the low, gloomy chambers, the host leading the way.

Suddenly a fearful cry left Holland's lips.

"Gracious heaven!" he exclaimed, raising aloft the lantern, and pointing to a certain part of the stone flooring. "Look—look!"

His great cry of horror was echoed by every man there present, for they saw a white figure stretched full length upon the flags—the figure of the unfortunate Mistress Montague.

A terrible sight she presented.

All around her head and shoulders was a great pool of blood.

The first few moments of horror over, Holland knelt down, and placed his hand upon the body.

"It is still warm," he cried, "and that shows she has not long been there! By the holy saints, a terrible tragedy has been committed."

"Who could have done it?" asked Captain Greenaway; "and for what purpose? Robbery?"

"No; certainly no robbery has been committed," said the butler. "But it puzzles me how she could have got here."

"Fallen through the—," began Captain Greenaway, casting his eyes upward, but he abruptly stopped, for apparently the ceiling above was as solid as a rock.

"No; she cannot have fallen," said the butler, "since there is no place for her to fall from. It is a mystery—a mystery that I cannot hope to fathom."

"You say your master and his secretary are absent?" queried Captain Greenaway.

"Yes, they are gone on a long journey, though whither I cannot tell."

"Leave the matter to me," said the captain. "And now, my men, procure something to place the poor murdered lady on—for murdered she certainly is. Place her very tenderly upon something, and convey her above. Two foul murders have been committed here to-night."

"Depend upon it," said Holland, "the hand that struck the maid the blow, struck the fatal blow here. Who knows," he whispered to Captain Greenaway—"who knows whether the master of the house himself is not concerned in the affair? It is well known how brutally he has ill-treated his lady."

* * * *

In the meantime, Barber made his way out of the house by the same way as he had entered. He was now greatly terrified; for he had not the slightest intention, when he entered the manor, of murdering the maid as well as the mistress.

He had to use the greatest caution, for he had not proceeded very far when the alarm-bell commenced to ring, and it had not rung five minutes before the appearance of many people in the streets warned him that if he attempted to use the open thoroughfares, he would most likely be seen, perhaps seized upon as a suspicious character, and eventually recognised.

Master Montague awaited his

"tool" in Windsor Forast, and on Barber joining him, Montague said—

"Stay not to tell me aught now. Mount and let us away. Even here I can hear the alarm-bell. Was the murder discovered, John Barber?"

"Yes," replied Barber; "but not the murder of Mistress Montague. I was forced to slay the meddling maid."

"What! you have murdered Jane?"

"I could not help it."

"Well, perhaps it is just as well. She knew too much. But let me ask this question—did you search Mistress Montague?"

"Te be sure. I descended to the vaults at great peril, for the whole of the servants were about, and I searched her without result."

"What?"

"I say, without result. She had no papers whatever on her person."

"Confusion!" cried Montague, savagely. "But no doubt I shall find them secreted in her apartments. Now let us on. We must not return to the manor for a few days."

CHAPTER III.

OF THE ARRIVAL OF THE HEADSMAN AND QUICKSILVER, AND OF THE DESPERATE CONFLICT IN THE WOODS.

It was the night after the strange murder of the lovely Mistress Montague, and the assassination of her maid, and the little town of Richmond was wrapped in slumber, for the hour of eleven had struck.

But though the majority of persons were in their beds and asleep, such was not the case at Garth Castle, a magnificent building, whose towers commanded an extensive view of the country around.

Garth Castle was the residence of Master Garth, one of the "fine old English gentlemen" of the days long past, and the owner of a good many hundreds of acres of English soil.

Master Garth was seated in one ot the fine lofty reception-rooms, busily engaged with his steward, Francis Fullmore, a man who had grown old in the service of the Garths.

Master Garth touched a bell standing upon the table.

It was at once answered by one of the serving-men.

"Jackson," said Master Garth, "has not Dudley yet returned?"

"No, sir."

"No signs of him?"

"Not at present, sir."

"Gracious powers! what can have happened to him? Let three or four of the men go out in search of him. And in the meantime, if he should return, let him— Hist! what is that?"

The unmistakable sound of a horse's hoofs was heard in the courtyard.

"'Tis he, master!" said Jackson; "'tis he!"

"Thank heaven, he has returned! Quick, Jackson! Tell him that I am most anxious to see him. Tell him to delay not a moment."

Jackson departed, but he returned in a few moments accompanied, not by the person expected, but by two totally unexpected individuals.

One was a tall, muscular, broad-chested man, attired in an elegant black velvet costume; the other was a very little fellow.

They were Jerome Lomew and Quicksilver.

Though there was little or no alteration in Quicksilver, the headsman was, in all outward respects, a different person to the man we saw at the Tower.

The astonishment of Master Garth was intense, though it was but momentary.

Rushing forward, he eagerly seized both his visitors' hands, and warmly pressing them, said—

"Thrice welcome, Master Lomew

—thrice welcome. And your little friend here, I give him also a hearty welcome."

"Thank you," replied Jerome.

"As for myself," said Quicksilver, "allow me to return thanks. Master Garth, here's to you."

And doffing his mite of a cap, in which was a feather a foot long, Quicksilver placed one hand on his breast, and bowed in the most graceful fashion.

"Your kind reception to these historic halls," he said, "overwhelms me with emotion. Were it not for the fact that my mouth is so parched that I can scarcely get a word out, I would thank you with—"

"Silence!" cried the headsman, impatiently. "Dry or wet, your tongue is always just as much inclined to wag. But if, as you say, it is now very dry indeed, get you downstairs into the kitchen, and, unless I mistake not, the numerous maids below will make you right welcome."

"Maids!" repeated Quicksilver, now standing erect and lightly touching his breast. "Numerous maids, say you? Then shall I have much pleasure in retiring. Your name, sirrah?"

This query was addressed to the astonished steward.

However, he was not long disconcerted.

Though his hands at that moment were full of papers, he quickly placed them down, and, touching his breast as Quicksilver was doing, he replied, with much mock solemnity—

"Francis Fullmore, Master Garth's steward, and very much at your service. May I ask who does me the honour to demand my name?"

"Oh, of a surety," replied Quicksilver, promptly, "though I had already been announced. My name, Master Fullmore, is Sir Quicksilver. And now be good enough to lead the way below."

Despite Master Garth's anxiety, he couldn't help smiling at Quicksilver's coolness and assurance, as well as his conceit.

"They will make much of him below," he said, "for though they have heard of him, this will be the first time they have seen him. And now let me ask you, have you seen aught of Dudley?"

"Of Dudley! I came here on purpose to see him, for the hour has come, Master Garth."

Master Garth started violently, and his face turned pale.

"Has it indeed come—so soon?" he said, in low, quivering tones.

"Soon!" replied the headsman; "soon! Why, Master Garth, nineteen years have passed. But Dudley --you asked me whether I had seen him?"

"He has been absent for hours."

"Hours! And you have no idea where he is?"

"Not the slightest. Would that I had."

"Have you no idea whither he went when he set out?"

"Oh, yes; though he gave no hint, I am certain that he set out with the intention of visiting Madeline Maynard."

A shade—as it seemed of anxiety —crossed the grave face of the headsman, and after a few moments' reflection, he said—

"I am much afraid harm will come of this. If the young girl has learned to love Dudley—and what maiden could help loving so handsome a youth?—her heart will surely break, when she is told that it is necessary they must part for ever! I have said, Master Garth, that the time has come for me to reveal the secret of his birth. But let us set out in search of him. He may be still at the smith's cottage.

"I well know that both you and Mistress Garth love him dearly; but in a letter that I sent you, I made you acquainted with all that has occurred, and I told you that it was absolutely necessary that he be now publicly acknowledged, lest that murderer, Marcus Montague, comes into possession of the property. The tragic occurrences at the manor have reached your ears?"

"Yes, I received all particulars. Dudley, of course, learned all; but he little dreamt how nearly they concerned him."

"He will learn all that directly. And now let us off."

They were quickly in the courtyard, where their horses awaited them, and jumping into the saddle, they set off for the wood, whither it is necessary to precede them.

* * * *

The beautiful wood, which at the period of our romance, ran round the outskirts of Richmond, then but a little village, had a broad road in its centre, and, as it was a near cut to London, it was largely used by travellers. Hence the only occupant, a farrier of the name of Thomas Maynard, got an excellent living.

His house was a pretty picturesque cottage, with workshops adjoining, and within that cottage, the weary traveller could rest while his horse's shoes were attended to.

Many a traveller stopped at that cottage, not because his horse's shoes required attention, but rather because he longed to gaze upon the lovely face of Madeline, the farrier's daughter—his only child, so it was said.

A more beautiful creature than she could not have been found—not even at Court.

She was a vision of loveliness, and her person was a striking contrast to her surroundings. Moreover, she was as unlike her parents as could be.

Her huge, brawny father—"a man of iron," as the travellers called him—was as dark as night, so was her mother, whereas Madeline's complexion, as well as her hair, was exceedingly fair; and, though the features of her parents were unquestionably handsome, Madeline's features in no way resembled theirs.

However, this was not so very remarkable, as it is a matter of frequent occurrence, and yet many considered it somewhat strange.

Her age was eighteen, so that between her and her lover, Dudley Garth, as he had ever been known, there was a difference of a year only.

It was close upon eleven of the clock—just the hour when the headsman arrived at the castle—when Dudley reached the cottage.

The reader already knows that Dudley was the twin-brother of the ill-fated Walter Herbert, to whom, so far as features are concerned, he bore a most extraordinary resemblance.

But whereas Walter had ever been somewhat delicate, Dudley's frame was robust and powerful.

A single glance at the broad chest, the erect figure, the firm decisive step, told the observer that this was a young man of tremendous strength, while but a short look at the finely chiselled face, and the piercing black eyes, would have convinced the observer that he was a person of strong will and determination.

That this was his character the course of our romance will show.

The farrier was waiting before the door of his workshop, the dull glow of the furnace showing Dudley that his face wore an anxious expression.

"Dudley—Dudley!" he cried; "is it indeed you?"

"It is, Master Maynard. And Madeline?"

"She was to pay a visit to her sometime nurse at 'The White Horse,' which, as you know, is the other side of the wood. She should have returned three hours ago. I was but this moment thinking of starting off in search of her. But I am astonished to see you abroad at such an hour."

"Naturally so, Master Maynard. And no doubt those at the castle wonder at my absence. But the fact is, I have been engaged in a most important undertaking. Chancing to pass within a mile, I thought I would call and bid Madeline good-night if she had not retired. And she is absent at this hour! Who would bring her home?"

"Mistress Nutter's sons. I begin to think that the reason Madeline has not returned is because the sons have not yet reached home."

"I will set off to find her," replied Dudley, promptly. "I shall not be long."

So saying, he darted off, and was quickly hidden from the farrier's sight by the dense overhanging foliage.

With hasty strides he pursued his way through the wood, his anxiety increasing with every moment, lest Madeline, fearful of not reaching home at all that night, had set out alone, for he remembered that Mistress Nutter herself was too infirm to walk.

He must have proceeded at least half-a-mile, when, suddenly, loud shouts fell upon his ears.

They were instantly followed by two or three shots, and then the wood echoed with the wild, piercing scream of a woman, this again being followed by the rapid clashing of swords.

Dudley, with a loud cry, snatched his sword from its sheath, and rushed to the spot whence the sounds proceeded.

He felt certain that a fight was being waged not far off, and he soon saw that he was right.

A hundred yards brought him to a stile over which travellers on foot were in the habit of going in order to reach the high road.

Before this was a clear space, and in the centre were at least a dozen men engaged in a struggle for life.

What the meaning of it was, Dudley had then no means of ascertaining.

The faces of the combatants he was unable to see, on account of the darkness prevailing, but his quick eye told him that two men were being attacked by half-a-score, and he quickly ranged himself on the side of the weak.

"What!" he shouted; "five to one! Cowards, desist, or maybe it will yet go hard with you!"

"'Tis Master Dudley," cried one of the men whose side he had taken. "Master Dudley, quick—quick! Madeline has been seized by a wretch whom I recognised—by name Marcus Montague. Quick, I say—fight your way through these men, for the villain has gone on ahead!"

Dudley uttered a cry of dismay as these terrible words fell upon his ears.

He waited to hear no more, but with terrific fury he attacked the men before him.

No more skilful swordsman breathed than Dudley, but he found that the men with whom he was now engaged were no mean swordsmen.

They ranged themselves directly in front of the three—Dudley and the two sons of Mistress Nutter—and in the most determined manner prevented them from making a movement in advance.

Dudley wielded his blade to some tune. In a few minutes he had stricken down two of the ruffians before him, but this did not cause the others to waver.

They were urged to fight to the death by one who apparently took good care to keep out of the range of the three swords.

Dudley remarked the voice as loud, harsh, and peculiar.

It struck him that this man must be the leader of the others, and he tried every means in his power to get at him, but his efforts were fruitless for John Barber (for this person it certainly was) kept his men well before him.

Presently he tried a shot, and it was effective, for one of the Nutters was stricken down, grievously wounded.

The odds were overwhelming, and it would have gone hard with our young hero had not help appeared.

The galloping of horses was heard, and presently two horsemen dashed upon the scene.

The first was the headsman, the other Master Garth.

To leap from their horses was the work of but a single instant.

Lomew was the first to touch the ground, and his long blade at once leaped from its sheath.

Without a word he rushed upon the men.

But the villains, now panic-stricken, turned and fled—all with one exception, the tallest of the lot, who fell at the headsman's feet.

"Are you injured, Dudley?" asked the headsman.

"No," exclaimed Dudley. "Thank heaven, you arrived in time to aid me. But a villain has carried off poor Madeline."

"Carried her off!" exclaimed Master Garth. "Who can it be?"

"Marcus Montague."

"What!" thundered the headsman! "Marcus Montague here? Ha! I begin to see. Dudley, had you a rival?"

"No."

"But you have often mentioned to me that a strange-looking man was frequently hanging about the cottage—that, in fact, he had persisted in addresing Madeline?" said Master Garth.

"Yes, but can he have had anything to do with this brutal attack?"

"I know that he has," said the headsman; "for that person is the assistant to Marcus Montague—the notorious John Barber."

"Let us away," cried Dudley, excitedly, "to the rescue."

"Mount on my horse, Dudley," said Master Garth; "but, for the love of heaven, guard yourself."

"Fear not, I am with him!" said the headsman, significantly.

Both were quickly in the saddle, and were speeding away in the direction pointed out by young Nutter.

But not the slightest trace of the unfortunate young girl was discovered.

At last they rode in the direction of the neat little cottage of Master Maynard.

The farrier had been made acquainted with the particulars of what had occurred within the wood by Nutter, and he was found at the smithy, his wife by his side.

The poor woman was shedding bitter tears.

"Cheer up, I pray you," said Lomew, "for I swear that no stone shall be left unturned in order to restore your daughter to you. Master Maynard, will you accompany us to the castle? We can there deliberate as to what is best to be done."

"I will accompany you," replied the farrier, "and I rely upon you to assist us in the recovering of our daughter. But, alas! she is in possession of a most notorious scoundrel, who is one of the queen's favourites."

"Even so," replied the headsman; "but at present, Dudley knows not what this man is to him."

"To me!" cried Dudley; "to me? On my word, I understand not that remark."

"No; but Master Garth and myself will make it plain enough anon."

"I am determined as to this," said Dudley, fiercely. "Marcus Montague shall answer for his villainy at my sword's point."

"I doubt it not," said the headsman, grimly. "But now, Master Maynard, let us away. And you, Mistress Maynard, though your daughter has thus treacherously been stolen from your arms, forget not that there are those who will not rest until she is recovered."

Mistress Maynard made no reply.

She was too overwhelmed with grief.

Her husband was soon in the saddle, and then away towards the castle went the three.

CHAPTER IV.

OF WHAT OCCURRED AT GARTH CASTLE, AND OF THE IMPORTANT NEWS BROUGHT BY THE FOOTMAN.

In the meantime, Quicksilver had been enjoying himself and amusing the servants in no small degree.

The steward, with much solemnity, conducted him below.

One of the servants caught sight of them, and as soon as she recovered from the astonishment into which she was thrown at the appearance of such a diminutive specimen of humanity, she informed her fellow-servants as to who was about to visit them.

The servants at once came to the conclusion that it could be no other than the companion of the gloomy headsman, of whom they had heard so much, but never yet seen.

So when the steward was observed

descending the stairs, men and women collected at the bottom.

Quicksilver was no sooner observed than a hush fell upon all—a silence caused by intense astonishment; and then a mighty shout arose, that seemed to shake the hoary old walls to their foundations.

Then broad grins spread over the jovial faces of the men, and the eyes of the women beamed with pleasure.

As soon as he reached the bottom of the broad stone stairs, he was surrounded.

"This cordial reception," he said, as he bowed in the most graceful fashion, "puts me completely at my ease. It is highly gratifying to me to meet with so hearty a reception."

"Let me introduce our guest," said the steward. "Sir Quicksilver, of Her Majesty's Tower of London."

"Entirely at your service," added Quicksilver, with another bow.

"We shall make the little gentleman comfortable," said the housekeeper. "All of us have heard so much of Master Quick—"

"Sir Quicksilver," interrupted the steward.

"Your pardon. I meant to say Sir Quicksilver," replied the housekeeper.

"Oh, pray don't stand on ceremony," said Quicksilver, hastily. "I hope, mistress housekeeper, that the wines are as much in your charge as the butler's, who, I am informed, is at present absent."

"To be sure they are," laughed the housekeeper, "and I will presently place before you as much wine as you wish for. Sandy!" she cried to a little red-haired urchin, who had climbed one of the pillars the better to have a good look at the little guest, "come hither. Take this key and get a bottle or two of the best Rhenish—you can't mistake it."

"If he does, it is not likely I shall," said Quicksilver; "for good Rhenish and Quicksilver are most intimately associated one with the other."

"I trust, Sir Quicksilver," answered the housekeeper, "that you do not give way to wine?"

"On the contrary," replied Quicksilver, with the utmost promptitude, "the wine gives way to me."

"Instead of talking here," said the steward, "I propose an adjournment to the hall. Sir Quicksilver has just finished a long journey, and stands in need of refreshment."

"And he shall have it," replied the buxom housekeeper. "Bestir yourselves! Ransack the larders, and spread a banquet in the hall."

"I trust, master steward, you will honour me with your presence?" said Quicksilver.

"To be sure," answered the steward. "I shall be well pleased to sit at the same table with so popular a person as yourself."

The servants, highly delighted and amused at this unexpected break in the monotony of their lives, bestirred themselves with a will, and quickly the large table in the servants' hall groaned beneath viands of all descriptions.

The usual heavy high-backed oaken chairs were provided, but when Quicksilver was mounted on one of them, his little head scarcely reached the level of the table.

What was to be done?

The steward soon settled the difficulty.

"I trust you will have no objection to occupy an important post, Sir Quicksilver?" he said.

"No objection whatever."

"Come hither, Sandy," continued the steward; "go to Master Garth's study and bring a hassock and stool."

These articles were quickly procured, and the steward cleared a space in the centre of the table.

To this position Quicksilver was lifted, to the unbounded delight of the servants, whose laughter could have been heard all over the castle.

On the stool a napkin was placed, and thus Quicksilver had a neat little table all to himself.

Merrily the supper proceeded.

The best wine the castle afforded was provided for Quicksilver, and he toasted each of the servants in turn.

Presently the cloth was removed, and the servants prepared to pass a jolly time.

The Rhenish wine had certainly

made a very strong impression on Quicksilver, and he was now somewhat unsteady on his legs.

But nevertheless he had not lost the use of his voice.

The steward begged him to troll them a stave, and at once Quicksilver complied with the request, and he astonished those present with his voice, which, though small to a degree, was nevertheless remarkably sweet.

His efforts were highly appreciated, and were rewarded with rounds of hearty applause.

The servants consumed such enormous quantities of liquid refreshments, that even Quicksilver did not fail to notice it.

"On my life, my friends," he said, "you drink more beer in an hour than the Tower warders consume in two."

"And how much is the headsman, who is a big, powerful man, in the habit of consuming?" asked the housekeeper.

"He drinks no beer," answered Quicksilver.

"Then what does he drink?"

"Blood!" suggested Sandy.

"You are mistaken, my friend," said Quicksilver; "he does not drink blood—nor does he drink anything so red in colour as your hair. What he does drink is a mystery to me."

"Perhaps you drink your share and his too, Sir Quicksilver?"

"If I do, 'tis without his knowledge, I warrant you. He well knows my weakness for a cup of good wine, such as is this Rhenish, which is most excellent. Again, your healths!"

"Is your weakness for the fair sex as great as that for a cup of good wine?" put in the steward.

"My weakness for wine comes nowhere near my love for fair ladies, such as I see about me at this moment," replied Quicksilver. "I love them all."

So the time time passed pleasantly enough, but at last Quicksilver showed signs of weariness, and thereupon the housekeeper took him in her arms, and carried him upstairs to one of the bedrooms.

He showed no signs of waking; the fumes of the wine had completely overpowered him. And so there he slept, all unconscious of the troubles in which his huge, gloomy companion was placed.

Master Garth returned at length, and by-and-by the headsman, Dudley and the farrier reached the castle.

Master Garth at once saw that their efforts had been fruitless.

"Alas!" he said; "what dreadful fate may be in store for this poor girl? Only too well is it known what a monster of iniquity this Montague is."

"Fear not, Master Garth," cried the headsman; "we shall discover what has become of her, ere many hours have passed. We have a most cunning man to deal with, and cunning must be met by cunning. Let us consider what is best to be done. Our plans must be drawn up quickly, and each will have a share allotted to him. But for a few moments I must request you, good Master Maynard, to excuse us, for I have most important news to convey to Dudley."

Master Garth thereupon led the way to the study.

"Dudley," said the headsman, "the time has come when the mystery which for so many years has surrounded you, must be cleared up. Know then, my lad, that you are the lawful son of Lord Fitzwilliam Herbert."

"What!" cried Dudley in amazement; "do you tell me that I am a brother of the Walter Herbert murdered at Traitor's Gate?"

"You are, indeed, brother to that most ill-fated youth. You and he were twins, but you were the first born."

"Then the lady who has been here so many times—the lady who has ever paid so much attention to me—"

"Is your mother."

"And she has never told me so! In heaven's name, what has been her reason?"

"I will tell you the whole story, my dear lad. But calm yourself."

At once he plunged into the narrative.

"A day or two ago," concluded

the headsman, "I had a long interview with your distracted mother, and she told me that her principal reason for not acknowledging you was this: that Walter had always imagined himself the only son and heir, that his medical attendant had informed your mother that Walter could not possibly live many years, and that she had thought it would be cruel to undeceive him as to the property."

"She may have been right," answered Dudley, gloomily; "at any rate, the whole story is a strange and weird one. Oh, Lomew, how proud I should have been of that brother."

"Yes, yes," replied the headsman, much affected; "I am sure of it. But, Dudley, that brother fell by orders of Marcus Montague. You will avenge his death; it was John Barber who carried out that assassination. At your mother's house I met one of the footmen who had been commissioned by poor Mistress Montague to give certain letters to your mother. From what he said there can be no doubt that Barber was present at the attack on your brother. Then, also, the man informed Lady Herbert as to what he had overheard between Montague and Barber. He had his suspicions, and the world now knows how they have been verified. But listen to this, Dudley. The position you will hold will be one of great importance; it will be vastly different to that held by poor Madeline. Consider, my lad, whether your heart is fixed absolutely upon her."

Dudley gave a great start as this unexpected question was asked.

He did not hesitate, but at once replied.

"Listen to it," he said. "Were I offered the proudest position the queen could bestow, if I agreed to give up Madeline, I would renounce it in favour of being a poor peasant, compelled to toil from morning till night, and to live in the humblest cottage, did Madeline share my joys and my sorrows."

"Nobly said—nobly said!" cried Mistress Garth, rushing forward and folding Dudley to her breast. "It is my own cherished Dudley who thus speaks like an affectionate and brave man."

"Let no more be said on that subject," said the headsman; "and now let us return to the farrier."

He was interrupted by the loud ringing of the outer bell.

In a few seconds there rushed into the apartment the footman, Garvel.

His face, hands, and breast were covered with blood.

"Master Lomew!" he cried, in wild tones.

"What is it?" replied the headsman, coming forward. "Heaven's mercy on us, man, what dreadful accident have you met with?"

"Oh, sir," cried the footman, "I have been nearly murdered by Master Montague and John Barber."

"Where? When?"

"I had been this morning to Lady Herbert's again, and she charged me with a message to you, whom, she said, I should find here. I was proceeding along the Richmond road, about four miles from here, when I heard a loud cry for help. It was a woman's voice."

"Though I was unarmed, I dismounted, and rushed towards the spot whence the sounds proceeded. At some little distance I found an inn, and without was a rough-looking coach. Into this several men were brutally thrusting a lady.

"I seized upon a large piece of wood, and rushed upon the ruffians, demanding the lady's release.

"I was at once ferociously attacked, and the landlord of the inn bringing out a flaming link at the moment, I saw, to my astonishment and horror, that two of the men were my master, Master Marcus Montague (but master no longer) and John Barber. I was quickly overpowered and stretched senseless upon the ground.

"When I recovered, I found that I was within the hostelry. The host asked me if I recognised the lady. I told him no, but I recognised two of the men. He then informed me that his ostler had overheard the lady calling out her name, evidently in the hope that some customers at the hostelry would recognise and release her. He had also overheard Montague utter these words as the whole party moved off—'Hollow Ground.'"

"By heaven's mercy," cried Lomew, "we shall recover her."

"Not so," replied Master Garth, sadly; "for she is lost."

"Merciful Providence!" cried Dudley, "what means this mystery? What is this Hollow Ground?"

"One of the mysterious places owned by Marcus Montague," replied Master Garth, "and it is a place regarded with horror and dread by all. Whoever is placed in its underground vaults may just as well be placed in the tomb."

"Leave it to me," said Lomew. "Compose yourself, Dudley, and we will procure Madeline's release."

"We will," cried Dudley. "No place, however mysterious, or whatever its evil reputation, will deter me from attempting her rescue."

"As soon as morning dawns," said Lomew, "we will set out for London, for that is where Hollow Ground is situated."

The farrier, very fortunately, had not overheard what the footman had said, and Lomew thought it would be no wrong to tell him that a clue had been found, and that, if it were followed, his daughter would be safely restored to his arms.

The news comforted him, and he at once left the castle to impart the welcome intelligence to his wife.

CHAPTER V.

OF THE TERRIBLE MYSTERIES OF HOLLOW GROUND—OF MADELINE'S DEFIANCE, AND OF THE RESULT.

It is necessary that we follow Marcus Montague and John Barber, and we will commence with their leaving the hostelry of which the footman had spoken.

The story he told was a strictly accurate one, as far as he was concerned, but he had not witnessed the brutal treatment to which poor Madeline was subjected.

Finding that, in defiance of their repeated warnings, she persisted in crying for assistance, Marcus suggested to Barber that she should be gagged.

"Though it is a matter of but little importance along these roads," he said, "if she should be heard in the streets of London, it is likely that some romantic gallants might feel inclined to attempt a rescue."

"I have not the least objection to her being gagged," grinned Barber.

Reaching a dark part of the road, Marcus suddenly called a halt.

No sooner did the coach stop than Madeline shrieked for help.

This decided them.

The door was pulled open, and one of the men seized Madeline, and, in defiance of her frantic struggles, managed to fasten a silk kerchief over her mouth, and to tie her hands behind her back.

The party then proceeded.

During that journey, the precious pair conversed respecting the principal thing uppermost in Montague's mind—namely, the possession of the property which was now rightly Dudley's.

But though his conversation was somewhat animated, he was also thinking of another matter.

That was Madeline's great beauty.

"If I work my cards skilfully," thought this consummate scoundrel, "I shall easily get the girl out of Barber's hands. Even the beauteous Margaret is not so fair as this lovely maiden.

"And so this person called Dudley is really Dudley Herbert, Walter's twin-brother. By the rood! the story is a marvellous one. If it can be substantiated, I get not one fraction. But ho, ho, ho!" he chuckled; "I have the queen on my side, and it will go hard if I don't get her to believe my story and to laugh at the other."

In due course Charing Cross was gained, St. Martin's Fields were traversed, and presently the journey was finished, for Hollow Ground was reached.

Old London, at the period of our romance, abounded in remarkable and most curious places, but there certainly was no more remarkable place than Hollow Ground.

It consisted of about four acres of ground, with a large building in the centre.

The whole four acres were protected by a wall no less than twelve feet in height, and four feet thick.

It was built of huge pieces of granite, bricks, and monstrous flints.

If a person stood at the principal gate, and looked at the place, it would have struck him that the piece of ground looked as though it had been scooped out with much labour and great accuracy, and that in the very centre, and consequently the deepest part of the hollow, the "house" had been built.

A mystery—a profound, and, as it was always said, an impenetrable mystery—surrounded this dark, gloomy dwelling.

Just inside the wall we have described, there was a deep moat.

This was crossed by a heavy, oaken bridge of most ingenious construction.

By the simple turning of a screw it could be raised or lowered.

On reaching Hollow Ground, Montague rang the bell attached to the gate.

It was at once answered. A few words passed, and the enormous oaken gates rolled slowly back.

At the edge of the moat the coach stopped, while Montague and Barber, as well as the men, dismounted.

A loud, creaking sound was now heard, and what in the semi-darkness had looked like a gigantic tree slowly descended.

This was the bridge, which had been standing almost on end.

"Now," cried Montague, "pull the coach-door open."

One of the men at once did as desired.

"Now, my pretty Madeline," said Marcus, "will it please you to step forth?"

Madeline sprang from the coach, and Barber took the kerchief from her mouth and unbound her hands.

Her eyes rested upon the black waters of the moat, on which the dull rays of a single link were reflected, and then they wandered to the high walls and the huge building.

Bewildered and astounded at what she saw, she fixed her lovely eyes for an instant upon the handsome but sarcastic features of Marcus Montague.

Then, with a wild, piercing cry, she threw herself upon her knees.

"Sir," she cried, in passionate, heart-rending tones, "grant me your protection. I entreat of you—restore me to my distracted parents."

Montague smiled.

"My protection you shall have," he said. "But your liberty I am unable to give you."

"But, in heaven's name, what is to be done with me? Ah!" she said, as she suddenly leapt to her feet, and pointed to Barber, "you are responsible for this brutal abduction—you! But think not that I shall not be sought for. There is one who will leave naught undone to restore me to my parents. But, tell me this: Which of you two is master?"

With a majestic movement, Montague threw open his cloak and displayed a splendid doublet, richly ornamented with gold lace.

"Judge for yourself," he said.

"You, then, are the master," cried Madeline. "Then, again, I entreat—restore me to my parents."

"Silence!" interrupted Montague, sternly. "I can pay no heed to your entreaties. Listen. You know this young man, for he has repeatedly paid his attentions to you at your father's cottage. His attentions were not required—that I well know—but he took a fancy to you, determined to have you at all risks, and, in consequence of services he has rendered me, I gave him my assistance."

NOTICE.—A Coloured Picture for binding with the Work is Given Away with this Number. Another Picture with No 3.

"'HOW DARE YOU SPEAK WITHOUT MY PERMISSION,' CRIED MONTAGUE

"To your eternal disgrace! Perhaps you will tell me whom you are, for now that I look fully into your face, I fancy that I have seen you before this dreadful night."

"My name is Marcus Montague."

"What!" almost shrieked Madeline. "That monstrous villain! Then I am indeed lost!"

"To the world you are," replied Montague, grimly, "for not many who pass these walls by force ever again quit them—alive or dead."

"Say you so?" cried Madeline, recoiling from the terrible look Montague fixed upon her face. "Then I will not be in your power, monster! Away!" she shrieked, suddenly pushing Barber from her, and plunging wildly forward. "Thus do I escape from your clutches!"

Another second and she would have plunged headlong into the moat.

But Montague instantly divined her intention, and with a swift movement he seized her and dragged her backward.

"Fool!" he hissed. "What would you do?"

"Villain!" gasped Madeline, struggling to release herself; "unhand me! Let go your hold!"

"No! Be still, or it will go hard with you! Resistance is useless."

"Heaven aid me!" cried Madeline, bitterly. "The dark stories whispered about Marcus Montague are only too well founded! Holy Mary! what terrible mysteries does a place like this conceal?"

"Proceed," said Montague, impatiently, "proceed across this bridge! And you, Barber, see to the men. I will attend to this girl."

Madeline fixed a look of indignant scorn on the villain, and one of loathing on Barber and the men, and then proceeded slowly to cross the bridge.

There was no chance to renew the attempt to throw herself into the water, for the sides were too high.

Montague strode after her, taking care not to be more than a few feet from her.

Barber looked after the pair, considerably puzzled.

Had Montague taken a fancy to her? he asked himself.

"He would not dare to interfere with her," he chuckled, "for I hold too many of his secrets."

The bridge crossed, two men made their appearance, each carrying a lantern.

Madeline noticed that both were heavily armed.

She observed, too, how they treated Marcus Montague—how they almost grovelled before him.

It was too dark for Madeline to see the surroundings between the bridge and the house, but she felt that the ground was as hard as rock.

Presently they reached the front of the house, and, a signal being given, the broad, stone steps became alive with armed men, many of whom carried links, the light from which fell full upon the two principal figures—Marcus Montague and Madeline.

Scalding tears were falling down the latter's cheeks; her head was bent upon her bosom; while her hair, having become unbraided, fell in luxuriant profusion over her graceful shoulders and dropped to her waist.

Her little white hands were locked together, while the agitated movements of her tapering fingers showed in what terrible condition her mind was.

She was not greeted with smiles of derision, or with mock welcome.

Every man stood without taking the slightest notice.

They might have been statues for all the movement they made.

The hall of the house was of tremendous extent, with a vaulted roof, from which were suspended scores of grinning human skulls!

It was impossible not to see them, for the hall was brilliantly illuminated, and the skulls were the first objects which struck one on entering.

Montague fixed his eyes upon Madeline's face, as if to note the effect of those ghastly objects upon her.

A shudder passed over her frame, and she turned a shade paler, but otherwise she was not affected, much to Montague's astonishment.

"It is strange, indeed," he thought.

"Every woman who has ever crossed the threshold of this house has dropped almost senseless as soon as her eyes rested upon these skulls, and has at once offered to submit to anything so that her life was spared. But it is not so with this girl. By the rood! she has remarkable courage."

Marcus conducted her to the farther end of the hall, and motioned her into a small, but sumptuously furnished chamber.

"For the present," he said, "you will remain here, Mistress Madeline."

"And will you be my gaoler?"

Montague winced.

"No," he replied; "you may yet find that there are as many gaolers here as there are at the Tower of London."

"To which place you, Marcus Montague, will one day go, and not of your own free will."

"Confusion!" thundered Montague, starting back. "What mean you?"

"What I say. Know you not that there is such a place as Traitor's Gate?" asked Madeline, who was now singularly calm and collected.

"Madeline Maynard," gasped Montague, as he suddenly plunged forward and seized her arms, "let me warn you to beware of what you say. By the heaven above us! many a woman has fallen a victim to a man's vengeance for far less than the words you have uttered!"

"Does that include Mistress Montague?" asked Madeline, looking him straight in the face.

"I see," said Montague, fiercely, "that your tongue will ruin you yet!"

"It may be so; but your cunning and trickery will soon be your ruin!"

"Enough! For the present, Mistress Maynard, I will leave you."

Madeline made no reply.

Proudly and haughtily she, after directing a glance of scorn and loathing at the villain, turned her back to him.

Thus she did not observe the terrible glance Montague fixed on her as he closed the door, and placed the steel bar in position on the outside.

Poor Madeline no sooner found that she was alone, than she seated herself in one of the luxurious chairs, and, burying her face in her hands, burst into a passionate flood of tears.

They relieved her overcharged heart—that heart which was presently to be wrung with agony the most intense.

Montague proceeded up the stairs, and entered a large stone chamber, the ceiling of which was supported by massive stone pillars.

This chamber was used for various purposes.

In length it was sixty feet, and down the centre was placed a long, massive oaken table, on each side of which were two or three score of chairs.

At the farther end was a sort of raised platform, with a chair of state in the centre.

The high vaulted roof was hung with beautiful candelabra, while the walls were adorned with pictures, arms, and tapestry. The flooring was of oak, and highly polished.

Montague passed up this apartment, and he had no sooner reached the centre than he touched a silver bell, and instantly a heavy piece of stone in one of the pillars revolved, and a man stepped forth.

He was about sixty, and his height, had he stood erect, would have been at least six feet.

His hair was grey and unkempt, while the skin of his hands and face had a yellowish, sickly appearance, and his large, restless, bloodshot eyes, were sunk far back in their sockets.

His narrow waist was encircled by a broad belt, from which depended three or four heavy bunches of keys.

The name of this singular specimen of humanity was Joseph Hockley, and he was chief of the men within that mysterious building.

"We have brought a visitor, Joseph," said Marcus.

"So I am given to understand, your worship," replied Hockley; "a lady visitor."

"Yes."

"I hope she's not dangerous, your worship," leered the fellow.

"I don't know that—I am unable to say at present."

"Do you think you will require my services?"

"I may. Look you, Hockley—a word in your ear. The girl we have brought here is a beautiful creature."

"So I am informed."

"She is one to whom John Barber has taken a fancy."

"Not yourself?"

"Barber does not think so. But, as a matter of fact, I have taken a strong fancy to the girl. But I don't want Barber to be suspicious of me, so if the girl is obstinate, and is conducted below, don't let Barber know of it at present."

"I understand."

"And I will see that you lose nothing by it."

"Thank you, your worship."

"And now, what of the meeting?"

"It takes place in twenty-four hours. Lord Galloway will preside. There will be at least sixty gentlemen present, most of them noblemen. They look to you, your worship, to form the plan."

"What plan?"

"The murder of the queen!"

"That requires a vast amount of consideration, Hockley. And besides, the question is, to what extent should I benefit?"

"To be sure—to be sure. Though, of course, I know but little of political matters."

"You know far more than you would care to openly say, Joseph Hockley—chief of hypocrites."

"Fellow chief, I bow to you," replied Hockley, with a curious twinkling of his eyes, as he made a profound bow.

"But the matter at present occupying my attention is this young lady," continued Montague. "As soon as you have seen John Barber comfortably settled for the next few hours, be ready to obey my summons."

"I shall be ready. You know how to communicate with me."

Montague repaired to an upstairs room, and there he attired himself in another costume—a costume far more gorgeous than the other.

He was thus prepared to pay Madeline a visit.

In the meantime, Madeline had been visited by a hag named Gitto, a repulsive, horrible, dissipated wretch, whose bloated face and blear eyes conclusively proved that sobriety was a virtue little known to her.

She no sooner entered the apartment than she surveyed Madeline from head to foot with the most insulting deliberation.

Madeline shrank from her as from some loathsome reptile.

Mother Gitto was thus narrowly examining her to see what articles of jewellery she had upon her person.

To her astonishment, she found she had none.

"Well," she sneered, "you certainly are not one of the richer sort of girls. Why, you haven't so much as a ring on any of your fingers. Marcus Montague is to be a lord, or an earl, or something like that, shortly, I hear, and is very wealthy, so if you don't have some of his riches, you are a fool."

"Tell me," cried Madeline—"tell me, where am I?"

"You are in a living tomb."

"Almighty Providence!" cried Madeline, "what do you mean? A living tomb! Explain."

"It is not necessary. You will soon know what I mean, if you do not comply with orders given you."

"Whose orders?"

"Montague's."

"Is Montague master of this great building?"

"He is not; but he has the same power as if he were. Ah, here he comes."

At this moment the door was thrown wide open, and Montague walked in.

For a moment or two Madeline felt dazed at the sight of his glittering ornaments, but at once coming to the conclusion that these had been donned to impress her, she turned away.

Montague looked remarkably handsome, and the costume in which he was now attired set off his shapely figure to the best advantage.

He fixed a look full of significance upon Mother Gitto, and that person dropped a curtsey and withdrew.

Montague then closed the door.

"Madeline Maynard," he cried, "I have come to make you an offer."

"What offer?" asked Madeline, in indignant tones.

"I have taken a fancy to you, and I presume I present a far more attractive appearance than my servant, John Barber."

"For some time," said Madeline, "I have been asking myself which is the bigger scoundrel of the two—you or John Barber."

"Beware what you are saying."

"Beware yourself, Marcus Montague! The indignities you have offered me will be avenged, and Dudley Garth will be the avenger."

"He will fail to trace you here. And even if he imagined that you were within this building, how is he to obtain admission?"

"He will find a way."

"Pshaw!"

"You may sneer, but you know him not yet. Wait, and, by heaven, you will find that you have no child to deal with in Dudley Garth."

"We will waive that matter for the present. I repeat that I have taken a fancy to you, and it is in your power to become a person of importance."

"Talk not to me, sir!" cried Madeline, stamping her foot with passion.

She paused and started back in wonder, for a remarkable noise was heard.

It sounded like the muttering of distant thunder, and suddenly the floor oscillated violently.

Montague dashed from the room.

"Hold!" he roared. "Hold!"

It was too late.

The signal which Hockley was accustomed to obey—namely, the stamping of the foot on the floor—had been given, and some machinery had been put in motion and could not be stopped.

With a loud, terrified scream, Madeline seized upon one of the heavy chairs, but even as she did so the lamp was extinguished, and the chamber was in total darkness.

Falling upon her knees, Madeline covered her face with her hands.

"Am I about to meet my death?" she gasped. "If it be so, let me die breathing your loved name, Dudley."

Suddenly she felt a great jolting beneath her.

She took her hands from her eyes.

Profound darkness still reigned.

But in a few moments, the deep tones of a man's voice were heard.

"Rise, girl!"

"Who speaks?" gasped Madeline, starting to her feet.

"'Tis I," was the reply.

Footsteps were heard, a light approached, and once more Montague stood before her.

But he was not now alone.

On one side of him stood Hockley, while behind him Madeline noticed several men.

But what was this she saw? Where was she now?

Dazed and bewildered, she looked about her.

No beautiful walls now met her eyes; no polished floor—no mirrors.

She found herself standing in the centre of a horrible dungeon, the walls of which were dripping with slime.

She had had her hand upon a beautiful chair.

But what had become of it?

In place of it stood a hard chair of deal, and the appearance of the whole place was horrible to contemplate.

A shudder pervaded Madeline's frame; and so violent was it, that Montague chuckled with satisfaction.

"No doubt you wonder where you are?" he said, mockingly. "Think you that Dudley Garth would be able to penetrate these massive walls? If he did, what would become of him? Would you like to know? Behold!"

Hockley made a movement with his hand, a loud clap rang out, a huge piece of the wall revolved, and some massive iron rails were revealed.

At the same moment, a wild, unearthly cry rang out—a cry which seemed to set Madeline's veins on fire.

Hockley seized a link, lit it at the lantern, and waved it before the bars.

A terrible sight was revealed.

On the other side of the bars stood a human being—a man.

It would have been difficult for anyone not well acquainted with him to have told his age, but it was certain that he was not very old.

He was wasted to a shadow, and his back was bowed, owing to the fact that the ceiling of the vault in which he was confined was not of a height to allow him to stand erect.

His hair (naturally curly) was as long as a woman's, and in parts matted with blood from wounds in his head, which he had dashed again and again against the massive walls in the madness of despair.

Seizing the bars, he shook them violently, while another fearful cry burst from his lips.

The prisoner's gaze fell for a moment upon Madeline's beauteous figure, and he uttered a deep pitiful groan; then his eyes were directed upon Montague, who stood erect, his arms folded across his breast, surveying the unhappy man with a sardonic smile.

"Fiend!" yelled the prisoner. "What do you here?"

"Does he not present a dreadful sight!" sneered Hockley, addressing himself to Madeline. "He is mad—hopelessly mad!"

"It is false!" roared the prisoner. "I am in the full possession of my senses, though over and over again have you tried to rob me of them. You have robbed me of the precious daylight—you have robbed me of the sight of *her;* yet you cannot rob me of my senses! But I would willingly end my days here, and be buried beneath the unholy stones, unwept for, did I know that poor Elise were free—free to use her efforts in bringing to justice the monster—Marcus Montague!"

The scene was of so affecting a character, that Madeline wept bitterly.

The prisoner noticed it, and exclaimed—

"Come hither, lady, while I whisper in your ear."

"Fool!" thundered Montague. "You might just as well ask those bars to open, so that you could walk forth."

"If I could force them open," replied the youth, "I would strike you dead at my feet, Marcus Montague!"

"Put a bridle on your tongue," hissed Hockley, as he dashed the flaming link across the youth's face.

As he spoke he set the stone in motion.

"Claude Wentworth!" yelled the prisoner, in ear piercing tones; "that is my name, fair lady! If you should get a chance—"

Madeline heard no more, for ere he could complete the sentence, the stone had resumed its previous position; and though, no doubt, the prisoner continued to shout, his voice was heard no more.

"A living tomb!" thought Madeline.

She now understood what Mother Gitto had said.

"That," said Montague, "would be the fate of Dudley Garth, if he attempted to force an entry into this building. Even his powerful friend, the headsman of the Tower, would be of no use to him. But, Madeline Maynard, this is what will happen to you if you do not favourably consider my proposals."

Again Hockley made a movement with his foot; this time on the opposite side, and again a huge block of the massive wall revolved and revealed a number of heavy bars.

Madeline was so overpowered at what she had already seen, that she would have refused to look at this aperture; but she thought that, perhaps, the prisoner within this vault might be the Elise of whom the youth had spoken.

Such was, indeed, the fact.

But the prisoner made no movement to the bars.

So Montague advanced to them.

"What ho!" he said. "Liberty at last!"

"What?" shrieked a woman's voice. "Liberty! Then heaven be praised!"

The next instant, a ghastly white face—the face of a skeleton, were it not for the long, unkempt hair, which once had been nut-brown in colour, but was now streaked with silver threads, and the sunken, but fiercely glittering eyes—appeared at the bars.

Montague laughed.

It was a laugh which seemed to send a cold current to Madeline's heart—a demoniacal laugh, which was fully understood by the prisoner.

"Ha!" she said; "you mock me! Liberty—liberty! Yes, when this poor heart ceases to beat for ever—when this wasted form is thrust beneath the cold earth—then shall I feel liberty, but not till then! But what would liberty be without *him?* Marcus Montague, outrager of humanity! traitor to your queen and country! may a dungeon in the Tower be your portion, and the headsman's axe—"

"Silence your raving!" thundered Montague. "What you have said now you have said for the last—"

"Hist, hist!" interrupted Hockley.

The prisoner had pressed her ear right to the bars as Montague spoke, no doubt to catch his last words, which would have told her how long she had been where she was, had it not been for Hockley's interruption.

The sentence was unfinished, and the prisoner uttered a deep sigh of despair.

And now she seemed for the first time to have observed Madeline.

"Yet another!" she muttered. "Yet another! Heaven! when will these terrible crimes be brought to light?"

"Silence, you ugly hag!" yelled Montague.

"Yes, ugly now," replied the prisoner, bitterly. "But once I was beautiful, and my beauty was such as to command the attention of Master Montague. Yes, lady," she cried, directing her unnaturally brilliant eyes upon Madeline. "I was beautiful once. And I had a happy home. How long ago it is, I cannot say—but it seems years to me. My Claude—and—I wonder whether he still lives?"

"Yes!" cried Madeline; "he does!"

"Stand back!" shouted Montague, seizing her savagely by the arm and thrusting her backward; "how dare you speak without my permission?"

"Your permission!" replied Madeline, proudly. "You may withhold it if it so pleases you; but that will not deter me from speaking."

"Then what you have here seen, you would tell me, has made no impression upon you?"

"Yes; it has made a deep impression. It has convinced me that you are a fiend in the shape of a man. What I have seen has strengthened my resolve not to give way to you, John Barber, or any of the loathsome reptiles who obey your orders."

"Enough!" muttered Hockley, fiercely. "I, then, am one of the reptiles. Is that what you would say, mistress?"

Madeline's reply was a glance of bitter scorn.

The unfortunate creature behind the bars had not been allowed to again speak, for the stone had been returned to its position.

After a short consultation with Hockley, Montague said to his lovely captive—

"I have determined to allow you time for reflection."

"It is not necessary," replied Madeline; "did you give me days for reflection, my resolve would not be shaken."

"So you now say; but you know not what darkness and solitary confinement are."

"I well know the result," replied Madeline.

"You are worse than mad," said Montague. "Would you prefer darkness and solitary confinement, to light, luxury, and liberty within these walls?"

"To your society, yes!—ten thousand times yes!"

"Let her taste it," grinned Hockley; "she will change her mind, depend upon it."

"As much as yonder poor victim has changed her mind," replied Madeline; "for I see only too plainly that she has been one of Montague's victims."

"Words are only wasted on the obstinate girl," growled Montague.

Hockley held the link aloft, and signalled to the men.

Two of them ranged themselves one on each side of Madeline, while the others, with Montague, brought up the rear.

The farther end of the vault being reached, a low door was opened, and the party descended some stone steps.

Another vault was thus entered.

It was a large one, with a low ceiling.

Madeline's attention at once became fixed on a most peculiar-looking object in the centre.

In shape it was something like a huge crate, but in the centre was a marble slab, with a hole in the middle.

On each side of this was a solid mass of iron, which must have weighed at least a ton.

That it was a diabolical contrivance of some description Madeline at once saw.

From it to the ceiling, and from the ceiling to the floor, were a number of pulleys and ropes.

In the ceiling, exactly over this extraordinary affair, was a trap-door, which, judging from the fact that no bolts could be seen from the vault, opened on the other side only.

In this vault Montague called a halt, and once again he conferred with Hockley.

What was said Madeline was unable to overhear, with the exception of these words, uttered by Hockley—

"Yes; you are right. No better plan could be thought of. It would have a magnificent effect."

Montague nodded, and again the party proceeded.

Another door was opened, and a small chamber was revealed.

"Here will you remain," said Montague, "for a few hours, when I will visit you with the hope that—"

"Hope for nothing," interrupted Madeline, sternly.

Montague bowed sarcastically.

He appeared fully persuaded that darkness and solitary confinement would have the effect he desired.

"If at the expiration of a certain time," he said, "I find that you still keep to your mad resolve, by the rood! you shall be a witness to that which shall cause you to do as I wish you to."

"I will be a witness to no more of your terrible revelations," replied Madeline, "for I will cover my eyes, that my heart may not stop its beating with horror."

"We shall see to that," said Hockley, with a sneer.

"Calm yourself, Hockley," smiled Montague, "and depend upon it that time will work wonders with her. Listen to me, Madeline. A word, and you will at once be conducted from these vaults and placed in the room above—"

"Fitted with a diabolical contrivance," interrupted Madeline. "No, I shall feel more secure here."

Montague scowled, and motioned to Hockley to close the door.

On Madeline, the effect of the clanging of that heavy portal was terrible.

"I feel that my death-knell is sounded," she muttered. "I feel that this will be the place of my death. 'Tis indeed a living tomb, but it will not long be a living tomb for me—death will speedily end all my sufferings. Ah, Dudley, that you knew where I was, you would freely risk your life for mine."

CHAPTER VI.

WHEREIN DUDLEY AND THE HEADSMAN PROVE THEIR VALOUR.

Morning dawned, and the party, consisting of Dudley, the headsman, and Quicksilver prepared to set out.

Already the horses were saddled, and Dudley was standing ready, the reins in his hands.

On the broad steps stood the magnificent figure of Jerome Lomew, while beside him was Quicksilver, who was receiving the final attentions, so far as his boots and tiny gold spurs were concerned, from two or three of the servants.

The headsman was awaiting Master Garth, who was tarrying above in order to bring down his almost heart-broken wife.

Presently a movement of the servants crowding the hall for a last look at Sir Quicksilver, showed that the pair were advancing.

The headsman turned his head away, for he saw that Mistress Garth was sobbing bitterly.

Master Garth, without a word (for he was too affected to speak), led her to Dudley, who passed his arm round her waist and kissed her again and again.

"Grieve not!"

But even as he uttered the words, the tears rushed from his own eyes and mingled with Mistress Garth's.

"Dudley, my boy," said Mistress Garth, as she placed her hands on his cheeks and looked into his eyes, "you will not forget your foster-mother?"

"May heaven forget me if ever I forget you, beloved mother!" replied Dudley; "but fear not; I shall not long be absent."

"Dudley, be careful of yourself. Remember that Marcus Montague is not only a man of great cunning—a man who will stop at nothing to effect his purpose—but that he is a favourite of the queen."

"Which," said Lomew, gravely, "has ever been a mystery to me as well as to others."

"It proves that he is a consummate hypocrite," said Master Garth. "But rely upon it, he will be brought to justice. A charge of abduction can be preferred against him."

"But such a charge, against so powerful a man," said the headsman, "requires powerful influence to support it."

"He shall answer to me," cried Dudley, sternly.

"Did he abduct one on whom I had been pleased to bestow my affections," said Quicksilver, as he loftily touched the hilt of his sword, "I would challenge him to mortal combat."

"Bravo, Sir Quicksilver!" cried the servants, admiringly.

"As he could not reach the villain," said the housekeeper, "I'd willingly raise him in my arms, so that he could give him a thrust or two."

"Which I would supplement with the heaviest rolling-pin I could lay hands on," added the cook.

After a long parting, Dudley mounted his horse.

The headsman followed, and Master Garth was about to hand Quicksilver up, but he declined, saying that there was one way only in which he mounted with his companion.

The headsman held out his whip Quicksilver seized the thong, and in the twinkling of an eye was across the pommel of the headsman's saddle.

He then took off his feathered cap, bowed to Master and Mistress Garth, and in the most gallant fashion kissed his hand to the servants.

Then, amid a loud cheer, the party moved off.

It was not far off midday when they arrived in the neighbourhood of what is now Hyde Park.

"Whither now?" asked Dudley, wearily.

"Why, my lad," replied the headsman, "I have been thinking. But you look worn and weary?"

"And I am too, for I slept not last night."

"Well, 'tis not to be wondered at. But you must recover your strength to face and fight your enemies."

"Fear not," replied Dudley, in almost fierce tones. "I shall be ready—am ready at this moment."

"I would that we could go straight to the accursed house, force our way in, and secure the poor girl's release. But that would be a matter of utter impossibility, for we can do nothing by daylight, and at night what we do must be by cunning, for the house and the approaches are most carefully watched. In the meantime we will think out our plans."

"What say you to a disguise?" asked Dudley.

"That would not do, for, though a disguised person might manage to get within the gates, he would not be permitted to cross the moat."

"And where do you propose to stay all these dreary hours?"

"At a friend's. Come!"

They soon reached Chelsea, and the headsman led the way through several curious turnings, until, at last, he halted before a large wooden building abutting on the river.

On a huge signboard, which projected far out from the house, was the inscription — "The Black Dragon."

"Is this a hostelry?" asked Dudley.

"No; nor was it ever a hostelry. Have you never heard of Alexander Rodney, the great chemist?"

"I have; he is chemist to her majesty."

"Yes, one of them; for Elizabeth thinks proper to have several, just as she has more than is required of all trades or professions—especially courtiers."

"Thank heaven she has but one headsman!" exclaimed Quicksilver.

"Yes," replied Lomew; "she has but one at present, but there is never any telling when State affairs may demand more. But, Dudley, the gentleman to whom we are now going, is a noble-hearted man. He will receive you with open arms, for he was a firm friend of the father you never knew. And he knows as well as I do that your father died an innocent man."

By this time the three had dismounted. High up over the door the headsman reached his hand.

His fingers touched a bit of wire; this he jerked, and the result was, that, in a few moments, the door was thrown wide open by a tall elderly man, wearing a dark mantle, and whose broad forehead was surmounted by a skull-cap.

Despite the fact that he was of great age, and that his back was somewhat bowed, his eyes were keen and penetrating.

His white, curling hair flowed in graceful ringlets over his shoulders, but he wore neither beard nor moustache, being, in fact, clean-shaven.

"I trust, Master Rodney," said the headsman, "that you have no difficulty in recognising me?"

Master Rodney smiled gravely as he held forth his hand.

"I at once recognised you from above," he replied, "though the costume you wear alters you considerably. And I think I can recognise your companions. This is the Dudley of whom we have so often spoken?"

"It is."

"He is right welcome to my poor abode."

Dudley warmly returned the pressure of the old man's hand.

"As for this one," continued Master Rodney, with a smile as he looked at Quicksilver, "I think he and I are already acquainted."

"We are indeed," replied Quicksilver. "'Twas you, Master Rodney, an I mistake not, that once gave me a vile compound."

"It was," said Lomew, "and thus saved your life; for, if you remember, you had drank poison in mistake for wine. Thus you are much indebted to Master Rodney."

"If that is so, I am afraid 'twill be long ere the debt is rubbed out, for in these days 'tis hard to get enough to live upon, let alone pay debts," returned Quicksilver.

"Pray enter," said Master Rodney. "Ho, there, Patrick."

"Yes, yes," returned a deep voice from the regions below.

"Come hither."

Patrick, Master Rodney's only servant, quickly appeared.

He was a middle-aged Irishman—honest, warm-hearted, and true.

What his costume was it would be difficult to say, seeing that it had in it as many colours as Joseph's coat is said to have contained.

His face was almost as black as a negro's.

At the sight of him Quicksilver burst into an uncontrollable fit of laughter.

"Heaven's mercy on us all, Master Patrick, what have you been doing with your face?"

"Ye may well say that," replied Patrick. "Why, it's compounding charcoal I've been, and it's about as black a task as ever man had."

"Well, after all," said Quicksilver, "you had better have a black face than a black heart."

"True for you; there's already too many black hearts about."

The party were now ushered into the dwelling, while Patrick took charge of the horses, taking them round to the shed at the back.

The greatest caution was necessary in traversing the passages and rooms in "The Black Dragon," for not only the walls and tables, but the floors as well, were crowded with bottles, large and small retorts, crucibles, and the like.

But at last the parlour was reached, and when Pat had seen to the horses, he placed before our friends a substantial repast.

During its discussion, Master Rodney was made acquainted with all the particulars of the abduction, and he promised his advice.

But observing that Dudley required rest, he persuaded him to take a draught for the purpose of procuring sleep.

Dudley at last drank it, and the result was that within half-an-hour, he fell into a profound sleep.

It was night when he awoke, feeling greatly refreshed.

"Let us now set out," said the headsman. "Master Rodney, into your safe keeping I place Quicksilver. And look you, sirrah," he added, turning to Quicksilver, who was busy with his hair before an elaborate mirror, "I charge you to keep your meddling fingers off the various things in this house, for if you don't, depend upon it you will never return to the Tower alive."

"The night favours you," said Master Rodney, drawing aside a curtain, and revealing the dark waters of the Thames, "for 'tis as black as ink. There is not much chance of your being recognised, unless you act rashly."

"Which is not likely," replied Lomew. "I think that Dudley fully recognises the necessity of using the greatest caution. But hark! Someone knocks upon the door."

Master Rodney summoned Patrick, and in another moment he was heard ascending the stairs.

But a few seconds had elapsed when there rushed into the parlour a tall, elegantly dressed young fellow of about twenty.

Judging from the fact that his clothing was splashed with mud, and that his hair was stained with blood, as well as from numerous other signs, including the paleness of his strikingly handsome face, he had got mixed up in some brawl.

"Gracious Providence!" exclaimed Master Rodney, starting back; "it is Walter Raleigh."

"Yes, yes," was the reply; "'tis even so, and I am pursued by half-a-dozen men, who have vowed to take my life. There were eight," he added, bitterly, "and the cowards beset me on the river—or, I should say, me and my friend, young Chandler. Him they have slain, but I avenged him, for with this good blade I sent two of them to their last account. I then pulled in for the shore, but they followed me—landed almost as soon as I did—and I believe they have guessed where I have taken refuge."

"Now may heaven have mercy on us," exclaimed the old man. "If they come here they may force their way in, and, not finding you, they may pull this old house down about my ears."

While the old man had been speaking, Dudley had been earnestly looking into the face of the new-comer, and in that brief space, he conceived a strong liking for him.

With a sudden impulse, he drew his sword from its sheath.

"If you require help," he said, "command me. My name is Dudley Herbert."

"Son of the once powerful lord of that name," added Master Rodney.

"So far as help goes," cried Lomew, "I pray you count on me. I will not ask you the reason of the attack made upon you, for I feel sure that the warm-hearted youth of whom I have heard so much—if you are the same

Walter Raleigh*—could descend to nothing mean or unlawful."

"By heaven, you but do him justice," cried Master Rodney, warmly.

"Master—master!" cried Patrick, suddenly appearing at the door, his face showing every sign of the greatest agitation. "A number of men are advancing from the river."

"Let us go forth to meet them," said Dudley. "As soon as they come before the door, let us dash out."

"By my faith!" cried Raleigh, in enthusiastic tones, as he seized Dudley by the hand, "you are, indeed, a true Englishman. We will do as you say."

"Hist!" cried the headsman, who had thrown back his cloak, and bared his huge muscular arms the better to wield the ponderous blade he held in his hand; "let them not hear our voices."

"Patrick," whispered Master Rodney, "take these pistols, and see if you can render any assistance from the windows above."

"Now, may I never again see the Old Country if I do!" replied Patrick. "I'll use my stick when I see the chance, but I could not fire straight if it was to save my life."

Suddenly a shuffling of feet was heard without.

Raleigh gave the signal, and a dash was made to the door, which was flung wide open, and the three abreast, Dudley being in the centre, stood before the astonished men.

"Perdition!" growled one of them. "The hound found his way to kennel in order to rouse the cubs—eh? Have at you! Cut them down!"

The three took a few paces forward, while the six men placed themselves abreast, and the next moment a tremendous fight was in progress.

Though Raleigh's thoughts were directed to getting rid of his pursuers, he nevertheless devoted great attention to Dudley, and he was astonished at the dexterous and determined fashion in which he wielded his blade.

Suddenly a fearful cry rang out as the man immediately in front of Dudley fell, pierced to the heart by a thrust from our hero's sword.

At the same moment, almost, the man who had spoken dropped, his skull cloven in twain by the sword of the mighty headsman.

Raleigh succeeded in driving his blade through the arm of one of his foes, who, however, did not fall back.

On the contrary, he fought with stubborn determination, and his attack, as well as that of the man next him, was directed exclusively against Raleigh, whose life they seemed determined to take.

Presently one of them managed to force Raleigh back a few paces, and then the two attacked him with redoubled fury, while the others kept the headsman and Dudley well employed.

Suddenly Raleigh's opportunity came, and with the swiftness of lightning one of the men attacking him fell to rise no more.

But even as the fatal blow was struck, the young fellow's foot slipped, and he fell.

The other man dashed forward.

His sword was raised, and a fatal blow would have been struck, had not a strange thing occurred.

As it seemed to Raleigh, a small bundle suddenly sprang from the threshold.

Then the man before him, uttering a terrible cry, dropped his blade, and, reeling back a few paces, fell into the roadway.

The thrust he had received was from the tiny hand of Quicksilver.

The fight was over, for it was terminated by Lomew delivering upon the man opposed to him a blow, which, though it did not deprive him of life, would mark him for the remainder of his days.

The one fighting with Dudley turned and fled, and thus the three were left masters of the field.

A terrible sight was presented to Master Rodney as he came forth.

From one of the windows he had been watching the progress of the fight, and though he was not apprehensive as to whose the victory would be, he was fearful lest one of his

* Afterwards Sir Walter Raleigh.

friends would receive some serious injury.

Indeed, when he saw Raleigh fall, he felt certain that he had received —perhaps a mortal wound.

But as soon as he reached the threshold, Raleigh was on his feet and warmly thanking the headsman and Dudley for the great service they had rendered him.

"Though I am still very young," he said, "I have, for the past few years, been intimately associated with military life, and I have seen some fighting. But I never saw a young man fight with such coolness, such skill and ease, as Dudley. As to you, Master Headsman—well, I once saw you strike the head from a traitor, and by heaven! you use your sword much after the same fashion as the axe."

"What of me?" asked a small voice.

All hastily turned, and there was Quicksilver, leaning against the shutters of the house, calmly wiping the blood from his sword.

"My little friend," said Raleigh, picking him up, "your courage is far more weighty than your body. Master Headsman, and you, Dudley, I owe my life to this small specimen of humanity; for one of the ruffians, when I fell, was about to strike me what, perhaps, would have proved a fatal blow, when this little fellow plunged forward with his tiny blade, and passed it clean into the fellow's body."

"Well done, Quicksilver!" cried the headsman; "and though I cannot raise you in height, on my soul I raise you in my good estimation."

"Gentlemen," broke in Master Rodney, "would it not be as well to see if you can recognise any of these men?"

"I have been glancing at them," replied Raleigh, "and though I can trace in their features one or two persons I have seen before, I know not their names, nor where they came from.

"Chandler and I were near the Temple, partaking of wine.

"There was a lot of gambling going on, and hearing a great noise, we left the place and took boat.

"And then we found that a number of men were after us.

"There had been some cheating, no doubt, and we were taken for two of the cheats.

"Some enemy must have assumed the name of Raleigh, for it was shouted time after time by the men.

"We at first thought of stopping, and, indeed, I should have done so, but Chandler, laughing, said—

"'Oh, give them a row, Raleigh.'

"'Twas not long after this that poor Chandler was shot through the head.

"He was standing at the time laughing at the men, and when he was shot he fell into the river.

"The boat came up, I fought and struck two dead, and then, in the confusion, managed to get clear once more.

"But the ruffians quickly gained upon me.

"They reached the shore almost as rapidly as I did, and we all know the result. Poor Chandler is terribly avenged."

"My suggestion as to the disposal of the bodies," said the headsman, "is a simple one. Place them in the river."

"It shall be as you suggest," returned Master Rodney. "Patrick, see that the bodies are consigned to the river."

The party having once again entered the house, Master Rodney said—

"It has just struck me that your arrival here was most opportune, Master Raleigh. They say that one good turn deserves another, and unless I mistake not, it is in your power to render these friends of mine great service."

"I hope 'tis as you say," replied Raleigh. "Any service it is in my power to render shall be rendered promptly."

"Then listen, and I will tell you the story, which principally relates to no less a person than your rival at Court—Marcus Montague."

"Is the villain in London?"

"He is at Hollow Ground."

"Ha! Then my man did not tell me wrong. By heaven! Hollow Ground and its mysteries shall be laid bare before her majesty ere I am much older. But I pray you, tell me this story."

Master Rodney told him all.

His story was added to by the headsman and Dudley, and on its conclusion, Raleigh said—

"I well know the bravery and determination of Lomew, and I know how brave is Dudley; but that bravery would not open the gates at Hollow Ground.

"I have never entered that mysterious place, but I know that there are many armed men within the building.

"The same activity and watchfulness prevails at Hollow Ground as at the Tower of London, and I am sure that no man, however clever he may be, would gain admission by stratagem.

"In order to get that unhappy girl from the clutches of Marcus Montague, a bold stroke must be made.

"Now, if a breach could be effected in the wall which surrounds Hollow Ground, and fifty determined fellows were to make a rush through, success might follow."

"I had thought of the plan myself," said Master Rodney, "but feared to propose it."

"The plan is an excellent one!" cried Dudley. "By all means let us attempt it. No danger would be too great if poor Madeline could be rescued. But what of the fifty men?"

Raleigh smiled.

"That is the very least difficulty," he said. "I can within a few hours summon fifty as determined young fellows as could be met with in a day's march."

"But how will you make a breach in the walls?" asked Master Rodney.

"With gunpowder. Then there will be the moat to cross. We could take two or three long stout beams of wood for that purpose."

"I see that you are already a soldier, Walter," smiled Master Rodney. "With you, Dudley, and Master Lomew as leaders, success is almost certain."

"Let there be no delay," cried Raleigh. "I will, at once, go to collect my friends, and we will all meet here in three hours."

"Agreed!" replied Dudley.

"And in the meantime," said the headsman, "we will watch the exterior of Hollow Ground. It may be to our ultimate advantage."

"The idea is good. Watch it closely; but above all, do not show yourselves, for you may be recognised."

Fastening his cloak closely about him, Raleigh left the house, turned towards the river, and jumping into his boat, he pulled as hard as he could in the direction of the City.

CHAPTER VII.

WHEREIN THE HEADSMAN AND DUDLEY MAKE AN IMPORTANT CAPTURE—OF THE EXAMINATION, OF THE SHOT FIRED BY DUDLEY, AND OF THE PART PLAYED BY QUICKSILVER.

DUDLEY and Lomew set off for the neighbourhood of Hollow Ground on foot.

It was quickly reached, and Dudley had a long look at the exterior of this extraordinary and most mysterious building.

"It looks much like a prison," he said.

"Yes, and for that purpose it has frequently been used," replied Lomew; "but I think that I would sooner prefer to be a prisoner within the Tower than a prisoner in that place. In the Tower, the lieutenant, or those beneath him, have to give an account of every prisoner committed to their charge. Nothing of that is done here, Dudley. You cannot ever make a firmer friend than

Walter Raleigh—a braver heart could not be found. He will be your friend at Court, where you will meet Marcus Montague face to face."

"Unless," said Dudley, "I meet the villain face to face within yonder gloomy walls. If I do, Lomew, you may guess the result. I beg that, if fortune so smiles upon me, you will not offer to stay my hand for fear of the consequences to myself. Let me fight."

"My lord, if you cross swords with the villain," replied Lomew, "I will not attempt to stay your hand."

At a distance of some three hundred yards from the walls, and towards the left, was a clump of trees, and beside that a little building, used long before as a watch-house, but now fast falling into ruin.

Here the pair watched the gates, or, rather, the ground before them, for owing to the darkness the gates could not be seen.

For a long time nothing was heard.

Had the whole of that huge place been a vast burial-ground, deeper silence could not have prevailed.

But suddenly Dudley, who had been lying upon the ground, leapt to his feet.

"I saw a person issue forth," he said, in low tones; "but whether it is a man or woman, I cannot tell."

"Lie close—lie close," replied Lomew; "and let us both keep our eyes fixed in that direction. Be assured that we shall presently see whether you are correct."

A few minutes passed, and it was then seen that Dudley was indeed correct.

A person had issued from the gates; that person was a woman.

On she camé, but very cautiously, for the ground was very uneven in many places.

She passed within a stone's throw of the spot where Lomew and Dudley stood.

Dudley would have sprung forward and captured her, but Lomew restrained him.

"Wait," he whispered; "let us follow her and see whither she goes."

"Who can she be?"

"Most likely it is the woman Gitto. A very fiend in human form, this same Gitto, I have been told, and you may depend upon it that she has something to do with Madeline."

"There can be no doubt about it."

On went Mother Gitto, and the pair followed her at a distance.

That she was followed, never for an instant entered the old woman's mind.

Presently she arrived at Charing Cross, and, turning sharply to the left, she reached a row of small houses, the various signs on which, showed that they were shops.

Now all were closed, but Mother Gitto, going to the middle of the row, stopped before one of the houses bearing the name of "James Greene, Haberdasher to her Majesty," and from the top of which swayed a golden lamb.

Without hesitation, she knocked on the door, which was quietly opened by the proprietor, a grave, elderly man.

"Well," he queried, "what seek you, madame?"

"Oh, oh!" chuckled Mother Gitto. "What seek I? Why, to do you a good service, Master Greene."

The haberdasher started.

"Why," he said, "I think I recognise you. You are Mother Gitto."

"You are right."

"On whose business are you come now?"

"Why do you ask me that question?" demanded Mother Gitto, savagely.

"Why, for the simple reason," replied Master Greene, calmly, "that you are on one person's business one day, and another's the next."

"I do the same as you," said Mother Gitto. "I work for whosoever pays me best. But now I've half a mind to transfer my custom to a more civil and obliging person."

"Well, to be sure, you are quite at liberty to do so, my good woman. But as to one more civil and—"

"Enough!" interrupted Mother Gitto, as she impatiently snapped her fingers in the haberdasher's face. "Get aside, so that I may enter and transact my business I have something for one of your apprentices to do."

"'LOOK AT THIS MAN'S FACE. DOST RECOGNISE HIM?' CRIED WALTER RALEIGH."

"'BEHOLD THE MURDERESS!' CRIED MASTER RODNEY."

"Indeed, madame?" said the haberdasher. "Well, pray enter, and make me acquainted with the nature of your business, which I presume is urgent."

"Very urgent. A lady's needs must always be supplied."

The haberdasher nodded stiffly, and passed into the shop, followed by Mother Gitto.

The headsman and Dudley placed themselves in such a position that they could overhear all that transpired.

Mother Gitto fumbled amid the folds of her garb, and presently produced a piece of paper.

This she spread out, and handed to the haberdasher, who, carefully adjusting his glasses, examined it.

"This," he said, "is a list of articles required by a certain gentleman."

"Lady!" snapped Mother Gitto.

"Why, madame," said the haberdasher, sternly, "do you tell me that I am unable to distinguish between a lady's and a gentleman's handwriting?"

"Oh, I've little doubt as to that," grinned the old woman; "but the articles are required for a lady."

"Well, madame, a large number of articles like those named here, would come to a large amount."

"Who said they wouldn't?"

"Patience! patience! You have not told me yet who orders these articles?"

"Certainly not."

"Well, I am unable to supply them without the money."

"I was quite prepared to hear you say that. And so, as you see, I have come prepared with the money."

And she banged upon the counter a heavy purse, though she did not loose her hold of it.

"That alters affairs," replied the haberdasher. "I will at once procure the desired articles."

"They must all be placed within the best box you have, and the box perfumed, because it is to be placed in the hands of a dainty lady."

This she said with a bitter sneer.

"Be pleased to wait here," said the haberdasher; "I shall return in a few moments."

Then, list in hand, he hurried off.

The haberdasher soon returned, carrying a box in which were the desired articles; but in the meantime, Mother Gitto had taken from a shelf a box of silk kerchiefs, which she had placed in her dress.

The haberdasher emptied out the contents on the counter, and then setting them out, one by one, replaced them, set the lid of the box in position, corded it, and over all placed a small piece of canvas marked with his name and address.

"That will do," said Mother Gitto; "but I have other business to transact, and therefore you must send the box to Hollow Ground."

"What!" cried the haberdasher, looking suddenly up. "Hollow Ground!"

"Yes, Hollow Ground. Is there anything strange in that?"

"Strange that a 'dainty' lady should be within such a place."

"If a dainty lady is within Hollow Ground, master," said an apprentice, entering, "be assured that Marcus Montague is not far off."

"Impertinent rascal!" cried Mother Gitto. "Look you, Master Greene, you must not send that youth with the box."

"I will send another," replied Master Greene, calmly. "This youth certainly does talk somewhat fast."

"Now, Master Greene, tell me what is the amount due, and I will pay it and go."

"There is the amount. I have put it down at the bottom of the list —twenty nobles."

"Well, here are the twenty nobles. Are you satisfied?"

"Perfectly."

"Then I am not. You will scratch out the twenty, and put twenty-five nobles."

"In heaven's name, why?"

"Five for myself."

"I never transact business like that."

"Fool!" cried Mother Gitto, as she savagely snatched up the bill, and crumpled it in her horny fist. "I will soon get someone to alter it. Now, when will you send the box?"

"At whatever time it may suit you."

"Then say an hour."

Another moment, and Mother Gitto had left the shop.

We need not say what had passed between the headsman and Dudley.

It is sufficient to remark that a plan had already been projected by them.

Both well knew that the articles were changes of toilet for a lady within that house of mystery, and no doubt Madeline was that lady.

Dudley waited at the haberdasher's, while the headsman followed Mother Gitto.

Whither and on what errand she was now bound, the headsman did not wait to see.

No sooner had the old woman reached a dark and lonely spot, than Lomew pounced upon her.

Like a great black shadow he suddenly appeared, and so startled was the wicked old hag that a great cry left her lips.

Perhaps she thought that the Evil One had suddenly come to claim his own.

"Heaven!" she gasped, "what is this? Is murder intended?"

"No, woman," replied Lomew, "murder is not intended. Information is sought. That information shall be furnished by you."

Mother Gitto groaned dismally.

"I thought you were some horrid fiend," she said; "you look it. Stopped by the headsman! Holy Virgin!"

"The information I seek," repeated Lomew, "must be furnished by you."

"Never—never!"

"If you do not accompany me quietly, I shall use force."

"Dare to do so at your peril."

"Dare! You will quickly find that I dare do anything. If you refuse to go with me, I will hurl you to the ground, gag and bind you, and carry you."

"Well, since there is no help, I will go with you. But though I go, I tell you that you will get no information out of me."

"Come."

"I am ready. Lead on."

Determined that she should have no opportunity of procuring assistance, the headsman led her down to the river, where he called for scullers.

One was soon forthcoming, and the pair were speedily being rowed up the river.

In the meantime, Dudley had lingered about the shop, the door of which had been closed.

But he determined to watch for the apprentice who was to carry the box.

More than half-an-hour passed ere the door was opened and the apprentice, with the box on his shoulder, passed out.

Dudley saw that it was the same apprentice who had been in the shop.

Before he had got a hundred yards. Dudley laid his hand on his shoulder.

With a start the apprentice turned.

Despite the darkness, he saw that the one who had thus touched him wore a rich costume, and looked a person of some importance.

"My friend," said Dudley, "with your permission, I should like a little conversation with you."

The apprentice stared.

Then shifting the box from his shoulder, he placed it upon the ground, and sat upon it, saying—

"Well, whoever and whatever you are, as you are so civil, why I will give you permission to have a few words, though what may be your business with such as I, I am at a loss to conceive."

"I will soon ease your mind."

"Very good, sir. As long as you don't ease me of this box I sha'n't complain."

"What is your name, my lad?"

"My name—the name I am proud of—is Merlin."

"Well, Master Merlin, would you like to rattle in your pockets the sum of fifty crowns and call them your own?"

The apprentice, a remarkably sharp and shrewd youth, opened wide his eyes, and then gave vent to a low, prolonged whistle, expressive of intense astonishment.

"It's a shame to tantalise a poor apprentice," he said.

"I am not doing so, I assure you.

Stand up, my young friend, and look at me."

The apprentice promptly did so.

"Do I look like a person who would deceive you?" asked Dudley.

"Well, I'm bound to say that you don't. But all this sounds so mysterious. Do you say that you can really put so large a sum in my way? If so, hasten and tell me, for, on my soul, fifty crowns would be a fortune to my old mother."

"Will you accompany me as far as Chelsea? We can take a boat."

"But where can I leave this box?"

"Bring that with you; it is by means of the box that you can earn the fifty crowns."

"You surprise me. This is quite romantic. Well, sir, I will go with you. But you will at least give me an inkling as to what you want of me."

"Most assuredly. You are about to take that box to Hollow Ground."

"How do you know?"

"I will tell you as we go along. I will tell you a story that will cause you great surprise. I heard all that passed between the haberdasher and Mother Gitto."

"Ha!"

"Yes. And I know well enough that that box contains articles intended for a lady who is confined against her will within the strong walls of that mysterious place."

"And is Master Montague at the bottom of it?"

"He is."

"I thought so. He is indeed a villain."

"You know him?"

"By sight—yes. But I and my comrades know him better by reputation. And I suppose, sir, that this poor lady is your sister."

"No, she is my betrothed."

"Well, sir—here's my hand on it—if I can be of any service, you can command me."

The riverside was soon reached.

A boat was secured, and the two, with the box between them, were soon being pulled towards Chelsea.

* * * *

When the boat, containing the headsman and Mother Gitto, arrived at its destination, the former landed first, and then having assisted Mother Gitto out, and paid the waterman, he proceeded with his prisoner to the house of Master Rodney.

The door was opened by Patrick, who led them into the parlour, and whispered to Lomew that Master Rodney, who was then busy upstairs, would descend in a moment.

A most extraordinary change had come over the hideous face of Mother Gitto.

The headsman's keen eyes were watching her.

Presently an opposite door opened, and Master Rodney made his appearance and came forward.

No sooner did the old gentleman fix his eyes upon Mother Gitto than, uttering a loud cry of wonder, he abruptly stopped.

The expression on Mother Gitto's face was now awful.

The headsman saw that the pair recognised each other.

For the space of some moments they continued to gaze upon each other.

Mother Gitto was the first to drop her eyes.

"Here!" she muttered, hoarsely—"to be brought here, and thus come face to face after so many years! Had I known it, I would have sooner died."

"You here!" said Master Rodney, slowly; "you, Mary Kenyon, the murderess—here in my house! Then it seems that justice at last will claim you."

"I came not of my own free will."

"That is true," said Lomew; "I compelled her to come."

"Then you did not mention my name?"

"I did not."

"Had you done so she would never have accompanied you. Sooner than that, she would have undergone the tortures of the rack, or the scavenger's daughter. Lomew, you know somewhat of my history. I told you my wife was murdered. Behold the murderess."

And he pointed his trembling fingers at the haggard, cowering wretch before him.

Mother Gitto (*alias* Mary Kenyon) made no attempt to deny the terrible accusation.

"Rather than have revived so dreadful a recollection," replied Lomew, "I would have done anything. But I knew not that you were acquainted with this vile woman."

"This is the Mother Gitto, of Hollow Ground?"

"Exactly. We saw her leave the gates."

"Her right name is Mary Kenyon, and to this day the warrant for her apprehension holds good, though it was issued twenty-five years ago."

"Twenty-five years ago!" repeated Mother Gitto, as we shall continue to call her. "Twenty-five years ago!"

"Yes," said Master Rodney, sternly; "and despite the terrible life you have since lived—for now that I know you as Mother Gitto, the whole of your profligate career is brought before me—your hand committed that terrible deed. Besotted, depraved wretch! No riotous living could cause you to forget that terrible crime. What you have since been guilty of, heaven and yourself alone can tell. But, at last, justice shall overtake you."

"Mercy!" shrieked the old woman, throwing herself on her knees before the chemist; "mercy, mercy! Yield me not up to justice after all these years. Surely you could not wish me to suffer for a crime committed so many years ago?"

"Avaunt!" cried the chemist, shrinking back with disgust and loathing. "Does the lapse of time tone down a base, heartless, and cold-blooded murder? No, no! When that crime was committed, I swore to avenge my wife's death, and I will."

"Sir, when I lived in your house you were but a poor, struggling man, and now you are a great one. Surely—surely you can well afford to grant me mercy?"

"No mercy should be shown the murderess," said Lomew.

"No, for the murder," said Master Rodney, "was committed under circumstances of more than ordinary coolness and deliberation."

"My love for you made me mad," cried Mother Gitto.

"No, woman, there you lie! 'Twas not your love for me. It was the love you bore what I then had, and what you predicted was in store for me in the future."

"And that prediction has been fulfilled."

"To some extent—yes."

"But why have I been brought here?" interrupted Mother Gitto, suddenly leaping to her feet; "why was I brought here? What question does this man want to put to me? I see that I was not brought here by your orders; what, then, is the reason?"

"I know not," Master Rodney replied, coldly; "but now that you are here, I will see that you do not depart unless in the custody of those who will place you in gaol. Master Lomew, what seek you at the hands of this murderess?"

"She shall now know. Woman, what of the lady placed by order of Marcus Montague within the walls of Hollow Ground?"

"Ha! Madeline Maynard!"

"The same."

"I know nothing of her!"

"Beware! You will perhaps find it to your advantage to speak the truth," said Lomew; "you know all about her, else you would not have uttered her name."

"What do you seek to know?"

"What has been done with her."

"And if I refuse to answer you?"

"You will take the consequences."

"And suppose I choose to answer you?"

"I shall say that, for once, you have proved yourself wise."

"How so?"

"The box you ordered at the haberdasher's was for this lady, was it not?"

"I see," growled Mother Gitto, "I have been watched."

"You have, and so is Hollow Ground."

"I will tell you what," said Mother Gitto, after a pause of a few moments. "If Master Rodney will swear to let me go free, I will answer truthfully every question you may ask, as well as give information. If he refuses, I will still answer you, but all I say will be false!"

The headsman glanced at Master Rodney's stern, impassive face, and then, in low tones, which were inaudible to Mother Gitto, he said—

"For Dudley's sake."

"Yes," replied Master Rodney, addressing himself to Mother Gitto, "I will let you go. But I warn you, now that I know Mother Gitto to be Mary Kenyon, I will leave no stone unturned to capture you and bring you to justice."

"I take you at your word. I will go."

"Does the bear ever leave its old haunts?" asked Master Rodney, bitterly. "No; nor will you."

Lomew was about to ask a question, when Patrick announced the arrival of Dudley and a companion.

Master Rodney bade him usher them in.

The first to cross the threshold was the apprentice with the box on his shoulder.

Mother Gitto saw that she had been, indeed, very closely watched—that a plot was hatching, and that the apprentice had been bribed to play a part.

She looked daggers at him.

But the youngster was in no way disconcerted.

He smiled blandly, doffed his flat cap, and bowed.

"You, then, have succeeded, Dudley?" said the headsman.

"I have," replied Dudley. "Ah, now, Marcus Montague—now is a web being woven, and if you fall not into its meshes, then my name is not Dudley Herbert."

"I pray you let Master Rodney into the secret of the plan so hastily formed," said Lomew.

"It is this, Master Rodney," said Dudley. "We watched and followed this woman to the haberdasher's, and we soon arrived at the conclusion, that this box of articles was intended for Madeline. There can be no doubt, that Montague intends to try what a little kindness will do towards bringing her to his views, or the views of his assistant, John Barber."

A low chuckle left Mother Gitto's lips, and she said—

"Marcus Montague has taken a strong fancy to the lady, but I admire not his taste."

"Wretch!" thundered Dudley, "Stand aside!"

"Proceed, Dudley," said Master Rodney.

"My idea is to use that box as a means of conveying to Madeline positive assurance that firm and powerful friends are working to procure her release."

"By addressing a letter—I see."

"No, no; something better than that. Where is Quicksilver?"

"Here!" cried the well-known little voice of Quicksilver, who had been lying in a small recess, out of which he now jumped with amazing rapidity.

Mother Gitto remembered the talk about this little fellow, and as soon as she saw him, she knew what was intended to be done.

The apprentice was directed to place the box upon the table.

It was then opened, and the contents—with the exception of a few articles—were taken out.

The headsman had lifted Quicksilver upon the table, and the little man, his arms akimbo, was surveying matters with great interest.

"Quicksilver," said Dudley, "think you that you have the courage to be placed in this box, and to be thus conveyed into Hollow Ground?"

"Whatever you order me to do, Dudley," was the reply, "I will do without a moment's hesitation—that is, if my undertaking meets with the approval of Master Lomew."

"It would be unnecessary to ask whether that undertaking would meet with my approval," said Lomew; "but let us not forget that a few holes must be made in the box to admit of free ventilation. But, listen, Quicksilver; what you are about to do is a most perilous thing, and you might lose your life. I well know your small body is full of courage, but Dudley will agree with me, that no one should risk his life without his free consent."

"Most true," said Dudley. "Let Quicksilver reflect."

"No, no!" cried Quicksilver, his little heart palpitating with excitement at the idea of being the principal in an adventure at once romantic and perilous; "reflection is quite unnecessary. I will do as Dudley asks me. All I desire is, that I may be permitted to have my sword with me."

Lomew felt inclined to laugh at this request; but, remembering that the tiny blade had but lately done such good service, he refrained.

"You shall have it," he said.

"And if he will carry it," added Master Rodney," I will make him a present of a pistol."

"No pistol was ever yet made small enough for his hand," said the headsman.

"Wait!" answered Master Rodney, who, opening a drawer in the table, took out a small leathern case.

Opening this, he produced one of the smallest pistols ever seen.

Quicksilver was delighted.

"And here," said Master Rodney —"here in this little bag are bullets to fit it. 'Tis yours, Quicksilver; and may it be of service to you in an hour of need."

"A thousand thanks, Master Rodney!" cried Quicksilver. "Be assured that I will make good use of it, if necessity requires. I hope I shall have the opportunity of burying a bullet in Marcus Montague's heart, and thus rid the world of a cruel villain, and Dudley of his greatest foe!"

"Let us no longer delay," said Dudley, "for the apprentice must at once be rowed back. If he does not quickly present himself at the gates of Hollow Ground, they may refuse to take the box in."

"They have orders to take it in, I presume?" Lomew asked Mother Gitto.

"They have," was the reply.

"Tell us—does it go straight to Mistress Madeline?"

"I think there is no doubt as to that. It is the intention of Marcus Montague to subdue her by terror."

"To subdue her, woman!" cried Dudley. "What mean you?"

"Where is she now?" asked the headsman.

"Below."

And Mother Gitto pointed her thumb downward.

"In the vaults?"

"In the chambers of mystery—yes."

"Ah, no doubt poor Madeline is not the first who has been placed there," said Dudley, sternly.

"You are correct," chuckled Mother Gitto. "Some have died; others have lived through it."

"Some have died—in what way? You mean by violence?"

"I am not at liberty to say."

"Master Merlin," said Dudley, turning to the apprentice, who had not once taken his admiring eyes off Quicksilver, "are you ready to go?"

"Yes."

"In a day or two the promised reward shall be furnished you."

"Good."

"You, Patrick," said Master Rodney, "might accompany him, for it is necessary that you, Dudley, and you, Lomew, remain here."

"Rather let me go with him," said Mother Gitto, "and then there will be neither delay nor difficulty."

"Fool!" cried Master Rodney. "Though these present know not your true character, it is well known to me. I would trust you no farther than I could see you."

"My character has changed in twenty-five years," said Mother Gitto.

"For the worse—yes, for the worse indeed," retorted Master Rodney.

"I would not trust her on any account," said the headsman.

"Nor would I," added Dudley.

"No, nor would I," said Quicksilver, "for one has only to look once to see what sort of a woman he is dealing with."

The bottom of the box having been duly prepared, Quicksilver entered, it being first understood that no word was to be said by either, in the boat or the streets.

Quicksilver shook hands with all, and bade them good-bye without a quiver in his voice; but the voice of the headsman trembled as he said—

"Good-bye, little playmate—good-bye, and heaven guard you well."

Quicksilver was then covered with the articles (several of which were of course left out), the lid was placed on, and once more it was secured.

The apprentice placed the box upon his shoulder, then Patrick took his hand, and led him forth.

"And so," said Mother Gitto, savagely, "I am to remain here until it suits your pleasure to let me go, Master Rodney?"

"Yes, and beware! Let me caution you to guard well your tongue, lest I be tempted to hand you over to the officers of justice."

"Listen to me," cried Mother Gitto, with a sudden burst of passion; "let me tell you this: that though that sprig of humanity of yours obtains admission—and there is little doubt of that, since the box is expected—he will never come out, either alive or dead. He may be able to speak with the girl, truly, but of what use will it be? What friends, however powerful, will be able to pass the walls of Hollow Ground?"

"We will say to you, wait and see," retorted Dudley.

"For the next few hours," said Master Rodney, "you will remain in the chamber to which you will now be shown."

"You mean to keep me a prisoner, then?"

"For the present it is my intention to take care of you. When it is no longer necessary to keep you here, then shall you depart, according to my promise; but the other part of the promise was that I would eventually hand you over to justice, and, in the name of my murdered wife, I mean to keep my word."

"And I swear to slay you as I slew her," muttered the wretched woman.

In another few moments she was taken by Dudley and the headsman to a chamber at the top of the house, and there safely placed under lock and key.

And now the three prepared for the reception of Raleigh and his friends.

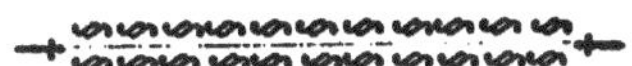

CHAPTER VIII.

SHOWS HOW THE "GAYONNE CRANK" WAS PUT IN MOTION—WITH WHAT RESULT—OF HOW THE BOX WAS BROUGHT TO MADELINE—AND WHAT FOLLOWED.

BUSINESS of an important character at Whitehall commanded Montague's attention, and therefore poor Madeline received the visits only of John Barber and Joseph Hockley.

Barber's protestations of love made no impression on Madeline. She, crouching on the stool provided, shut her ears to all he said, until at last Barber finished with threats of an appalling character.

Hockley was well aware of the fact that Montague was playing a double game with his factotum. And he well knew, too, that John Barber was standing with one foot in the grave.

John Barber, after a last interview with Madeline, had come to the conclusion that, though the maiden refused to entertain his proposals, her mind was coming round to view Montague with favour, and loud and bitter were his imprecations on the "traitor," as he called him.

"Wait—wait a few hours," said Hockley, in encouraging tones, "and you will, I think, find that you are mistaken."

"No, no; there can be no mistake about it. But I will retire to my room."

As he proceeded, he muttered—

"I will at once commence to write a full confession to the queen. I know who would be only too glad to peruse it—Walter Raleigh. By heaven! I will give the most minute particulars of everything, including the murder of his wife. But then—what would become of me? Ah, I cannot pause to think of that; I must risk all."

So he proceeded to his task of making a full confession, when Montague returned, flushed and excited; for once again his lucky star had been in the ascendant, and he had received more than one favour at the hands of Elizabeth.

"Where is Barber?" he asked Hockley.

"Within his room," was the reply. "I don't think he is in a very good humour."

"I would have instant speech with him, for I want to send him on important business to the Lady Herbert."

"It strikes me, Master Montague, that you will not be able to get John Barber to budge an inch from this building unless you consent to let the girl go with him."

"That I will never do. I have resolved, Hockley, thus: You have heard of my projected marriage?"

"I have heard something of it. But what says the queen respecting the death of your late wife?"

"As yet, nothing. She has not even hinted at it. Indeed, she has been more than usually pleasant."

"But, of course, she knows all about it. For, unfortunately for yourself, you have plenty of enemies at Court—more enemies than friends."

"I have, thanks to Walter Raleigh, who, however, I will take care does not cut me out. I have money, Hockley; he has none."

"That is true. But, by the Virgin, what he lacks in money, he makes up for in coolness and cunning. But look to it, Master Montague—I believe that your greatest enemy at the present moment is John Barber."

"Ha! You do not say so with the object of earning the thousand nobles I promised you, in case I decided that it was necessary to put him out of mischief?"

"No, no! But I will tell you that I heard him mutter threats against you. He is of opinion that you are not only neglecting him now that, as he says, he has done your principal dirty work, but that you are also seeking to take from him the only girl he ever loved."

"Vile dastard!" hissed Montague; "did he say dirty work?"

"In very truth he did. Now, do you, Master Montague, really think that it would be wise to allow a man like that to become acquainted with the plot which is presently to be formed here?"

"No; you are right," replied Montague, an expression of fear passing over his face. "No; I have decided, Hockley. You shall at once earn the thousand nobles. He must be put out of the way, for I know that he has the devil in him, and that it only wants raising."

"The crank must be used, then?"

"Yes."

"You see, the girl could witness it. And you could tell her, that since Barber is obnoxious to her, you thus remove him. At the same time, it will show her that you are not to be trifled with. Believe me, the operation of the crank will have more effect on her than months of imprisonment."

"Have you supplied her well with food?"

"Yes. She has had the best of dainties; and she has been removed from the dungeon to the Oak Chamber."

"Has Mother Gitto procured the change of clothing?"

"She has, no doubt, ordered it by this time, but it has not yet been brought."

"When it arrives, let it be at once taken to her."

"Good; and you will now take action?"

"I shall, at once."

"Well, you know how to signal me. I will be in readiness with half-a-dozen men."

"You are sure no one is with Barber?"

"Certain of it."

"And he has been in his apartment, you say—how long?"

"He must have been there three or four hours."

"What can the villain be doing?" muttered Montague.

"There is never any telling what

a dangerous man may be doing," replied Hockley. "Now, look you; why not enter the apartment by the secret passage, and come suddenly upon him?"

"But does he not know of the secret passage?"

"He does not."

"If he happened to hear my footsteps—"

"Oh, there is no danger in that. Come, I will lead you to the passage. Then I will get the men, and stand ready at the end, awaiting your signal."

"Bring ropes to bind him."

"Fear not. All shall be well arranged in my hands," chuckled Hockley, who now led the way.

John Barber had already written a mass of matter—every line of which was a tale of villainy in which Montague had been the leading, and himself the second actor.

He had already got to the shocking murder of the "Windsor Rose," and was in deep thought.

"I shall have to fly the country as soon as I have placed it in the hands of Raleigh," he thought; "but here are names of persons of whom her majesty can make inquiries, and she will soon find that what I have written can be amply corroborated."

Then, taking up a bottle of wine, he poured himself out a glass, and, holding it aloft, he said—

"And here's confusion and death to Marcus Montague! Here's to his arrest, and may but a few days pass ere Traitor's Gate opens to receive him!"

He raised the glass to his lips, but before he could swallow the contents, a heavy hand fell upon his shoulder, the glass fell with a crash to the ground, and he leaped to his feet and placed his hand on his sword as he turned—to see Marcus Montague standing beside his chair.

Only one look was necessary to see what humour his "master" was in.

Montague had overheard what he had said.

His rage was great.

His face was deathly pale.

Nevertheless, he endeavoured to keep a calm exterior.

"Checkmated!" he exclaimed.

"Eh?" queried Barber. "I don't understand."

"But I do, ungrateful scoundrel! So you had determined to betray me. But you are foiled. I will frustrate your intentions. What is this?"

And Montague strode towards the papers.

At once Barber threw himself before him.

"Touch them not!" he cried.

"Away," shouted Montague, "lest I strike you at my feet!"

"Touch them not, I tell you!" yelled Barber, snatching his blade from its sheath. "Touch them not, or you force me to kill you!"

"What would you do—murder me?"

"No, I would not murder you; for though you gave the order for the murder of your wife, I don't suppose you will give an order to the same effect as regards yourself."

"Heaven's mercy, this from you! You, than whom viler hound never existed! But I will look at your handiwork."

"At your peril touch them, Marcus Montague."

"Why, what has made you so brave, assassin—eh? Is it the wine?"

"I will answer you not, except to say again that you shall not touch those papers. If you force me to fight with you, then—"

"Fight!" interrupted Montague, with a sneer; "fight with you? Now, indeed, I must have descended low enough in your estimation! Draw blade to fight a worm like John Barber! Ha, ha!"

"A worm you have made crawl into many foul deeds, which shall ere long reach the queen's ears, Marcus Montague. A worm you have trodden upon, and a worm that now has turned."

"A worm that I can crush!" hissed Montague. "A worm that I *will* crush."

"I give you not the opportunity, for hence I go at once."

"Not so fast—not so fast. Listen. I overheard your devil's boast."

"Devil's boast?"

"Yes, devil's boast. For they say

that he who boasts aloud, thinking that no one hears him, boasts to the devil."

"I care not what you overheard."

"You said, 'Confusion and death to Marcus Montague.' And you hoped that Traitor's Gate would open to receive him. Well, John Barber," and here Marcus folded his arms across his breast and fixed a keen, sardonic look on Barber's face, "you will never live to see that come to pass."

"Yes, I shall," replied Barber, who had no suspicions of the plot formed between Montague and Hockley. "Let me tell you that I will try hard enough to live and see the end of it. I know that were I to lodge information against you, I should have to quit the country; but the news of what befalls you will quickly spread."

"John Barber, I see that you are under the impression that I have never thought of taking measures to put a stop to that tongue of yours whenever it so pleased me. Fool, you mistake!"

So fiendish was the expression on Montague's face as he said this, that it at once struck Barber that the villain had been prepared for this outburst. But up to now, no mention was made of Madeline.

Again Montague pointed to the documents.

"This is your handiwork," he said, "and as I have no remembrance of having set you so prodigious a task, what you have there written must be on your own account. So I say, let me look at it."

And he strode forward again.

Instantly Barber, with a cry of rage, raised his blade; but just as quickly, Montague threw himself upon him, wrested the weapon from his grasp, snapped it in two across his knee, and hurled the pieces in opposite directions.

"That blade is like your spirit, John Barber," sneered Montague—"not very strong! But I have no further time to waste. All is over between us. We part for ever!"

"I am willing," replied Barber, eagerly, as he snatched up the papers. "Do but give me the sum which is properly mine, and I will go."

"Yes; we part, and for ever, John Barber," continued Montague; "but I assure you, that I could never think of allowing you to go hence, and enrol yourself under the banner of a new master. Briefly, John Barber, you have sealed your own doom. What ho!" he roared, stamping his foot.

John Barber saw all now, only too plainly. Danger loomed ahead.

Self-preservation was everything to him, and, with a desperate rush, he tried to gain the door.

But Montague prevented him, for he reached the door first.

At the same moment, the rattle of arms and the tramp of heavy feet were heard in the secret passage, and presently Hockley, at the head of half-a-dozen men, made his appearance.

"Hockley," said Montague, "to work with this man!"

"Ah!" yelled Barber, as he picked up half of the sword and held it dagger-wise in his hand, "I will defend myself to the last!"

"I doubt it," sneered Montague; "you were never very good at open fight."

"You had better place that blade down," said Hockley, glad of something threatening to say, "or if you don't, we must use our weapons, and you know what the result will be."

"Ha! I have been betrayed!" cried Barber.

"Put down that blade!" shouted Hockley.

Barber saw that resistance would be madness, and so, with a fierce cry, he flung the weapon at Montague's feet.

"As this blade is broken," he said, "so may your dastard career—so may your black heart be broken!"

"Ah, ah" chuckled Hockley; "we do not fear you."

"What are your orders with respect to me?" asked Barber of Hockley.

"You will see before another half-hour has passed," replied Hockley, grimly. "Bind his arms behind his back, my men."

A cold perspiration broke out all over Barber's body.

For a moment he seemed as if he would resist being bound, but second thoughts decided him to submit.

So he was quickly pinioned.

The papers, which had fallen to the floor, were picked up and handed to Montague.

He ran his eye over the commencement, scowled darkly, and said—

"As I suspected—a confession! By heaven! I was only just in time. Well, it is exit John Barber, instead of exit Marcus Montague. These papers I will peruse at my leisure."

And he thrust them within his doublet.

"Better destroy them," suggested Hockley; "it would be the safer plan."

"No, no; I must read what the dastard has written. And now away with him. When you hear the signal, proceed."

"Yes, yes," replied Hockley.

"Let me have a word or two," cried Barber, now in a state of the greatest terror; "let me have a word or two; let me apologise to you, Master Montague; let me, here on my bended knees, apologise and vow to serve you faithfully."

"No," replied Montague, sternly; "the snake whose fangs are found ready to discharge poison, should be destroyed."

"Oh, heaven! then you mean to murder me?"

"I murder you! I soil my hands with such vile stuff as you! Never! Away with him to his doom, I say. Away with him!"

Another moment, and Hockley, with his prisoner, had vanished into the secret passage.

And even when he had traversed its whole length, the voice of John Barber could be heard alternately begging and reviling Hockley and his men.

Into the great hall went Montague, and inquired of one of the men-at-arms whether they had seen aught of Mother Gitto.

She had not returned.

"Who have arrived?" asked Montague.

"Five gentlemen, masked."

Soon after this the bridge was lowered, and presently a man with a box on his shoulder approached Marcus.

"An apprentice has left it," he said. "Know you aught of it, master?"

"Yes; it is from the haberdasher's. Follow me—'tis to be taken to the Oak Chamber."

He turned to proceed thither.

The Oak Chamber was situated in the vaults, being simply one of the numerous apartments there.

Though it was neither so cold nor so dark as the one she had just been placed in, Madeline was just as miserable.

The ceiling, walls, and flooring of this chamber were of black oak, hung with faded tapestry. The walls looked solid enough, but owing to many sounds of a peculiar character which had reached her ears, Madeline was under the impression that more than one secret passage was connected with the room, and accordingly she was well on her guard.

The custodian of the vaults at present on duty hastened forward with the keys, and the door of the Oak Chamber being thrown open, Montague strode in.

A small taper burned upon the little table, and beside it stood Madeline, pale, broken-hearted, but resolved.

Montague bowed in courtly fashion, and said—

"I trust I find you in a better frame of mind, Mistress Madeline?"

"I am in no better frame of mind, nor shall I be."

"Say not so. Are you not more comfortable? When I thought of how dreadful must be your sufferings in the other vault, I at once resolved to change it."

"I do not thank you for the change," replied Madeline, in freezing tones. "A cage is a cage, call it what you may."

Of this Montague took—or pretended to take—no notice.

"Here is a box," he said, "full of articles which I thought might be necessary to you. You see it is from the haberdasher."

Madeline looked.

"Yes, I see," she said; "and I see

something else. I observe the address, Charing Cross, so that there can be no doubt that I am close to that spot."

Montague frowned.

"For that matter," he replied, "you may be a dozen miles from that neighbourhood. However, here is the box. The list of the contents was prepared by one who is qualified to know what you may want."

"I desire it not."

"It shall be left with you. No doubt you will find much within it to please you. Accept it, Madeline, as proof that I am devoting my attention to you. You have but to utter the word, and your removal to the beautiful apartment above is instantly done. And I am now going to give you further proof of my devotion."

"What with you and John Barber—"

"Speak not his name, sweet maiden," interrupted Montague, "for he is about to be removed from your path."

"What mean you?" cried Madeline, startled at his demeanour.

"Saw you not the machine in yonder vault?"

"Yes, I noticed it."

"He dies by that means."

A wild shriek burst from Madeline's lips.

"You are about to commit murder!" she gasped.

She was horror-struck at his consummate coolness.

"No, 'tis not murder, 'tis justice. Barber has been for years my slave, sweet Madeline; but he has proved himself a traitor. As a matter of fact, it is his life or mine."

Madeline answered him not.

She could but fix her startled eyes on his handsome face, and marvel that any man could speak of a contemplated tragedy in such off-hand tones.

Before this brief conversation, Montague had waved the two men aside.

He now beckoned them forward.

"Come hither," he said, "and conduct this lady after me."

"No, no!" cried Madeline; "spare me—spare me! You would force me to witness this terrible scene. Oh, no, no! Let me retain possession of my senses, I implore you. If you force me to be present in that chamber, I shall go mad."

"No, I have no fear of that. Come."

Madeline found it next to impossible to move.

"No doubt she is weak," said Montague, in sarcastic tones, "and, therefore, pray assist her."

His meaning was plain enough.

It was—

"Thrust her forward."

One man took her by the arm, and "led" her forward.

In a few moments she was led into the fatal vault.

The infernal machine appeared very much as she had seen it before, but now the vault—the dreadful chamber which had "murder" stamped on its every stone—was illuminated by flaming links thrust into wall-brackets.

At each corner stood two men, brutal, degraded - looking ruffians, with drink-besotted faces.

Each was thoroughly well armed —they were always well armed, but whether they were used to the arms they carried was another thing.

But the time was rapidly approaching when all their valour would be put to the most severe test.

Neither John Barber, Hockley, nor the men who had seized Barber were present. They were above.

"Madeline," said Montague, as he pointed to the terrible instrument of death, and his tones became threatening, "sometimes a man finds himself foiled and insulted by a woman. Then—here is the remedy."

"Your words are vague, but I well understand their meaning," returned Madeline. "You mean to convey to me the intelligence that if I do not conform to your wishes, that diabolical contrivance will be my fate. I tell you, Marcus Montague"—and here she drew herself proudly erect, and fixed a defiant, scornful look upon the stern face before her—"I tell you that, sooner than be crushed in life and humbled by you, I will be crushed to atoms, if that is the action of yonder machine."

Montague moved back a few paces, and folded his arms across his breast.

"Stand back, in yonder recess," he said, "and remain there."

"As a witness to a murder, you mean?" replied Madeline.

"If you so like to call it," said Montague, in low, fierce tones. "If you do not do as I command, it will go hard with you."

"As you command me!" replied Madeline. "Villain, I will not obey!"

"Seize upon her!" thundered Montague; "and stand beside her!"

This command was promptly carried out, and then Montague gave a signal in the form of a shrill whistle.

But before giving an account of what followed, we will ascend to the room above.

It was a chamber about half the size of the one below.

The ceiling was high and vaulted, and in the centre was a circular glass dome.

Across this was a monstrous iron bar, from which depended a piece of heavy chain, and to this again was joined a thick rope.

The end of this was hooked on the wall.

Round the room instruments of all sorts were placed, as well as arms, and in one corner were several kegs of powder and bags of bullets.

In that chamber were John Barber, Hockley, and his men.

The appearance of Barber was now abject in the extreme.

He was seated upon the floor, unable to move either arms or legs, for both were securely bound.

For some time nothing had been said.

Barber had listened intently to ascertain whether he could overhear anything respecting the fate in store for him.

But no sound fell upon his ears.

Presently, however, he heard voices below.

He strained his ears, and fancied he heard a female voice.

"Go," cried Barber—"go, I implore you, to Master Montague, and appeal to him in my behalf. If you are successful, I swear I will reward you."

He might just as well have appealed to a stone wall.

"You have gone too far, John Barber," replied Hockley, "and therefore you must die."

At this moment Montague's whistle was heard.

At once Barber was pounced upon and dragged to his feet.

This was no sooner done than Hockley and the men stepped aside.

The former stooped, touched something, and, like a flash of lightning, that part of the flooring on which Barber stood shot downward, and the doomed wretch, of course, went with it.

Straight as a dart he went, and shot clean into the hole in the marble of the infernal machine.

And now a fearful yell of terror escaped his lips.

Again and again did he frantically appeal for mercy.

"To work!" Montague thundered, as soon as the trap went down.

Four men rushed forward, and the next moment a great creaking and groaning of the pulleys showed that the machine was at work.

The two enormous pieces of iron moved slowly forward across the marble slab.

Barber's body was on a level with the slab, while his legs were below.

And now the chamber was filled with his shrieks, and his appeals to Montague for mercy.

He vowed that if he would order his release, he would for ever be his most abject slave—he would even be as humble and submissive as a dog—but Montague heeded him not.

John Barber was doomed.

Marcus Montague thought of the papers within his bosom, and of what their effect would have been had they fallen into the hands of Queen Elizabeth.

His blood ran cold at the idea of how his rivals at Court would have mocked him, and there loomed before his mental vision the black outlines of gloomy Traitor's Gate.

Madeline had shut her eyes—but not before she saw a human figure shoot through the trap—and she saw nothing of how Barber met his doom.

But those dreadful cries rang in her ears for months afterwards.

The huge blocks of iron continued to move, but so slowly, that their movement was almost imperceptible; and, in the meantime, the unhappy wretch endured the most horrible mental agony.

Then suddenly the irons touched his body, and his cries were redoubled.

Closer, closer pressed the irons—closer, until a terrible feeling of compression seized upon him.

Hockley, by this time had entered the chamber, and directed the fiendish operations.

Closer still came the irons, until, at last, it seemed as if Barber's whole body was seized in a monstrous vice.

His cries for mercy changed to horrible imprecations.

In the space of a few moments, Madeline had learned from his lips the whole of a fearful history—the history of himself and his murderous master, Montague.

Terrible words left Barber's lips; but they were stopped by a sudden rush of blood, which flowed over the white marble of the infernal machine, and tell around him on the stone floor.

Still the word to stop was not given.

The pulleys continued to creak and groan for some little time longer.

Then, at a signal from Montague, they stopped.

"Now, Madeline," said the monster, "as Barber has been released, return to your chamber?"

A sigh of relief left Madeline's lips.

She opened her eyes.

And the first object on which they rested, was the mutilated figure of John Barber.

The shock was too much for Madeline.

A low, bitter sob left her lips; she tottered back a few paces, and fell insensible at the feet of Montague.

"The sight must have surprised her!" he chuckled; "and so, now she's seen him, let him be taken out, Hockley, and then bury him where you think proper."

"And the girl?"

"I'll attend to her."

Montague lifted Madeline in his arms, and carried her from the vault.

He had scarcely crossed the threshold, when a man whispered to him—

"Your worship, several masked men have arrived."

Hockley overheard this.

"Lord Galloway is among them, I'll be sworn!" he said.

"Perdition!" muttered Montague; "this is an unlooked-for interruption. It is important that I should see to the girl."

"It is of more importance that his lordship be not kept waiting," whispered Hockley.

"Well, I'll carry her into her chamber. And, mark you, Hockley, close the door, but don't lock it, in case I should feel disposed to see how she progresses. The sight she has seen may affect her greatly, therefore I will see to her now and then myself. Lead the way, I will follow you; but keep silent."

* * * *

It was a considerable time after Montague had taken his departure, that Madeline regained partial possession of her mental faculties.

She tried to reflect calmly upon all the horrible events which had transpired.

And ere long she remembered all, and a deep sigh of despair left her lips as she recalled the dreadful tragedy at which she had unwillingly been present.

"Where am I now?" she thought.

She placed her hands to the right and left, and, by means of the objects with which they came in contact, she ascertained that once again she had been placed in the Oak Chamber.

She rose, and, finding the tinderbox, kindled a light and lit the lamp.

The first thing which met her eyes was a tray of refreshments.

Sorely she stood in need of them.

"Yet I will refrain from partaking of them," she murmured, "for it is possible all are drugged."

She drew back, as if to resume her seat, when her eyes fell upon the box.

"What can be the contents of this?" she thought. "I will see."

"'NOW, SWEET MADELINE,' CRIED MONTAGUE, 'RETURN TO YOUR CHAMBER.'"

She held the lamp over it, so as to have a good look at the address upon the canvas.

"After all," she said, half aloud, "this may be but some fiendish trick. I will not open it."

"In heaven's name, mistress, I pray you open it, at once!"

These startling words fell upon the ears of the astounded girl.

She started back, and seemed as if about to give utterance to the terror which had seized upon her heart.

But the cry issued not forth—and, well indeed was it that it did not; for Hockley and some of his men were at the top of the stone steps, almost opposite the door of the chamber.

"Mistress Madeline," continued the voice, "I conjure you, in heaven's name, to open the box. I am within it—I am sent by Dudley."

That beloved name had an electrical effect on the trembling maiden.

"Dudley!" she gasped. "What mystery is this? Whence comes the voice?"

"From the box—it is Quicksilver who speaks."

"Quicksilver!"

Instantly Dudley's description of the headsman's tiny companion occurred to her, and with hands which trembled as if the owner were afflicted with the ague, she untied the cords, and wrenched the lid from the box. This was no sooner done than the articles on the top went flying off, and Quicksilver was erect before her.

He was deathly pale—the result of insufficient ventilation; and the same reason caused his hands to tremble.

Never before had Madeline been so astonished.

The sight of this tiny, though perfect specimen of humanity, drove, for a short space, all other thoughts from her head.

With hands clasped to her heaving bosom she stood, her wide-open eyes fixed upon this courageous little fellow.

Then suddenly springing forward, she clasped him to her breast, and kissed him again and again.

"There can surely be no harm in a maiden kissing her deliverer!" she whispered.

"Well," replied Quicksilver, "I don't know what Master Dudley might say. But all my sufferings while in this box—and they have been something worth remembering—are amply compensated by the pressure of your sweet lips. But let us not forget the peril we are in. Replace the lid, mistress. That is right. Now I will get beneath this bed, and from there I can speak in whispers with you. Do you sit down as if in an attitude of meditation, and move not your head as you speak. Thus, if the door is suddenly opened—"

"Nay, I should hear the key," interrupted Madeline.

"By no means. No key will have to be used, for I heard Marcus Montague's orders—which were, that the door on no account was to be locked."

By this time Quicksilver had got beneath the bed, and Madeline had resumed her seat.

"Mistress Madeline," said Quicksilver, "just now you said that I was your deliverer. I would to heaven that were the case."

"Tell me—tell me," replied Madeline—"for my heart is bursting to know it—what of Dudley?"

"He is not far from you, being—at least, when I left him—at Chelsea. This is Charing Cross, or close by. But I presume you are well aware that you are within that mysterious dwelling known as Hollow Ground?"

"No!"

"When you are released from this building—if Providence so pleases—you will, I think, be taken to the Tower of London."

"You speak of rescue," said Madeline, in great excitement. "Keep me not in suspense! Tell me the whole story, including how you came to be placed in this box."

Quicksilver informed Madeline of everything he could think of, including what had occurred at Richmond, and of Dudley's right position in society.

While she was rejoiced that such strong action was being taken to effect her rescue, Madeline felt somewhat saddened when she knew what position Dudley would occupy.

Yet this lowering cloud was somewhat dispelled when Quicksilver told her that no change of fortune could ever turn the tide of Dudley's love for her.

"Listen, Mistress Madeline," resumed Quicksilver. "While in this chamber—you being absent—I heard voices, and listening, I gathered a lot of information relative to the proceedings in this house. It is the meeting-place of conspirators—of noble lords and gentlemen of position. I heard one name mentioned; it was Lord Galloway. This will be most important information for the one who has so courageously given his great assistance to Dudley—I mean Walter Raleigh. He and Montague are deadly enemies at Court."

"And Dudley and he, you say, are now friends?"

"Yes. But let us not waste time by further talk on these matters. Look you, Mistress Madeline, here is a tiny pistol which Master Rodney presented me with. I pray you take it, and use it if necessity requires."

"But suppose you are seized upon."

"I have my sword and a dagger."

"Both would be useless here. The house is full of armed men. Though few of them are seen at a time, the place must swarm with them, because I so frequently see fresh faces."

"Well, if I am surrounded, I must trust to my activity and the good luck of which the headsman says I am possessed, to make good my escape. But fear not, mistress; take the pistol. That's right; and now place it within your bosom."

"I will do so, my little friend. But you think a terrible fight may be waged between my rescuers and their foes?"

"Of that there can be hardly a doubt. This Walter Raleigh is a most determined fellow, who laughs danger to scorn; and I am sure the same may be said of Dudley Herbert. But, hush—footsteps!"

The door was flung suddenly open, and Hockley stood on the threshold.

A dark scowl rested on his face, but it quickly changed to a hideous grin.

"What, sweet lady, as Master Montague is pleased to call you," he sneered, "is it one of your tricks to speak to the Evil One?"

"What mean you, ruffian?" asked Madeline.

"I heard you, an' I mistake not, speaking."

Like lightning it occurred to Madeline that if she denied it, Hockley might become suspicious.

"I may have been muttering," she faltered.

"May have been! I am sure you were. Still, it matters not to me what you mutter. I have come to tell you that you cannot be waited upon by Mother Gitto, for the hag has not returned. Moreover, Mistress Madeline, I am come to tell you that Master Montague has altered his mind with respect to the door of this chamber, which, of course, you found open."

"I did not try it."

"Well, he orders me to see that it is securely locked, as he will not have the pleasure of paying you a visit for some hours."

So saying, Hockley backed out of the chamber, and the next moment the key turned in the lock.

CHAPTER IX.

OF THE ATTACK ON HOLLOW GROUND—OF THE TERRIBLE AND DETERMINED FIGHT WAGED BY DUDLEY AND RALEIGH—OF MONTAGUE'S AMAZEMENT, AND OF HOW MADELINE WAS RESCUED FROM DEATH BY QUICKSILVER.

It was soon after the appointed three hours that Patrick, looking from one of the windows, saw a tall, cloaked figure rapidly advancing towards the house. A few paces from the building, however, it paused as if at fault.

Then it gave utterance to the name, "Raleigh."

"Begorra!" muttered Patrick; "that's one of the fifty, I'll be sworn."

Down he went and opened the door.

"Follow me," he said, "and I'll make you comfortable."

"Thank you, my Irish friend," was the laughing reply; "but don't shut the door yet, for I have companions behind me. They are following me like Indians, one after the other, and each at least twenty paces apart."

Another moment and up came another cloaked and mysterious-looking figure, then another and another, and all passed into the house.

Dudley strongly wished to join them.

He would have done so had not the headsman restrained him.

"Be patient, Dudley," he said. "When Raleigh himself arrives, it will be time enough for us to make their acquaintance."

The men began to arrive so rapidly, that Patrick was driven to his wit's end to know what to do with them all.

Pat was a bad hand at counting, and moreover, many of these young gentlemen seemed very much alike.

At last there were no less than three of the cellars filled with them.

Suddenly appearing before our three friends, Pat said—

"How many did ye say would come?"

"Fifty, Raleigh said," replied Dudley.

"Well, then, on me sowl, if there ain't about twice that, I'm a Dutchman. Why, the whole three cellars is full of 'em. It's a surrounding party they are with a vengeance. Hist, there's another."

Off went Pat, and presently he returned.

"It's Walter Raleigh," he said, "and he requests you to go below."

The headsman and Dudley at once descended to the cellars.

At a single glance both saw that there were considerably more than fifty young fellows present.

"Friends," cried Raleigh, "behold him of whom I spoke—Dudley Herbert."

At once every eye was directed upon Dudley, and then a loud cheer made the rafters ring again.

"And here," continued Raleigh, "is our other friend, Jerome Lomew, the Headsman of the Old Tower."

Again a cheer rang out.

"As you can see," continued Raleigh, turning to Dudley and his friend, "I have brought more than the number I spoke of, for here there are eighty, and each is ready to risk his life in the attack to be made on Hollow Ground."

"I have an interesting story to tell you of what has occurred during your absence," said Dudley.

Thereupon he told the story of the capture of Mother Gitto and of the sending of the box.

Raleigh's handsome face at once became very serious.

"I do not think that will be productive of much good," he said, "but I sincerely trust that Quicksilver may escape danger. And now let us to business. In a boat which is at the edge of the river, I have a large barrel of powder. Also we have four heavy planks, by which we shall endeavour to cross the moat. We will divide the men into three sections, and each of us will take charge of one."

"By all means let it be so," replied Dudley.

So the eighty were divided into three parties, and it was arranged that each should go towards Hollow Ground in a roundabout direction, so as not to excite attention, and then meet at the back of the mansion.

The gunpowder and the planks having been secured, the whole proceeded on their errand of danger and of death.

* * * *

It was one o'clock, and the streets were entirely deserted.

Moreover, the heavens were as black as pitch, a fact which was of the greatest importance to the eighty-three daring spirits bent upon storming the house of mystery.

Raleigh was the first to arrive.

It was his party which carried the

powder and the planks, and these were placed against the wall.

Then Raleigh stationed his young and eager friends at a safe distance.

The next to come up was Dudley, and he was quickly followed by the headsman.

Raleigh at once took Dudley to the wall.

"Behold," he said, "here is the powder and here are the planks. And here," and he took a flask of powder from his belt, "with this I lay the train."

So saying, he sprinkled a quantity of gunpowder on the ground, and then carried it to some distance ahead.

Returning, he pulled a plug from the bottom of the barrel, and thus the deadly preparation was ready to be exploded.

"I would suggest," said Dudley, "that the planks are held in readiness by our party, and the moment the breach is made they can rush on with them."

"Good," replied Raleigh; "that shall be done; for if left here they may be blown away or rendered useless.

"And now listen to me, Dudley. Though each of us is in charge of a party, I hope that we shall fight as near as possible together."

"You think," replied Dudley, "that those inside will resist?"

"I am sure of it."

"Well, I sincerely trust they will do so, for I long to come in contact with the scoundrel leader—if Montague will lead them."

"I think it quite likely that he will be one of the leaders, at any rate. But I have gathered some information relative to several individuals who make this house their headquarters, that may bring Montague to the block."

The pair now rejoined their comrades.

Everyone was standing eagerly awaiting the explosion and the word to advance.

With cloaks thrown right back, and each with a naked sword in the right hand, and a pistol in the left, they stood, not a whisper being passed among them.

But the most striking figure was the headsman.

His huge form towered above all the others.

His sleeves were rolled back, and in his right hand was the heavy blade which he had so often wielded with deadly effect.

His left hand held a pistol, while a long poignard glittered in his belt.

He presented the appearance of a powerful, determined, and most dangerous enemy.

Ascertaining that all was perfectly ready, Dudley took from Raleigh a small piece of tow.

Lighting this, he advanced and placed it against the powder trail.

He then returned and stood at the head of his party.

Every eye was fixed on the tiny flickering light proceeding from the tow.

Every breath was, as it were, held in anxious expectation.

Suddenly, with a slight puff, the powder ignited, and rapidly trailing along, that in the barrel was reached.

The black heavens were for an instant lit up with a most dazzling brilliancy, and then a mighty report rang out.

It shook the ground for a considerable distance around.

The wall trembled, and then a portion of it toppled and fell with a mighty crash, a large proportion of it falling into the moat.

"Forward!" cried Raleigh.

His cry was instantly echoed by Dudley and the headsman, and then there burst from the lips of the brave young fellows, a ringing, exultant shout, repeated again and again.

On they went with a mighty rush, and quickly the gap in the wall was reached.

And now we must, for a brief space, return to the interior of the house.

When the attacking party reached the walls, a dozen gentlemen were assembled in the great room already described.

The raised chair was occupied by a tall, elderly man, of grave aspect.

This was Lord Galloway.

Beside him sat Marcus Montague, who had before him a pile of papers.

Before each of the other gentlemen were plans and drawings.

Not one person in twenty thousand could have understood the meaning of these plans; but had one been shown to the queen, she would, at once, have known that a dangerous plot to depose her was afloat.

The conspirators, with the exception of Marcus Montague, had all entered masked; and these masks were only thrown off when they entered the room, the doors of which were kept by several men under the control of Hockley.

An animated conversation was in progress, when the ears of the party were assailed by the noise of a fearful explosion.

Instantly every man was on his feet, and before a single word was spoken, the black masks were resumed.

The masks now covered faces of ashy paleness, for a great terror had seized upon every conspirator present.

"Betrayed!" said Galloway, in low, trembling tones.

"Caught in a trap!" murmured another.

"Not so," replied Montague, drawing his sword. "We have not been betrayed, gentlemen; but I should say that we have been attacked."

"Ah!" said Galloway, sharply; "this, then, has reference to your private affairs?"

"No doubt of it," replied Montague.

"This comes of using this house for other purposes than as at first proposed. Good; if it is as you surmise, Montague, I must decline to have anything to do with the matter."

Montague's face became perfectly white as these words were uttered.

"You have but to please yourself, my lord," he replied; "but decline to lend me your aid should it be required, and I cease my connection with this business. More, I will take means to— But I am sure you do not wish me to threaten."

"No," replied another. "My lord, since we are here, we cannot refuse to lend our aid. Ha! Who is this?"

The secret entrance in the pillar was pushed violently open, and Hockley, sword and pistol in hand, appeared.

"Master Montague—gentlemen!" he cried; "we have been attacked by a large number of men. They have blown down a portion of the wall, and through the aperture made are swarming into the grounds."

"A large number of men, say you?" replied Montague. "By whom are they led?"

"By one we have every reason to dread."

"Ha! Who is that?"

"Walter Raleigh."

Not only Montague, but every gentleman present, gave utterance to a startled cry, and, at once, every sword leapt from its scabbard.

"You are wrong, Montague," said Galloway, "and I am right, or Raleigh would not be at the head of the attacking party. We have been betrayed! and yonder, I would almost wager my head, stands the betrayer!"

And he pointed to Hockley.

"I?" gasped Hockley. "It is false! But let me tell you, Master Montague, that with Walter Raleigh, is Dudley Garth, and the headsman of the Tower. You well know their object—the release of the girl."

"As I thought," replied Montague, in tones of great relief. "Nothing is known of our conspiracy, gentlemen, so I pray you do not needlessly alarm yourselves. I will explain all anon; but, in the meantime, let it be our work to repel the invaders. You certainly have no need to trouble yourselves with my private concerns; but when you consider that one of us might, at a single stroke, remove from our path such a dangerous enemy as Raleigh—well, then, I've no doubt you will require no urgent pressing. A hundred and fifty men are here, gentlemen, and all are well armed."

"Away, then!" cried Galloway. "But, above all things, gentlemen, let me urge upon you the great necessity of retaining your masks.

Raleigh has a sharp eye, as well as a sharp sword."

Montague gave a few directions to Hockley, who at once hurried off.

Then, placing himself at the head of the conspirators, Marcus led the way to the grounds, where an extraordinary sight met their eyes; for, right away at the western extremity, a great fire was burning, the ruddy glow of which lit up the grounds, and showed them that a desperate battle was in progress.

So rapidly were shots being fired, that at a distance they resembled the roll of a kettle-drum.

Ever and anon, as the wind, which was slight, blew the sulphurous smoke aside, the flashing of the blades could be seen, while high above all was heard the clash of the steel, and the cries of the combatants.

In the meantime, the attacking party had made but little progress into the grounds, and this fact was owing to the moat, which, as before remarked, was deep and dangerous.

A huge mass of masonry—if the composition of which the great wall was constructed can be so called—had fallen into the moat, and of this both Dudley and Raleigh took advantage, for both jumped upon it, and lightly sprang safely on *terra firma;* but their eager comrades behind were not so fortunate.

Too many jumped upon it, and the result was, that the mass toppled sideways, and glided deep down in the mud, and it was with the greatest difficulty that several of the youths were rescued from a horrible death.

The delay occasioned by this incident enabled Hockley to summon his men—many of whom issued from the mansion in an intoxicated condition—and to place them in such a position that they could aim at the daring invaders.

For the first time the ruffians' bravery was put to the test.

At the outset they proved themselves arrant cowards.

They were speedily thrown into a state of terror and consternation, and Hockley's furious threats had no effect on them.

They fired and fired, it is true, but their aim was wild and erratic.

And yet, as might be expected, some of their bullets found their billets; for, before five minutes had elapsed, no less than eight of the brave young fellows were stricken down, either wounded or slain outright.

Presently the planks were placed in position, and the attackers proceeded to cross.

This occupied no little time, owing to the fact that they had to go in single file, and at some distance from each other.

As they proceeded, Dudley and a number of those under him covered them, and steadily poured their shots into the ranks of the ruffians under Hockley.

The effect was deadly.

Notwithstanding Hockley's repeated commands, the men would persist in keeping close together, and the result of this was, that almost every shot fired from the other side, told.

One of the ruffians, a tall, burly man, who was drunk, wishing to distinguish himself, seized a link and rushed forward, his object being to upset the planks.

Dudley met him.

Raising his pistol, he dealt him a fearful blow in the face with the butt-end, felling him to the ground.

He then seized his link and rushed to the right, where stood a small shed.

As he expected, it was a wood-shed, and it was nearly full.

Dudley plunged the link into the midst of it, and soon the dry wood ignited.

A bright flame shot upward, and the grounds in that part were illuminated.

The act was a daring one, for the shed was not far from where Hockley and his men stood, and Dudley had thus boldly risked his life.

His action met with the cordial approval of Raleigh, who was fighting against odds, but he found time to warmly press his hand and say—

"Bravo, Dudley Herbert! That was well done."

It was when the shed was on fire

that Hockley caught sight of, and recognised the faces of the headsman and Raleigh—heard the latter utter the words given above, and rushed off to inform Montague.

The battle proceeded, the three leaders proving themselves possessed of great bravery, and their actions stimulated those they led to perform deeds of valour.

But for some considerable time, before they became engaged hand-to-hand, the superior numbers of the ruffians told, and as Raleigh and Dudley were as yet uncertain as to what their numbers really were, they led their men cautiously.

But, at last, and just as Montague and the conspirators made their appearance, they became engaged hand-to-hand.

Had not Marcus put in an appearance, the fight would have been decided at once, and in favour of the attacking party.

But Montague's voice was no sooner heard than the aspect of affairs became changed.

His men roused themselves, and blindly threw themselves forward, the result being that many of them were cut down before Montague's eyes.

The shed was now burning with great fury, and the flames lit up with much distinctness the faces of the combatants.

Montague's eyes became riveted upon a tall, fine young man, who, bareheaded, was calmly issuing instructions, while at the same time his gory blade was never at rest.

He did not want to be told who this young man was, for in his features he recognised Dudley Herbert.

"It is all true," he thought; "there is no lie in this. He is more like his father than Walter. But, nevertheless, I will dispute his claim, if he is not slain, and will, if it comes to it, denounce him to the queen as an impostor."

Assuming the command, and being aided by his co-conspirators, Montague fought with determination.

Well acquainted with the weapons he yielded, he speedily laid low more than one youth who, attracted by the splendour of his costume, rushed upon him.

"Yonder is Montague," Raleigh said, pointing him out; "I leave him to you, Dudley, though I fear me you will not be able to reach him. Heaven's mercy on us! Though victory will be on our side—see, they are giving way—our loss will be severe."

"Yes," replied Dudley, as for an instant he allowed his eyes to rest upon the bodies lying in all directions; "many a brave fellow will meet his death this night."

"Look yonder at those masked men," cried Raleigh. "Observe how eagerly they are issuing directions. Depend upon it, these men are some of the gentlemen of whom I have heard, and, on my soul, I intend to unmask as many as possible; so follow me, Dudley."

The next moment Walter Raleigh had crossed swords with the first of the men in the masks.

The masked men knew Walter Raleigh well, and they shrank from before him, as if, while not afraid of fighting him, they were anxious to conceal their identity.

The one Raleigh attacked, a man of fine physique, fought with great fierceness and skill.

Not a word was uttered by either of the combatants.

The roar of the fight raging around them distracted not their attention.

The battle was quickly decided in Raleigh's favour.

He suddenly dealt his masked antagonist a mighty blow on the head, which instantly struck him dead.

At once Raleigh snatched the mask from his face.

"By heaven!" he muttered, "'tis Sir Francis Compton!"

"Die with the knowledge yet on your tongue!" cried a voice. "Die, you meddling foo—"

The sentence was not finished, for the speaker uttered a fearful scream, threw up his arms, and dropped dead at Raleigh's feet, his head cloven in twain by a single blow from the sword of Dudley Herbert.

"By the rood!" cried Raleigh,

"you have saved my life, Dudley. This man whom I have slain is Sir Francis Compton. I will take his signet-ring from his finger. And now— What ho, Jerome Lomew!"

"Yes, yes!" replied the headsman, who was at this moment dashing past. "What will you?"

"Look at this man's face. I have just slain him. Do you recognise him?"

"I do. 'Tis Sir Francis Compton!"

"What will his precious son think of this?"

"Heaven only knows! But, see, the villains are fast retreating to the house. Let us make a sudden dash upon them."

"Good. But where is Montague?"

"He has disappeared. Let us be careful, for now that he sees the battle is lost, there is no telling what villainy he may be up to."

"True. Let us be wary. Now, to re-form our brave comrades."

It was, indeed, a fact that Montague had withdrawn.

"Hockley," he said, "the fight is all against us. Where one of these youths is slain, two, or even three, of our own men are laid low. But," he added, savagely, "even while I fought, I formed a plan to foil our enemies. Call off six men. By St. Joseph! if I don't have the girl no one else shall! And you have not succeeded in slaying Dudley Herbert?"

"No," growled Hockley; "nor have you. In a fight he is more like a demon than a human being. Had I tackled him 'tis likely enough that I should not now be speaking with you."

"Come—six men—quick—quick! The fight is being waged nearer and nearer to the house."

The six men were called off, and they hastily followed Montague and Hockley.

Hurriedly the house was entered by a side door, Hockley snatching a lantern from the wall as they proceeded.

The appearance of these eight men as they rushed from corridor to corridor, from chamber to chamber, up one staircase and down another, until the great, gloomy vaults were reached, was terrible.

Montague had entered into the thick of the fight with his fine clothes unsoiled; now in many places they were torn and blood-stained, and he had received a severe wound on the head.

But his appearance was nothing compared with that of the men who followed, panting and breathless, and filled with wonder as to what Montague was now about to do.

That it was something fiendish, they could tell from his chuckling and his excited cries of "Revenge! revenge!"

Presently the Oak Chamber was reached.

Hockley inserted the key, flung the door open, lifted high the lantern, and Montague entered.

Madeline was seated at the table, her face buried in her hands.

"Rise!" thundered Montague, seizing her by the wrist and dragging her to her feet; "rise! Danger threatens!"

"Danger!" repeated Madeline, with well-affected surprise. "Whence would come danger to me, except—"

"Silence!" thundered Montague; "silence, I command you! Listen. No doubt you have heard the shots and the cries without, and no doubt you fancied that a rescue was being attempted. Such is the case, and one of the leaders of this attack is Dudley Herbert, whom I will yet crush and disgrace, as well as his mother. Proof will I now give him of what mercy he may expect if ever good fortune sends him into my hands. Come."

"Would you murder me!" gasped Madeline, terrified at his dreadful appearance.

"You will soon know what I intend to do," was the reply. "Hockley—to the roof, through the wainscot."

Hockley advanced a few paces to the left, stooped, and pressed a spring, and a portion of the wainscot flew open.

"Lead the way," cried Montague; "and you," he added to the men bringing up the rear, "forget not to close the panel."

Another second and he had forced Madeline through the aperture, and the men having followed, the panel was closed behind them.

And it was no sooner closed, than the tiny form of Quicksilver slipped from beneath the bed.

First, he snatched his little sword from its sheath, and, advancing to the door of the chamber, he pushed it.

It fastened by itself, and could only be re-opened from the other side.

The next thing he did was to go to the spot where he had seen Hockley touch the spring.

He quickly found and pressed it; and the panel once more flew open.

And now Quicksilver paused.

"It is probable," he thought, "that though they have gone to the roof this way, they do not intend to return by the same route. I will make my way up the passage. If there are any recesses in it, I shall certainly feel the safer, and, moreover, if either of the men, or if Montague himself comes along the passage while I am in it, may heaven have mercy on him!"

He found that the passage, which was exceedingly narrow, contained many recesses—not large enough for an ordinary man, but quite so to contain Quicksilver's small body.

Using the utmost caution, he advanced until he stood where he could see all that was taking place on the roof.

As soon as the other end of the passage was reached, Montague again seized Madeline by the wrist, and rudely pulled her forward.

The portion of the roof on which they stood was flat.

To the left, and at the edge of the parapet, stood a gigantic iron flag-staff, and to this Montague dragged Madeline.

Dazed and bewildered, she looked below—a distance of at least sixty feet—and saw that a terrible fight was being waged.

Madeline felt bewildered at the rattle of the shots, the clashing of steel, the smell of the powder, and, above all, by fear as to the safety of Dudley.

"Listen, Hockley!" cried Montague. "Fasten this girl to the flag-staff. Quick—quick! for 'tis a thousand chances to one, that this will turn the tide of the battle in our favour."

Madeline was speedily tied to the staff.

"Now, one of you," cried Montague, with a fiendish chuckle, "draw your dagger and stand beside her—thus! You observe this whistle? If you should hear it blown three times, plunge your dagger into her heart, cut the cords, and hurl the body over the parapet."

A wild, heart-rending shriek burst from Madeline's lips, but it was lost in the din below.

"And bear in mind," said Hockley, "that if you fail to do as you are told, your life will pay the forfeit!"

But there was no fear of the ruffian not doing as he had been bidden.

"Now, follow me," cried Montague, and turning, he was followed by Hockley and the five other men.

Passing across the roof, they lifted a trap-door, descended a ladder placed beneath it, and passed into the grounds, which now presented a terrible spectacle, for the dead and the dying lay in every direction.

The first person on whom Montague's eyes rested was Raleigh, who, like Dudley, not far from him, was fighting as calmly as when the battle was commenced.

"Hold—hold!" shouted Montague.

"Ah!" cried Raleigh, "at last the villain admits he is beaten! Hold, my men—hold!"

In less than a minute the sounds of strife ceased, and the combatants, panting and breathless, stood still, glaring fiercely one upon the other.

"Well, Master Montague," said Raleigh, "so you admit you are beaten?"

"No!" was Montague's thundering reply. "It is you who are beaten!"

"Not so! Cast your eyes round, appeal to those left of your own men, and you will have reason to change your opinion."

"Look you, Walter Raleigh, let me tell you, and the impostor who goes by the name of Dudley Herbert, that I can now compel you to withdraw."

Raleigh cast his eyes round.

It struck him that, perhaps, Montague had obtained reinforcements.

But nothing of the sort met his eyes.

"Dudley Herbert," continued Montague, "you came here to rescue Madeline Maynard! But, unless you instantly withdraw from these walls, her death will be laid at your door."

Dudley started.

"What do you mean, vile caitiff?" he asked, stepping forward a pace or two, his sword clutched fiercely in his hand.

"Look up at the roof," replied Montague.

Instantly all, leaders and men, looked upward.

At that very moment, the shed burnt with a fiercer glow than ever, and the bright flames lit up with great distinctness the figures on the roof.

Dudley—and, indeed, everyone else—understood what had taken place, and what was intended, at a glance.

A deep groan left his lips.

Every eye was fixed upon the white figure above, every eye noted the pale face and the eyes upturned, as if pleading for mercy from heaven.

And then the eye wandered to the dark figure of the man beside her, and the long flashing blade in his hand.

"Monster!" cried Dudley, rushing forward, "what would you do?"

Raleigh placed his hand on his shoulder, and arrested his progress.

"Wait, Dudley," he said. "Rashness may plunge the poor girl headlong into eternity. And," he whispered, "what have they done with Quicksilver? I fear that our foes have triumphed, and that the little fellow has lost his life!"

"From what I can now see," replied Dudley, I am afraid you are right."

"There is no help for it," said the low, deep voice of Lomew. "Unless you consent to withdraw, Dudley, Montague will give a signal, and the man above will slay the girl before our eyes."

"Yes," muttered Raleigh. "And so all the dangers we have passed through, and all the lives which have been sacrificed, have been for naught."

"I again say," shouted Montague, who, with Hockley, had been eagerly watching their consultation, "that unless you instantly withdraw, I shall blow this whistle three times; the result will be that yonder man will slay Madeline Maynard, and her body will be hurled at your feet."

A loud, terrible cry left Dudley's lips.

The restraining hands of Walter Raleigh and the headsman had now no effect upon him.

With the fury of a tiger he darted forward, and in an instant his hand clutched Montague's throat with a vice-like grasp, while his sword was shortened to slay him.

And he would have slain him had not several of Montague's men rushed forward and seized Dudley's sword-arm.

Hockley snatched the silver whistle from Montague's hand, stepped back a few paces, and blew it three times before he could be prevented.

Instantly every eye was once more fixed above.

The ruffian had raised the dagger to strike the fatal blow, when a tiny figure darted across the roof.

Another second and the man, with a frightful yell, dropped his dagger, threw up his arms, staggered forward, and went clean over the parapet, falling with a mighty crash on the heads of two of Montague's men.

Both were killed outright, and thus, at one stroke as it were, three were slain.

"Quicksilver!" roared the headsman, almost mad with delight.

"Heaven be thanked!" murmured Dudley.

And his fervent exclamation was as fervently echoed by Raleigh.

Montague essayed to rise in order to see what had occurred, but the headsman observed his movement, and, rushing forward, he sent him backward again, while he held the blade which had done such terrible execution threateningly over him.

"Beware!" he hissed; "remain

where you are, lest Dudley Herbert forgets for an instant one which commands his attention, and drives his blade through your black heart; which would be a pity, since 'tis fit that you should walk to your doom through Traitor's Gate!"

Montague scowled darkly, but he was wise enough to hold his tongue.

A groan escaped his lips as, casting his eyes around, he saw that the remainder of the men were slinking off.

In the meantime, Quicksilver had cut Madeline's bonds.

She, however, was too weak to move unaided from the spot, and so he assisted her to seat herself upon the roof, while at the same time he tried to make his little voice heard below.

Suddenly, while speaking to Dudley, Raleigh rushed forward and seized a man who was trying to creep past them unobserved.

"Ah! I thought I was not mistaken," said Raleigh; "here is the villain Hockley! You may well look crestfallen, scoundrel, for I have a mind to have you run up to yonder flagstaff by the neck. Dudley, we require a guide within the house. This is the man. No one knows so much of the secrets of Hollow Ground as Hockley. Speak, scoundrel! Will you lead the way, or will you take the alternative?"

"What is that?" gasped Hockley, who was now terribly frightened.

"A bullet through your scheming brain!"

And Raleigh pressed the muzzle of his pistol to Hockley's forehead.

"I will lead the way if—if you will swear that no harm shall come to me."

"I will neither swear nor promise anything," retorted Raleigh; "lead the way, dog, or you die! And, mark it well—attempt the least treachery, and I will make you suffer for it!"

"I will attempt no treachery," replied Hockley. "But what of Montague?"

"Has he not enough to do to look after his own neck?" was the reply. "But look who stands over him! Do you know him?"

"Yes," was the sullen reply; "it is the headsman."

"Truly; and Marcus Montague could have no better guardian. One day, if all goes well, he will feel the sharpness of his axe and the strength of his srm."

"Say you so, Master Raleigh?" replied Hockley. "Well, we know not what may happen. Perchance you, too, will feel the keenness of the headsman's axe."

"That may be so," answered Raleigh, in tones which, as Dudley thought, had changed; "but if I do, 'twill be as an innocent man; for I love my country and my sovereign far too fervently ever to become such a traitor as to merit so infamous and disgraceful a doom. If ever Traitor's Gate opens to receive me, then, indeed, proof will be at hand that Walter Raleigh is sent to his death by bitter and envious enemies."

These last words were uttered rapidly and in low tones, as if he were speaking more to himself than those beside him.

But, suddenly looking up, he pointed his sword towards the house.

"Go!" he said! "we follow—and remember, dispatch is necessary, therefore pause not. Come, Dudley, let us to the roof. When I see you hold in your arms the girl you love, I intend to scour the building."

Hockley started as he heard these words, and a deathly paleness overspread his hang-dog face.

Raleigh called two of the young fellows who that night had proved of what mettle they were possessed, and the party proceeded to the front entrance.

Without a pause, Hockley led the way to the roof.

Dudley was the first to mount the ladder.

"Madeline!" he cried; "Madeline!"

The words acted like magic.

Madeline darted up with a wild cry, staggered towards him, and fell weeping into his arms.

"Are you safe, Dudley?" she cried.

"Yes, my darling. And you?"

"I feel completely broken down. I never thought to behold you again."

"Cheer up, Madeline," replied Dudley, his heart seeming as if about to burst, as he looked upon the ashy-pale face, the wild-looking eyes, and the long, beautiful, but now dishevelled hair. "Cheer up, my love. Happiness is in store for us, I'll warrant you. But perhaps Quicksilver has told you a great deal?"

"He has; but in our joy at again beholding each other, we have forgotten him."

But Raleigh had noticed the little man. For a moment he was at a loss to understand what he was doing.

But approaching closely to him, he observed that he was remarkably busy with his toothpick blade, which he was carefully wiping with a delicate and highly perfumed kerchief.

"Why, Quicksilver—why are you doing that?" asked Raleigh.

"Well, you see," replied Quicksilver, in matter-of-fact tones, "this good blade has been soiled by the blood of a villain. In that condition I could not sheathe it."

"Quicksilver, you are a hero."

"Coming from such an authority," was the reply, "I am bound to believe it. But I did no more than a little man should have done."

"My little friend, you have a large heart and a tender one, and no one would think that you were possessed of so much courage. Your place should be at Court. The precincts of the Tower are only calculated to make a light heart like yours pine away to nothing. You would like Court life, Quicksilver."

"That's likely," replied Quicksilver, slowly shaking his head; "but I would not leave Jerome for any Court, nor for any position. And I am sure that Lomew wishes for nothing else than to remain her majesty's headsman."

Raleigh smiled.

"Different men, different tastes," he said. "But now let us descend. Stand beside the trap," he added to Hockley, "and hold it. Yet wait. Dudley, your ear for a moment. Ah, this is Madeline Maynard. Sweet mistress," he said, doffing his cap and bowing, "I offer you my heartfelt congratulations."

"'Tis Walter Raleigh, Madeline," said Dudley, "and without him your rescue must have been hopeless."

"How can I thank you, noble sir?" faltered Madeline.

"By loving me as a brother."

Madeline placed her little hand his.

"That I will," she said. "And proud indeed shall I be to call you brother."

"And now, Dudley, let me whisper in your ear."

The two withdrew while Madeline went towards the trap.

She saw that Hockley was standing between the two young fellows who had come up with Raleigh, and she noticed that his eyes were glancing furiously on the two leaders as they talked.

From his attitude she felt certain that he meditated an attack and a dash through the trap; and not wishing to alarm Dudley, she took the tiny pistol from her bosom.

Hockley thought that the conversation between Dudley and Raleigh must be concerning himself.

He considered it more than likely that they were discussing what punishment they should inflict upon him.

The trap was open, and if he could succeed in dashing down and slamming the door behind him, he would be able to get away.

Suddenly he turned upon the young fellow on his right, and dealt him a terrific blow on the chest, striking him to the roof.

Then, like a flash of lightning, he plunged forward.

He would have gained the trap, had it not been for Madeline.

As quick as thought she raised the little pistol and pulled the trigger.

The weapon exploded, and its tiny bullet proved effective.

Hockley staggered back with a loud, gasping cry, and dropped like a log on the leaden roof.

At once Raleigh and Dudley rushed forward.

"Is he dead?" asked Raleigh.

"No," replied Dudley; "but he has received a shot in the cheek. See, here is the wound."

"The scoundrel deserves no mercy," replied Raleigh; "we will leave him to recover as best he may."

"I see that 'twas you, Madeline, who fired the shot," said Dudley; "for the smoking weapon is still in your hand."

"'Tis my pistol," Quicksilver cried.

"I return it to you," said Madeline; "it has served its purpose well."

The young fellow who had been so suddenly stricken down by Hockley's cowardly hand, had been seriously injured.

He, however, received every attention from Raleigh, who assisted him below.

When all had descended, the trap-door was closed and fastened.

"Let the scoundrel upon the roof recover as best he may," said Raleigh. "Mercy he does not merit, and none shall he receive."

CHAPTER X.

OF THE RELEASE OF THE TWO PRISONERS—OF THE DEPARTURE FROM HOLLOW GROUND—OF THE ATROCIOUS DEED COMMITTED BY MOTHER GITTO, AND OF HOW MASTER RODNEY WAS SAVED FROM DEATH.

BEFORE commencing the searching of the premises—to do which Raleigh and Dudley had thoroughly made up their minds, more especially as Madeline had given them particulars relative to the two unhappy prisoners—it was decided to return to the grounds.

So Madeline was left in charge of one of the young soldiers and Quicksilver, and by them she was conducted to the best room they could find.

Getting into the grounds once more, Dudley and Raleigh sped to the spot where stood the headsman, surrounded by what remained of the brave, young soldiers.

The shed had burned itself out, and the grounds were now illuminated only by a few links.

The dull glare of these fell upon the grimy, blood-stained face of the headsman, and they saw that it wore an expression of great gravity.

"The scoundrel Montague has escaped!" was his announcement to the two young heroes.

"Escaped!" cried Raleigh and Dudley in a breath.

"Yes, but perhaps you may not think it all my fault. Two of these brave young fellows had him tight enough, and I proceeded to attend to the many wounded in this terrible fight. Montague, assisted by three or four men who crept up unawares, threw the young fellows down and so escaped. But not so two of those who assisted him, who were shot dead."

"Well, though he escapes the headsman now, 'twill not always be so, I'll wager," cried Raleigh. "Had you managed to detain him, Master Lomew, it was my intention to have placed him in one of the rooms of this house, and there let the villain remain until such time as he chanced to be released by those in his and his confederates' pay.

"I think I have sufficient evidence to lay before the queen as to some of the proceedings at Hollow Ground. I have the signet-ring from the hand of Sir Francis Compton, and you, Lomew, and you, Dudley, will bear me out as to his identity. But I've no doubt the queen will learn of the death of this old meddler in State affairs through his son. But now, what of our loss?"

"A heavy one," replied Lomew. "Of the eighty, thirty are slain outright, while at least that number are wounded—some grievously."

"And what of the ruffians?" asked Raleigh.

"Behold them," replied Lomew, pointing to the slaughtered wretches, who lay in every direction. "Over a hundred men have been killed, and—"

He was here interrupted by loud shouts, which proceeded from outside the walls.

"What can that be?" asked Dudley.

"The walls are surrounded by hundreds of people," replied Lomew. "They would have crowded into the breach we made, had not I prevented them by posting a few of our youths beside it."

"Let us consider what should be done with the bodies of our unfortunate comrades," said Raleigh. "My suggestion is that they be laid beneath the grounds of this house. Dudley and I are going to make a search of the place, and as soon as this is done we will take our departure."

"Madeline is safe?"

"Yes, thanks to little Quicksilver," replied Dudley. "But when we leave here, Lomew, you will away at once to the Tower?"

"Yes. And there, for the present, accommodation shall be found for Madeline. You, Dudley, will have most important matters to attend to, and though I well know love is to the fore, your attention must be directed to the establishment of your rights. Your mother also anxiously awaits you."

"I shall forget nothing, Lomew. But I would that Marcus Montague had not escaped! The foul murder of my brother has yet to be avenged."

"I will aid you in whatever revenge you may take, Dudley," said Raleigh. "And now let us re-enter the house. When we have finished there, Lomew, I trust all will be ready for departure."

"All shall be ready."

Taking half-a-dozen of the young men with them, Dudley and his friend re-entered the mansion.

First, they proceeded to the chamber in which were Madeline, Quicksilver, and the young soldier.

Curiously enough, this room was the very one to which Montague had first taken our heroine.

She told them of the secret the room contained, but they did not wait to investigate it.

After some search, they found a small chamber which looked as if it was a living-room.

It was the apartment used by Hockley.

Over the desk near the door they found a bunch of keys, as well as several links and lanterns.

Three or four of the latter were lit, and Dudley taking the keys, they proceeded below.

Chamber after chamber was entered and searched.

Some were filled with arms of all descriptions, others were crammed with furniture, while one or two contained various costumes—evidently to be used as disguises.

At last Madeline paused.

"This is the place where the young man and woman are confined," she exclaimed. "Here are the ponderous stone doors."

Dudley proceeded to try the keys.

They were evidently duplicates of those in the possession of Hockley.

After several tries one was found to fit.

The door was flung open, and the face of the unfortunate young man appeared at the bars.

For an instant he fixed his startled eyes on the party, and then a wild shriek escaped his bloodless lips.

"Gracious Providence!" cried Dudley, "what fiendish deed is this?"

"Who are you?" shrieked the young man. "Has help at last come? Do I see friends before me? Yes, yes! I am sure of it; for I see the young girl—yonder," pointing to Madeline—"that beautiful face that hours ago was brought here by Montague. And you," he said, fixing his eyes on Dudley, "you have a kind face—it is the mirror of your heart. You will force these bars and release me; but no, no—what am I saying? There is one who should be released before me. She is within this building—"

"Yonder," interrupted Madeline, pointing to the other door.

"Both of you shall be set free,' cried Dudley.

"Both!" exclaimed the young man, falling on his knees, and raising aloft his wasted hands; "both! Heaven's choicest blessing rest upon you. Oh, hasten—hasten!"

"THE MAN, WITH A FRIGHTFUL YELL, DROPPED HIS WEAPON."

The same key was found to fit the other door.

This was quickly thrown open, and the young woman appeared at the bars.

The sight of this unfortunate creature had a horrifying effect on Dudley.

Uttering a low, startled cry, he let the bunch of keys fall to the ground.

"Providence guard us all!" he muttered, "can this be a woman?"

"No!" replied the woman; "only what remains of one—"

She abruptly ceased, for her eyes, had wandered to the other prison.

Slowly, she dragged her emaciated form erect, the while muttering sentences which were unintelligible to the listeners.

Her eyes remained riveted upon the object behind the other bars, and her gaze was returned by the other prisoner.

It was evident that, for the moment, they did not know each other.

But presently the brilliant glare in the hollow eyes of the woman died out, and an expression of indescribable tenderness took its place.

Her lips parted, and amid a silence which was profound, she whispered—

"Claude!"

A wild, passionate cry was the response.

Dudley found the key which fitted the lock in the rails, and the barrier was flung open.

Throwing up her wasted arms, the prisoner rushed out.

But her strength gave way before she could cross the vault, and she was sinking to the ground when Madeline caught her in her arms.

Dudley had sprung to the other vault and released Claude Wentworth.

Taking him by the hand, he attempted to lead him forward.

But he also was too weak to walk.

Dudley placed his strong arms about his waist and carried him forward, just as Madeline laid the poor girl tenderly down on a rug brought by one of the young soldiers.

No word was uttered by either of the unfortunate prisoners.

Kneeling beside each other, they were instantly locked in a warm embrace.

Madeline would have spoken, but Raleigh placed his hand upon her arm.

"Wait," he whispered, "wait."

At last Dudley broke the silence.

"I need scarcely ask by whom you were placed here," he said, "but can you tell me how long you have been here?"

"No," replied Claude, "that I cannot. But it must be years. And yet, the scoundrel Montague does not appear to have changed much in that time."

"Can't you remember the year when you were seized?" asked Raleigh.

"I can. It was 1570."

"Then, my poor friend, you have only been here two years."

"Two years!" repeated both prisoners, opening wide their eyes in astonishment. "Two years!"

"That is all," said Dudley.

"Gracious powers! it seems to me as if we must have been here at least ten years."

"Yes, no doubt. But now do you await us here, Madeline. We will proceed a little farther."

So on again went Raleigh, Dudley, four of the young soldiers, and Quicksilver.

The keys on the bunch were found to fit every door they came to except one.

This was a low, narrow door at the end of a flight of stone steps.

A brief examination showed them that the door was of iron.

No lock was visible, nor were there any bars or bolts.

"Depend upon it," said Dudley, "this chamber contains a mighty secret."

"Yes," replied Raleigh, who for a few minutes had been lost in reflection; "I believe it does. And look above. Behold that ventilator. The difficulty as to how we are to enter is solved. Quicksilver's little body can pass through that."

"But he may fall into some terrible trap."

"I will tell you what we can do. Let us fasten our belts together—

since the procuring of a rope may take a long time—and on the end let us place a lantern. We will then hoist little Quicksilver up, and he can lower the lantern, and tell us what he sees."

Quicksilver was most anxious to see what the place contained, and, the belts being arranged as Raleigh had described, and the lantern attached, he was hoisted up.

With the greatest care and judgment, he lowered the lantern, and then raised himself in such a position that he could see within the chamber.

Presently his little voice was heard.

"Holy Virgin! what think you is within this vault?"

"The remains of many an unfortunate wretch," suggested Dudley.

"Nothing of the sort," replied Quicksilver; "it is full of bags of money."

"Money!"

"Yes, money! I see many of them marked with the amount, while over them are cards with the words, 'From Chester,' 'From Nottingham,' 'From Birmingham,' and a lot of others."

"On my soul," exclaimed Raleigh, "I can see the true meaning of this! Dudley, it is as I suspected. A gigantic plot is in progress, it is rapidly extending all over the kingdom, and this money has been contributed by the already disaffected quarters. For the present let us keep silent."

"What!" cried Quicksilver, "don't you mean to try and break the door open and take this treasure? Heaven save us all! see how handy it would be."

"No," replied Raleigh; "I have already thought of a better plan than that. Descend, Quicksilver, and let us return to the chamber above.

Proceeding in another direction, for the vaults seemed to have no end, they came to the chamber where stood the hideous machine which had as its last victim—John Barber.

Madeline had given them a brief account of his death, and the party examined the machine with great attention.

The next apartment was the one above this chamber, and here Quicksilver strutted proudly into the centre of the room.

"Behold!" he said, pointing above.

"What is this rope?" asked Dudley.

"Why, that is how I reached the roof," replied Quicksilver, proudly. "Yonder lies the piece of iron I carried in my doublet, and which I used to smash the glass above. I climbed up this rope to reach it."

"You are a brave little fellow," said Dudley; "and if I live I will one of these days make you a present worth having."

"Thanks," replied Quicksilver. "I shall take care to remember your words."

"Do so. You will find I never make a promise without its being fulfilled."

In a few more minutes they had rejoined Madeline.

They found that during their absence, the maiden, after searching various rooms, had discovered enough articles of attire to clothe the unfortunate young man and young woman.

In one of the outhouses two sedan-chairs were found, and into one of these the long-parted lovers were placed, while Madeline occupied the other.

The headsman, with what remained of the party, joined them, and all proceeded towards the breach, around which many hundreds of people were still assembled.

"You saw no more of the masked men?" asked Raleigh.

"No," replied Lomew. "All made off as soon as they saw the battle was against them."

"Which showed that they were beaten. And now, I propose that we all go to Master Rodney's. After this, you, Lomew, together with Dudley and Madeline, will, I suppose, repair to the Tower?"

"We shall."

"So far as I am concerned, I will, first of all, see the poor people we have rescued placed in some hostelry for the present, and then my attention must be directed to my comrades."

Master Rodney's house was quickly reached.

They found it in total darkness.

Dudley was about to touch the wire over the door, when the headsman suddenly placed his hand on his shoulder.

"Hush!" he excitedly whispered. "Something unusual is occurring within the house. See, a light suddenly appears. Let us get into the shadow. Our services may be required. Do you be ready to force your way into the house, Dudley!"

"Silence!" whispered Raleigh. "I remember; we left Mother Gitto here. Maybe it would have been better had we allowed her to go."

* * * *

Our readers will remember that the vile hag, Mother Gitto, was confined in a chamber at the top of the building.

That chamber was a strong one; and the door was not only locked, but bolted on the outside by Patrick, who, for the time being, constituted himself as gaoler.

The first thing Mother Gitto did, was to examine the chamber in order to ascertain whether there were any means of escape.

She thought: "If I can but escape, what an amount of information I could give Montague! And what a price I could command for it! Perdition on the headsman! The murderous-looking hound! His very look would suffice to kill a prisoner, let alone his axe! And Dudley—Dudley—something, I forget what. And may all earthly torments seize old Rodney!" she hissed through her thin, clenched lips. "I would give half the years left me on earth to drive a blade into his heart! After all these years he has not one spark of sympathy for me. He hates me as of old! Well, well, I return his hate quite as heartily."

Every nook and corner, the walls, the floor, and the window she searched, but it was of no use—no secret exit met her eager eyes or hands.

The only place which seemed likely to prove a means of escape was the fireplace—one of those huge old-fashioned places up which many a man had made his way.

For a long time she surveyed this chimney, then stood on the hearth, and looked up.

"Broad enough," she muttered, "and there are enough projections to place one's feet upon. But then I am not a man. Ah, what is this?"

She had been turning over some wooden embers on the hearth, and suddenly, she heard a sound as of steel touching the stone.

The miserable taper with which Patrick had provided her she brought forward, knelt down, and carefully examined the embers.

She was rewarded for her trouble, for she found a large white-handled "wood" knife—an instrument such as was used by gardeners in cutting branches.

No doubt the man who had tied the sticks up to be used as firewood had in mistake fastened up the knife as well.

Mother Gitto darted upon it as if it had been a bag of gold.

It was a godsend to her.

It was black from having been exposed to the action of the fire, but nevertheless it was strong enough.

Mother Gitto ascertained that by bending the blade backward and forward.

"Ah, ah!" she chuckled, a fiendish glitter in her eyes; "escape is now almost certain. I see what to do: And should I hesitate? No. That man Patrick is not a man that Mother Gitto, at any rate, should be afraid of. But then—when is it likely that he will come? He left here this loaf and this water. Water for Mother Gitto! Ho, ho! I will wait—wait as patiently as I can, but I will have the knife ready."

She drew one ot the chairs to the table and sat down.

To wait patiently! There was little patience about Mother Gitto. Again and again she rose and paced the apartment, heaping bitter words on the heads of Master Rodney and all concerned with him.

And as she paced that chamber, her impatience turned to terror, for she remembered what Master Rodney had said.

He would keep his word certainly, and let her go by-and-by.

But then he had sworn to hunt her down, and hand her over to the law.

Of the law she had a fearful dread.

"If I do but get into the clutches of the law," she thought, "my life is surely lost."

Presently, as she sat, sleep stole over her.

She tried her hardest to resist it, but it was impossible.

The great amount of liquor she had that day consumed had its effect, and she was quickly sleeping as soundly as it is possible for a person to sleep.

It is likely, though, had she had anything on which to fix her attention, she would have remained awake.

But not the slightest sound fell upon her ears.

All below in the house, and without as well, was as silent as the tomb.

Moreover, nothing was to be seen from her window but the black waters of the Thames.

No moving thing had met her eyes, repeatedly as she had looked without, except the dull light fixed in the stern of a skiff or other vessel, as it glided on its journey up or down the river.

Mother Gitto presented a remarkable figure, as she thus slumbered.

Her hideous face was pillowed on her arms, while her coarse hair fell over her shoulders in the wildest disorder.

How long she had thus slept she had no means of ascertaining, but she was awakened by being roughly shaken.

"Now then," shouted a voice with a strong Irish accent. "Now then, wake up—wake up. What d'ye mane by upsitting the taper? Why, ye might have burned the house down wid yer foolery! Wake up, I say, or I'll christen ye wid this cold water."

"I'm very sorry to have put you out of temper," whined Mother Gitto.

"Are ye? Well, get up while I light the taper again."

Mother Gitto rose, and as she did so she instantly remembered the knife.

Patrick had brought up a lantern.

Holding it up, he was unfastening its door so as to relight the taper, when Mother Gitto glided noiselessly beside him.

What followed was as swift as the lightning flashes.

From the folds of her dress she took the knife, held it daggerwise, and with all the force she could muster, she plunged it deep into the unfortunate Irishman's heart.

Never was a blow given with more accuracy than this.

A wild cry left the poor fellow's lips—or, we should rather say, partly left his lips, for the cry was stifled by the rush of blood from his mouth.

He staggered back, and fell with a thud across the hearth.

Had Mother Gitto not pounced upon the lantern as it rolled from his hand, she would have been in total darkness, and this might have been a serious thing for her, knowing nothing of the construction of the house.

Her heart was palpitating violently, but not with horror at the deed she had perpetrated.

This was not the first terrible crime she had committed—no, nor the second, nor the third.

Her wicked heart was palpitating with apprehension of being caught red-handed.

The noise made by poor Patrick in falling had been somewhat loud.

But no sound as of persons alarmed fell upon the ears of the wretched old hag, and yet it was some time before she could persuade her trembling limbs to move.

The first thing she did was to partly shade the lantern and advance to the door of the room, which Patrick had taken the precaution to fasten on the inside.

Hearing no one moving, she advanced to the dead man.

The knife was still buried deep in his breast.

Twice Mother Gitto raised her hand to withdraw it, and twice did she draw back.

"But I had better take it," she thought, "since he has no arms about him. Yes, I had better take it; for if I can manage it, I will put Master Rodney beyond the power of placing me in the embrace of the hateful law.

"No one moves below; 'tis evident that they have not returned from the Hollow Ground. Yes, nor perhaps will they ever return. If they succeed in rescuing that girl, then Master Montague is not the man I have always thought him."

Stooping suddenly, she made a snatch at the knife and withdrew it.

She then searched poor Patrick's body.

The first thing she found was the key of the door.

The next was several pieces of money, as well as a few charms and other little knick-knacks, and lastly, a crumpled letter.

Mother Gitto was curious enough to read this.

The writing was remarkably good, and the spelling excellent; the document was, in fact, from the village schoolmaster at Pat's native place, on the outskirts of Waterford.

It said—

"PATRICK,—This by my hand, but from your parents and from your dear little motherless child. They greet you with the fondest love. The letter written by your master, Alexander Rodney, whose fame is known even in this most remote village, was read to them by me, and was received with tears and blessings. They return you their heartfelt thanks for the money—all your earnings—you so kindly and thoughtfully enclosed, and all of which was safely brought to the cottage by a gentleman you mentioned as a friend of the celebrated Walter Raleigh, of whose deeds in this, our unhappy country, I will not speak, since he was acting under the orders of his queen.

"I am informed that London swarms with assassins, both men and women. But I need scarcely warn you to be careful.

"So, for the present, Patrick, we must bid you adieu, the while commending you to the keeping of the Holy Virgin.—Your devoted friend and old schoolmaster,

"MICHAEL KAVANAGH."

"So he's a father," chuckled Mother Gitto; "and his parents pray for his safety! Umph!"

She replaced the letter, and then, advancing to the door, opened it, and passed on to the landing.

Here she halted, and listened intently.

But she heard no sound.

There were two or three other apartments on this landing, and, having taken off her boots, she passed into them one after the other.

It was while thus engaged that the light of the lantern was observed by the headsman.

Mother Gitto now descended the stairs.

Halting on the next landing, she tried the doors.

All here appeared to be locked.

Again and again she listened, but not the slightest sound fell upon her ears.

Consequently she arrived at this conclusion—that Master Rodney was absent from the house, or that he had retired.

She now commenced the descent of the last flight, and she had reached the turn, when she noticed a long streak of light on the wall.

That light was reflected from the apartment opposite.

Instantaneously the hag shut off the rays of her lantern, and creeping to the door, looked in.

She found herself before a chamber filled with articles used by the great chemist in his profession.

At the farther end were a pair of folding-doors, and through them she saw Master Rodney's bedroom.

In the first apartment was Master Rodney.

He was in a stooping attitude before a huge glass instrument standing on the floor, the top nearly touching the ceiling.

Round this experimenting glass was fixed a small charcoal fire, and the old man was intently watching the bubbles which rose and fell in the glass.

Right and left were scattered the different bottles and cases, the contents of which he was using.

The chamber was like an oven, but

nevertheless, no perspiration rested upon Master Rodney's face.

A cry of joy rose to Mother Gitto's lips as she thus saw the old man.

"All my anxiety—all my fear is at an end!" she muttered as she clutched the murderous knife tightly in her blood-stained hand. "I will lay him low on the floor of his own chamber! But I will try hard not to slay him outright, as I did his man above; for I would taunt him, laugh at him, and revile him in his agony. Strange, though, that I should slay the wife, and then, after the lapse of many years, slay the husband. He is already a great man; but here is an end to his greatness."

During this soliloquy, Master Rodney had never moved an inch, nor, indeed, had he turned his head.

His eyes had remained intently fixed on the dancing, sparkling bubbles.

Evidently the experiment he was now conducting, was one of the highest importance.

It was an experiment on which the whole of his thoughts were concentrated.

Mother Gitto raised her hand, and began to gently push back the door.

There was great danger of detection here, because if the door creaked, the occupant of the room would be instantly alarmed.

In the right-hand corner of the apartment, and near the folding-doors, was fixed a large mirror.

In that, the dark figure of Mother Gitto was plainly reflected.

And yet the old man saw it not.

Slowly the door moved back in response to the pressure of the hag, and in a few seconds it was open, and she crept cautiously into the room.

She stood behind the old man, and with a demoniacal glitter in her eyes, she raised the knife.

Even as the deadly blow was descending, there was a sudden dash, a startled cry, a bitter exclamation from the lips of Mother Gitto, and, turning, the astonished chemist saw her in the clutch of Dudley Herbert.

His startled eyes marked the weapon in the old woman's hand.

Indeed, he saw all at a glance.

Yes, it was. indeed, Dudley, who had entered the house thus noiselessly and secretly.

Mother Gitto did not lose her presence of mind.

Well knowing that now it was not very likely that Master Rodney would let her leave the house without a proper escort, she frantically struggled to deal Dudley a fatal blow, and thus, at any rate, get rid of one who would be inclined to bar her progress.

Strangely enough, though she recognised Dudley, she never considered as to whether it was not more than likely that the friends she had seen him with were below.

Dudley found to his astonishment that the wretched woman was possessed of a strength quite uncommon among women of her age.

She fought and struggled like an old tigress, the while uttering the most terrible imprecations.

But despite her struggles, Dudley held her firmly by her skinny wrists.

She hissed like the most venomous serpent, spat in his face, and attempted to use her shoeless feet to a dangerous purpose.

"Give in, vile hag," said Dudley; "give in, I say, or I shall be tempted to forget that you are a woman, and fell you to the floor."

"Let her go—let her go, Dudley!" shouted Master Rodney, who seemed to have suddenly found his tongue. "Let her go—for the love of heaven, let her go! Quickly—as you value your life!"

But for a minute or two Dudley heeded him not.

He was intent upon getting possession of the knife the woman held in her hand.

"Had you been a man," he said, "I would have struck you dead long ere this."

"Wretched upstart!" shrieked Mother Gitto; "if I can but get my hand free, I will plunge this knife into your heart. Let me go—let me go! Let go my hands, or I will fix my teeth in your face and tear it to pieces."

"Horrible wretch!" thundered Dudley, his grip on the hag's wrists becoming tighter than ever. "Loathsome hag, drop that knife!"

"No, no, no! I will have your life first."

"Dudley," shouted Master Rodney, now frantic with excitement; "Dudley—for heaven's sake release her! In another few seconds, if you are in this chamber, death will overtake both of you! Look, Dudley—look: The glass—the glass!"

Dudley did look, certainly; or, rather, he cast a glance at the experimenting instrument; but he seemed to pay but little heed to it.

The contents of the glass had nearly reached the top.

When Mother Gitto had first looked into the chamber, no noise proceeded from the strange-looking glass, although it then bubbled as it did at this moment.

But now, high above the noise made by the determined struggles of our hero and this depraved wretch, could be heard a loud, strange hissing noise.

It sounded like the escaping steam from a large piece of modern machinery.

Every second Master Rodney became more and more excited.

Presently, he could not longer contain himself, and, dashing forward, he seized Dudley by the collar to pull him away.

It was then that Dudley realised the fact that Master Rodney was apprehensive of danger from the huge glass.

He, therefore, suddenly let go of Mother Gitto.

The result was, that the old woman went violently backward.

Clutching at a table, she prevented herself from falling to the floor; but in another second she found that her dress had become ignited at the charcoal fire we have spoken of.

Instantly the dry material was a mass of flame, and, giving utterance to a piercing shriek, Mother Gitto dashed towards the bedroom.

Forgetting, in the excitement of the moment, the character of the old woman, as well as the bitter and horrible imprecations she had hurled at his head, Dudley would have rushed after her and have attempted to extinguish the flames, but Master Rodney once more seized him with one hand, while with the other he banged the door to.

"Too late, Dudley," he said, hoarsely; "too late—too late! Death has overtaken her. No human power could save her now. Ha!"

He was interrupted by a tremendous report, as if a huge barrel of powder had been exploded within the chamber.

So terrific was the shock, that the whole of the house seemed violently shaken.

That the contents were shaken, was only too evident, for the report was at once followed by the loud, crashing of glass in various parts of the house.

"Had I not pulled you out, Dudley," said Master Rodney, whose voice trembled with excitement, "you must have been slain. But hark! the noise has alarmed someone without. I suppose 'tis your friends returned."

"Yes; but in the name of heaven, sir, what has caused this fearful explosion, and what is this vapour which is filling the whole of the house?"

"Wait—wait but a moment, my lad," was the reply; "if we enter at this instant, both of us would be stricken dead. The room within is filled with a deadly vapour. But in a few seconds, the poison contained in the vapour will evaporate, and that left within will be powerless to inflict injury upon us."

"You think, then, that the wretched woman is dead?"

"Unquestionably; but she died not by fire. No. Had the whole chamber been on fire, that vapour which left the glass when it exploded, would have instantly extinguished it. Unless I mistake not, we shall find her body horribly mutilated."

"Your experiments, then, are attended with great danger?"

"Danger attends many of my experiments; but no accident has ever befallen me, nor would this have occurred had I been able to properly attend to what I was doing without interference. But let me call Patrick to open the door."

He shouted for poor Patrick again and again.

"I will open the door," said Dudley, descending the stairs.

"Unfasten the bolts at the top and bottom. You will find it unlocked," said Master Rodney. "One instant—what of the maiden?"

"Safe!"

"Thank heaven!" was the fervent reply.

Dudley quickly had the door open, and loud and eager were the questions put to him.

Dudley led the headsman and Raleigh up the stairs, and as they reached the top, Master Rodney pushed the door open.

Then, rushing to a little window on the landing, he pushed that up.

"Close your mouths an instant!" he cried.

This was done, and after a brief pause, the remaining vapour had disappeared, though it left behind it a strange, nauseous smell.

In the meantime, the headsman, by means of his tinder-box, had lighted part of a link—an article which was now wanted, for total darkness prevailed in the chamber.

Master Rodney took the link, and, passing into the room, held it aloft.

A marvellous sight greeted the eyes of the beholders.

The contents of both rooms were a complete wreck, not an article being left on the walls.

As for the glass, that was smashed into thousands of pieces, which were scattered all over the place, and no trace remained of where it had stood.

At the farther end of the apartment lay the remains of Mother Gitto.

She was nothing but a blackened, distorted piece of humanity.

Quickly Master Rodney informed the astonished and horrified party of all that had occurred.

"But," said Dudley, "what has become of your man, Patrick?"

"That is what I am next going to ascertain," replied Master Rodney.

"Depend upon it," cried Dudley, picking up a lamp and lighting it by the link, "that something has happened to him. He was this woman's gaoler, and before she could have got out, Patrick must have got in."

Up the stairs he went, followed by Raleigh.

The fatal room was soon reached, and there they saw the body of Patrick.

Shocked beyond measure, they remained for some few seconds without uttering a word.

And while they stood Master Rodney joined them.

"Gracious heaven!" he exclaimed. "Murder has been committed!"

"Yes," replied Dudley, "and the vile hag below—the creature of the villain Marcus Montague—was the murderess. 'Twas a pity that such a sudden death overtook her, for the public hangman should have operated upon her."

"Poor Patrick!" murmured Master Rodney. "The most devoted servant I ever had! His heart was as true as it is possible for a man's heart to be. He has no friends here, but in his native place he has father, mother, and a little motherless girl, to whom he gave all his savings.

"He died in my service," continued Master Rodney, sadly, "and it is therefore my duty to make provision for those left behind. This shall be done."

"I hope you will allow me to be a contributor," said Dudley.

"And I trust to share also," added Raleigh; "though the amount I can give will be necessarily small, for my sword, though it has won a few trifling honours, has, as yet, brought me no gold."

"We know where there are a few bags of gold to spare," said the voice of Quicksilver, who, unperceived, had joined them, "and it will be a downright shame if Montague and his masked friends are allowed to take it away."

"We will give our attention to that matter at a future time, little Quicksilver," replied Raleigh. "At present this terrible deed commands our attention. I will tell you what it is in my power to do, Master Rodney.

Several of my friends are commanders of vessels, and if you think it should be done, I will make arrangements with one of them to convey poor Pat's remains to his native place. It would at least be a satisfaction for his relatives to place his body beneath the shadow of their own house of prayer. To us it is a satisfaction to know that his awful fate has been most terribly avenged."

"A timely suggestion," replied Master Rodney. "By all means, Master Raleigh, let that be done."

Soon the whole party once more stood in the chamber to which they had been first conducted, and then Master Rodney was made acquainted with the particulars of all that had occurred at Hollow Ground.

While thankful that Madeline had escaped, he became serious over the great loss of life, and expressed his opinion that when the particulars should reach the ears of the queen, Raleigh would get into serious trouble.

"I have been in many difficulties," said Raleigh, with a grave smile, "and have managed to extricate myself."

"May you be as fortunate with regard to this matter," answered Master Rodney. "My influence with the queen is, as you well know, great. If it should be required, you can rely upon me to say a word in your favour."

"A thousand thanks, Master Rodney," said Raleigh. "And now, I suppose the time has arrived for us to take our departure."

"You, Lomew, will to the Tower," said the old man; "and for safety, you will take Madeline Maynard. I should be pleased to welcome her here; but I would suggest your instant departure for the fortress. Marcus Montague has escaped. Heaven alone can tell what he will do."

"Yes," said Lomew; "I propose to take both Madeline and Dudley to the Tower. They will be warmly received by Sir Edward Warner, the lieutenant. On the morrow, Dudley can set off to his mother. When he explains all, no doubt she will take charge of Madeline until she can be sent in safety to her father's cottage."

The leave-taking was hurried, for Raleigh was most anxious to set off with his brave, but now exhausted comrades, and Lomew was just as anxious to reach the Tower.

"Adieu, Sir Walter Raleigh," cried Quicksilver, with a low bow, "for it will be 'sir,' one of these days, I'll warrant me."

"And it will be your own fault if you are not made a baronet in real earnest," replied Raleigh.

"If he is not created a baronet," said Lomew, "it will not be because he is in want of impudence. He has several times made the queen's acquaintance."

In another quarter of an hour the friends had separated, and had gone their several ways, and the neighbourhood of the chemist's residence was once again silent and deserted.

This was not the case with Hollow Ground.

The grounds of the mysterious residence were filled with many persons—men and women.

A strange sight was presented.

Every third person was provided either with a link or lantern, and as they moved from spot to spot, they appeared like a number of restless will-o'-the-wisps.

Many of these too curious individuals met with sudden and terrible deaths.

Some fell into the moat, never to rise again, while others dropped through concealed traps that were placed in various artfully concealed positions beneath the wall on the eastern side.

But long before morning dawned they were driven off, for Marcus Montague once again took possession.

He found Hockley on the roof, had him attended to by a surgeon, and then both of them set to work.

Men were procured, and the breach was rapidly made good.

And while this work was in progress, Montague and Hockley made a thorough inspection of the premises.

The first place visited was the money vault.

"Thank heaven!" said Montague; "that vast treasure is safe."

"Yes," returned Hockley. "When they first said they would search the house, my heart sank; for I made certain that cunning Master Raleigh would smell it out. But it's safe."

He added to himself—

"If all goes well, that money will become mine. Montague use it in the way it was intended! Pah! Though he dare not touch it at present, it would eventually go into his private chest. So, after all, it's only diamond cut diamond."

Marcus Montague's thoughts were—

"I will take the earliest opportunity of removing this vast sum. The fortunes of ten men are here."

Book the Second.—"The Maiden Queen."

CHAPTER XI.

OF THE DUEL BETWEEN MONTAGUE AND DUDLEY—OF THE RESULT—OF THE SUDDEN APPEARANCE OF ELIZABETH, AND OF HER DENUNCIATION.

A WEEK passed away, and during that time news of what had occurred at Hollow Ground got wind, and was soon carried over London.

The queen heard many accounts.

She had many a conference with one of her chief and most valued statesmen; and that gentleman was always careful that these conferences should be in private, for the subject on each occasion was no sooner broached than Elizabeth burst into a fearful rage.

She vowed that whoever was wrong she would bring to the block.

She would have sent for Raleigh and Montague, had she not been strongly advised to wait until she should reach the Tower.

It was at the end of a week after what had occurred that the Court moved to the Tower of London; but even then not a word was breathed as to what the queen would say respecting Hollow Ground.

No one knew better than Raleigh that the clouds had been gathering for some days, and that now the storm was ready to burst.

Though his position of a courtier had not been of any great duration as yet, he nevertheless well knew the violent temper of the "Virgin Queen," especially when she considered herself insulted, as she did in this case.

For a battle to be waged in the very heart of London—what was that but an insult of the grossest description?

St. Paul's had struck the hour of twelve; the guards on duty at the various points in and outside the fortress had been changed, and now silence prevailed.

It was a deep, solemn silence.

Gates and doors were closed with the utmost caution, and all this showed that the queen was occupying apartments within the Tower.

The night was a most beautiful one.

From a cloudless sky Mistress Moon sent forth her glorious rays, and flooded the dark, sullen Thames and part of the huge fortress, though the remainder of it was in semi-darkness.

It was a strange thing that Traitor's Gate always looked gloomy and forbidding.

When the moon's rays shone full upon the ponderous gate of oak, it seemed to cast many a strange shadow on the black walls.

Many of the warders said that, when the moon was in a certain position, and gleamed across the stout posts, the shadow of the axe and the block was most distinctly visible on the walls.

All within the Tower, except those on duty, were supposed to be in their beds and asleep.

This was not the case with at least

one person, and that person was the hero of our romance, Dudley Herbert.

The room allotted him was a small one, not far removed from the headsman, and it was as prettily furnished a chamber as one could expect in such a place as the Tower of London.

He was fully dressed, and certainly he looked very handsome in the costume he had chosen.

And about his waist he had fastened a beautiful sword and dagger, presented to him by Lomew.

"All ready now!" muttered Dudley—"all ready to stand before the proud Elizabeth, and assert my rights; for though the scoundrel Montague has taken possession, he shall be ousted! Oh, for a little fresh air! If I went forth, no doubt the sharp eyes of that villainous Barcally would detect me. And yet, why should I fear? I am a guest, not a prisoner. I will go forth. If Barcally attempts to intercept me, I will question his rights."

The window of his chamber looked out upon a narrow strip of ground, which led, on the right, to the staircase leading to St. Thomas' Tower and on the left to the steps and the archway of Traitor's Gate.

Extinguishing his light, he opened the window and passed out, being careful to make no noise.

For some time he paced the ground, and inhaled the fresh air.

But presently he approached close to the staircase.

Then he paused.

The curiously fashioned, well-like stone staircase, up which many noble men and women had gone, to be finally passed on to Tower Green, attracted his attention.

The whole of the entrance was distinctly visible in consequence of the moon's rays.

Wondering what sort of place it was, he, after a little hesitation, mounted the steps.

In a moment he was in semi-darkness; but, attracted by the moon's rays at the other end, he passed on, and presently found himself in a large vaulted chamber, filled with long stained-glass windows.

No sentries were here, but looking from one of the windows, he saw a couple of them in earnest conversation on the strand below.

Slowly he crossed the apartment, and reached a low door.

He touched it, and it at once flew back, but without making the least noise.

He found himself in a chamber similar in appearance to the other, but with a lower roof, and smaller in every way.

It was also in semi-darkness.

There was just sufficient light for him to notice that the chamber was furnished—or what the authorities of the Tower called furnished.

Impelled by curiosity, he passed on, and opening a door opposite, he found himself standing on the top of a flight of stone steps.

He could see that he was now in quite another part of the Tower, but he knew not its exact position.

Still no sentries obstructed his movements.

The moon was shining just as brilliantly, but the steps on which he stood were in the shadow, and he could see but little of the Thames over the huge embattlements.

Suddenly he started.

Standing against one of the cannon were two persons.

One of them was Marcus Montague, and the other was the warder, Barcally.

They were engaged in earnest conversation.

"Marcus Montague here!" muttered Dudley. "Then Lomew was mistaken. "By the heaven above us! we shall come face to face. I've no doubt now that the furnished apartment through which I have just now passed was the one set aside for him.

"Face to face! But what am I thinking about? I should bring the guard about my ears, and find myself inside one of the strong chambers in quick time. But can I resist this great temptation? Is it possible that I can stand before that man, a sword at my side, and never attempt to draw it? No, no! A thousand times, no! My hand itches to clutch the blade now.

"And when I think of what he has

done—that by means of his wealth and cunning lawyers, he has succeeded in wresting my lawful rights from me, and plunging my mother into poverty, I feel that he must die. But would it not be as well to stay my hand for a few hours? And yet—let me think an instant."

He backed noiselessly through the doorway; but getting on the other side of it, he kept it open for the space of half-an-inch, so that he could watch the pair of plotters.

His watch was rewarded, for he saw Montague place a purse in Barcally's hands.

After this a few words passed between them, though Dudley caught not one syllable of what they said.

And then Montague sauntered towards the door behind which Dudley stood.

As he lifted his face, our hero noted the expression upon it.

It was one of fiendish delight, as if he had just settled the points of some devilish plot entirely to his satisfaction.

Dudley at once remembered Lomew's warning—

"Beware of Barcally, one of the chief warders. He is in Montague's pay."

Before Montague's foot had touched the steps, Dudley had closed the door.

Then he retreated to the furnished chamber.

He was at a loss where to conceal himself, but he quickly found a spot, and that was behind the curtains of the bedstead.

Another few seconds and Montague entered the apartment.

The first thing he did was to bolt the door, the second to advance to the table, take up a tinder-box, and set light to a small lamp.

"There was one most important thing," he said, half aloud, "that I had fortunately not forgotten—or, rather, not forgotten to order—and here it is. Without it I should be lost, though who says that Lord Marcus Montague—ho, ho! it sounds quite natural enough—who says that Montague gives way to creature comforts would speak falsely."

With this he picked up a basketed bottle standing beside the huge fireplace, and stood it on the table.

From the opposite side he took up a small black travelling trunk, opened it, and brought out an exquisitely chased silver drinking cup.

Having filled this from the bottle, he pushed one of the massively upholstered chairs beside the table, and first taking off his sword, seated himself with just as much grace as if he were in the presence of the queen herself.

"So that is all settled," he chuckled, after having drunk part of the contents of the cup, "and if things go dead against me at the first court, there will be nothing of the sort at the second. Presently I shall be joined by young Compton, who is only too eager to avenge his father's death. Raleigh slew him, he thought, but then it was to my interest to tell him that I saw Dudley Herbert strike the blow."

After a few moments, during which he became so excited with what was passing in his mind that he rose and proceeded to pace the chamber, he said again, half aloud—

"And so this girl is actually within the walls of this fortress! What is she here for? What but to bear testimony against me? But they little know that I have a complete answer to the whole charge, which is certain to be made against me. The answer to it will come upon all like a thunder-clap. Dudley Herbert has a powerful friend in Raleigh, though. Yet if I don't manage to get him apartments which he will not leave for some considerable time, then my name is not Marcus Montague, and I have no influence in the proper quarter.

"I would to heaven that I had engaged with Dudley Herbert! I could have slain him beyond all doubt."

"Slay him now, scoundrel!" cried Dudley, as, like a lightning's flash, he darted from his place of concealment.

Snatching Montague's blade from the table, he hurled it violently at his feet.

"Draw!" he said; "draw, and

slay Dudley Herbert if you can, villain!"

Montague turned deathly pale as he saw who actually stood before him, but he was so skilled in the concealment of his emotions, that in another second he appeared perfectly calm.

"You here!" he said, in low, hissing tones, as he fixed his large eyes on Dudley; "you here—in my private apartment! What! has the redoubtable Dudley Herbert, the so-called eldest son of the beheaded traitor, Lord Herbert, descended so low as to steal into the chamber of a courtier to rob him? On my soul! I must issue a warning to my brother courtiers, lest they be robbed."

"Your satire is wholly lost upon me, Marcus Montague," replied Dudley, sternly. "I am proof against irony such as proceeds from your lips. Pick up your sword, draw it, and make the attempt to slay Dudley Herbert."

"You are a fool! You are worse than a fool; for he who dares to draw a weapon within sound of the queen forfeits his right hand. At present my right hand is valuable to me."

"Indeed! What would you tell me, Marcus Montague? That if you lost your right hand, you could not commit murder with the other?"

"Look you," said Marcus. "A man of my age does not feel inclined to stand still and listen to the idle words of a boy. If you do not at once quit my chamber, I will call the guard and have you arrested as a thief."

"What would you say, Marcus Montague—that I robbed you of your honour? Pick up your blade. And I swear that you will have some work ere you slay me. As regards fighting within sound of the queen, that would here be impossible. The sound of the clashing of a couple of blades would never penetrate these thick walls."

"I decline."

"You decline—eh? Then, Marcus Montague, you are a coward. Here is my challenge, however."

And striding suddenly forward, he dealt Montague a tremendous blow on the shoulder with the flat of his sword.

Nothing but this could have made the villain draw his blade from its sheath.

This blow roused all the savage fury in his breast.

Giving utterance to a loud, passionate cry, he stooped, picked up the sword and plucked it from its sheath, which latter he hurled from him.

"I will risk it, you impertinent bravo!" he hissed. "Come on, and, by the heaven above me, it will be strange indeed if I don't stretch you lifeless at my feet."

Dudley replied not.

He met Marcus Montague's furious onslaught with calmness.

A strangely hollow sound had this vaulted chamber, from the effect of the clashing of the swords.

The sound was heard in the chamber above, but very indistinctly, in consequence of the enormous thickness of the stone dividing the two apartments.

This duel, within the very walls of the Tower of London, was a sight that would have interested every man who was acquainted with the use of the sword, because the fight was waged between two persons who had a thoroughly scientific knowledge of that weapon.

Both presently warmed to the work—both fought with the determination of slaying; and more than once Dudley said—

"If I avenge my brother's death, Marcus Montague, I shall be satisfied."

"And if I for ever silence a hound like you," replied Montague, on one of these occasions, "I shall save others a task."

By which was meant that he had made arrangements for Dudley's assassination.

Suddenly, in the midst of a violent exchange, the lamp was swished off the table, and the chamber was thus only illuminated by the moon's rays.

This light was not great, but there was sufficient to enable them to proceed.

Yet, as if by mutual consent, both stopped to rest a few moments.

No sound as if anyone were alarmed was heard.

Dudley was the first to resume the conflict, but there was not the slightest hesitation on Montague's part.

Indeed, he resumed the fight with increased energy, and this, no doubt, was owing to the fact that he heard no sounds of alarm.

But before two minutes had passed, a sharp cry of pain left his lips.

His sword was knocked from his hand, and he received a wound in the breast, and not an inch from the heart.

"Hold!" he gasped; "hold your hand!"

"No! I stay not my arm. You die!" replied Dudley, fiercely, as he drew back his arm to give the fatal blow.

But Montague drew his dagger, and flung it into Dudley's face.

Fortunately, the blade did not strike him, but the hilt did.

The steel cross struck him on the cheek.

The unexpected blow sent him reeling backward a few paces, but it did not cause him to drop his weapon.

Montague, finding himself disarmed, and seeing that he could not pass Dudley, or dash through the door he had bolted, turned round and pulled at the other, which was unfastened.

He was soon upon the top of the well-like flight of stairs which Dudley had at first traversed.

Down these he dashed, but Dudley was after him.

"Hold, you accursed plotter—hold, this is murder!" cried Montague.

Most certainly the next instant would have been his last, bécause, owing to loss of blood, he was sinking rapidly.

Dudley had drawn his arm back to give the fatal blow, when a strong hand was laid on it from behind, and a voice cried—

"Hold! hold! What—murder under the very eyes of the queen! Can this be possible? 'Tis Dudley Herbert!"

Dudley turned and saw that he who had arrested his arm was the Lieutenant of the Tower, Sir Edward Warner.

At the same moment were heard the clanging of the alarm-bell, hoarse calls to arms, commands as to the mounting of the cannon on the embattlements, rushing of heavy feet, the clashing of arms and accoutrements, and, above all, the stentorian voice of a man standing on a part of the White Tower, who shouted—

"GOD SAVE THE QUEEN!"

A cry which was responded to by the men on duty, and others who were turning out.

From the way the officers and men looked at the river, it seemed as if an attack was expected from that quarter.

Bur Sir Edward soon caused a great deal of this excitement to subside.

"Nothing is to be apprehended," he said. "But if the queen is awakened, we shall have to answer for it. Let us see what all this is about—links and lanterns, quick!"

"Do not alarm yourself, Sir Edward," cried a sweet, but ringing voice—a voice which caused Sir Edward and nearly everyone present to turn deathly pale; "the queen is awakened, and she is here to investigate the cause of this disturbance herself."

It was Elizabeth!

She was enveloped from head to foot in a black velvet gown, lined with rich fur.

The hood was thrown back, so that her proud head was displayed.

Never before had the lieutenant seen the look which now rested upon her clear-cut features; never before —not even in the midst of the most heated discussion—had he seen the light of passion which now blazed in her eyes.

The crowd respectfully made way, and Elizabeth, amid a profound silence, came forward.

Behind her was her favourite maid, the lovely Margaret Meecham—the lady we have heard Montague speak of as "the beauteous Margaret," and upon whom he had evil designs.

"'HOW CAME YOU HERE?' DEMANDED BARCALLY."

It was this lady who was sleeping in the chamber above that in which the duel had been fought, and it was she who had aroused the queen.

The red glare of a dozen links lit up a most striking scene, the most prominent figure in which was Dudley Herbert, who stood proudly erect in the very centre of the steps, his sword still clutched in his hand.

At the foot lay Marcus Montague, now totally unconscious.

The queen, for a moment, looked down at the fallen man, and then she fixed her flashing eyes on Dudley.

"Sir Edward Warner," she said, "who is the youth who thus dares to stand before his queen with a naked blade in his hand?"

"One Dudley Herbert, may it please your majesty."

"It is very far from our pleasure," said Elizabeth. "Disarm the wretch who thus outrages us! Disarm him at once!"

Instantly half-a-dozen men sprang upon Dudley, wrested his blade from his hand, and placed him under arrest.

"And this man at my feet?" continued the queen.

Sir Edward held a lantern in such a position that the features could plainly be seen.

"Why, by all the saints," cried Elizabeth, "this is Marcus Montague!"

A sharp cry left the lips of the maid, and she would have fallen upon her knees beside Montague had it not been for the queen.

Elizabeth caught her arm, and gently but firmly drew her back.

"Wait—wait!" she said, sternly; "duty before everthing."

"Oh, your majesty," Margaret sobbed, "he may be dying!"

"And what of it? What does a man deserve who draws blade under the very eyes of his queen?"

"May it please you," said a whining voice, "he drew no blade."

"Who speaks?" queried Elizabeth, turning her eyes in the direction whence the voice proceeded.

"'Tis one of the chief warders, your majesty," said Sir Edward.

"Well, well—what knows he of it? Let him come forward."

Barcally was thereupon hustled forward.

"Well, sirrah," said Elizabeth, fixing such a look upon Barcally that the villain wished he had never spoken, "what know you of this?"

"I saw the affair, your majesty."

Dudley started.

That the man had told a falsehood he well knew.

"So you, one of the chief warders, saw the affair, and yet stopped it not!" cried Elizabeth. "You are as much to blame as those who drew blade! But you said that Montague did not draw?"

"I did say so, your majesty, and I repeat my statement. This young man suddenly attacked him in his chamber, and—"

"Villain—" commenced Dudley.

His voice was lost in the shouts of "Silence!"

"I begin to understand," said the queen. "I see well what enemies these two are, these two of the principals in the disgraceful outrage at Charing Cross. But give us the particulars. Listen carefully, Sir Edward, and catch well what he says; for if aught he utters proves to be a falsehood, a dungeon shall be this chief warder's portion, so long as Elizabeth sits upon the throne."

After this declaration Barcally had the greatest difficulty in controlling his agitation, so as to give a clear statement.

After a short pause, he said—

"I was in this walk, your majesty, and saw Dudley Herbert leave his chamber, creep up to the top of the stairs, and draw his blade. After a brief pause he passed the door. I crept after him, and through a chink in the door saw him suddenly spring upon Master Montague, who started up and dashed from the room, the prisoner after him. I was alarmed, and ran down the stairs again. Just before Master Montague reached the bottom of the stairs, he chanced to turn, and it was then that the prisoner plunged his blade into his breast."

"But do you tell us that our maid is mistaken in saying that she heard the clash of steel?"

"She must have been, your majesty."

"Well, it does not sound feasible that Marcus Montague attempted not to defend himself. Search for his weapon."

A dozen searched, but no weapon met their hands.

"That man has spoken falsely!" cried Dudley. "If the chamber above is entered, Montague's sword with which he fought will be found there, as well as his dagger."

"Sir Edward," said the queen, "hasten to that chamber and search it. And if a drawn sword is there found, the owner, injured though he be, shall, like this youth, be cast into the lowest dungeon this Tower contains."

Up went Sir Edward, followed by two or three of the assembled lords.

They returned in two or three minutes.

"Well?" queried the queen.

"We can find no weapon unsheathed, your majesty," replied Sir Edward. "All we can see is a sword standing beside the wall, duly sheathed."

"And," said Lord Morehen, "it has not recently been drawn, for the cord is wound fast about the handle and the sheath."

Dudley felt almost stupefied.

At once he saw what had been done.

Barcally had removed Montague's weapons.

Elizabeth stood silent for a few moments.

One or two of the Court physicians pushed forward, as if about to render the fallen man some assistance, but the queen fixed such a look upon them that they were glad to retire.

"Sir Edward," said Elizabeth, at last, "you have said that this man is one of the chief warders. Throw a light on his face."

The rays of a link, held by the nearest soldier, were instantly thrown upon Barcally's morose countenance, and upon it Elizabeth fixed a keen glance, as if she would penetrate to the very depths of his soul.

"You have a face that I would not trust," said the queen, in low, measured tones. "'Tis not an open face, and the eyes seem to denote a treacherous disposition; but then, that may come of his frequent association with the many who pass Traitor's Gate, my lords," she said, sarcastically. Then suddenly drawing herself erect, she added—

"Yet, under the circumstances, I am compelled to believe what you have said. But be warned. If you are found guilty of having told us false, nothing shall save your life. And now, Sir Edward, into your hands do I commit this traitor."

"Your majesty, I would speak a word or two in his behalf," cried a voice.

And Walter Raleigh stepped forward.

Instantly Elizabeth's face became white with passion.

"You speak!" she cried—"you! Unless we mistake, you will require someone to speak very strongly in your favour ere many hours have passed. Stand back, Walter Raleigh, lest you also find yourself a prisoner! Since when has he been in our tower, Sir Edward Warner?"

"Since eleven, may it please your majesty."

"Like other traitors who fear to meet their queen in the broad daylight, he steals here under cover of the darkness. 'Sdeath! it seems as if we are surrounded with traitors. But there are the block and the axe—unless, indeed, the man Lomew—"

"He is here, your majesty."

It was Lomew who spoke.

Elizabeth started as she turned and beheld the tall, grim figure of the headsman, and a shudder agitated her frame as she saw that beneath his arm he carried a glittering axe.

"What does the headsman mean by coming into our presence with the axe, Sir Edward?" asked Elizabeth.

"I will answer the question, if I may be permitted," said Lomew. "Hearing the alarm-bell, the rattle of arms, and the tramp of feet, and thinking that an attack was about to be made on the Tower, I seized an axe and rushed forth to Traitor's Gate, which spot I would have defended until this weapon dropped from my hands."

"We accept your explanation, Master Headsman," replied Elizabeth; "but put that axe behind you—the very sight of it makes our blood run cold. And yet heaven only knows how many heads around us will fall beneath it."

As she said this, she fixed a significant look on Raleigh.

"You observe, Master Headsman," said Elizabeth, "that your friend—your guest—is under arrest?"

"I have just learned it, your majesty," replied Lomew.

"Have you anything to say on his behalf?"

"Yes, your majesty," replied Lomew, "I have much to say."

"Then reserve what you have to say until to-morrow; for hark! St. Paul's strikes the hour of two, and we have already tarried too long in the night air. Sir Edward, let the prisoner be securely confined; I look to you for his safety. The traitor shall be examined in a few hours."

"Traitor!" cried Lomew.

"Yes," said Elizabeth; "traitor."

"Your majesty," ventured Lomew, "there lies the greatest traitor you ever yet had within your realms. I appeal to Master Raleigh."

"Silence!" cried the queen. "How dare you appeal to anyone? Begone, Master Headsman. We first deal with traitors, and you have the last of them. Therefore, be satisfied."

Thinking that very likely it would go all the harder with Dudley if he did not at once take his departure, Lomew moved away.

"Rash Dudley!" he muttered. "It was this rashness which brought your father to the block. It is rashness which has lost many a king a crown; it is rashness which will lose you name, fame, and fortune. What shall I do in the matter?"

In the meantime Dudley was placed in charge of Barcally and a few soldiers, and Sir Edward led the way.

Dudley had to pass Elizabeth, who was surveying him with a stern expression.

"He is a very handsome youth, Margaret," she said—"the handsomest within these walls, I'll warrant me. Strange it is that beauty, daring, wilfulness, and even treachery go hand-in-hand."

Before the queen Dudley halted.

Barcally was about to push him onward, when Elizabeth said—

"Wait!"

To Dudley she added—

"You would speak. Well?"

Dudley sank upon his knee before the queen.

"Madam," he said, "I am no traitor. There is no subject who loves his queen better than Dudley Herbert. I swear to you, by all my hopes of salvation, that this chief warder has lied to you."

"Well, well, we shall see that," replied Elizabeth, harshly. "In the meantime, our orders are to be obeyed. Depart."

Dudley rose, bowed gracefully, and was then hurried off.

"And now, my lords," added Elizabeth, "we had best beget ourselves to our chambers once more. Unless we hasten, yon moon will have given place to her more brilliant brother, and the sun will find us haggard and drowsy, and not at all fit to conduct State affairs. Disperse, my lords, disperse!"

No more was said, and queen and maid passed onward between two files of soldiers and warders, and followed by the lords and officers.

The latter were presently joined by Sir Edward.

The good-hearted lieutenant was evidently affected at what had transpired.

On inquiry, he found that Marcus Montague had been removed to the chamber in which the duel had been fought.

Sir Edward paid him a visit.

Finding he was being well attended to, he descended the steps, the blood on which had not yet been removed, and found himself face to face with Walter Raleigh.

"I am in disgrace, Sir Edward," said Raleigh.

"You are indeed, Raleigh. And I thought you well on the road to fame and fortune. Alas! who can tell what a few hours will bring forth?"

"If I am committed to your care, Sir Edward, I trust you will find me as decent a place as possible."

"Rely upon it I will do my best," answered Sir Edward, in kindly tones.

"It looks as if I shall be shut up in the Tower, Sir Edward?"

"I cannot answer that question, Raleigh. Go to your chamber. I suppose you have a friend with whom yau can consult?"

"At present none that I should care to confer with are in the Tower. The Earl of Sussex does not arrive until eight or nine. Would it be too much to ask you to grant me an interview with Dudley Herbert?"

"Far better leave him to his own reflections for the next few hours, Raleigh."

"Then I will to the headsman, and— But, no; I will wait a few hours. Adieu, Sir Edward."

"Adieu, Raleigh, and fortune be with you at the Court."

CHAPTER XII.

OF HOW DUDLEY WAS BROUGHT BEFORE ELIZABETH, AND OF THE INCIDENTS WHICH OCCURRED IN THE COUNCIL CHAMBER OF THE TOWER OF LONDON.

NIGHT'S dark mantle had been drawn aside, and the sun lit up the gloomy Tower, until the arms and accoutrements of the men swarming the battlements glittered and flashed right merrily.

The Thames, the streets approaching thereto, and the chief thoroughfares wore an animated aspect.

It was known that after a considerable absence in the country, the queen was about to hold her Court.

Barges, ornamented in a costly and superb fashion, revealed the rank and wealth of their owners.

As without, so it was within the Tower.

Margaret, on making her appearance, was at once surrounded by eager peeresses, all of whom were most anxious to know the state of the queen's temper.

What Margaret told them was not by any means calculated to raise their or their lords' spirits.

The queen had risen at six; had passed two hours in writing and pacing her apartments; and as far as her appearance went, she was very pale, but calm. This, in fact, meant—

"Prepare yourself for a troubled day."

Just after eight the Earl of Sussex arrived by water, as also did Earl Dudley, and many other wealthy noblemen.

Raleigh made haste to have an interview with the Earl of Sussex, who for a long time had been his firmest and best friend.

It was owing principally to the earl that Raleigh had obtained his present position at Court.

To Raleigh's consternation, he found the nobleman cold and stern.

"I have heard all about Hollow Ground," said the earl, "and nothing you can say, Raleigh, will cause me to alter the opinion I have formed with reference to this matter. It is a gross insult to the queen, as well as to her peaceful subjects. Such terrible deeds frequently lead to fearful riots, and even revolution. To the best of my power I will shield you, in remembrance of what you have already done in the queen's service. More I cannot promise."

The earl was joined by Sir Edward, who at once made him acquainted with all that had taken place in the early hours of the morning.

The earl was astonished.

At last he said—

"Someone's head will surely fall for this."

"I fear so," muttered the lieutenant.

"But yet," cried the earl suddenly, "you have witnesses as to Montague's conduct, Raleigh?"

"Many, so please you, your grace."

"Good. Then forget not to put

the whole of the particulars before the queen. And the story this Dudley Herbert has to tell—has he witnesses? I mean with reference to his birth and his property."

"He has."

"Well, you may depend that the queen will give him fair opportunity. Though passionate, she is, like all women, curious, and the story which will be told must interest her. So, Raleigh, gird up your loins, and go to the prisoner Herbert."

"I will do so," replied Raleigh, with a grave smile.

At eleven, Elizabeth took her seat upon the throne in the council chamber.

When all had arrived, and silence at last reigned, the scene presented in the council chamber was one of unparalleled splendour, filled as it was with the wealth and beauty of proud and honoured England, whose virgin queen, looking every inch a woman born to hold the sceptre of a mighty power, now sat beneath the gorgeous canopy of State, and whose noble head was surmounted with the small diamond-studded crown.

Close to the right hand of the queen stood Sussex, while at her left was the magnificent Earl Dudley.

As the queen sat, haughty and stern, her fair brow somewhat contracted, many anxious eyes were fixed upon her.

At last she spoke.

"What is our first business, Dudley?" she asked. "Did we not say it was with reference to the affairs which agitated our minds concerning the fighting at Hollow Ground? What think you of it all, my Lord Sussex?"

"My opinion is, madam, that the proceedings were disgraceful, and in the highest degree treasonable."

"Your grace is right. But where is Sir Edward Warner?"

"Here, your majesty," was Sir Edward's reply, as he came forward.

"Come hither, Sir Edward; nay, hold yourself erect. If murder is committed within the Tower, we shall not deem you responsible. Now, Master Lieutenant, what of Montague?"

"He is grievously wounded, your majesty."

"Grievously? Humph! Master Grant."

"Here, most gracious madam," replied one of the Court physicians.

"Your report said, 'progressing favourably'?"

"That was so, your majesty."

"Favourably! That means, then, that he is able to appear here?"

"I do not apprehend any danger if he attends here, madam."

"Good. Let him attend, Sir Edward. And what of the prisoner, Dudley Herbert?"

"He is ready to be conducted before your majesty."

"Good. Let him be brought hither. And now come forth, Walter Raleigh."

The words were delivered in sharp, stern tones, and they went to Raleigh's heart with the keenness of a dagger.

Halting some dozen paces from her majesty, he bowed gracefully.

Then he stood erect, his fine face pale, but unflinching in its expression.

Elizabeth surveyed him some few moments in silence.

She seemed to be weighing in her mind what he had done for the Crown and what against.

Presently she said—

"We have been waiting for this opportunity, Master Raleigh, just as much as you have been expecting it. Walter Raleigh, you are a disgrace to your queen!"

Raleigh started as if shot.

Then suddenly falling upon his knees, he cried, in low, but fervent tones—

"Oh, your majesty, say not that. Place me in irons—in the worst dungeon within this fortress—but say not that I am a disgrace to my beloved queen."

"What else are you, who, without the warrant of your queen, openly wage war in the very heart of her capital?"

"Gracious madam, hear the story before you condemn me. It was done solely for the purpose of rescuing one of your own sex from destruction."

"Eh? At whose hands?"

"At the hands of Marcus Montague."

"'Umph! We have heard many accounts, I warrant you, but we'll sift the lies from the truth presently; and by all that is just, the one I pronounce a traitor shall lay his head on the block ere the suns of many days shall shine upon this fortress. Now, Walter Raleigh, let us know the whole story. But wait, let the prisoner and Montague be brought forward."

Sir Edward Warner departed, and took his way to the White Tower, where, in one of the chambers, Dudley had been placed.

As he proceeded, the warders followed him.

In a few moments he was joined by Barcally, who, knowing whither he was proceeding, held the keys ready in his hand.

"What!" said Sir Edward. "I thought you were off duty?"

"I should have been, Sir Edward," was the reply, "but Champion" (the chief of all the warders) "is ill. He begged of me to take his place, and I have done so."

"Without consulting me or the deputy lieutenant, eh? Well, sirrah, you have exceeded your duty. Beware, Barcally, lest your increasing insolence causes me to sign my hand to your dismissal."

"Pardon me, Sir Edward, you have no power to sign anything of the sort."

Sir Edward was astounded at this announcement.

At last he said—

"As soon as the queen has taken her departure, I will prove to you what power I possess."

"Sir Edward," whispered Barcally, placing his lips close against the lieutenant's ear, "what think you of this?"

And he uttered in a rapid manner a dozen words.

The effect was electrical.

Sir Edward turned as white as the roses in his shoes.

For the space of a few seconds he appeared to be overwhelmed with astonishment.

Then he said, in low, hoarse tones—

"You are a dangerous man, Barcally, and one of the greatest villains that ever trod these stones. But lead the way, and dare not breathe those words in my ears again, or, old as I am, I will find strength to plunge my dagger into your black heart."

Barcally smiled and bowed low.

He now led the way to the stone chamber. Dudley had shared it with another prisoner, a tall, gaunt-looking youth of good birth, who was accused of singing a ballad the words of which were stated to be of a treasonable character, in the public streets, with the object of holding her gracious majesty up to ridicule and derision.

He had been imprisoned some few months, and the officials began to think that he had been forgotten.

He did not seem to care.

He was the liveliest and merriest prisoner in the Tower.

The name of this lanky ballad-singing young gentleman was Solomon.

The heavy oaken door was thrown open by Barcally, and beside Dudley, who stood close to the door, was Quicksilver.

"How came you here?" thundered Barcally, fixing a ferocious look upon the little man.

"How came I here?" repeated Quicksilver, as he placed his tiny hands on his hips, and looked disdainfully upward. "Why, look, shockhead, and you will see that I have an excellent pair of legs—'twas these which conveyed me hither."

"Lomew must have a duplicate key, Sir Edward," said Barcally. "And yet I knew it not."

"You already know too much," said Quicksilver. "If you charge your heavy head with too much, it will burst, and then what would be the result? Why, the Tower would get a better man for a warder."

"You ape!" growled Barcally. "If you are not careful I will stamp on you, and crush out what little humanity there is in your carcase."

"Attempt it," said a deep voice, "and there will instantly be a vacancy for another warder, and one who is not filled with monstrous lies."

It was the headsman who spoke.

"Let us have no quarrelling," said Sir Edward; "no time is to be lost, for the Court waits."

"Will you conduct me, Sir Edward?" asked Dudley.

"I would, my lad, were it not that I have to conduct another person into the queen's presence."

"Then, Sir Edward, let me entreat you to provide me with a man to lead the way—not a villain like this Barcally."

Sir Edward glanced keenly at Barcally.

"I am sorry indeed," he said; "but Champion is ill."

"Do not trouble yourself, Dudley," said Lomew; "I will follow up."

"But you dare not enter the presence chamber," said Barcally.

"You will see that I do dare."

"Sir Edward will prevent you—'tis his duty."

"Sir Edward will do nothing of the sort. He knows that I have business of importance there."

"Yes," said the lieutenant; "I will not prevent your entrance, since I know the value of your business; and feel sure the queen will call upon you. Go, Dudley, and may heaven grant you patience."

"Dudley Herbert," said poor Solomon, "remember my request. Assure the queen that I have no treasonable intentions. Tell her that if she will order my release, I will sing her praises everywhere. By Jove's thunder, Master Dudley, I will laud her to the very skies if she will but say, 'Depart, Solomon—depart, you ballad-monger, and be hanged to you!' But perhaps you, little Quicksilver, may chance to get a word with her."

Away went the party, and the rear was brought up by warders and soldiers.

There was a great stir as soon as Dudley made his appearance.

A buzz of surprise among the gentlemen—a murmur of admiration from the ladies.

What wonder? Dudley looked remarkably handsome, and even the queen was taking stock of his elegant figure.

"Dark Dudley!" whispered Elizabeth to the Duchess of Abercorn. "An excellent name for the youth, eh?"

Then, turning to Earl Dudley, she said—

"A namesake, my lord; and I think there is a strong likeness between you."

It was noticed by all. The likeness, most assuredly, was striking.

The proud and aspiring young earl looked hard at the object of the Court's attention, and a smile spread over his fine face.

"By the rood!" he muttered, "there is a strong likeness. And so that is Lord Herbert's son, he of the strange story which has been whispered in connection with Montague."

Dudley was placed in the centre of the presence-chamber and there left.

Presently arose another buzz, and Marcus Montague came slowly in.

He was deathly pale.

Elizabeth, for some few moments, counselled with her lords; then she said—

"First of all, we will listen to the story of the outrage at the mysterious residence called Hollow Ground. Dudley Herbert, speak."

Dudley did so clearly, and the story being told, silence was called.

Elizabeth, her eyes fixed downward, was thinking.

Sussex ventured to approach her, as did Earl Dudley.

Impatiently she waved them aside.

"Marcus Montague," said Elizabeth suddenly, fixing her flashing eyes upon him, "what have you to say to the atrocious charge which has been preferred against you?"

"I contradict the whole of it, your majesty."

"Eh—what? How's this? You contradict the whole of it! What mean you?"

"I am not, and never was, connected, directly or indirectly, with the place called Hollow Ground."

Dudley opened wide his eyes.

"Heaven's mercy defend us!" exclaimed Elizabeth, impatiently, "what are we to understand?"

"This, madam—and I will bring witnesses to prove it—there is in this city a man who, for a long time past, has personated me. The likeness he bears to me is remarkable. His voice is as like mine as he is like me in person. I saw him once—but once only. This, gracious madam, is the man who has wrought all the mischief for which I am blamed."

A look of incredulity rested for some few moments upon the queen's face; but apparently impressed by Montague's earnest manner, she said at last—

"By my father's head! never have I heard so strange a story. My lords, have you ever seen a man like the one described? If either of you said 'yes,' that man might be Montague himself. But then, Montague could instantly reply, 'The person you saw was the man of whom I speak—my double.' By heaven! there is a mystery here."

Our hero looked confused.

"Dudley Herbert," said Elizabeth, "what think you of this?"

"Your majesty," replied Dudley, firmly, "I assure you that he is telling a monstrous falsehood."

"Sir Edward Warner," continued Elizabeth, "you told us that this young girl—this farrier's daughter—What is her name?"

"Madeline Maynard, so please your majesty."

"Ah, Madeline Maynard. A pretty name is Madeline. Well, Sir Edward, you told us that this young girl is within the Tower."

Sir Edward bowed.

"We seek to know how it is that Madeline Maynard occupies apartments within this fortress?"

"Your majesty, she has been the guest of the headsman."

"What! another guest of the headsman. Well, it seems as if we shall have to find another place in which to hold our poor Court, my lords, for by-and-by, Master Headsman will require all the chambers within the Tower. But let her be conducted hither. I am anxious to look upon the girl for whom a battle was fought in the heart of our capital."

Again there was a general stir, and this time a loud and emphatic buzz of admiration left the lips of the gentlemen present as Madeline passed slowly up the chamber.

She was attired in a simple white satin dress, well open at the throat, so as to show the upper portion of her fine bust, but she wore no ornaments of any description, unless a little red rose twined in her beautiful and well-arranged hair could be so called.

A glance full of love she fixed upon Dudley as she passed to the front of the throne, before which she knelt humbly, but gracefully.

"Rise, child," said Elizabeth, in kindly tones; "rise, and tell us your name?"

"Madeline Maynard, most gracious queen," was the reply, in a low voice.

"And we hear you are the daughter of a worthy farrier residing at Richmond, eh?"

Madeline had no time to reply.

There was a sudden rush, a rustling of costly silks, and a beautiful lady prostrated herself before the throne, crying in low, agonised tones—

"Noble queen! Gracious madam! Listen to your poor servant."

"Heaven's precious mercy on us all!" cried Elizabeth, now starting to her feet and standing erect, "what is coming to us? What ails you, Montrose? Have your senses left you?"

"No, no, gracious madam! This Madeline Maynard—this supposed daughter of the farrier—is my child."

"Heaven and earth! is this true?" exclaimed Elizabeth.

Silence no longer reigned in the council chamber; all was confusion and excitement for some time.

But at the queen's command, silence was once more restored.

The host of courtiers and others who had swarmed forward fell back, and the Duchess of Montrose was seen fervently clasping Madeline to her bosom.

Elizabeth had extraordinary powers over her emotions.

It was now seen that she had

reseated herself, and was apparently calm, though deathly pale.

The revelation had come upon her like a thunderclap, for the Duchess of Montrose had long been a cherished friend, and she had no idea that she had a child.

"Madam," she said, in cold tones, "be good enough to inform us how this thing can be."

"Oh, not now—not now," pleaded the duchess.

"Where is the duke? I will have no secrets in my Court, by heaven! Where is the duke, I say?"

He came forward at once.

"Well, your grace," said Elizabeth, "know you aught of this astounding revelation?"

"This morning, your majesty, I heard it for the first time."

"Ah, by the Virgin, a father is generally informed of his happiness ere the child is hours, let alone years old."

The thrust was a keen one.

"It is not my child, your majesty," replied Montrose; "and the secret of its birth is known to few. I think it better at once to tell your majesty that the beautiful girl is the daughter of the villain Marshalton, of whom your majesty has no doubt frequently heard."

"Marshalton! What, Lord Marshalton who was slain in Paris by his valet?"

"The same, gracious madam."

"He was a murderer?"

"He was."

"And what was the Duchess of Montrose to that wretch?"

"She was his wife."

"Ha! A secret marriage?"

The duke bowed.

"We will hear more another time," said Elizabeth, hastily. "At present we are satisfied so far, inasmuch as we know that this girl was born in wedlock. But of a truth, our nerves are somewhat unstrung. And now, Madeline, turn and fix your eyes on the gentleman yonder. Do you recognise him?"

"Madam, I do."

"As whom?"

"Marcus Montague."

"Or his double?"

Madeline knew not what was meant by this.

Consequently the tearful and trembling duchess explained to her the story told by Montague.

"It must be false," replied the maiden.

"Can you prove it is false, good Madeline?" asked Elizabeth.

Madeline started.

How could she prove it false?

Again silence reigned for some few moments, when suddenly Elizabeth looked up.

"One moment, Montague," she said. "Are we to consider you, or this double you speak of, responsible for the murder of a certain lady at your residence?"

"Assuredly, your majesty, I am not responsible."

"It is said that the lady was your wife, whom many supposed to have died long ago. I know one who so supposed. But within the last hour she has changed her mind—I mean Margaret, who stands close beside me."

Montague started violently.

"Lost!" he thought. "She and her fortune I have lost."

"Whatever story the Lady Margaret has heard against me," he said, "is false. But this man must be discovered immediately."

"Yes, he must indeed," replied Elizabeth; "it is of the highest importance to you, Master Montague. But, then, the one who told us a certain story is prepared to prove it."

"Ah! And that person, your majesty?"

"Is here!" said a deep voice—the voice of the headsman.

The soldiers opened out, and Lomew came forward, leading by the hand Lady Herbert—Dudley's mother—a lady who, despite the sorrow and suffering through which she had passed, still carried unmistakable signs of being at one time very beautiful.

"Yes," said Lady Herbert, "I can substantiate it; for I have here papers written by his wife a few hours before her death."

"By whom were they brought to you?" asked the queen.

"Gracious madam, in public I cannot say."

"Well, well, leave that. Hand the papers here. Sussex, take them, and look at the date."

Amid a silence the most profound, Sussex opened the papers.

"There is no date," he said; "nor is there any address."

"Then it is likely they are forgeries," said Montague, boldly.

"I swear they are genuine," cried Lady Herbert; "for I well know the handwriting."

"Give them to me, Sussex, and I will peruse them presently," said Elizabeth. "And now, Lady Herbert, have you heard the story of Montague's double?"

"I have, your majesty."

"Well, and what think you of it?"

"It is an ingenious falsehood."

"Can you prove it?"

"At present—no. But time will prove it."

"Maybe! But now, Lady Herbert, I beg you will tell the story you spoke of to us. I suppose we are to hear just such a strange tale as has been told by the Duke of Montrose,"

"Your majesty," said Lady Herbert, "I would beg that Lomew be allowed to stand beside me as I relate it."

"What! Lomew, the headsman?"

"Yes, your majesty."

"In heaven's name, what has the headsman to do with it?"

"A great deal, most gracious queen."

"Humph! Perchance this headsman has a story to tell of himself."

The headsman's eyes glittered strangely for one instant, but the next he dropped them with a sigh, as much as to say—

"Alas! of what use would it be?"

Lady Herbert and Lomew told the story narrated in the commencing portion of this romance.

The queen did not appear surprised at this strange history.

When it was concluded, she sat still and spoke not for some minutes.

Lady Herbert and her son regarded Elizabeth with anxious looks, for the time had at last arrived when it should be proved as to whether Marcus Montague was the villain Dudley had denounced him to be, and our hero the rightful heir of the hapless nobleman who had been sent to a traitor's doom on Tower Hill.

"Men say that women are strange beings," said the queen at last, "and I begin to think they are. This story, my lords, is wild and romantic enough for the very wildest of German romances. I will not ask the opinion of anyone respecting it. I have formed my decision. Lady Herbert, can you produce the surgeon who was present at the birth of your twins?"

"Alas! he is dead. He died years ago."

"Well, the nurse?"

"She, too, is dead."

"Then who was present?"

"Those that were present at the time are dead!" sobbed Lady Herbert, who now indeed saw the property slipping for ever from the hands of her son.

"I took the child, your majesty," said Lomew, deeply affected by Lady Herbert's despair. "Most gracious queen, believe me, I took the child away."

"To whom?"

"To Master John Garth and his wife."

"Yes; but words are words only. Nothing is so good as black and white. Have you no registration of birth, your ladyship?"

"The registration was of my murdered child, Walter, and of him only."

"Foolish woman! Your judgment, if what you say is true, was blinded by the wild nonsense spoken by a heaven-forsaken, ignorant gipsy. Though it must cut you to the heart to hear it, I must tell you that I can pay no attention whatever to the story. Montague produces a copy of the will, his lawyers have carried it through, and the property is adjudged to be lawfully his. So far as we can see, it can never be your son's—if son he is—unless Montague's death places it in his hands. And now we see some reason—and a strong reason—why Dudley Herbert sought to slay Marcus Montague."

Montague's face lit up with triumph as these words were pronounced.

A deep silence had fallen upon all.

The majority of those present fully believed all that had been said by Lady Herbert and the headsman, but no one dared to say a word.

Suddenly Dudley advanced a dozen paces, so that he stood close to the foot of the throne, and said, in loud, passionate tones—

"Your majesty, you think that I am a nobody, whereas Marcus Montague is a man of wealth and influence. You believe his story, made up of infamous falsehoods. Who, after what has passed, shall say that Queen Elizabeth is the soul of honour?"

Had a thunderbolt fallen at the queen's feet, she could not have been more startled.

Sussex, Lord Morehen, and many others started forward to seize Dudley, but Elizabeth, leaping to her feet, said—

"Stand back, my lords—stand back instantly, I command you! Now, my lords, you have seen that this Dudley Herbert has shown his true colours. Since we have ascended the throne we have dealt with men and women whom we have caught in their treasonable designs, but this is the very first time that a black traitor has actually thrown down the gauntlet of defiance at the foot of the throne. Sir Edward Warner, seize him, and let his chamber be the lowest dungeon this fortress contains!"

Madeline would have broken away from the embraces of the duchess had she not been restrained, and would have thrown herself before Elizabeth and begged for mercy for Dudley, upon whose face now rested a look of bitter scorn and defiance.

In less time than it takes to write, Dudley was being hurried away by Barcally and a host of warders and soldiers.

Lomew, who had stood as if rooted to the floor, turned, and was just in time to catch Lady Herbert as she fell insensible.

"And now," said Elizabeth, "let the Court be cleared of those concerned in this disgraceful business. But Montague is not to quit the Tower without our permission. We must get at the truth of this double of his. And this command applies also to Walter Raleigh. Let him stand forward."

Raleigh once more came forth.

"I hardly know what to say to you, Walter Raleigh," said Elizabeth. "Sussex has been reminding me of the services you have already rendered us in Ireland, and I assure you and all here present, that I think most highly of those services. We withdraw what we said but a short time since; but we cannot exonerate you from blame. Be always prompt and faithful, Walter Raleigh, but never rash."

Raleigh bowed.

Looking up, he said—

"Gracious madam, will it please you to hear a short story from me?"

"By the Holy Virgin! yet another story? But as you are good at story-telling, we will listen. What is it?"

"In searching the vaults of Hollow Ground, madam, we came, not only upon poor prisoners who have been brutally treated by Marcus Montague—"

"Or his double," interrupted the queen.

Raleigh started, and looked confused.

Then he proceeded—

"But we came upon a certain iron vault, in which are large numbers of bags of money. Each of these bags is labelled with the name of a certain town in the kingdom. There must be enormous sums."

Elizabeth glanced at her lords, frowned, and then beckoned to Raleigh to proceed.

"There can be no doubt, your majesty," he went on, "that a great plot against the Crown is in progress."

"Indeed! And who, think you, is at the head of this plot?"

"Marcus Montague."

"Again, Marcus Montague or his double. By heaven! we will find this out ere long. Who else, think you?"

"Many are mixed up in the plot."

"Did you see any of them?"

"I did; but all wore black masks.

They aided in the defence of Hollow Ground. I engaged with one. We fought hard, madam; but I at last slew my antagonist. I then took off his mask."

Raleigh paused here, for the buzz of expectation had risen almost to a disturbance.

"Proceed," said Elizabeth. "Did you recognise the man?"

"I did, so please you. It was Sir Francis Compton."

"Sir Francis Compton!" cried Elizabeth, in loud tones. "Never!"

"'Twas he, your majesty."

"One of my advisers? Impossible!"

"Your majesty will recognise this, perhaps?" replied Raleigh.

So saying, he took the signet-ring from his pocket, and handed it to Sussex, who passed it to the queen.

"I do recognise it," said the queen, in hollow tones. "I remember it well. Sir Francis continually wore it."

"I, too, recognise it," said Sussex. "There can be no doubt that the hand from which this was taken was the hand of Sir Francis Compton!"

"Gracious Providence, place your shield about us; for if Sir Francis Compton was really a traitor, who shall say what traitors are about us at this moment?" cried the queen.

More than one of the noblemen present trembled at these words.

"This is a serious business," continued Elizabeth, uneasily. "But who is the owner of Hollow Ground?"

"That is not known with certainty, may it please your majesty," said Raleigh. "I have vainly endeavoured to find out."

"Walter Raleigh," said Elizabeth, excitedly, "I know you too well to regard what you say lightly. Listen: Into your hands shall be placed our warrant, and you, with a hundred men, shall proceed to Hollow Ground. The whole place shall be secured, and each door shall bear our seal. Let him who dares force admission; and mark you, Raleigh, whosoever you find there, take into custody, and let them be passed into this fortress by Traitor's Gate."

Raleigh bowed. Then he asked—

"And what of the money, your majesty?"

"Seize it. But take a sketch of the vault in which it is contained, and the exact way in which the money and the names of the towns are mentioned. We will find a vault at Whitehall, and there, Raleigh, you shall place the bags as they are at Hollow Ground. Sussex, into your hands I place the matter. You are a true man, or I am no true queen."

"I trust your majesty's opinion of his grace of Sussex is as high of myself," said Earl Dudley.

"Why, you know it is, Dudley," replied the queen, half smiling, "and therefore, why ask us?"

"Madam," whispered Dudley, "the exchequer is rather low, owing to your majesty's liberality towards the unhappy Huguenots; this great wealth of which Raleigh speaks would do wonders at the present moment."

"No doubt. I trust you do not require to borrow any of us?"

"On the contrary, if your majesty will allow me to say it, my purse is ever open, and you have but to command."

"Depart, Raleigh," said Elizabeth, "and set about our commands at once. Look to Sussex for what you may require. And bear in mind, all here present, let not a word of our commands be breathed outside this chamber."

Too late!

Barcally had overheard the queen's commands with respect to Hollow Ground, and he at once sought Montague and told him all.

Raleigh departed full of joy.

Once more his lucky star had shone, and most brilliantly.

"Heaven knows I am sorry for Dudley," he thought, "for I have become strongly attached to him. Whatever I can do I will. And I will pay him a visit ere I depart."

No sooner had Raleigh departed, than there arose another loud buzz.

It was accompanied by shouts of hearty laughter.

The cause was seen in a few seconds by Elizabeth and those around her.

Up the centre of the chamber, with the utmost gravity and solemnity, was walking little Quicksilver, and he was leading by the lower portion of the doublet no less a person than Solomon.

Quicksilver had waited close to the chamber, and had ventured to ask more than one nobleman whether he would be so kind as to undertake a commission.

Being so great a favourite, they readily agreed to do what they could for him; but he no sooner mentioned Solomon, than they declined to have anything to do in the matter.

Quicksilver was determined to lay Solomon's case before the queen, and so he possessed himself of the duplicate key Lomew had, and succeeded in opening the door of the prisoner's chamber.

At once he proposed to Solomon that he should be taken before the queen.

For some considerable time the ballad-monger could not be persuaded, but at last he was hurried away to the council-chamber by Quicksilver.

The contrast between our diminutive friend and the tall, ungainly balladist was so humorous, that the courtiers could not refrain from laughing.

At last, after considerable difficulty, silence was restored, and Elizabeth said—

"Come forward, Quicksilver."

At once Quicksilver went forward, and bent the knee in true courtier fashion.

Bidding him rise, Elizabeth said—

"You have taken a bold step, Master Quicksilver. We don't remember issuing instructions for you to escort yonder person to our presence."

"Gracious queen," replied Quicksilver, "since no one else did so, I was compelled to take compassion on him."

"What is his name?"

"Solomon, so please you," replied Quicksilver.

"Ah! we have heard of him. He was accused of singing vile ballads. We have never heard of this man's trial."

"May it please your majesty," said Earl Dudley, "there was a council held, and it was decided not to bring this man to his trial at all, but to let him remain in the Tower by way of punishment, until it suited our pleasure to release him."

"But you cannot punish a man unless you find him guilty of some offence against the laws of the realm," said the queen.

His grace frowned slightly, as much as to say—

"Trouble yourself about the Court, and we will look after offences against the Crown."

"Come forward, Solomon," said Elizabeth.

Solomon stirred not an inch.

Had his life depended on it he could not have moved.

But Quicksilver stirred him.

Plucking him by the doublet, he whispered—

"Forward with you, you fool! A fortune may be trembling in the balance."

Certainly Solomon was trembling violently, and with the greatest difficulty kept his balance.

Quicksilver gave him such a sharp pinch, that he moved with a jerk and a gasp.

Casting a helpless, scared look around him, he went forward a few paces.

"Why," said Elizabeth, "surely this man has not committed any offence worthy of a special council? Why, he's the greatest craven on whom we ever set eyes. Hold yourself up, man! Now, what do you want—liberty?"

Down with a stunning crash on to his knees went Solomon.

"Great and mighty madam," he said, "wingless angel from yon realms of light, deign to cast your glorious countenance for a brief space on a poor ballad-monger. Liberty! Yes, liberty is what I crave."

"The man's a poet," smiled Elizabeth, "or else Will Shakespere's wild lines have driven him mad. We give you your liberty; 'tis a shame to keep so poor a bird within a cage. Go. Are you wealthy?"

Solomon opened wide his eyes and mouth—a tremendous aperture—as this question was asked.

"I am not worth a groat," he replied.

"Go back to prison, then," said Elizabeth, "and wait; and I have no doubt that, despite the poorness of our exchequer, we will find at least a few pieces for you. We would not send you from our Tower a beggar."

"Heaven prosper you, most gracious queen!" Solomon exclaimed, in fervent tones.

"Come," whispered Quicksilver. "Come back to your chamber. No longer as a prisoner, though, for you are now the queen's guest. Bear that in mind."

"Since I am to stay until the exchequer finds a few pieces," whispered Solomon, "I should like to be with Dudley Herbert."

"That is very kind of you. But mention it not here. I don't know that the lieutenant will allow you to stay with him, for Dudley is in irons."

"Heaven save us! Let me plead for him."

"Pah! it would be useless. Come away."

CHAPTER XIII.

OF THE MANNER IN WHICH DUDLEY GETS OUT OF THE CHAMBER—OF THE STRUGGLE IN THE CELLAR—OF THE LEAP OVER TRAITOR'S GATE, AND THE PISTOL SHOT ON THE THAMES.

DUDLEY had been conveyed to one of the most terrible vaults in the Tower of London.

It was one of a number in what was called the "Iron Corridor," from the fact that the door of each chamber was of iron.

This corridor ran beneath the moat, and the consequence was that the vaulted ceiling of the chamber and the walls were always damp.

Even in the middle of the summer, these chambers were always damp and cold.

Barcally opened the door of the one he had selected for Dudley, and pushed him in.

"You are here, Master Herbert," he growled, a savage smile lighting up his coarse features, "and you need not trouble about being brought to trial. Here, in this chamber, you die. I have sentenced you to death, and I will carry that sentence into operation."

"Your words have no effect on me, inhuman monster," replied Dudley. "I do not despair, for I have friends within this fortress."

"That may be, but you will see who is the most powerful."

"I well know what you mean," said Dudley. "You mean to say that by Montague's orders I shall be slain—that, like so many more poor unfortunate prisoners, I shall be found dead, perhaps with a knife in my hand, and shall be buried as a suicide. But let me caution you, you will be watched—yes, and closely."

"You will not have to be watched, for this reason—that you will be ironed. You see those rings in the stone at your feet? You will there be fastened, as soon as the blacksmith is disengaged."

So saying, he stepped back and pulled the massive door after him.

Alone in this wretched place was Dudley left to his thoughts, and bitter thoughts they were.

Despite the tremendous noise made without and within the Tower, no sound fell upon his ears.

The deep waters of the moat effectually deadened all.

Before half-an-hour had passed, the door was again opened, and Barcally reappeared.

He was accompanied by the blacksmith and his assistant, a heavy, burly fellow, rejoicing in the name of Death.

Between them they carried a small iron anvil, while a soldier beside Barcally bore a pair of heavy chains.

"'YOU HAVE TAKEN A BOLD STEP, MASTER QUICKSILVER!' CRIED THE QUEEN."

At once Dudley, without being told, placed himself in position, a fact which elicited the good opinion of the chief blacksmith, who declared that he had more sense and good judgment than many prisoners of his acquaintance.

"Lighter irons would have done for this youth," said the blacksmith. "'Tis absurd, Barcally, to give a youth of twenty such irons as these."

"Do as you are bidden," growled Barcally. "He was ordered irons, and irons he has got."

"I should like to see the biggest man that ever lived get out of this chamber, even if he was not ironed," replied the blacksmith. "Even if it were possible for him to climb up to yonder grating—which it isn't, since there is no place for a foothold—he couldn't file the bars without files."

"They might be supplied by friends," replied Barcally.

"Yes; well, we'll suppose they might. What then? He couldn't squeeze his body out. I'd wager my head that little Quicksilver could barely squeeze himself out. But here we are, and here are the irons. Get to, Death, and here, young sir—What's your name?"

"Dudley Herbert."

"Any relation to 'Dudley the Great'—Earl Dudley?"

"Not that I am aware of," replied Dudley, with a faint smile.

The anvil was set beside our hero, and he was directed to place his legs upon it.

Then the chains were slipped on, and two or three blows from Death's hammer completed this part of the operation.

The heavy chains were next fastened to the rings in the stone floor.

No wild beast was ever more firmly secured than was Dudley Herbert.

"Thank goodness, we don't often have to do this," said the blacksmith; "and I say again, that it wasn't necessary in this case."

"Perdition!" thundered Barcally, "what do you know as to what was, or wasn't necessary? You are to obey orders, and not trouble yourself as to what they are. You earn your salary easily enough."

"That's true, Barcally," replied the blacksmith, calmly; "I can't deny it. But it's well known that you earn more than your salary very easily indeed."

"Your work is finished," replied Barcally, savagely, "therefore, depart!"

"We'll do so. But I think it's within my right to ask whether you or Champion is chief?"

"You will very soon know that," was the reply.

The blacksmith took no notice of this reply at the time.

But a circumstance occurred that recalled the words, and warned him that Barcally was indeed a man to be feared.

"Once again," cried Barcally, when the blacksmith and his assistant had gone. "Once again, upstart, I—"

He never completed the sentence.

A heavy hand fell suddenly upon his shoulder, and the next instant he was hurled violently backward, his head coming in contact with the wall, and partially stunning him.

Yet another instant and a heavy fist was dashed into his face, and with such force that he was felled to the ground.

"Coward!" cried Lomew, for it was he, "take that, and remember that while in the Tower of London Dudley Herbert has a friend in the headsman. Dudley, my poor lad, I trust he has not ill-treated you?"

"Except with his tongue—no."

"What has he said?"

"He threatens me."

"With what?"

"Death."

"Ha! Depend upon it, Dudley, that his threats come of his conversation with the scoundrel Montague. But fear not; you will be well watched."

"I will report your treatment of me to the lieutenant," hissed Barcally.

"Report what you like, fool. But I warn you to be careful what you do here. If anything happens to Dudley Herbert, you will be responsible with your life to me."

"Lomew," said Dudley, "what of my dear mother?"

"She is but sadly."

"And what of Madeline?"

"Her ladyship—for she bears this title—is completely prostrated by what has overtaken you. But she relies greatly on her mother's and the duke's influence with the queen. But now I cannot stay, Dudley, for I have much business to undertake on your behalf. But in a few hours, perchance, I shall get the lieutenant's order to visit you—as I know Raleigh is about to do. And I can then stay with you for a time."

"Adieu then, Lomew."

"Adieu, Dudley," replied Lomew, in affected tones, as he took the hand offered him. "And may heaven sustain you in your hour of trouble."

Letting his hand fall, he suddenly embraced him, and at the same time he contrived to whisper—

"Keep awake, Dudley—on your life sleep not!"

Another minute, and once more Dudley was alone—alone to think over the meaning of what the headsman had whispered.

One more visitor he had ere night set in, and that was Raleigh.

As his visit was limited to a quarter of an hour, not much passed between them; but when Raleigh departed Dudley felt that he had indeed found a friend to be proud of.

"He has a noble soul," he thought. "I wonder not that people think he is cut out for a great man. Long may he be spared to serve his country."

* * * *

Again midnight!

Who, to look upon the calm waters of the Thames, and at the thoroughfares leading to the great and mighty fortress, would have thought the Tower had been the scene of so much excitement during the day?

Within, the utmost silence prevailed, for though many of her lords and ladies had departed *pro tem.*—there not being sufficient apartments within the fortress for their accommodation—the queen was still there, and would remain for a few days.

Many of the prisoners within the Tower were asleep, as St. Paul's chimed the hour of midnight.

But Dudley was awake.

He required not the urgent exhortation of the headsman.

He could not have slept under any circumstances.

But what did the headsman mean?

Surely he could never mean to aid him in escaping?

"No," he thought, "that cannot be, for it would be a dangerous, if not an impossible task. At the end of the corridor, and close to the steps which I descended, I noticed one of the boxes used by the soldiers, and therefore am I certain that sentries are always stationed there. No; brave Lomew must have something of a highly important nature to tell me.

"But how is he to get here without permission? And surely permission would not be granted for midnight. But then, he may have a duplicate key.

"Hours must have passed—hours—and no one comes! This is indeed a living tomb.

"And all this is Montague's doings. He can now laugh at me, for what I had thought would be mine has passed into his hands for ever.

"But, despite the great fortune which has overtaken her, Madeline will not forget me, stay how long I may here.

"This darkness — this silence! 'Tis beyond human endurance. If I could but hear a human voice! Ah, what was that?"

A faint and most curious sound had fallen upon Dudley's ears.

It proceeded from the fireplace; and while he looked in that direction the strange sound was repeated.

Then a voice—low it was true, but Dudley instantly recognised it as the voice of Quicksilver—said—

"Dudley, Dudley, do you sleep?"

"No," whispered Dudley, excitedly; "no one was ever wider awake than am I."

"Move not, and whisper low, as you value your life, Dudley."

Another moment, and the rays from a tiny lantern illuminated the dark chamber, and strange and ghastly indeed were the shadows which crept hither and thither as that lantern was moved.

At first the aperture whence this light proceeded was very small, but in less time than it takes to pen the words, Dudley was astounded to see the whole of the massive oaken chimney-piece move upward, and there was Quicksilver.

Completely spellbound, as it were, Dudley could only stand and look.

"You may well be surprised," whispered Quicksilver, "for your knowledge of the secrets of the Tower of London is exceedingly limited. But Lomew and I are well acquainted with many of them, though I think I have the advantage of the headsman, because I can creep where he cannot. But, Dudley" — and here Quicksilver turned and dropped noiselessly to the ground—"can you guess what I am here for?"

"Perhaps to convey to me some dreadful tidings. Perhaps Madeline, or my dear mother—"

"Fear not as to them—both are as well as can be expected. No, Dudley, I am not here to speak of them; I I am here to aid you to escape."

"Impossible!"

"It is true."

"Attempt it not, Quicksilver, or your life, as well as mine, may pay the forfeit. Besides—"

"Dudley," interrupted Quicksilver, who for the time had shut off the rays of the lantern, "hear me, and then form your decision. I am not here of my own accord—I am here by orders of Lomew. This is exactly how matters stand. Lomew is not afraid that you will fall a victim to your rashness—and it was rashness to speak to her majesty as you did—no, he feels sure the influence of the Duke and Duchess of Montrose is sufficiently powerful to cause her majesty to order your release within a few days. But he has proof that Barcally has Montague's instructions to destroy you. The villain has many ways of accomplishing his object, so that no suspicion of any kind could be attached to him.

"He would allow you to remain here, ironed as you are, for a time, and then suddenly you would be found dead. Brave as you are, Dudley, you could not raise your hand to help yourself. You will thus see how necessary it is that you escape."

"Yes, yes; I feel that what you have said is but too true. I do indeed feel that Montague will attempt to make away with me; but I would rather die than be the means of bringing sorrow and trouble on those who love me."

"A most excellent sentiment, but if you will follow the directions I shall give, you will bring no trouble on those who love you."

Quicksilver spoke thus, though he well knew that to attempt to escape, Dudley would be compelled to pass through many dangers.

"Look you," he continued, "the articles I have brought with me are these: four excellent files—I took them from the blacksmith's shop even while he slept; a dagger; this little cloth bag—for what required I will tell you presently; and a flask of brandy. Now, Dudley, hesitate, and your life pays the forfeit."

"I will not hesitate, then, Quicksilver, for why should I die when a bold stroke may procure me liberty?"

"Well asked, by the rood! Now place the dagger beside you—so. Let me fasten the strap about your waist, and then tuck this flask inside your doublet; and now the files. Take two, and let us set to work."

"It will take a long time to cut through these links."

"Not at all. Work with a will, Dudley, and don't fear the noise you will make."

"You, then, are not afraid we shall be heard?"

"No; because I managed to drug the soldiers' beer—that is, the four who are on duty at the end of the corridor—and at this moment, they are sleeping as if for a wager."

"But what of the scoundrel warder, Barcally?"

"He is fast asleep in his chamber. Would that he would never wake again! His place is at present taken by Champion, the chief warder. He is a kind-hearted man, but, poor fellow! he is like a ghost. I fear me that Barcally is playing a deadly game there. If Champion died, Barcally would reign in his stead."

"I understand you. What a place of mystery and horror is this Tower!"

"It is indeed, and you do not know as much of it as I do. But now, Dudley, let us work a little harder, for Barcally will presently relieve Champion."

During a great part of the foregoing conversation the pair had been working on the links.

Dudley had a strong hand, and the sharp teeth of the file cut through the iron with wonderful speed.

As for Quicksilver, ere many minutes had elapsed, his arm ached violently, and great drops of perspiration stood out on his brow.

Nevertheless he had made good progress.

Dudley observed his distress, and took the file from his hand.

"You are already exhausted, Quicksilver," he said, "and rest you shall, whether you like it or not. But while I work tell me the whole of the plan for my escape, for as yet I know nothing, and you have not told me about yonder mysterious mantelpiece."

"Of a truth I haven't. But I will at once. In order to escape, you must go through a long series of vaults and corridors, all of them deep below the dungeons of the Tower."

"I have given you my word, Quicksilver, that I will attempt the escape—I have started upon it, and I will not now relinquish it."

"Good, good! But then, Dudley, you will be entirely alone."

"Ah!" and Dudley looked wonderingly into Quicksilver's face. "Alone? I thought, perhaps, you might show me a little of the way."

"That you cannot mistake, Lomew said, when I suggested to him that I should show you the way. 'No, that must not be, for if discovery should be made, Dudley would be seized and taken back to his chamber; but if Barcally happened to see you he would make that an excuse for putting a shot through your brain.'"

"Lomew was right. He hates you, Quicksilver, I believe."

"He does indeed. And his hatred is returned. But let me continue. Bravo! one of the links off, and the other is partly cut. 'Now,' said I, 'suppose I take a bag full of buttons, and place them at intervals along the route Dudley is to take?'"

"Excellent," said Dudley; "and so that is what this little cloth bag is for?"

"Exactly."

"Bravo, Quicksilver; your brain is as sharp as your tongue. But go on, for you see I am nearly through this other link."

"The secret of the chimney-piece," continued Quicksilver, now speaking rapidly, "is only known to Lomew and myself. It was I who discovered it. Beyond the chimney-piece is a small trap-door, large enough to admit me only. But between that and the chimney-piece are two or three heavy bolts, which I cannot shift from their position, but you can. When they are pulled back a large piece of the wooden wainscot slips down, and then you can pass through. You will find yourself in a narrow passage."

"There are no turnings right or left?"

"None. At the end of this passage the buttons commence, and they are placed quite close to the wall. Each one is of brass, and with this lantern you are bound to find them. You will pass through many vaults and cellars, and finally you will reach a flight of stone steps. These you will at once ascend. At the top you will come to a trap-door. Raise that, and you will find yourself on the flat portion of the roof beside St. Thomas' Tower. And then, for heaven's sake, shut off the rays of the lantern, for 'tis there that your principal difficulty will occur. On the left of the roof you will see a somewhat high part of the wall, and from that is hanging a rope, which I securely fastened to the top by a heavy iron hook. It is perfectly safe, so hesitate not to climb it.

"Reaching the summit you will find yourself on the very top of Traitor's Gate."

"Traitor's Gate!"

"Yes. Go across it with a rush, Dudley, and spring into the river, which is at full flood—or will be when you get to Traitor's Gate. The moon is at the full, too, and you will be seen from the river. Keep your eyes to the left, and strike out for the spot whence you hear the report of a pistol shot."

"Friends, then, await me on the river?"

"Exactly."

"Who are they, Quicksilver?"

"A gentleman of the name of Cleary—Captain Cleary."

"No others?"

"Two or three watermen."

"I know no such a person as Captain Cleary."

"No doubt; but a braver fellow never lived; so now on for Traitor's Gate! And then—bravo! free!—free so far, Dudley!"

The second link was cut through, and Dudley stepped forward a few paces unfettered.

The block of wood which served as the prisoner's seat was used by Dudley to stand upon.

By means of this he was soon above the chimney-piece, and through the aperture.

He then assisted Quicksilver into it, and the chimney-piece was restored to its usual position.

In the lieutenant's private room was a curious book, with ivory covers and parchment leaves, and it contained a list of the various secret chambers.

Many a secret trap and staircase was not entered in this book, and certainly nothing was said of the chimney-piece we have described, and which was as ingenious as anything in the Tower, though we may observe that no one, even if acquainted with the secret, could have opened it from the chamber.

Our hero soon drew the bolts, and the wainscot acted as Quicksilver had said.

Dudley passed through, and Quicksilver, with much difficulty, managed to shoot the bolts again. Then he got through the little aperture and stood beside our hero.

"Dudley," he said, "here I will bid you good-bye, and may heaven grant you courage and safety."

"Good-bye, Quicksilver, and may heaven bless you!"

"Dudley, you will promise me that you will take no human life unless absolutely compelled."

"I promise."

The pair pressed hands, and parted at the end of the passage, Quicksilver turning sharply to the right, and disappearing up a flight of steps.

Dudley turned the rays of the lantern only partly on, and first taking off his shoes he tied them to his waist. Then onward he went.

The vaults were very numerous, and in his progress he disturbed more than one human bone.

He found the buttons, every one of which had been most carefully placed, bright side up, against the wall, and about twelve feet apart.

As he went he picked them up and placed them in the bag.

On and on he went.

The length of some of the passages he traversed was tremendous.

Frequently he grew sick and faint, and his feet ached by reason of their contact with the many pieces of stone and other rubbish which they encountered.

Under these circumstances the brandy proved of incalculable benefit.

At last a large cellar was reached.

It was completely filled with empty barrels.

He passed through this cellar, and through another also filled with barrels.

He was about to pass through the door of this when the sound as of the falling of water fell upon his ears.

Instantly he shut off the lantern's rays and listened.

The sound was not only repeated, but he saw whence it came, and how it was produced.

The vault before him was one of the beer vaults, and beside one of the barrels were two burly assistant warders.

Unless they moved Dudley could not pass.

"Well," said one, "what number is this?"

"This makes the third we have tapped," rejoined the other, with a laugh; "and now before we go to our quarters, let us try that one over which the drawer makes so great a fuss."

"What! Murrel's October?"

"Yes."

"Phew! we would never mount the steps after it. No, comrade, let us be content this once."

"Well, at least let us taste it. Just a tankard between us."

"Ah, well! Let us do so."

As they took their lamp with them, the place where they had previously stood was in darkness.

"The chance has come," thought Dudley, "and if I bend my body I can creep round them."

No time was to be lost.

Dudley stooped, and keeping close against the barrels, proceeded through the cellar.

He was half way through when an accident occurred.

A couple of spades had been placed against one of the barrels, and Dudley, not seeing them, sent both with a crash to the ground.

Instantly the two guzzling warders, snatching their blades from their sheaths, rushed towards the spot, and owing to the state into which they had drunk themselves, they more than once nearly fell.

Besides the spades was a heavy wooden bottling hammer.

This Dudley snatched up, and the first that reached the spot received a tremendous crack from it.

The man dropped to the ground, without a groan.

Struck fair on the forehead, he fell like an ox.

The other man, now completely terrified, opened his mouth to send forth a tremendous shout of alarm, but Dudley, dashing upon him, seized him by the throat.

"One cry," he whispered, "and by heaven, you die!"

This threat did not terrify the burly warder, who now saw that it was an attempt, and a daring attempt, at escape.

What he saw was that if he could succeed in capturing the prisoner, he stood an excellent chance of rapid promotion.

Since he could not use his blade, he dropped it, and then proceeded to struggle.

But Dudley, nearly maddened at the thoughts of being recaptured after having got so far, held on to him like grim death.

Gradually he forced him backward, and at last the man, with a deep groan, fell with a crash.

His ponderous head came in contact with the stones with a violence that stunned him.

On again went Dudley, who presently reached the steps, and quickly he was on the roof of St. Thomas' Tower.

The soft fresh air at once acted most beneficially upon him; he felt his exhausted frame strengthened, and hope rose high in his breast as he saw a rope hanging down the wall.

He took hold of it and tried its strength by throwing all his weight upon it.

Then he commenced to climb.

Gradually, very gradually, but surely, he reached the top.

During all this time he was in semi-darkness, but he no sooner reached the top of that wall than a mighty shout awoke the echoes of the night.

"An escape! an escape!" was the shout—a shout no sooner uttered than it was taken up by every sentinel on duty, until the cry was heard in every part of the Tower.

In a very few moments were heard the sharp roll of the kettle-drum, the hoarse yells of the officers in command, the clanging of arms, and, above all, the ringing of the alarm-bell.

In the meantime, Dudley was drawing up the rope.

In this he had some difficulty, so fast to the wall was the iron hook.

But he was determined not to leave it.

At last it was clear, and holding it in his hand he turned to fly.

At that moment a shot was fired at him, and that shot was followed by a perfect volley from the White Tower.

But though he heard the bullets clattering against the leaden roof, none hit him.

With a mighty rush he sprang forward, clear over Traitor's Gate, and fell with a loud splash into the water.

The desperate act was witnessed by the soldiers, and loud were their shouts of astonishment and horror.

Almost as he dropped into the water a bright flash illumined the river, and the report of a shot fell upon the soldiers' ears.

It was the signal for the escaped prisoner.

Almost all who had witnessed the daring leap had come to the conclusion that Dudley would never rise to the surface.

But when a figure was seen gliding through the water, louder than ever became the clamour and the shouts for boats.

Confusion was everywhere, and several minutes passed before boats were manned.

The search was continued for upwards of two hours without the slightest success.

In the meantime, Dudley struck out with a will, and he was soon at the side of the wherry whence the shot had been fired.

Four watermen seized him, and pulled him into the craft; then picking up their oars they turned the head of the boat and proceeded towards Westminster at a rapid pace.

Dudley had now time to look at a gentleman standing in the stern of the vessel, and urging on the watermen.

Since he had a pistol in each hand, it seemed evident that it was he who had fired the shot.

He was a tall, active-looking man, with a bronzed and bearded face.

From his shoulders depended an enormous cloak, richly furred, while his countenance was partly concealed by a huge hat.

He spoke with a distinct foreign accent, as he said—

"All is safe, so far, Master D. But you can see from the glare of the links and lanterns that those within the Tower are searching for you. But they can't overtake us."

"I believe I am addressing Captain Cleary?" asked Dudley.

"The same, monsieur; in England, Captain Cleary; in *la belle* France, Capitaine Jean Clanquot—entirely at your service."

And he bowed gracefully.

"Captain Cleary, though I cannot conceive why you should take so great an interest in me, I return you my heartfelt thanks for the great service you have rendered me."

"Mention it not, monsieur. Anon, I trust, we shall be better acquainted. Pull hard, my merry men, for your reward is great."

It was impossible that the oarsmen could pull faster, for they were working with might and main.

Again and again did Captain Cleary and Dudley look at the river beyond, but no signs of anyone pursuing them could they see.

The darkness had hid them from sight.

"It's a thousand chances to one," laughed Captain Cleary, "that our turning round so sharply and keeping close to the Surrey side misled them. It is likely enough that they have gone seaward."

Battersea was at last reached, and Captain Cleary directed the watermen to a certain point, where they stopped.

He then fired another pistol.

The signal was returned, and in a few moments after a horseman, holding spare horses on his right and left hand, galloped up.

"Let me assist you, monsieur," said Captain Cleary, springing lightly ashore; "soh!—steady, my men! That's right. And now, my merry watercocks, here is your reward—catch!"

So saying, he took a small but heavy bag from the folds of his cloak, and flung it into the boat.

Striking one of the seats it burst and scattered its contents—a number of golden pieces.

"Are you satisfied?" asked Captain Cleary.

"Perfectly!" was the joyous reply.

"Then, adieu, messieurs, and remember that a still tongue makes a wise head."

The man who had brought the horses had jumped down, and having assisted Dudley into the saddle, Captain Cleary leaped upon his horse, and directed the man to follow up behind.

Then telling Dudley to keep close to him, he turned, and having selected a safe path, shot across the marshes like the wind.

CHAPTER XIV.

IS ONE OF SURPRISES—MARCUS MONTAGUE SEES THE WARNING IN LETTERS OF FIRE ON THE WALL OF HIS CHAMBER—THE ASTOUNDING DISCOVERY AT HOLLOW GROUND.

ON went the three, through dangerous and most intricate turnings, all of which, however, appeared to be perfectly familiar to the captain, for not once did he hesitate.

Dudley would have conversed with this dashing Frenchman, but he felt so completely exhausted, and so dazed at the tremendous speed at which they were travelling, that he found himself unable to utter a sentence.

More than once the reins fell from his hands, but Captain Cleary had hold of a guiding-rein, and therefore there was no danger of his horse becoming unmanageable.

Presently they came to what looked like a small wood, but which was in reality the grounds surrounding a large and noble-looking mansion.

All was so dark and gloomy, that it did not seem as if anyone was expected.

Down the avenue at a smart gallop went the three, and the broad steps being reached, Captain Cleary was the first out of the saddle.

As he assisted Dudley to dismount, the door was opened by a tall, elderly man, whose face and voice betrayed the fact that he was in a state of great excitement and anxiety.

"Thank heaven," he cried, "all is well!"

Dudley was now indeed intensely mystified.

What did all this mean?

Who was this grave, white-haired old gentleman?

And why did he seem so concerned?

It was certainly a great mystery.

But, despite his anxiety, Dudley concluded—and very wisely—that at present it would not be advisable to put any questions.

Captain Cleary, taking his arm, conducted him up the steps and into the hall, when the door was closed.

"Now you need fear nothing," said the captain; "you are with those who are your firm friends, and in a few minutes you shall see someone whom you well know. Ring the bell," he added to the old gentleman.

A bell on a massive oaken table was touched, and a man-servant made his appearance.

"Stephen," said Captain Cleary, "conduct this gentleman to the Crimson Room. Supply him with a bath, and whatever clothing he requires."

Stephen bowed, and said to Dudley—

"Pray follow me, sir."

Having indulged in a bath, and a steaming jorum of punch, Dudley was himself again.

A costume was found that fitted him admirably.

In a few minutes he stood in a magnificent drawing-room.

From the richly ornamented ceiling depended a crystal chandelier, and the soft glow of its many lights fell upon the figure of a beautiful girl, who was reclining on an elaborately embroidered couch, and attentively perusing a work printed in a foreign language.

She heard Dudley's approach, and at once started to her feet.

Embarrassed at first, Dudley

quickly recovered his self-possession and bowed.

His bow was gracefully returned, and the young lady said, as an amused smile lit up her beautiful features—

"Welcome, Dudley Herbert—thrice welcome! Ah, here is my dear father!"

As she spoke an elderly gentleman entered the apartment.

"Let me introduce myself," he said, "I am Lionel Abercrombie—a student of heaven, an astronomer."

"Abercrombie!" exclaimed Dudley, excitedly. "Do I indeed see the great Abercrombie before me?"

"Men call me great," smiled the old gentleman. "This is my daughter—my only child, Margaretta."

Again Dudley and the lovely girl exchanged glances.

"And Captain Cleary?" asked our hero.

"Is my brave nephew—my sister's only child."

"I trust, sir, he is about to join us?"

"No; he has left the house. But a friend you well know will join us. Hark! footsteps. 'Tis he."

As he spoke the folding-doors were thrown back, and a graceful figure passed through.

Had a thunderbolt dropped at Dudley's feet he could not have been more astonished.

So overwhelmed with amazement was he that it was some few seconds before he could speak.

At last he rushed forward, his hands outstretched.

"What!" he cried, in loud, joyous tones. "It is Walter Raleigh!"

Bowing with the utmost gravity, Raleigh said—

"Captain Cleary, at your service."

Then observing the state of consternation into which Dudley was thrown, he seized his hands and pressed them warmly.

"In the name of heaven!" cried Dudley, "what is all this? Would you tell me that Captain Cleary is Walter Raleigh?"

"Assuredly. And now, Dudley, behold my dear betrothed, my sweet cousin, fair Margaretta."

Again our hero bowed.

Raleigh now told Dudley that he had arranged with Lomew as to what he had done, and he then informed him as to the commission given him by Elizabeth.

"But," he said, "the doing of all this requires time. Sentries, however, are posted without and within Hollow Ground, so that we can reckon the place and the money are safe enough. And now, Dudley, what say you? Will you let me disguise you when the time comes, so that you will be able to accompany me?"

"Willingly!" cried Dudley.

"But you must have another name—let us say Jonas Halyard, a seafaring cousin."

"As you will," smiled Dudley.

"The disguise shall be an effectual one," said Raleigh, "and not even Montague will know you. Speaking of Montague reminds me of his monstrous story. Your time will certainly come, Dudley. Whatever hopes he has of being created a peer of the realm will be dashed to the ground. I am certain that the queen strongly suspects him."

"You do not think that she believes in his story?"

"Assuredly not! But her curiosity has been excited, and she will find out the truth, and then Montague's head will fall beneath the headsman's axe."

* * * *

Montague, on leaving the queen's presence, had gone straight to his chamber, and there he remained the whole day. But from time to time Barcally brought him news of what was transpiring.

In his chamber he could prepare his plans, and could, at intervals, confer with the villainous warder without fear of interruption, and, as he and Barcally thought, without being overheard.

Here were they mistaken, for much of what passed between them was overheard, first by Lomew, and then by Master Rodney, who entered the Tower entirely unannounced and almost unnoticed, in consequence of the state of confusion caused by the dissolving of the Court.

He sought Lomew first, and with him held a long consultation.

Lomew then led him, by a series of passages, to a certain portion of the Tower.

"Here," he whispered, "you observe a small handle. If you were to pull that, a huge piece of masonry here would revolve, and on passing through you would be within the chamber occupied by Marcus Montague. But to overhear at least something of what might be said, it is only necessary to listen at that little grating above. I have done so, with the result I told you of. And here, you see, is the little ladder I used."

At the ventilator Master Rodney listened for some time.

But the information he gleaned was of the most meagre description.

The reason of this was that he did not hear the whole of the conversation.

A few words were wafted to his ears as the speakers, Montague and Barcally, occasionally raised their voices, but that was all.

"If he stays within this chamber another night," thought Master Rodney, "I will cause him to have a horror of a Tower chamber for evermore."

It was Montague's intention to stay another night, and that was all.

For, in defiance of what Elizabeth had said, he was determined to leave the Tower.

It had been his intention to have left that night, but the prying Barcally learned that Raleigh would not march into Hollow Ground for a couple of days or so, and therefore Montague found that he had plenty of time to fully mature his plans.

The villain's consternation was great when he learned of the escape of Dudley.

But it did not deter him from denouncing Lomew as the one who assisted him.

Lomew declared that he knew nothing about it.

Elizabeth made every inquiry, and by her orders every portion of the prison chamber was closely searched.

With no success, however.

The soldiers whom Quicksilver had drugged were soon sobered by the clanging of the alarm-bell, the shouts, and the general state of disorder and confusion into which everything and everybody were thrown; and they declared most emphatically that the door had not been tampered with, because they had been patrolling the corridor the whole night.

Again night came round, and at ten of the clock, Montague was sound asleep.

Barcally had received instructions to attend upon him at midnight.

In and about the Tower all was hushed.

Time passed on, and at length the taper burning upon the table in Montague's chamber flickered and went out.

The apartment was, therefore, only partly illumined by the moon, whose rays stole through the curtains, and rested upon the bed.

No sound was heard, save the measured tread of the sentinel pacing the gravelled walk below, and the heavy laboured breathing of the sleeper.

Suddenly, and without the slightest noise, a huge piece of the masonry within the chamber, and close by the foot of the massive bed, moved inward, and the figure of a man emerged.

He advanced with noiseless tread to the centre of the chamber.

Then he halted, and placed something upon the floor.

He then moved to the wall, over which he slowly passed his hands.

His movements were so ghost-like, his appearance was so weird, that had the sleeper awakened and fixed his eye on him, he must have been filled with terror.

Having passed his hands over the wall, the mysterious figure glided through the aperture, and the masonry resumed its former position.

Something like five minutes passed, and then a tiny streak of smoke—or what looked like smoke—rose slowly from the stone flooring.

In a short space of time it died out.

But the chamber was filled with a

strange smell, and the sleeper, with a gasp and a choking sensation, awoke, stared round him, and then, with a low cry, leapt from the bed.

He was about to shout "Fire!" when his eyes were suddenly riveted upon the wall.

Wildly were they staring upon a circle of dazzling light, which appeared as suddenly as if directed by the lens of some powerful instrument.

Again he tried to shout, but it was useless; he was too terrified to form a word.

Just as suddenly as the circle had come into view there now appeared a number of words.

Of a fantastic character they were; but Montague had no difficulty in deciphering the letters of fire.

His heart seemed to stand still, his hair to stand upright, as he read—

"Marcus Montague, you have offended against your Creator, and against man! Murderer of the beautiful Windsor Rose, and of Walter Herbert, your end approaches! Prepare to meet it!"

No sooner had he read this than the words disappeared.

Then Montague found his tongue.

"It is false!" he gasped; "and this is some fiendish juggling to frighten me! But, by heaven, I am not so easily frightened. If the hand which traced those letters—"

His voice had risen to a wild shriek, when he was interrupted by the opening of the door, and entirely forgetting his appointment with Barcally, he was so terrified by the sound, that, uttering a wild shriek, he fell unconscious to the floor.

It was thus Barcally found him.

The warder was astonished.

Turning on the rays of the lantern he carried, he directed them hither and thither, and then walked from one side to the other of the chamber, as if seeking the cause of Montague's alarm.

"This is incomprehensible!" he muttered.

Kneeling down, he raised Montague's head.

"Totally unconscious," continued Barcally; "but he has spirits of one kind and another here. I will— But wait! What has he worth taking in this trunk?"

Seizing upon the trunk, he opened it.

No doubt he expected to see a lot of jewels or money.

If so, he was disappointed.

What met his eyes was a packet of papers, carefully tied.

"No telling what value these may be," he thought; "I may as well pocket them."

He thrust them into his doublet.

Those papers were the very ones penned by Barber.

Barcally quickly found some spirits, and, after some little difficulty, succeeded in restoring Montague to consciousness.

Then he assisted him to a chair.

"What is the meaning of all this, Master Montague?" he asked.

"Ask me not—ask me not," groaned Montague. "Some accursed trick has been played upon me."

"Or have you seen the Evil One?"

"Fool! trifle not with me. Can you not see the state I am in?"

"Yes; you might have died but for my timely arrival."

"Go to yonder wall and tell me whether you can see anything."

Barcally did so, and carefully looked where he had been directed.

"I see nothing," he said.

"No trace of fire?"

"Fire? No!"

"And yet on that wall there suddenly appeared letters of fire!"

Barcally burst into a loud laugh.

Shaking his head, he exclaimed—

"Such a tale will not pass with me."

"You doubt me, then?"

"I am compelled to doubt you."

"You are a consummate dolt?"

"Probably, then, that is the reason I obey you so well."

"No; gold pieces is the reason of that. But disbelieve what I have said if you will. I tell you, nevertheless, that letters of fire appeared on the wall—letters which conveyed to me an awful warning."

"What was the purport of this warning?" asked Barcally.

"It matters not. Give me more brandy, for I feel dazed and bewildered. You are sure there is nothing on the wall?"

"Quite."

"Is Merlotti, the magician, within the Tower?"

"No; he is at Rome, I believe."

"Then it could not be he, bribed to commit an outrage."

"If he had been here, I question whether Merlotti could produce letters of fire on the wall."

"Perdition! Do you, then, still doubt?"

"I should have felt more sure about the matter had I seen this mystic writing. But 'tis past midnight. I told you that Jordan, one of the warders who acts as night messenger, was about to set out for Whitehall; I bribed him to change clothes with you, and he agreed to do so. He now awaits."

"Then assist me to dress, for I am anxious to depart."

"And you will return, secretly, as agreed upon?"

"No, I must risk the queen's displeasure. What I have to do will take a long time."

"I trust you will be successful."

"Successful! How can I be otherwise?"

"Do not forget that a number of men are posted within and without the place."

Montague smiled grimly.

"Depend upon it we shall go fully prepared," he said.

"We?" queried Barcally.

"Yes, we. I shall take with me one on whom I can fully rely. It is to his house that I shall first repair."

"The son of Sir Francis Compton, you mean?"

"I do."

As soon as Montague was ready he followed Barcally, who took his way to one of the rooms attached to the great stone kitchen.

There the messenger awaited them.

Jordan was of about Montague's height.

The change of clothing was effected, and then Barcally once more led the way.

It is not necessary to describe the many tricks he adopted to get Montague past the sentries in such a way that they would not see his features.

At length Montague passed out of the Tower Hill gates without its being suspected that a treacherous act was being performed.

What Barcally had done during the day by Montague's orders was quickly evident; for the villain, with rapid strides, passed into Tower Street, and when near the cross he was accosted by a tall man, whose costume showed him to be an ostler.

"Pray assist a poor beggar who starves for a crust," whined this man.

"Are you alone?"

"No, honoured sir; I have a charger with me, and have left it under yonder archway."

"Here is a noble for you. Depart and procure food."

With many thanks the man accepted the coin, and with a series of jerks intended for bows, he shuffled off.

To the archway went Montague, and there he found a charger saddled and bridled.

It came from the stables of Redmond Compton, only son and heir of Sir Francis.

Montague led the steed out, and vaulting into the saddle, he proceeded towards the west.

Up Fleet Street, up the Strand he rode, the horse's hoofs ringing a merry tune on the rough, uneven pavement; and skirting Spring Gardens, he paused before a large house standing beside the park, and which bore on its portals the name "Compton House."

He had no sooner reached the broad steps than the door was opened by a man attired in livery.

Montague dismounted and strode into the hall.

"My master awaits you in the study," said the footman, at once leading the way to a heavily curtained door.

Throwing it open, he announced—

"Lord Marcus Montague."

Montague looked hard at the footman, as if to find out whether he was laughing at him.

But no. The man's face was as

calm and as void of expression as a man's face could well be.

Montague entered, and was now in the presence of one of his greatest "friends."

Young Compton and he were old acquaintances.

Redmond was somewhat tall and slender, and his features would have been very passable had it not been for the marks left on them by dissipation.

He was elegantly apparrelled.

"Well, my noble friend," cried the young blood, "and so you managed well, eh? How went the horse?"

"Like a shot from a bow. But why am I announced as Lord Montague?"

"Is not that right?"

"Certainly not."

"Then my friend told me false."

"What friend was it?"

"One you know not. But he is an old friend of my late father. He was in the neighbourhood of the Tower, and he informed me that he was told the queen had created you a peer of the realm."

Montague shook his head.

"I fear I must give up all hopes of that," he said; "but it is not a matter which will trouble me. So that I have the wealth, I can do without distinction."

"My sentiments exactly. If the queen thinks proper, let her take the 'Sir' from the name of Redmond Compton, and give it to Raleigh, or some such poverty-stricken fool; I care not so that the property is left."

"By heaven, Redmond! Elizabeth may give the property, as well as the title, to Raleigh."

Redmond's face turned ashy pale.

"Whoever she gave it to," he said, "should never live to enjoy it, for with my own hand would I slay him."

"Well, well, let us not anticipate. I see you are all ready."

And he pointed to swords, daggers, and a number of pistols lying on the massive couch.

"Yes," replied Redmond, "all is ready. And now, let me hear all about it. Your message—which was mysterious—was to the effect that I should procure twenty or thirty powerful men, that they were to be well armed, and you and I were to be leaders in a dangerous expedition, the result of which would undoubtedly be successful, and I should be enriched to a very large amount. I procured all you desired."

"And the men?"

"Are below. Thirty of them."

"Good. And did you succeed as to the other part of the message?"

"As to the man Hockley? No. High and low have I and my servants searched, but in vain. At every hostelry within a circle of four miles have inquiries been made, but without result. It is likely enough that he has met with his death in some drunken brawl."

"I do not think so," answered Montague. "Hockley was not a man to indulge in brawls. His interests were centred in Hollow Ground. There he was chief."

"So you have told me. But he can be chief no longer, since the place is now in possession of the queen's troops. To-morrow Raleigh marches in, and every door will be sealed. And now, tell me of the expedition. Where is it to?"

"Hollow Ground."

"Impossible!"

"Not at all; but let us be seated. Where is your wine?"

"Here at your service."

So saying, Compton took the cloth off a small table, and disclosed a number of decanters and goblets.

When both were seated, and had pledged each other, Montague said—

"Redmond, I am about to tell you a mighty secret."

"Indeed!" was the reply. "I thought that I knew all your secrets, except that which has reference to this upstart, Dudley Herbert."

"That upstart, Redmond, should fall by your hand."

"My hand?"

"Yes, for 'twas his which laid your father low."

"Great heaven!" cried Redmond, leaping from his seat, "how do you know this?"

"Was not Dudley Herbert one of the leaders in that daring attack on Hollow Ground?"

"So I heard."

"Was I not present?"

"To be sure you were."

"Very well; I saw him dash upon your father, who chanced to be unarmed, and drive his blade through his heart."

"The coward! But why did you not prevent this deed?"

"My dear friend, I was lying helpless not far from the spot."

"May title and fortune vanish if I do not have revenge!" cried Redmond, in low, passionate tones. "And my father, Marcus, was the only one among the noblemen present who lost his life?"

"'Twas so."

"Fool that he was to have anything to do with the plot."

"Of which you knew little?"

"Nothing. My father would not allow me to dabble in such matters."

"No," replied Montague, calmly, "such things require brains."

"At least," said Redmond, unheeding the sneer, "now that the plot has come to an end, you will give me the names of those concerned?"

"I am sworn to secrecy."

"Then I shall know the name of one only."

"And who is that?"

"Marcus Montague."

Montague smiled grimly.

Tossing off another goblet of wine, he said—

"I never enter into these matters, Redmond, until I have calculated all the *pros* and *cons.*, and unless I am certain that my coffers will be enriched.

"If anyone thinks that Marcus Montague cares whether the land is 'governed' by king or queen, he is mistaken. But when others of power and influence, dissatisfied with having no honours bestowed upon them, make up their minds to break into revolt, I join them when I see a way to make money—or, rather, my double—ha, ha!—joins them.

"It was so, Redmond, in this case, but I had a struggle for supremacy. It was, however, at my suggestion that the principals in the various towns were communicated with in reference to the raising of money for the arming of a large force of men."

"And where were these men?"

"Heaven only knows!" replied Montague, with a loud burst of laughter; "but it was supposed that they would be gathered from all parts of the provinces.

"That, however, troubled me not. What I wanted was the money. It came in quantities which astonished me, and was placed in the iron vault, a place I once showed you."

"So you did—when it was empty."

"It was then empty because there was nothing of value to be placed there."

"And you would tell me that the money is now within that vault?" cried Redmond.

"Yes, it is there safe enough. But Raleigh has orders to remove it."

"From whom?"

"From the queen."

"But how did she know that 'twas there?"

"Raleigh told her. He managed to smell it out in some extraordinary fashion."

"And so you intend to forestall him? I understand. It is an excellent plan! And now, Marcus, let us understand each other. What am I to have for my share? I will not ask how much money this iron vault contains—"

"But I intend to tell you. I have all the important papers with me."

Montague had brought with him from the Tower the small trunk from which Barcally had abstracted the papers, and as he finished speaking he opened it.

All the colour forsook his face, and left it as pale as death.

He trembled violently.

"In the name of the Virgin," said Redmond, "what ails you?"

"I miss certain papers!" exclaimed Montague.

In a state of intense agitation he snatched every article from the bag.

The papers he sought were not there.

"Confusion!" thundered Montague, "I have been robbed."

"'One cry,' whispered Dudley, 'and you die!'"

"Robbed! Who robbed you?"

"I see it all now—yes, yes! I see it all. Dudley Herbert has those papers."

"Let us hope you will recover them."

"No, if he has them—which I doubt not—they will never again reach my hands."

"Are they highly important?"

"So important, that if the queen's eyes rested on them, she would at once order my arrest. Yet wait," he muttered, "the story as to my double would again confuse her. But is it possible that Barcally, and not Dudley Herbert, has them? While I was unconscious he had time to steal and secrete them. I will find out. If he did take them, I will first purchase them of him at a heavy price, and then drive my dagger into his heart."

Aloud, he continued—

"And here, Redmond—here is the paper; and here is the total in the iron vault. Read it."

"Four hundred thousand nobles!" gasped Redmond. "Is it possible?"

"Yes; and to prove that I am your best friend, I swear that if you will work hand-in-hand with me for its recovery, I will give you half."

"Agreed!" cried Redmond. "Your hand on it."

"Then, come, let us at once prepare; and bear this in mind, Redmond: every man on duty at Hollow Ground must be slain. Not one must remain alive to give the alarm or tell the tale!"

"A wise plan; and, I assure you, the men below will have no hesitation about the matter. We shall pay them between us."

"Exactly."

"Before we arrange our plans, tell me, has aught been heard of Dudley Herbert since his escape?"

"No; but I suppose the news has been ringing all over London?"

"Yes, indeed. May fortune lead me to him, so that I may plunge my dagger into his heart. And now for your plans."

* * * *

Once again in Hollow Ground.

It was two o'clock in the morning, and as black as pitch, for the moon had disappeared behind dense masses of inky black clouds.

The sentries without the mysterious mansion were slowly pacing backward and forward, though occasionally they paused to exchange a few words.

There were ten without, and the same number within, while over them was placed a man with whom our readers are already acquainted—Captain Greenaway, whose men had removed from Windsor to the Tower.

A more shrewd and careful officer Raleigh could not have selected.

Greenaway well knew the great trust which was reposed in him.

And so anxious was he respecting it, that it was very little rest which he took.

He was ever on the alert.

The hour of two had just struck when the gate opened, and Captain Greenaway, with two men, came forth, and passed slowly round the walls, stopping to speak a few words to each man.

He found that the sentries were well on the alert, and just as eager and anxious as he was himself.

Satisfied that all was right, Captain Greenaway re-entered the grounds, and with his men proceeded to search every portion of the place.

For during their searches they had come upon so many extraordinary secret passages, that Greenaway considered it likely that they might discover one the end of which might be some distance away outside the walls.

The last place he visited was the iron vault.

The secret of how it was opened had not been discovered.

But against the door a ladder had been reared, and so the captain was enabled to see that all was right within the strange chamber.

Half-past two struck, and it was just at that time that one of the outside sentries fancied that he saw the figure of a man at some distance from him.

He called a comrade, who likewise fancied he saw something.

Feeling uneasy, both men got their arms ready.

But they were soon satisfied that, though they saw two men advancing, they were not enemies.

In a few seconds two voices singing the chorus of some bacchanalian song were heard, and it was evident that the owners of those voices were drunk.

Presently they were within a dozen paces of the wall.

Arm-in-arm they were staggering hither and thither.

"Hold!" cried one of the soldiers—"hold!"

The drunkards, whose costumes showed them to be persons of some position, stopped, looking foolishly before them.

But they could not keep still.

Each frantically endeavoured to keep the other up, but at last both, with a crash, fell to the ground.

The noise attracted the attention of some of the other sentries.

In a few moments several men were on the spot.

They were picking up the drunkards when suddenly a score of men dashed from the darkness.

There was no time for resistance.

A few oaths passed, there was a faint clash of steel, and then the sentries lay weltering in their blood.

The other men had been served in the same way.

In but a few minutes every man that was on duty lay still in death, and not one had had the satisfaction of returning a single blow.

The fearful tragedy was not witnessed by anyone but those concerned.

Montague, who, like Redmond, was disguised in such a way that his best "friends" would not have known him, called the assassins back as soon as the dreadful deed was consummated, and at some distance waited, for two reasons.

First, to see whether their movements had been observed; secondly, to ascertain whether the little noise that had been made had been overheard by those within the grounds.

Satisfied that all was right, Montague took from a man beside him a thick rope, having an enormous hook at one end.

A long pole was next brought forward, and with this the hook was quickly fastened to the top of the wall.

Montague was the first to ascend.

Redmond was the next.

In like manner did the men, to the number of thirty, climb the rope.

All were soon within the grounds.

Montague took the lead.

Acquainted as he was with every inch of ground, he led them in such a direction that it was hardly likely that they would be observed, the darkness so well favouring their movements.

Some dozen yards from the house were two of the sentinels.

Totally unconscious of the close proximity of a terrible danger, they were chatting quietly over the recent extraordinary events at the Tower.

Montague quickly arranged his plans.

"Redmond," he whispered, "let us two deal with these men. Get your blade ready, and when I give the word, dash upon them and cut them down."

"Yes, yes," whispered Redmond; "I am ready."

Montague picked up a stone, and giving the men the word to remain where they were, he crept forward, Redmond at his side.

Getting behind a small shed, Montague threw the stone at the wall of the house.

The noise, though slight, attracted the attention of the sentries, and they turned and looked in the direction whence it had done.

And while they thus looked the two murderers crept forward.

Quickly reaching the men, they raised their blades, and brought them down on the heads of the soldiers.

Both men fell dead, for so tremendous had been the blows that their heads were cloven in twain.

No sooner had they fallen than two more soldiers rushed to the spot.

They had been attracted by the noise of the fall.

Both were about to shout for help, when Montague and Redmond dashed upon them, seized them by the throat, and threw them upon the ground.

Both the men were instantly murdered by the brutal assassins.

Montague now produced a key.

"This, Redmond," he whispered, "will conduct us into the house in such a way that we are not likely to disturb those within."

"Yes, but it is important that we discover in what particular part of the house they are."

"True, and we shall discover that as soon as we gain admission. Get your lantern ready."

"I have it here—quite ready."

"Good. One moment, and I shall also be ready."

Montague posted twenty of the ruffians about the house, and gave them strict orders to shoot down any man who attempted to leave the premises.

Then taking ten men with him, he led the way to a side door.

Set deep in the wall, it was almost hidden by a mass of ivy.

Inserting the key, he soon had the door open, and he, Redmond, and the ten men were presently standing in a long narrow passage.

"Now," whispered Montague, "follow me, and bear this in mind—the man who makes a noise loses his reward. We shall presently come upon the remainder of the soldiers guarding this house. When I give the word, fall upon them, and slay every one!"

The men replied with a grunt.

As a matter of fact, there was not a man among the lot who had not been wondering what all this butchery was for. They knew not that there was any treasure within this gloomy residence.

It was well for Montague and Redmond that they did not, for had they been aware of it, the lives of the two would not have been worth much.

Montague had considered it likely that the remainder of the men would be occupying the chamber which, when introducing this mysterious building to the notice of the reader, we first described.

Consequently he, Redmond and the men made their way to the vaults.

When all had crept into the place, Montague held up his hand.

Another moment and he said—

"Yes, I am right! They are above. Be ready, my men, for they will presently fall at your feet!"

Captain Greenaway and the remainder of his men, to the number of six, occupied the elaborately furnished chamber.

The arms of officer and men lay ready to hand on the table.

They were laughing at a comical episode one was relating, when, without an instant's warning, they were precipitated into the vault below.

The flooring had given way with the rapidity of lightning.

No time was left them even to cry for mercy.

The assassins, themselves electrified for a moment at the rapidity of what had taken place, fell upon and butchered them.

Redmond plunged his dagger into the throat of Captain Greenaway, and the poor fellow, with a bitter cry, sank back, but not dead.

He was the only one who was not killed.

He, however, like the others, was examined by Montague, and since he was thought to be dead, no further attention was paid to him.

"Now, my men," said Montague, producing three or four bags of money, "open them and count the contents."

One of the men, who acted as leader, declaring that the amount agreed upon was there, Montague continued—

"That is all we require you to do, my men. I am once again in the possession of my property, and therefore, I am satisfied. Go hence, and remember that the sum you have received purchases your silence. But ere you depart take the bodies of the slain, both those outside and inside the walls, and throw them into the moat."

This order the men proceeded to carry out, but ere its completion they took their departure.

Montague and Redmond once again entered the house.

First, they adjourned to the wine-cellar, and when Montague had selected a bottle of the best and filled a couple of goblets, he said—

"Success, Redmond—success!"

"Yes, indeed!" replied Redmond, whose face was flushed, not with the excitement through which he had passed, but with the thoughts of an immense sum coming into his coffers. "Our success has indeed been swift and sure. And now for the next secret."

"Yes, the secret of the iron vault. You see, Redmond, how wise we were to get the men away ere we touched the money. Now, as soon as we have feasted our eyes on the contents of the vault, we will return to the Park and summon the others."

By the "others" he meant half-a-dozen of the men-servants at Compton House, who were awaiting the order to go to Hollow Ground to remove the money.

The mysterious iron vault was quickly reached, and Redmond held the lantern.

Montague inserted the point of his dagger in a scarcely perceptible crack in the side of the passage.

He pressed the weapon backward and forward, his movements being watched with profound attention by Redmond, and a small portion of the stone presently flew outward.

Placing his hand within the aperture, Montague pulled a handle.

The result of this was that a portion of the ceiling immediately over and touching the iron door, was displaced.

Montague now placed his hand at the bottom of the door.

Just where the portion of the ceiling had been displaced was an iron roller, and upon that the top of the door worked.

The slightest touch was now only necessary, and the door flew open; then Montague and his comrade eagerly entered the vault.

But little noise was made, so well kept was the action of this extraordinary contrivance.

The walls of this vault were of solid granite, and of great thickness, and, therefore, scarcely liable to penetration by thieves, no matter how clever they were.

"Behold!" almost shouted Montague. "Behold, Redmond! Look at the bags full of gold and silver!"

Redmond was too overcome with excitement to reply.

He did not require telling to look, for his eyes were riveted upon the scores of bags within the vault, every one of which was duly labelled as Quicksilver had seen them.

The first of these was somewhat larger than the others, and the card upon it was marked—

"BUCKS.—INST. V.—T. 6000."

The proper reading of this was—

"Buckinghamshire. Fifth instalment. Total, six thousand."

Montague tore the card off, and seizing the bag pulled it forward.

It toppled over and fell, and part of the contents were at once scattered at the feet of the assassins.

But they were not bright gold pieces. Nothing of the sort!

What fell at their feet was nothing but stones and sand!

The villains looked into each other's starting eyes with ashy-pale faces, chattering teeth, and trembling limbs.

Then their eyes wandered to the bag at their feet, and then to the other bags, every one of which was exactly as Montague had placed it.

Suddenly, with a yell, that sounded like the despairing howl of a madman, Montague seized the bag at the bottom, and emptied it of its contents.

And as he emptied it, Redmond suddenly pounced upon something which had caught his eye. That something was a card, on which a number of words in a sprawling hand were written—

Montague snatched it from him, and while Redmond held the lantern, he read aloud—

"TO MARCUS MONTAGUE.—Greeting. Four hundred thousand nobles is an enormous sum. It has taken me a long time to remove it, but the task has been accomplished at last, and the whole is now on a vessel lying off London Bridge, and which only awaits the tide and a stiff breeze to bid adieu to this country for ever. The bags I have refilled in order to give them their usual neat and trim appearance.

"JOSEPH HOCKLEY."

"Traitor!" yelled Montague, as he threw the card to the ground; "may all the foul fiends seize you!"

And uttering the most awful cries, he went wildly round and round the vault, raving like a madman.

Redmond stood looking helplessly at Montague, at the bags, and at the satirically worded card.

He realised the fact that all that had been done had been for naught.

Money had been spent, lives had been sacrificed, dangers innumerable had been encountered, and for what?

Hockley had the whole of the vast sum.

"While I was planning with Barcally," roared Montague, "that scoundrel was taking the money away. Taken to a vessel! I'll not believe it. By the Virgin! every vessel within miles of London Bridge shall be searched."

Then his voice dropped, and in low, bitter tones he exclaimed—

"All gone—every coin. Redmond, there is not a piece left!"

"No," was the sullen reply, "and I am out of pocket by the transaction."

"What you are out of pocket I will refund."

"Well," said Redmond, "out of all this you have one cause for satisfaction."

"And that is?"

"That Raleigh will be taken in in the same manner as we have been."

"You are right," replied Montague, eagerly. "By heaven! that certainly is cause enough for some satisfaction. Let us burn this card, and I will write another. Thus it will seem that Montague's double had seized the treasure. Excellent idea! It shall at once be done. But after this we will leave no stone unturned to discover the scoundrel Hockley; and when we *have* found him, we will exact a terrible revenge!"

"What Hockley did must have been done before the soldiers took possession," observed Redmond.

"Exactly," agreed Montague. "The scoundrel must at once have set to work."

The pair now took another of the cards, and proceeding to one of the upper rooms, Montague, in a feigned hand, wrote upon it.

Hockley's card was burned.

The stones and sand were replaced in the bag, and on the top the card was affixed.

Then the door was placed in its proper position.

"How will Raleigh open it?" asked Redmond.

"I know not," replied Montague. "But that he will open it I have no doubt. He lets nothing stand in his path. But now let us begone."

The two scoundrels made their way out of the grounds.

Little did they fancy that almost the whole of their conversation had been overheard.

The listener was Captain Greenaway, who had managed to crawl near to the spot, and conceal himself.

When they had gone he crept to one of the upper rooms.

But when there he found himself unable to move again, for he had lost so much blood that he had become as weak as a child.

CHAPTER XV.

IS OF WHAT FURTHER EVENTS TRANSPIRED AT HOLLOW GROUND, AND HOW JONAS HALYARD SETS OUT IN SEARCH OF THE TREASURE.

It was about nine of the clock on the next evening that a hundred of the queen's guards left Whitehall, and marched to Hollow Ground.

Behind them came a waggon drawn by eight powerful horses, and it was guarded by soldiers, ready to resist any attack which might be made.

Inside sat one of the State clerks, while at the bottom of the waggon was a profusion of crowbars, axes, and other formidable implements.

At the head of this party were two horsemen.

One was Raleigh, looking every inch the brave and determined young soldier he was, while the other was Dudley, disguised as a sailor, and known only as Jonas Halyard.

The gates being reached, Raleigh looked around him in some surprise.

For it was to be expected that the soldiers would be on duty.

The bell was rung, but no answer came. It was rung again, and yet again, but still no answer was received.

"Most singular!" said Raleigh. "What think you of it, Jonas?"

"I fail to understand it," replied the disguised Dudley in an assumed voice—"it is strange that the summons remains unanswered."

Again was the bell rung, and there being no reply, three or four of the men were despatched for a ladder.

When this was brought it was placed against the wall, and Raleigh first ascended it.

Jonas followed him, and then both, with the assistance of the soldiers, pulled the ladder on to the top of the wall and lowered it on the other side.

Links having been handed to them they descended into the grounds.

The bridge was down over the moat, but this did not call for any expression of surprise, either from Raleigh or Jonas.

Lighting the links, they unfastened the gates.

Thereupon the soldiers entered, and the waggon followed them.

All having passed through, the gates were closed, and the crowd of gazers who had collected saw no more.

The links were lighted, and Raleigh, Jonas, and Master Elliman, the clerk who had ridden in the waggon, and who carried the necessary materials for sealing the doors in the queen's name, went on to the house.

The front door was wide open.

Raleigh shouted.

No answer being returned, all three began to think that something terrible had happened.

"Let us at once descend," said Jonas, leading the way.

Down went the three, and presently Jonas was the first to come to a halt.

He did so with a great cry of horror—a cry echoed by Raleigh and the clerk; for there on the ground lay the bodies of a number of the unfortunate soldiers.

In all attitudes they were, and it was at once painfully evident that they had met their deaths without a chance of resistance, for not a single hand grasped a weapon.

The sight was indeed a terrible one.

The clerk, unaccustomed to horrifying spectacles, stood like a man petrified, and was only called to his senses by Jonas, who, placing his hand on his arm, told him, in kindly tones, to remember that he was on the service of the queen.

In the meantime, Raleigh turned the men over in order to see whether their brave captain was among them.

"These are not all the men," said Raleigh; "there were twenty of them. In heaven's name, what can have become of the others?"

"They may have escaped," suggested the clerk.

"No, or I should have heard. Jonas, what are your thoughts with regard to this slaughter?"

"Why," replied Jonas, sadly, "that Montague and a horde of ruffians have done this."

"Or his double?"

Jonas shook his head.

"Let us at once make a thorough search," continued Raleigh; "and now— Ha! listen! What is that? By heaven, 'tis a human voice!"

"Yes, 'tis plain enough," said the clerk, excitedly, "and it proceeds from above."

At once the three turned, and with the flaring links held high over their heads, they dashed up the stairs.

As they proceeded the voice became plainer, until when the hall was reached they could distinctly hear a man's voice pleading for help.

Another moment, and a small room on the right was opened, and the rays of the links fell upon the figure of Captain Greenaway stretched full length, looking a ghastly object.

The upper part of his clothing was

saturated with his blood; so also was a portion of the flooring beside him.

His face was ghastly white; his eyes, now glazed and glaring with the light of fever, had in a comparatively few hours, sunk deep in their sockets.

As Raleigh, who, like Jonas, had drawn his sword, entered the apartment, Captain Greenaway uttered a feeble cry of joy.

"Just in time!—just in time!" he muttered. "I pray you give me a drink."

Jonas quickly took a silver flask from his pocket, and placed it against his parched lips.

Like a drop of water to the dying plant was that drink of wine.

The stagnant blood once more coursed, though feebly, through the poor fellow's veins, as again he said—

"Just in time, thank heaven! Raleigh, I am dying!"

Raleigh was deeply affected.

"Alas!" he said, "fortune has indeed served you unkindly, my brave comrade!"

"Yes," replied the captain. "I have always prayed that, if I died suddenly, it would be on the field of battle, within sight of the standard of our beloved country, and with the cries of 'Victory' ringing in my ears!

"Raleigh," continued the captain, after a brief pause, during which Jonas again moistened his lips with the wine, "you have guessed who has done all this? You have seen my slaughtered men?"

"I have, and I can indeed guess who has done this," replied Raleigh, "and his object, of course, was the money."

"Yes, the money! the money!" said Greenaway; "but he has been foiled, Raleigh—foiled."

"Foiled! How?"

"He was forestalled, and by the man of the name of Hockley.

"Montague thought that I, like the others, was dead, but I managed to creep sufficiently near to overhear all that was said. Montague was disguised, and he was in company with one you well know. Can you guess who it was?"

"I cannot."

"It was Redmond Compton!"

"Ha, I am not surprised," exclaimed Raleigh. "Then this Hockley—you remember him, Jonas?"

"I do," was the reply; "I well remember his villainous face!"

"This Hockley," continued Raleigh, "has taken the whole amount. Gracious heaven! How and when did he contrive to do it?"

"It was done before we took possession. How he contrived to do it I can't say. But oh, I feel so faint and weak! Raise me, sir," he said to Jonas; "and I will relate the whole of what transpired."

With the greatest difficulty he continued to tell the story.

He remembered a great deal of the card, Hockley's card, the contents of which Montague had read aloud to Redmond, and he also mentioned that he heard Montague speak of placing another card in its place with the object of getting Raleigh to believe that his "double" had got possession of the money.

"Did you chance to discover the secret of the way the vault is opened?" asked Raleigh.

"No; though I heard the movements as of machinery, I did not see how it was worked."

"Bear up, my poor friend!" said Raleigh, "and we will carry you to a skilful doctor."

"Useless—useless, Raleigh," was the sad reply; "it is too late! But of death I am not afraid. Yet my heart aches for the wife and the little ones I shall leave behind."

Raleigh seized the captain's hands.

"Greenaway, old comrade," he said, "if aught happens to you, I here swear that I will be a friend to your wife and children. At present I have little, but of that they shall share."

"A thousand thanks! Heaven bless you, Raleigh!" exclaimed Greenaway. "Now you can leave me."

Raleigh and Jonas turned to go.

"Would it not be as well if I stayed with this most unfortunate man?" asked the clerk.

"It would indeed," replied Raleigh. "Not long will it be ere we return."

Some of the men were called in with the axes and crowbars, and the vault being reached, Raleigh carefully took stock of the place.

"No doubt," he said, "it is an ingenious piece of mechanism; but, ere we go, it will be so displaced that no man will be able to use it again."

Having carefully looked on each side of the door, he gave instructions for the men to set to work.

But though they worked until their arms ached, very little progress was made, so massive and firmly placed were the walls.

At last Raleigh called "Hold!"

This order was very much to the satisfaction of the soldiers.

"Jonas," said Raleigh, "what say you if we attempt to make a hole in the cell here with gunpowder?"

"It is our best plan," replied Jonas.

"Look you, my men—empty your powder-flasks into this iron pot."

And he pointed to a large iron pot used for carrying hot water, and having a screw lid.

It was now perfectly dry, and the soldiers at once emptied their flasks into it.

Raleigh then proceeded to lay a train of powder.

This he carried through several of the vaults so that no danger to the men might ensue, and then, having called the soldiers to his side, he fired it.

Away like lightning went the bright flash, and a violent explosion shook the place, and sent the dust flying in volumes about their ears.

Raleigh, with Jonas at his side, went forward.

The powder had been perfectly effective; the iron door had given way, and was now hanging sideways by its chains.

But the powder had not only done this.

It had sent the bags within the vault all over the place, and in a state of woeful confusion.

The flooring of the vault was covered with sand and stones.

Search was at once made for the card, which Jonas quickly discovered, and aloud he read as follows—

"Foiled, foiled! The money is mine! Fool that you are, to think that Marcus Montague is the one who frequents this house! Fool that you are to think that this money is his! It seems that I am called his double. Let it be so. Certain it is that I have the money."

This was all.

Raleigh smiled, and so did Jonas.

"Well, Marcus Montague is indeed completely charged with impudence," said the former; "but it will not do, for here he has betrayed himself."

"Yes," replied Jonas, "and we have the satisfaction of knowing that the money was not his. We have also the satisfaction of knowing that while he wrote that his heart ached."

"Yes, indeed!" replied Raleigh.

Turning to the men, he bade them join their companions.

Then he said to Jonas—

"Captain Greenaway has told us the contents of Hockley's card. Now there can be no doubt that Hockley is somewhere in London. If he had really taken a vessel and was about to leave the country, he would have written on that card that he was in London, and *vice versâ*. Jonas, here is an opportunity for you to distinguish yourself and to get the queen's favour."

"I understand what you mean. You mean that I should make the attempt to recover the money?"

"Assuredly. Let me tell you that the queen's exchequer is very low. Gladly would she and her ministers welcome any addition. What say you?"

"I will make the attempt."

"Good! But you must retain your present disguise. It is impossible that anyone can recognise you Let us now ascend to the captain."

Poor Greenaway! he was dead.

As Raleigh and Jonas were about to enter the chamber, they caught sight of two of the soldiers, each of whom held aloft a flaming link, and at the same time they heard a low voice speaking in solemn tones.

Both at once felt that Greenaway was dead, and they removed their hats.

At the bedside knelt the clerk—who was a deeply religious man—and in his hand he held that of Captain Greenaway, while in low tones, and with the tears streaming down his face, he was saying the prayers for the departed.

One by one the soldiers came and crowded round the door.

Presently, when the clerk rose, Raleigh said—

"I will trouble you to place the seals on the doors as the queen has directed. We will then depart. But several men shall be left to guard the captain's body, which I will see placed in charge of his wife. My men," he added, "the captain was a brave Englishman and a good soldier."

In an hour from this the party returned to Whitehall, and then Jonas bade Raleigh adieu for the present.

"Raleigh," he said, "you will not forget your promise with regard to dear Madeline?"

"Forget! It would be impossible. News that you are safe, with all information it is right she should know, shall be quickly conveyed to her as well as Lomew. So now, adieu."

"Adieu, Raleigh."

The friends shook hands warmly, and parted, Raleigh to pursue his duties of courtier and soldier, and Dudley Herbert—*alias* Jonas Halyard—to attempt the recovery of the mighty sum taken from Hollow Ground.

Book the Third.—Old London Bridge.

CHAPTER XVI.

SHOWS HOW MONTAGUE RECEIVES IMPORTANT INFORMATION—OF WHAT OCCURRED IN THE "CASKET."

MONTAGUE and the young villain, Redmond Compton, had discovered that Hockley had not sailed in any vessel, as for three days no vessel of any kind had left Gravesend.

Where, then, had he concealed himself?

Where had he placed all this vast sum of money, the actual weight of which was enormous?

It was a mystery.

The two villains had employed men to search for Hockley, and they did not despair of being successful.

The first thing the queen did was to issue a warrant for the apprehension of Montague and his "double."

It was about ten of the clock, and London was, at that time, wrapped in silence.

In the studio at Compton House sat Montague and Redmond, and they were discussing the flavour of the various bottles of wine before them.

"Marcus," said Redmond, "a month has gone by."

"Most true; but let us not despair," replied Montague, "for I place great faith in the cunning of old Famburg. That he has a clue there can be no doubt whatever. But you smile."

"I do."

"You have lost faith in him, then?"

"I have—entirely," replied Redmond. "He was to have been here two hours ago—that is, if he had anything of an important character to communicate to us. It is now past ten of the clock, and you may, therefore, depend that he has—"

He was interrupted by a hurried knock on the door.

"Enter," said Montague, rising in some excitement.

A servant threw the door open.

"Master Famburg!"

Master Famburg, an elderly man, entered the apartment, lightly treading the carpet as if afraid his rough shoes would soil it.

Redmond pointed to a chair.

At the same moment Montague cried—

"The news—quick!"

"Success!"

"Thank heaven!" muttered Montague, sinking into his chair.

Redmond's unbelief now gave way to intense excitement.

Pouring out a goblet of wine he tendered it to Famburg.

"Drink!" he said; "clear your throat, man, and out with your news."

"Where is he?" asked Montague; "where is Hockley?"

"At this present moment I cannot tell you where he is," replied Famburg; "but I can tell you for certain that the money is at London Bridge."

"Ah!" ejaculated Montague.

"Yes," continued Famburg; "obedient to your instructions, I have watched the river—and one day I chanced to be in a wherry, the sculler of which was remarkably clever with his sculls, and remarkably lively with his tongue.

"Seeing that I was very well dressed—for I was then disguised as a courtier—he wished to make himself appear as large as possible, and after some conversation, he told me that his father was keeper of a hostelry at Greenwich; the name of the house—'The Ship'—was well known to me, and I asked him his father's name.

"Imagine my surprise when he told me that it was Hockley!

"I had the greatest difficulty to control my astonishment. Of course there are many Hockleys in the kingdom; but by-and-by I led him out. I learned that his father had a brother.

"Where was this brother? And what was his occupation?"

"The young waterman told me that he very seldom saw his uncle, and that neither he, nor any of the members of his family, knew his occupation.

"This was enough for me. I went to 'The Ship' in disguise, and remained there altogether a week.

"In four days—you remember my message—I got a clue. Yesterday I had positive proof that the man I sought was the brother of the host of 'The Ship.'"

Another excited cry left Montague's lips, and this time it was echoed by Redmond.

"Proceed," said Montague. "You recognised him?"

"I recognised his voice."

"Then he was disguised?"

"He was, and so cleverly, that I should never have recognised him had he not spoken. His brother invited him into the parlour. I crept to the window and overheard the principal part of their conversation. Under the name of Herr Wagstaff, Hockley occupies a chamber at the celebrated "Casket" at London Bridge, and there the treasure is no doubt placed."

Montague leapt from his seat.

"The 'Casket'?" he cried. "Famburg, you have indeed proved yourself worthy of my trust."

Famburg bowed.

"And," continued Montague, as he placed part of the contents of his purse in Famburg's hands, "if Redmond will agree to it, we will each give you a thousand nobles on the recovery of the treasure."

"I agree to it," said Redmond. "The attempt had better be made tonight."

"Certainly."

"Shall we require any men?"

"But one, and that is Famburg here. Having got possession of the treasure, we can remove it at once in a barge."

"To be sure we can," replied Famburg.

"Then you had better depart at once," said Montague. "Bring a barge to Whitehall Steps, and there await us."

"Good!" said Famburg. "I will at once set out."

So saying, he left the room.

"What is this so-called 'Casket'?" asked Redmond; "for I have heard a great deal about it."

"Yes, so has everyone. It is a hostelry in the centre of the bridge, and called 'The Casket,' on acoount of its chief room being in the middle of one of the buttresses. But now let us don complete disguises, for some of these Tower warders are clever at detection."

"Tower warder! By the Virgin, I trust we shall have nothing to do with them."

"'The Casket' is their chief rendezvous. It is, in fact, kept by a man who was once chief warder."

Before half-an-hour had passed, the precious pair set off.

Reaching Whitehall Steps they found the barge awaiting them.

"I must get you to aid me," said Famburg, "for it is impossible for me to get this craft single-handed to the bridge."

"Where shall we moor the boat?" asked Redmond.

"At the centre buttress. But now off we go."

In about half-an-hour Old London Bridge was reached.

In the centre of the bridge, perched on a long pole, a large lantern was burning.

On the glass, in curious characters, were the words—

"THE CASKET."

Above the whole was a large hand pointing to the broken and dirty wooden steps leading to the foul cellars.

This tavern was kept by a man of the name of William Golf, nicknamed "Sweet William," on account of the sourness of his disposition.

The flight of wooden steps, which was long and steep, led in the first place to a small apartment, satirically called a parlour.

The furniture of this "parlour" consisted of barrels of all sizes, and containing all sorts of liquor.

The walls were adorned with measures, principally of pewter, and the dents in many of them showed that they had been put to other uses besides drinking purposes.

But the principal room in this hostelry was the chamber immediately beneath the parlour.

A short flight of steps led to it, and there was space for one person only at a time to descend.

The walls were hung with specimens of all the instruments of torture in the Tower.

The curiously coloured wooden ceiling, now dingy with the smoke of years, was covered with arms and other instruments from all parts of the world, civilised and uncivilised.

A most extraordinary effect was obtained when a large fire was burning on the broad hearth, for then the flames reflected themselves in the murderous-looking knives, daggers, swords, and other weapons on the walls and ceiling.

The barge being drawn up to the buttress, Famburg quickly secured it to an iron ring.

Then he aided both his companions out on to the buttress.

Round to the front they went, and Redmond was surprised to see a rope-ladder hanging from just below the parapet.

Montague was the first to ascend.

He was at once followed by Redmond, and Famburg brought up the rear.

They passed round the house and descended to the parlour of "The Casket."

Several men, the majority of them being warders, were here drinking, and were being "entertained" by the savage-looking host with a most improbable story.

"Here," whispered Famburg, "I am known as Captain King."

Addressing the host, he said—

"So here I am once more, Master Golf."

"Right glad to see you, Master King," was the reply. "And just as glad to see your friends."

"My friends are the two travellers I spoke to you about."

"Yes, yes. Welcome, my masters. I trust you are both glad to see yourselves in the old country once more."

"Yes," returned Montague, flinging down a gold piece; "as you say, we are indeed glad enough to get back to the old country."

"Ha!" said Golf; "merry England's the place to spend your money, and the place to get your money's worth."

"Indeed it is!" observed an old warder, in significant tones. "And it sometimes happens that one gets more than one's money's worth. Now I know a man who got a great deal more than his money's worth."

And he fixed a pair of glittering eyes upon Golf's face.

Golf understood him.

He knew well enough that he referred to the manner in which he had gained possession of the "Casket."

The host made no reply, for his attention was directed to King and his two travelling friends.

King whispered—

"Look here, Master Host, my friends are very rich. I have told them of the excellent 'Casket' below, and they agree, if you will let us have the exclusive use of the chamber, to pay you the full value for whatever they may require, and besides, they will give you five nobles."

"On my soul, the offer's very fair—very fair indeed. They shall have the chamber, and welcome. But here—look you, King—a word in your sharp ear; show them not the secret entrances and exits—I can trust you for that."

"You can—most assuredly."

"You and your friend—I mean your former friend—are the only two besides myself who know all the ins and outs, and my very place depends upon your secrecy."

"I and my former friend—that friend who is my friend now," replied King, "will be careful to place seals upon our lips."

King turned to Montague and Redmond, who in the meantime had been closely scanning the faces of the individuals who came dropping into the house, and said—

"I have arranged with him for the exclusive use of the 'Casket.' Give me five nobles, Master Montague."

Montague handed over the money.

King took it, and handed it to the host.

King then took three or four bottles of wine, and led the way to the "Casket" below—the Casket of Arms.

Montague had been here before, and on many occasions, but as he never met with any company suited to him, his visits were brief.

Redmond had never before crossed the threshold.

Having entered, King locked the door, and the three seated themselves beside one of the tables.

"So far, Famburg," said Montague, in low tones, "you have done well. You have shown me that you are a clever and shrewd man. So clever a man should never want for employment, and therefore, when I offer you a position of constant attendant, I trust you will see your way to accept it."

"I will, with many thanks."

"And now that we have got thus far, how are we to proceed?"

"The next thing to discover, I should say," said Redmond, "is the whereabouts of the treasure, for I cannot imagine where so large a sum could be put in a place like this."

Famburg smiled.

"One moment," he returned, "and I will show you things which will surprise you."

"But wait," said Montague, "do you think that that savage-looking host is in league with Hockley?"

"Most certainly," was the reply.

"Ah, I thought so!"

"Listen," continued Famburg. "I think you said you have been here many times, Master Montague?"

"I have."

"But you have, I feel sure, never suspected that this place is full of secret traps and passages?"

"No."

"Such is the case. I am one of the two or three who are acquainted with this place. Look here."

He rose, followed by Montague and Redmond, and stepped to the side of the "Casket."

Here there was a large square case of stuffed foreign birds.

To protect it from accident the glass was crossed by strong iron bars.

Famburg moved a short iron rod beside it, and then pushed it in a peculiar manner.

Instantly the cage, and the stand upon which it was placed, moved outward, and the astonished pair saw before them the bleak river, and just below was the very barge by which they had arrived.

The fact was that a portion of the massive masonry had been taken away, and in its place an enormous door, constructed of oak with iron facings, had been put.

"I am astonished!" exclaimed Montague.

Famburg, with a smile, replaced the case, saying—

"This is but one secret door. Look!"

He removed a rug at their very feet, and there was a heavy brass ring set in the flooring.

This was attached to a trap-door.

Lifting it up, a short ladder was revealed.

"Yet another chamber!" said Montague. "The place is as mysterious as the Tower itself."

"Yes," replied Famburg, dropping the trap and replacing the rug, "it is."

"And how did you get to learn these secrets?"

"From the host when he was drunk. But now let us resume our seats. I may tell you, Master Montague, that the place below is a passage which turns in the most remarkable fashion.

"At some distance on the left of the passage is a chamber, which is reached by descending a trap on the other side of this house. It is called the Black Room, on account of the woodwork of which it is constructed being of black oak."

"Is it your opinion that Hockley has placed the treasure there?"

"He could place it there without difficulty, because the chamber can be reached in the same way as the one in which we now are—that is, beneath the arch. The Black Chamber, you understand, is entered from the next archway."

"I understand. But it can also be reached by descending the short flight of steps beneath this flooring and by traversing the passage?"

"Exactly. Four times have I started upon the journey with the intention of satisfying myself that the treasure was there, but on each occasion I have heard the voices of men proceeding from the Black Chamber.

"But," continued Famburg, "now that there are three of us, there can be no further difficulty in the matter. We will wait here until we hear the men, and then descend and dash upon them."

"What name did you say Hockley has assumed?"

"That of Herr Wagstaff, a German."

"Let us see that our arms are in proper condition," said Montague; "and remember, Redmond, we will not spare him."

An hour passed.

Presently a dull thud was heard.

The three started to their feet, for that noise had certainly emanated from below.

It was repeated at an interval of a few seconds, and then rapidly.

It was the sound of a hammer driving nails into wood.

Montague and Redmond were ready for action.

The instant Famburg raised the trap, each firmly grasped a pistol in his hand.

Having lifted the trap, Famburg whispered to Montague and Redmond to descend, which they did.

Famburg then unhooked a lantern, lit it, and followed them.

"Follow the passage," he whispered.

Montague and Redmond at once pressed forward.

Presently Famburg whispered—

"Hold! the door is reached. But look! there is a little hole on your left. Peer through it and tell us what you see."

Montague stooped and peered through the hole. What he saw set his fingers nervously grasping his pistol, and his heart beating violently.

He saw within the chamber, not half-a-dozen men, but one only.

That one was attired as a German.

On all sides of him were boxes.

But it was to a spot just before the door, in the full light of the lantern by which the man was working, that Montague's eyes were riveted.

For there, just turned out from a leathern bag, were a number of nobles!

Here, then, within his reach, was the vast treasure.

The man before him would be able to offer no resistance, though he was well armed.

No; they would fire upon him at once, without giving utterance to a single word.

Rapidly Montague communicated to the anxious Redmond what he saw, and Famburg said—

"Place your hand gently down the door. On the right of it, about the middle, you will find a small knob. Pull it, and the door will instantly open."

"And do you, Redmond," said Montague, "hold your pistol ready. As soon as the door opens, fire!"

Redmond nodded, and Montague placed his hand on the door.

The critical moment had come!

Montague quickly found the knob, and pulled it.

The result was as Famburg had said—the door opened with the speed of lightning, and "Herr Wagstaff," with a wild yell, started back, snatching a pistol from his belt.

Redmond raised his pistol, and pulled the trigger.

Click! was the only sound heard.

The charge had not exploded.

Amazed, Redmond drew back a pace, while at the same moment, Montague raised *his* pistol.

With the same result.

Giving utterance to a maddened yell, he snatched the other pistol from his belt, but even as he raised it, Redmond shouted—

"By the fiend, we have been deceived! We have been betrayed by Famburg! The flint of my pistol has been removed!"

"By heaven!" almost screamed Montague; "mine have been served in the same way. And the villain Famburg has vanished!"

This was the case.

Famburg, in some mysterious fashion, had disappeared.

Redmond and his friend advanced into the chamber.

"Villain!" cried Montague, "we know you, Hockley. Wretch, your life shall pay the forfeit of your dastardly conduct."

"Hold!" was the calm reply. "Hold! My pistol will not miss fire. Master Montague, you have been betrayed. Escape is impossible. You have been betrayed into a meeting with Dudley Herbert."

So saying, the false wig and beard were snatched away, and Dudley stood revealed.

Montague and Redmond were astounded.

Unbounded astonishment and savage rage agitated both hearts.

For some seconds both stood rooted to the spot, their starting eyes fixed upon Dudley's determined face.

Then a startling incident occurred.

Montague was no coward in the strict sense of the term, but on this occasion he proved himself to be one.

During that pause of a few moments he thus considered—

"Dudley Herbert here! Then this is a trap. He is not here alone! No, by heaven! he will have help if he but raises his voice. 'Tis not safe to stay and fight. No, I will make my way back, at all risks."

He thereupon turned, and dashed through the door and down the zigzag passage.

In total darkness he went, for Famburg had taken the lantern with him.

A great cry left Redmond's lips as he saw this, but before he could follow, the door closed with a bang.

Seeing that escape was thus cut off, Redmond turned, and at that moment, with vivid force, came the remembrance that he now stood face to face with the one who had plunged his sword into his father's heart.

This thought maddened him, and with a cry of frenzy, the young man rushed upon Dudley.

"One moment," said Dudley. "Though I know you but as a companion of Montague's, I would not slay you, since I know not that you have done me wrong. But—"

"Wretch!" screamed Redmond, "you it was who murdered my father, for you plunged your blade through his heart at Hollow Ground, when he was unable to protect himself."

"CAPTAIN GREENAWAY WAS DEAD."

"May heaven pardon the man who told you so infamous a lie," replied Dudley. "But who was your father?"

"Sir Francis Compton."

"I did not slay him."

"'Tis a lie!" cried Redmond, passionately. "I have proof positive that you slew him. Defend yourself."

"Rather let me bid *you* to guard yourself," replied Dudley, "for since you force me to fight, I warn you that I will show you no mercy."

"Nor I you!" was the hissing reply.

The fight proceeded, and with great fury and determination.

Each had to be very careful, for the place was so strewn with boxes—decoy boxes, we might call them—that it was with the greatest difficulty they could avoid them.

In but a very short time Redmond realised that he was fighting with no ordinary wielder of the sword, and before the fight had lasted two minutes, he would have given all he was worth to have made his escape.

Many times he opened his lips to cry aloud for mercy, but he found himself unable to utter a sentence.

At last, dazzled by the rapidity of Dudley's passes, and astonished at the ease with which our hero checked his furious lunges, self-possession gave way, and he fell at last pierced through the heart.

Whether he was dead or not, Dudley paused not to see, but throwing the door open, he dashed through it and along the passage.

But we must precede him.

Montague easily found his way to the steps, and his heart was filled with joy as he saw that the trap had not been closed.

No, it was wide open!

What, then, had become of Famburg?

Up the steps he dashed and into the room, which he now found in semi-darkness, for the faint glow of a taper was all the light in the extraordinary apartment.

He rushed to the door in which he remembered that Famburg had left the key.

That key was gone!

At once he ran to the bird-case and pushed it in all directions.

He was, at last, successful, for suddenly the strange case revolved, and in another instant, the rushing river was before him.

He looked down and saw that the barge was ready at hand, and that one stroke of his sharp sword would sever the rope by which it was moored.

But then, how could he, single-handed, manage that ponderous mass?

It was likely that it would be dashed into pieces.

While he looked, he heard a sound as of a key being forced in the lock of the door of the "Casket."

With a cry of joy he moved towards it.

He had scarcely reached it before it was thrown open, and Famburg appeared, followed by several men with drawn swords.

"Here he is!" cried Famburg. "Cut him down—cut him down!"

With a loud howl of terror, Montague turned, rushed to the aperture, and sprang through it, three or four shots being fired at him as he took the leap.

Another second, and he had plunged headlong into the seething waters; for the barge, there but a few moments before, had been removed.

But as his body struck the water, his hands came into contact with a piece of rope, a portion of that by which the barge had been moored; and to this, with a cry of despair, he clung.

Another moment, and two or three flaming links lit up the black arch and the mysterious doorway, and revealed Famburg standing at it, sword in hand.

"Save me! save me!" gasped Montague, "and half of my fortune shall be yours. Save me!"

"Drown, merciless dog—drown!" thundered Famburg, his voice sounding clearly and distinctly beneath the arch, despite the roar of the rushing river. "Drown! But if you live, it will be to pass Traitor's Gate as one of the greatest traitors Elizabeth ever dealt with. And you cry to *me* for mercy! Look, I have taken off this false wig, I snatch this beard from my wasted face, and stand before you as Claude Wentworth!

"Yes, you may well utter a cry of astonishment. It is indeed Claude Wentworth who for long has so imposed upon you. It is Claude Wentworth who confronts you. Monster, perhaps you would like to learn that I am now alone in the world! She whom, with me, you so brutally outraged because she would not conform to your wishes, is dead."

"Hold!" interrupted a voice; "hold! Is that Montague?"

It was Dudley who spoke.

They made way for him as, sword in hand, he rushed forward.

"It is," replied Claude; "the barge, according to your orders, was removed, and he leapt into the Thames, but, chancing to seize a rope, he has held himself up while I have revealed my identity."

"Good," replied Dudley. "Now, Marcus Montague, that in fair fight I have slain your companion, it would be useless to drag you from the river and endeavour to force you to fight. Go, therefore, upon a journey which may end in death!"

So saying, he drew his blade across the rope.

Montague was instantly whirled out of sight, and his shrieks of despair were drowned in the roar of the black river.

The door of the "Casket" being opened, the whole of those assembled, warders and watermen, rushed to see what the noise was about.

"Come within!" Claude suddenly whispered. "Come, or you are lost! Quick, assume your disguise, or—'Tis too late!"

Dudley had not stepped back three paces before a heavy hand fell upon his shoulder, half-a-dozen others seized upon his arms, and a deep voice—a voice only too well remembered—said—

"I arrest you, Dudley Herbert, in the queen's name! Resistance will be useless, you are surrounded by her majesty's warders."

It was Barcally!

And a look of fiendish triumph rested upon his villainous face.

This capture was really a most unexpected one, for he had no idea of finding the daring Dudley in such a place as this—so near to the very fortress whence he had escaped.

In imagination Barcally saw himself kneeling before the maiden queen, receiving from her her gracious acknowledgment of his prowess, and her promises as to the future.

It was indeed a triumph.

And, how he now could crow over the man he hated and detested with all his soul—the headsman!

Dudley was astonished.

He would not attempt resistance, surrounded as he was by such a posse of her majesty's officers.

In less than a minute, Dudley had his hands tied firmly behind his back.

"Do not give way, Dudley," whispered Claude; "do not give way. Fear not, I shall be near you, and if I see the slightest opportunity I will take it."

"Since this place is open," said Barcally, "we will take him to the Tower steps from here. But, then, how can we get a sculler?"

"There is a barge moored a few paces down," said one of the men, who had been standing on the ledge which ran from one end of the arch to the other, "and a man can easily get along this ledge to it."

This was exactly how Claude had reached it, using the rope-ladder to get from the bridge.

"Do you go along the ledge, then," said Barcally to the speaker; "and here's another man who will help you. Bring the barge, and help me to the Tower, and I will pay you well."

"Agreed," was the reply.

Both men very easily reached the barge by means of the ledge, and they soon got it to the aperture.

In the meantime, Claude had contrived once more to get close to Dudley, and in a skilful and most rapid manner, he managed to sever the cords which bound our hero's hands behind his back.

At the same moment he contrived to whisper—

"Keep your hands where they are, Dudley, and it will not be noticed. When you get the chance, jump into the river and swim for your life., I will prevent them from following if I can."

Dudley touched his foot by way of answer, and did not move his hands, so that it really looked as though the cords had not been tampered with.

A flaming link having been handed to Barcally, that wretch entered the barge first.

Dudley was then handed in, and the two warders brought up the rear.

"Let me go with you to the Tower steps," cried Claude.

"Who are you?" asked Barcally, contemptuously.

"That barge is my brother's property," was the reply.

"What is your name?"

"Swinton—George Swinton, waterman, of Westminster."

"Westminster! I don't know any barge-owner of that name."

"I don't care what you know," replied Claude, slowly. "Give me my barge, and I will not ask you to let me accompany you to the Tower."

"Jump in, you insolent varlet!" cried Barcally. "But if you think I shall pay a single groat for the use of it you will find yourself mistaken."

"I require my barge only," replied Claude, at once leaping into the unwieldy craft.

"Give way!" cried Barcally.

Then turning to Dudley, he added—

"If you escape from where I shall this time put you, may my head fall at the block."

Dudley made no reply.

He was sitting against the side of the barge, his head bent upon his breast.

To all appearance utter despair had seized upon him.

The two warders were unable to properly manage the barge, and therefore, when Claude offered to navigate it, he was readily permitted to do so.

But the barge rocked so violently, and occasionally was hurled with such force against some obstruction, that Barcally was filled with apprehension for its safety.

At last, however, the gloomy walls of the great fortress came into sight.

Dudley's opportunity had now come.

While Barcally was intently watching Claude's efforts to keep the crazy old barge clear of obstructions, our hero suddenly bounded forward, and with his clenched hand dealt the chief warder such a mighty blow in the face, that he was stretched at the bottom of the vessel.

One of the warders at once snatched his blade from its sheath.

But he had no sooner raised it than Claude, whirling a boathook over his shoulder, brought it down with awful force on the man's head.

Then turning, he followed Dudley, who had leapt into the river.

The other warder jumped upon the edge of the barge, and fired the only pistol he had at Claude.

Apparently without effect, since the young man still swam on.

Claude could just see Dudley through the darkness, and he saw that our hero was a powerful swimmer.

He was not a strong swimmer himself, and had not proceeded far before he found that his strength was rapidly giving way.

"Dudley! Dudley!" he cried, "I sink! I sink!"

Low as was the voice, Dudley heard it, and without an instant's hesitation he turned and swam back to Claude.

"Place me against one of yonder buttresses," whispered the latter, "and then go on. I would not be the cause of your recapture."

"No, no! I will not leave you," replied Dudley. "But look, Claude, see you not yonder boat? 'Twas that for which I was making. If we can but reach it we may be saved! Let me place my arm about you—so."

Their progress was very slow, but eventually they reached the boat.

Dudley was certain he had seen two or three persons in it.

Now they were gone.

It was therefore evident that they had been taken on board the large vessel, against the side of which the boat lay.

Dudley and Claude clutched hold of the boat's side and looked up.

All appeared to be very still and very dark, for, with the exception of one at the stern, no lights were burning on the ship.

"Help!" cried Dudley; "help!"

At once his cry was answered, for first a lantern, and then a head, were thrust out of one of the portholes.

Then a curious voice cried out—

"Saints alive! it is Dudley Herbert."

"It is!" cried Dudley; "and you are Solomon, the balladist."

"You are right. Wait but a moment. Captain, captain!"

"What now?" a gruff voice was heard to reply.

The next moment the head of the captain was thrust out, and his eyes opened wide indeed when he saw the two young men clinging to the boat.

In a few moments Dudley and Claude were in the cabin.

Quickly a change of attire was effected, and a stiff bowl of punch was placed before each of the rescued fugitives.

Dudley then told his and Claude's adventures.

At the conclusion of the narrative, the captain, an elderly, bronzed, bluff old tar, said—

"Well, it is a strange yarn. But the most curious fact is the swimming to this vessel. Solomon here is my nephew—and a very bad nephew he has proved himself.

"He got the sum of a hundred nobles from Queen Elizabeth. I accidentally met him on London Bridge, and like the fool he ever was, he was spending his money right and left. I took him under my wing, and persuaded him to invest his nobles with me. He consented, and so now, only this very night, he has joined me, and with the dawn we are off."

"May I ask whither?"

"To Rotterdam; and if you are wise, you and your friend, who looks very ill, will go with us."

"I think that it would be a very wise plan to go with you, captain," returned Dudley. "Claude, what say you?"

"Where I go is a matter of no importance," was the reply. "I have no one to think of me."

"Poor lad!" said the rough old mariner. "But let no more be said. You shall go with us to quaint old Rotterdam. We don't stay there long, for after landing our cargo and reloading, we shall come back to Deptford, and you will then be at liberty to go ashore for good if you feel so disposed. But there's no telling, lad—this Rotterdam is the place for refugees of all sorts; and—who knows?—this very man Hockley may be in that town. Such a thing is not impossible."

"No, indeed," replied Dudley; "stranger things than that have occurred."

"Yes; for instance, your escape from the Tower," said the captain, bursting into a loud roar of laughter.

With the first streak of dawn all hands went to work, and the big vessel glided down the river, and quickly old London was left in the dim distance.

CHAPTER XVII.

IS OF A SURPRISING CHARACTER.

THE mariners generally of the days of "good Queen Bess"—and braver men never lived—were not familiar with the "science" of navigation, and the consequence was that they frequently got themselves into the most curious "pickles."

It was so with Solomon's uncle, Captain Hawser.

He reached Rotterdam some considerable time after leaving London.

He would have arrived long before had it not been for the fact that he had had a number of collisions with various vessels since leaving the Great City.

In more than one of these Dudley distinguished himself by his calmness, his bravery, and his great determination.

His conduct completely won the captain's heart, and secured for him the admiration of the whole crew.

It was night when the vessel glided into the crowded port, and so Dudley had a fine view of Rotterdam by moonlight.

"Captain," said Dudley, "I feel a strong inclination to go ashore to-night."

"What!" cried the captain; "to-night! Holy Mary! 'tis near midnight."

"I know it."

"But you don't mean that you would like to go ashore alone?"

"I did think of it."

"I would not allow it. But I'll tell you what—if you don't mind Jameson going with you, why, well and good. Jameson knows the place well."

"If he would accompany me," replied Dudley, "I should be very thankful to you, and to him."

"He will be very glad," smiled Captain Hawser, "for he will have a chance then of kissing his sweetheart—or, perhaps I had better say, one of his sweethearts; for, to my certain knowledge, he has at least one in every port we call at."

Jameson was the mate of the vessel, a young man of about one-and-twenty, as hardworking, as brave, and as jolly a sailor as ever walked the deck. Moreover, he was a remarkably well-looking fellow, so it was not to be wondered at that he had a number of sweethearts.

Very readily did he jump at the chance of accompanying Dudley, who now proceeded to don the clothes Raleigh had provided him with.

They had passed through many adventures, but were as good as ever.

The wig he had worn, had, of course, vanished, but Claude had seen it, and he, with Solomon for a companion, went off in search of a costumier.

One was discovered and aroused, and being offered twice its value for the article required, his ire at being woke up was quickly appeased, though for the life of him he could not understand why it was that Solomon went into convulsions over his broken English, which he had been told by many sailors was simply perfection.

The article obtained was a very fair counterpart of the one Dudley had lost, and he was well satisfied.

Aided by Claude, the disguise Raleigh had provided was once more assumed, and Dudley said—

"And now, gentlemen, I beg you to remember that I am simply Jonas Halyard, the sailor."

"On my soul, a good sailor, too!" cried the captain.

"Yes, I fancy I shall have to look to myself," said Jameson; "for though disguised, he will meet with the approval of the maids of Rotterdam."

"No, I know not the language," smiled Jonas, as once more we shall call him.

"I know a fair amount," said Jameson; "and what I don't know I'll willingly translate—at least, to my own and your satisfaction. So now we will be off."

"Jameson," said Captain Hawser, in serious tones, "I look to you for his safety, remember."

Jameson bowed.

"Nothing would cause me to leave his side," he said. "Nothing—that I swear.

"I can trust you," answered the captain.

Dudley, with Jameson at his side, now went ashore, and threading their way through mountains of boxes, and bales of merchandise, they passed through many narrow and curious turnings, the houses in which were decidedly of a more picturesque character than those in London—and, it is scarcely necessary to say, they were more dirty.

"Captain Hawser," said Jameson, "has been in the port of Rotterdam scores of times, for he has traded between here and London for twenty-five years. But though he has often been asked, he has never yet been to the place where I propose to conduct you, Master Dud— I beg your pardon, Master Halyard."

"What is the name of the place?" asked Dudley.

"The 'Rotterdam Hades.'"

"Holy Mary! what a title."

"It is a very suitable one, I assure you. And you will be of the same opinion when you get there. I would not take you there, only that I think if this man you are in search of chances to be in Rotterdam, there is no doubt that he will be at the place I speak of."

"Has it no other title?"

"No."

"I mean, is it not known to Englishmen by any other title?"

"It is known as Darvill's."

"Darvill's! Is that the name of the proprietor?"

"Yes."

"Then he is an Englishman?"

"Yes. But he calls himself a naturalised Dutchman!" laughed Jameson. "I will give you his character. He is the most cunning knave I have met with on all my voyages. There cannot be a greater knave than Darvill—except this Montague of whom you speak, and who I trust has been drowned. But we are close to the place. Now, bear this in mind: a man will question you in Dutch. If you don't answer him in that language, he will speak in broken English. Whatever he says don't answer him. What you will do is to hold forth the thumb of your left hand."

"I understand."

"And you are sure that your pistols are all right?"

"Quite. Are yours?"

"They always are when I chance to be in a neighbourhood like this. But here we are."

So saying, he paused in the midst of a clump of large houses, dark, dismal, and forbidding.

There was not a sign of life here.

Jameson now took the lead, and descending a flight of crooked stone steps, he knocked softly on a small door, while Dudley looked in vain for any signs of a hostelry.

The door was quietly opened by a big, robust Dutchman.

In an instant, he thundered out some words in Dutch, the while scowling on the pair in a furious manner.

No answer being returned, he said, in broken English—

"Scoundrels! thieves! whom do you seek to rob?"

Dudley put forth the thumb of his left hand, as did Jameson.

At once the Dutchman stood aside, the pair passed in, and the door was closed without noise.

Jameson pushed open a door just before him, and there was darkness no longer.

They were in the midst of a flood of light, and both could hear the distant hum of many voices, the rattle of glasses, and sounds of hearty laughter.

Before them was a steep flight of stone steps.

Descending these, they stood in a large, vaulted, roofed cellar.

This was one of the many places which were devoted to the worship of Bacchus.

One side was divided from the rest by a broad oaken counter, behind which were the liquors and the man who sold them—Darvill.

The cellar was illuminated with all manner of things, from lanterns to tapers; and the effect of so much heat in such an ill-ventilated place, together with the fumes of the various beverages in use, was overpowering to Dudley.

Scores of men and women, apparently of all nationalities, were seated at the tables enjoying themselves after their own peculiar fashions; and of Jameson and Dudley they took not the smallest notice.

Had our hero and his companion been attired in other than sailor's costume, however, they would have been regarded with suspicion, and their lives would have been in deadly peril.

"By the sword," cried Darvill, extending his horny hand to Jameson, "do I indeed behold you once again?"

"Yes, I'm back once more," replied

Jameson, "and I have brought a friend with me—one of the real old school, Darvill."

"With such a conductor," replied Darvill, "I am bound to give him hearty greeting."

The fellow supplied both with wine, and then he said—

"And now, Jameson, shall I call Mary down?"

"Yes," was the laughing reply; "for my visit is principally to see her."

"And how many fathers have you told the same tale to, since you were last here?" asked Darvill.

"Not to one, I swear."

"Then your disposition must be entirely changed," laughed Darvill. "However, we are not all saints."

Passing through a door behind him, he was heard calling "Mary!" with all the power of his voice.

He was soon answered, and presently there passed through the door a pretty English girl.

This was "Mary Darvill," the adopted daughter of the host.

Her eyes brightened as she saw who was before her, and there was a joyful ring in her voice as she said—

"How glad am I to see you once again! But stay not here—come with me. I have such a sight to show you. You have seen much in your travels; many strange and unaccountable sights—but I have something which you have never seen—a something which will astound you."

"Indeed!"

"Yes—is it not so, father?"

"It is," growled Darvill; "but you want to take him away before we have had a dozen words. Why, lass, I was about to tackle him as to his intentions concerning you."

"Thank you," was the haughty reply; "leave that to me. Though I have been compelled to heed not my surroundings, I have not yet forgotten that I am an English maiden."

"Well said," muttered Dudley.

"She has more spirit in her than the whole of these barrels," said Darvill, with a loud guffaw. "Well, go—go, Jameson. Hear the story, and see the sight."

"May I bring my friend with me, Mary?" asked Jameson.

"Yes."

Thereupon she led Jameson and Dudley round the counter, and they followed her through the little door.

Passing through several apartments, all of them well, and, in some instances, handsomely furnished, she led them up a flight of stairs, and opening the door of a chamber before her, bade them enter.

Most superbly furnished was this apartment—so beautiful indeed was it, that a murmur of admiration escaped Dudley's lips, and was echoed by Jameson.

A bright smile lit up Mary's face as she saw the impression created on her visitors.

"For the first time," she said to her lover, "you visit the 'Tapestry Room.'"

"Tapestry! I never heard of such a place before. The chambers I have heard of here have very different names. For instance, one is called the 'Grindstone Chamber.'"

"True, from the fact that the headsman used to live there, and his grindstone is there to this day. His place is taken by a man who is infinitely worse than the headsman, who was a monster of iniquity."

"Not your friend Lomew," Jameson whispered to our hero.

"If the man of whom you speak," he added aloud, "is a greater monster than Scilitto, the once notorious headsmen of the City, then he must be a monster indeed. Of course, he is not an Englishman?"

"People are of opinion that he is. There is no telling; you may get a view of him anon. But listen.

"About a week ago my adopted father was out on a visit to a friend who lives across the Swlezer Cliffs.

"He had transacted his business, and was returning at night along an unfrequented road, when he heard a man's voice.

"The mist was thick at the time, and it was with difficulty he could get his mule along the dangerous road.

"As you know, he is a hard-hearted man, with no spark of

sympathy in his breast; and, therefore, why he should dismount and try to find whence that voice proceeded, is to me a mystery.

"For some time he searched, but he could not find the owner of the voice, which continued to call for help.

"So my father lit a link. This at once attracted the attention of the man, whose voice now became louder.

"Presently he reached a little covered waggon, harnessed to which was a mule, that had broken its leg.

"My father pulled aside the covering, and there was an old man lying within the waggon.

"The poor old fellow was in the last stage of illness, and my father says he appealed to him so earnestly, not for himself, but for his daughter, a young woman of twenty, that he took compassion on him.

"I do not believe this, but I fancy that the old man offered him a large reward, and it was this which induced him to bring the waggon to this dreadful house.

"It was taken to the stables, and the old man being unable to move, he was left within it, while the daughter was given into my charge.

"The name of this old man was—"

"An Englishman?" cried Jameson.

"Yes; and he had made the journey from Deedarm, a distance of one hundred miles. In a few days he died, and in my charge he left his daughter, and a box which he said was not to be opened until she had delivered a certain letter she has in her possession to a gentlemen in London."

"A most mysterious story," said Dudley. "And from what you say, the old man was evidently making his way to Rotterdam to take vessel for London?"

"Exactly. And now I will show you the daughter."

"Is it the daughter which is to cause us so much astonishment?" asked Jameson.

"It is," was the smiling reply.

So saying, she advanced to a door, drew aside the fine tapestry which covered it, and opening it, said—

"Come forth, Anna."

At once there issued from the apartment the tiniest specimen of humanity on which Dudley and Jameson had ever looked.

This young lady was considerably smaller than Quicksilver!

And yet she was a perfect model of womanhood, well proportioned in every way, and very pretty.

Dudley was astounded, while the expression on Jameson's face was most ludicrous.

"Anna," said Mary, "this is Master Jameson, mate of an English vessel, and this is his friend—er—"

"Jonas Halyard," said Dudley, hastily.

"I am very pleased to see them both," replied Anna, in sweet, clear tones, as she gracefully returned Dudley's bow; "and I hope that arrangements may now be made, so that the completion of my father's mission may be accomplished."

"She means," said Mary, "that she hopes that you, Jameson, being mate of an English vessel, will make arrangements for taking her to London."

"By my faith," cried Jameson, hastily, "I should be afraid of losing so small a lady."

Mary laughed heartily.

"You need have no fear as to that," she exclaimed.

"Well, by the rood, Mary," said Jameson, "do you want me to see her landed in London?"

"I do. I promised her that if I saw you, I would ask you to do this."

Jameson bowed.

"Your commands are captain's orders," he smiled, "and they shall be obeyed. But now listen to me, Mary. My friend here is really a gentleman's son, and I have only to ask him, and he will accept any commission this lady may be pleased to give him."

"Willingly!" cried Dudley. "I understand, Mistress Anna, that you have a letter to deliver to a gentleman in London. May I ask the name of that gentleman?"

"It is Matthew Jordon."

"Jordon! Of what part of London?"

"Ah, sir, you ask a question which

I am unable to answer. Again, there are a thousand chances to one that the gentleman is dead."

"What makes you think so?"

"My father had not seen him for twenty years."

"Nor heard from him?"

"No."

"He was a friend of your father's?"

"He was—a firm friend."

"In London?"

"No; abroad."

"Well, I will do my best when I reach London to trace the gentleman out. Do you know what his occupation was?"

"The same as my father's—that of a diamond merchant."

"Good! Leave it to me, and I promise you that I will do all in my power for you?"

"When do you sail, Jameson?" asked Mary.

"As soon as we have unloaded and taken a fresh cargo," was the reply. "I suppose your father will have no objection to this lady's leaving?"

"He will be very glad of it. He will allow me no permanent companion—time enough for that, he says, when I am married."

"Ah, Mary," said Jameson, "I would I had a home to offer you, I would ask you to be my wife at once."

"I should not refuse," replied Mary, with a smile.

"On my next visit here we will talk over this," added her lover. "I feel sure Darvill will have no objection to our marriage."

"No, he would not. But you have heard what he said respecting that: 'If you were to take Mary, you would take her with all she has in money'—I know not how much it is—'and you would go to yonder cathedral and there swear that you would ask no questions respecting this house and its secrets.'"

"Yes, yes, I remember; and I would willingly do as he demands."

"Would you—could you?" cried Mary, eagerly, as she seized Jameson's rough hands and looked earnestly into his face.

"Yes, Mary, I would."

"Then," she cried, the tears filling her eyes, "take me from this wicked house, and I will love you as woman ne'er loved before."

"I will presently speak with Master Jameson on the subject if he will allow me," said Dudley to the girl.

"Only too thankful shall I be to take your advice, Master Halyard," observed the young sailor. "And now let us go below."

Dudley bade adieu to both the ladies, and promised to make arrangements at once with respect to Anna.

Then he left the room to give Jameson an opportunity of a few private words with Mary.

Presently both went below and rejoined the host.

"Well," he said, "what think you of the sight?"

"A marvellous one."

"It is indeed! Did she tell you the story?"

"Yes."

"Did she show you the box the old man gave Anna?"

"She did not."

"Ah! she is very careful of it—very! My opinion is that it is full of diamonds, for the old man was a diamond merchant."

Dudley adroitly contrived to turn the conversation.

He was anxious to know who this mysterious Englishman was—this man who occupied the Grindstone Chamber.

But he rightly considered that it would not do for him to speak of the man, and therefore, he contrived to secretly urge Jameson to mention the matter.

So a fresh bottle of wine was ordered, and Darvill was invited to partake of it, an invitation which he accepted with alacrity.

"Here's to your good health, Master Darvill," said Jameson, "and I trust you have been lucky of late, and have let all chambers below to those who are able to pay for them."

"Yes, yes; I have been lucky for once, and yet unlucky."

"Indeed! How is that?"

"Have you been in the Grindstone Chamber?"

"Not to my knowledge."

"Well, the best chamber below is this Grindstone Chamber, or rather chambers, for there is a set of three, with an extensive vault, below which—But that is of no consequence. These, Master Jameson, were empty for a long period, and I could not help grumbling at the dead loss, the rent of this place being enormous.

"Suddenly I stumbled across a man who had just arrived from London. A most curious-looking fellow he is, I'll warrant you.

"Seeing that he had plenty of money, and hearing that he required apartments, I showed him the Grindstone Chamber. He was more than pleased, and seeing this, I tacked on twice the sum I was about to ask for them. Ha, ha!

"He closed at once, and then he told me he was a silk merchant, and on board the vessel in which he had come to Rotterdam, he had numbers of boxes of his goods. Could I stow them anywhere? he asked.

"I thereupon showed him the trap leading to the vault, and he went below to examine the place. He was more satisfied than ever, and so that same night, he and two of my ostlers brought the boxes from the vessel, and they were stowed away in the vault.

"I fancy they will eventually become mine, because from morning till night the man drinks nothing but spirits; and he has become so thin and so haggard, that I believe a deadly illness has already seized upon him."

"How long has he been here?"

"Nearly a month, and he has not been sober once during that time—at least, not to my knowledge. He's a fine customer, and pays liberally for what he has; and besides this, gives his money away in profusion."

"And the name of this eccentric man, Master Host?" asked Dudley.

"Ah, there you beat me. At one time he says he is So-and-so; at another he swears that he is someone else. But the name he gave me first of all was Yelkcoh."

"Yelkcoh! What a strange name."

"It is Jewish, I should say. But I should like you to see him, Jameson. I would take you to the chamber, but I cannot leave this place."

"But would he not resent the intrusion?"

"He would not see you. I'll warrant he is in his usual condition."

Darvill at this moment was called aside by one of his customers, and Dudley, in grave excitement, whispered—

"Jameson, the vast treasure is discovered."

"Holy Mary! what mean you?"

"The man in the Grindstone Chamber is the villain Hockley."

Jameson shook his head doubtingly.

"Then you saw nothing?" cried Dudley. "This man goes by the name of Yelkcoh—Y E L K C O H. Spell that backward."

Jameson did so, and was thunderstruck.

Darvill now returned, and continued—

"I once left this place for a few minutes, and when I returned, I found that at least a dozen bottles of wine had disappeared. But I trust you, Jameson; and if you would like to see this scarecrow of a man, why you may go yourself."

"But my friend may go with me?"

"Yes; but on your lives, make no noise. Come this way, and I will show you the staircase. When you reach the bottom keep straight along, and you will come to a small lamp. A little distance from that, on the left, you will turn off, and there is the first chamber. If you can pluck up enough courage, and if the door is not fastened, you will cross that; then through a little window you will see this man. Rouse him not, for when the drink is in him, he is a very demon."

Having promised that what they did would be done with the utmost caution, they once more went behind the counter, and the host passed them through another door.

Before them was the staircase.

"Take this lantern, Jameson," said

the host, "but keep its rays shut off as much as possible."

And now, in order fully to understand the extraordinary events which occurred, we will precede Dudley and his friend.

* * * *

Darvill's mysterious house was at one time the property of the State, and it was in communication with a prison.

When the prison was pulled down, the house passed into the hands of a man who turned it into a gambling den, and having passed through several other hands, it finally came into the possession of Darvill.

The communication between house and prison was, of course, underground; and the cellars, vaults, and passages leading hither and thither, together with horrible dungeons, were very numerous.

One end of these passages was beside the river.

A heavy oaken door opened on to a long flight of stone steps.

The other end was blocked by a brick wall, but the door had not been permanently secured.

On the inside were the bars and bolts, which could be removed by a man of ordinary strength, and there was no lock attached to it.

A few of these underground chambers were let to tenants, if such could be found, which was not very often; a few were used as wine and beer cellars, and the others were closed.

Entirely unknown to the host, his drunken tenant of the Grindstone Chamber had made a thorough inspection of the whole of the passages.

He had found the door leading to the river, and he frequently used it for the purpose of going and coming, unknown to anybody in the house, and occasionally he introduced a "friend" or two, sometimes more.

He was cunning in this respect; so much so that neither the host nor those in his pay had the least idea of his movements.

He was the greatest drunkard on earth, according to the host's idea.

Darvill, of course, went by his usual appearance, and by the vast amount of wines and spirits he was constantly ordering.

But his "usual appearance" was almost always assumed, while it was the "friends" he chose to smuggle into the premises who consumed the larger share of the vast quantities of the wines and spirits he procured.

The most prominent feature of the Grindstone Chamber was a monstrous grindstone, ingeniously contrived; for it was so constructed that it could be set in motion by the foot, or, by turning a great handle affixed to the wall, an immense volume of water from the river rushed through an enormous pipe, and so set the wheel in motion.

But this machine had long since been in disuse, and the ironwork was now covered with the rust of years.

The next chamber was a bedroom, and beyond that was another apartment.

Despite the closeness of the place a large log fire was flaring up the chimney, and the bright flames lit up the faces of three persons seated at a table before it—two men and a woman.

Upon the table were several bottles of wine, as well as eatables.

That the three were considerably the worse for drink was quite certain, but they were not too far gone to engage in a game of cards.

From the serious fashion in which they proceeded, it was evident that the stakes were large.

The man on the right of the table answered exactly to the host's description of Yelkcoh.

The man on his left was a short, stumpy individual of about forty, while the woman was of about the same age.

She was powerful-looking, with black hair and eyebrows, and a skin as tanned as a gipsy's.

Her accent at once proved her nationality. She was Irish.

In the meantime, Dudley and Jameson proceeded exactly as they had been told, and without making the least noise.

Passing through the two first chambers, they reached the third.

"Here is the window," whispered Dudley; "and see, the man is not in bed, for the place is well lighted. Ah, he is not alone! There are a man and a woman with him. Look."

"By heaven! you are right."

"Do you not think it strange that the host should not have said so?"

"Perhaps he did not know it."

"But how could anyone reach the vaults without his knowing it?"

"Can't say. But I've heard that this place is full of secret entrances and exits. This man may have found one unknown to the host."

"Jameson, we are foiled. There is the man who answers to the host's description. There is the man I had thought was Hockley disguised. But such is not the case I am convinced, for this man wears no disguise whatever."

"You are right. And it can't be the other man?"

"No, he is too short. By heaven! all my hopes are dashed to the ground. If there— Ha!"

His sudden ejaculation was caused by a loud crash at his feet.

On the little window-sill an earthenware jug had been standing; he had touched it, and it had fallen to the ground.

At once the three dashed from the next chamber, though the two men did not attempt to draw their weapons.

"Hillo!" cried Yelkcoh; "what mean this, my masters? What do you mean by this intrusion? And how did you get here?"

"They must have come by the river," said the short man.

"By no means," replied Yelkcoh, who spoke with a strong German accent, "for I never forget to fasten the door after using it."

"The fact is," said Jameson, "I am an old friend of the host, and he gave me permission to show my companion the vaults."

"Humph! the explanation sounds well enough, but how are we to know what you say is true?"

"Ask the host yourself."

"You are sailors?"

"Yes."

"What vessel?"

"'The Queen of the Thames.'"

"Ah, she has not long since reached Rotterdam?"

"That is so."

"Produce your papers, and we will then believe you."

Fortunately Jameson had his papers with him.

He handed them over.

They were eagerly scanned by Yelkcoh, who handed them to the Irishwoman.

"Here, Bridget," he said, "you can read English fairly—what think you of these?"

Bridget took the papers to the fireplace, stooped before the blaze, and attentively examined the documents.

"Yes," she said, "they are genuine enough. Here, take them, Master Jameson, and take a bit of advice with them. When you visit a strange place take notice you don't walk into private apartments."

"But now that they are here," said Yelkcoh, "what say if they join us in a game of cards?"

"Three's company and five's none," replied Bridget, which caused the short man (whose name was Collette) to utter a guffaw.

"We should be glad to join you in a game," said Dudley.

"To be sure we should," added Jameson.

"Well, I will join in one game," said Bridget, "and one game only."

Seats were procured from the bedchamber, and Collette having opened three or four fresh bottles of wine, the game was commenced, Collette winning.

It was next suggested that there should be partners, and the one who made that suggestion was Dudley.

This was agreed to by Bridget, who declared that she had had enough of play, and would watch the game.

This was exactly what Dudley required.

He proposed to have Jameson for a partner, and this being agreed to, the game commenced.

"Jameson," whispered Dudley, pretending to examine the cards his friend held, "ask me no questions, but when I start up, immediately seize

Collette, and point your pistol at his head."

"I will do as you direct," returned Jameson.

The game was proceeding, when on a sudden, Dudley started up, dashed upon Bridget, seized her by the throat, and hurled her to the ground.

"Attempt to stir," he cried, "and I will plunge this blade into your heart!"

At the same moment he drew a pistol, and pointed it at Yelkcoh's head.

Jameson had done exactly as Dudley had told him.

So completely overwhelmed with surprise and terror were Collette and Yelkcoh, that they did not attempt to draw the weapons with which they were armed.

"What means this dastardly outrage?" growled Bridget. "Coward that you are thus to take advantage of a woman!"

Jameson appeared quite as much confounded as the others.

He seemed to be wondering whether it was possible that Dudley had just taken leave of his senses.

"The meaning of this 'dastardly outrage,' as you call it," answered Dudley, "is this—that in defiance of your excellent disguise, in defiance of your wonderful and more than correct assumption of the Irish brogue, I have recognised you, Bridget. So sure as my name is not Jonas Halyard, so sure are you the villain, Joseph Hockley."

"Never!" gasped Jameson.

"Put your pistol to that man's (Collette) ear," said Dudley, "and if he answers not the questions I shall put to him, blow his brains out when I give the command. I am sorry to have to give utterance to such words, but they shall be carried into effect if I am not answered."

"Depend upon it I will fire if you but give the word," said Jameson, and in such cool, determined tones, that a shudder ran through Collette's frame.

"Answer me this," said Dudley. "Is not this supposed woman Joseph Hockley?"

"Yes."

"And who is yonder man who takes his name? for think not that we have not recognised that Yelkcoh is the name Hockley reversed."

"He is no more Hockley than am I," was the surly answer. "Hockley had the name of Yelkcoh for a long time, but, fearing that he would be suspected, he got my mate yonder, whose name is Turner, to take it, and to imitate him in appearance as much as possible."

"Oh, so you are comrades, eh? Sailors?"

"Sometimes, and sometimes not," was the curious, but significant reply.

"And what did you take this man Hockley for?"

"A silk merchant."

"Then you did not make his acquaintance in London?"

"No, 'twas first of all on the river, where, when he was drunk, we saved him from drowning."

"What was his story? Answer faithfully, and I will give each of you a handsome sum, and you shall leave this place without injury."

"His story—"

"Traitor!" thundered Bridget, or rather Hockley, for he it assuredly was. "Ungrateful scoundrel! breathe another sentence and you die!"

"Silence!" cried Dudley, raising his sword in a threatening manner. "Now," he continued to Collette, "proceed."

"His story," said Collette, "was that he was accused of fraud in England by his brother; that he had been forced to fly with all his goods, and that soon he intended to go to Germany, and there to open as an English silk merchant."

"Ah, a very plausible story. But I accuse him of a worse crime than fraud. What it is would be of no interest to you. My advice to you is this: Go from this place and leave Rotterdam by the first vessel, for if we see you about we shall accuse you of being associates of this man, who is wanted in England."

"It is false!" yelled Hockley.

"There is nothing false about it," said Dudley; "for a warrant for your arrest has been issued."

"Signed by whom?"

"Signed by the Earl of Sussex, and countersigned by Earl Dudley."

"They have me sure enough," thought Hockley, "but they know not where the treasure is, if that is what they have actually come after. The host cannot have said anything as to the boxes of silk."

"I agree to leave Rotterdam at once," said Collette.

"And I," added Turner.

"Very well," said Dudley, "you shall be conducted above."

"That is not necessary," said Collette, "for there is a door in these vaults leading to the river, and a boat is in waiting for us."

"Good. Jameson, conduct them to that door. Here is a purse of money, divide it between them; but, first, let them deliver up their arms."

This was quite an unexpected order, and since neither of the men made any attempt to give up possession of his weapons, Jameson calmly took them himself.

Then having divided the money, he took the lantern, and turning it full on, told Turner to place himself beside Collette, and in that fashion go on to the door.

Both very quickly proceeded to do this, and having reached the door, Collette opened it.

Jameson was astonished to see the river immediately before him, and so close that only a flight of steps separated them.

At the bottom of that flight was a boat, and the two men at once entered it, and pulled away.

Jameson watched them until the darkness hid them from sight.

"I will leave the door open," he thought, "for that will be an excellent way of leaving the house. It is likely that by this time Darvill is well on the road to intoxication, and therefore he will forget all about us."

Returning to the Grindstone Chamber, he found Hockley in exactly the same position in which he had left him.

"Now rise," said Dudley, "and listen to what I say."

Hockley rose.

"I listen," he said; "but before you speak, I would take off this gown."

"Take it off, then."

Hockley thereupon took off the gown, as well as a few other articles which had assisted in the deception.

Dudley and Jameson watched him narrowly.

No weapons were visible.

But he was armed nevertheless.

He was in the act of stooping to disengage his feet from the gown, when he suddenly started up, and with a wild cry dashed upon Jameson.

So sudden and so unexpected was the attack that not only Jameson, but Dudley also, was taken entirely off his guard.

Jameson put up his hand, and caught the wrist of Hockley as it descended.

In the villain's hand was a dagger, and this he would have buried in the mate's heart.

No sooner did Jameson seize his wrist than Hockley raised his fist and dealt him a blow in the face, which levelled him to the ground.

Dudley dashed upon him, but Hockley managed to elude his grasp, and stooping, he snatched up Jameson's sword.

Turning suddenly, he made as if about to attack Dudley.

Just as suddenly, however, he turned and rushed through the chambers.

Dudley was after him with the speed of lightning.

"Hold!" he shouted. "Hold, or I will fire!"

Hockley's reply, as he dashed onward, was a wild and savage yell of defiance.

Dudley at once snatched a pistol from his belt and fired in the direction he had taken.

But no cry followed; the ball had not taken effect.

Suddenly the open door leading to the river was reached.

An instant Hockley paused before it, his wild eyes glaring upon the black waters.

For a moment he had forgotten that the boat was gone.

"'ATTEMPT TO STIR, AND I WILL PLUNGE THIS BLADE INTO YOUR HEART!' CRIED DUDLEY."

Giving utterance to another yell of savage rage, he turned.

But Hockley, at bay, had no terrors for Dudley.

Both could now see each other fairly well, and in a moment their blades crossed, and a furious fight was in progress.

Hockley was in a state of frenzy.

He thrust and plunged, and howled like a wild beast, but whatever he did had no effect on his opponent.

He had not one opportunity of striking a blow, whereas he felt himself twice wounded.

At last, wearied with the fight, he resolved to risk a leap into the river.

He would trust to chance.

No doubt, he thought, he would be picked up just as he had been once before, and then in a day or two he would return and take the treasure to a place where it could not be traced.

His mind made up at this point, he suddenly hurled his sword at Dudley's face, though it did not strike him, and turning, he dashed through the doorway, and with a mighty spring he leapt into the river.

It was his last leap!

As he took the spring, Dudley again fired, and the ball this time found its billet, for it struck him at the back of the head, and he fell.

Dead!

The sharp report echoed over the silent river, followed by a few shouts, as from the watch on the different vessels.

Then all was still once more.

Dudley descended the steps, and looked ahead.

He could not see the body for a few seconds, the moon having disappeared.

Presently, however, it came forth again, and it was then that Dudley saw his shot had taken effect, for Hockley's body came up at his very feet, and with such suddenness as to cause him to start.

"Is he dead?" asked a voice.

It was Jameson.

"Yes," replied Dudley; "he has met with his deserts at last."

"It serves the scoundrel right. Has the shot attracted attention, think you?"

"No. I heard a few shouts, but they have not been repeated. I see nothing advancing this way. Do you notice anything?"

"By heaven! I am not able to see much at present, for the wretch dealt me such a mighty blow that my eyes ache. Still, I am sure nothing is advancing. These Dutchmen require a lot to rouse them. They say that nothing makes them so quick on their feet as the sight of English steel, and I believe it."

"So do I. But what of the body, Jameson?"

"Why, the finding of the body would mean inquiries. Let us drag it in and close the doors."

So the pair, between them, dragged the body of the man who had thus deservedly come by his death up the steps, and then reclosed the door, and placed the bars in position.

While Dudley held the lantern, Jameson rifled Hockley's pockets.

All that was found in them was a piece of paper.

Jameson handed this to Dudley, who opened it and read—

"MASTER YELKCOH,	THE MONARCH,"
"Passenger,	CAPTAIN DALTON,
"London to Rotterdam"	No. 2038.
"with Fourteen Boxes."	
"No s. 22 to 35."	

"These," said Dudley, "are the boxes which have been placed below."

"Exactly," cried Jameson. "And after all, Master Jonas, your fortune is made—or, rather, your pardon is certain."

"Now listen to me," continued Dudley. "We have as good as got hold of this treasure. The thing now is, how to take it away without its being seen by the host and his customers."

"Why, the thing is easy," replied Jameson. "We can take it away by yonder door. In the first place, I will get a boat, and bring it to the steps. We will then get three or four of the boxes, place them in the boat, and go to the ship. And in a very short time we shall have conveyed the whole of the fourteen boxes away."

"Good! Now, Jameson, I have

thought that this young girl, Mary, is very unhappy here."

"Unhappy is hardly the word. Look at the vile wretches Darvill compels her to associate with. But, despite all this, she is as pure as an English girl can well be; of that I am certain. I would make her my wife at once if I could."

"She has money."

"Yes, but then that isn't mine."

"It will soon be, Jameson, mark my word. I will tell you what I propose. It is that, before we get the treasure away, we take the two girls on to the vessel."

"I will do exactly as you advise—that is, if the ladies consent."

"Then let us, first of all, seek the treasure."

Entering the Grindstone Chamber, the ring of the trap-door was soon found, and the trap lifted. Dudley descended one short flight of steps, while Jameson leaned over with the lantern.

Dudley had not far to go.

Right before him were the boxes, all of wood, and heavily cased with iron.

There they were all in a row, and numbered from 22 to 35, and each bearing the word—

"YELKCOH."

"All are here!" cried Dudley.

"What sort of place do you stand in?"

"A damp cellar. On the right are a number of tools, such as spades and pickaxes."

"Ah, then I will tell you what—let us bring the body of Hockley here."

"Good! We will do so at once. Do you, then, drag the body here, Jameson, and lower it. We will then set to work and dig a grave."

In a few minutes Hockley's remains were dragged to the cellar and lowered, and in a short time he was buried, and the ground was made to look as if it had never been disturbed.

Both now ascended and carefully reclosed the trap.

"We must now," said Dudley, "find our way upstairs without going back to the host."

Both set to work to discover some secret way, Dudley proceeding on the one side of the place, and Jameson on the other.

Just as they were about to relinquish the search as a hopeless one, Dudley caught sight of a crack behind a heavy wooden bench.

This was pulled aside, and it was seen that a door was there.

There was, however, neither handle nor lock, so that it appeared as if it was fastened on the other side.

At last Dudley lifted a small square piece of stone at the bottom of the door, and there was revealed a square iron plate.

This, on being pressed, went downward, and the door flew open, creaking and groaning on its hinges.

"You deserve to succeed in everything," exclaimed Jameson. "I would I had one tenth part of your perseverance."

"Let us hope that Mary will teach you what perseverance is," laughed Dudley. "But here, you see, is a flight of stairs, and judging by the look of them, they have not been used for many a long day."

"It is more than likely that Darvill does not know of their existence," said Jameson.

"Yes. But though we have thus discovered these stairs, we as yet know not whither they lead. They may lead to the host's private chamber, and if we entered that, one of us might be shot dead; for Master Darvill is not a man to wait for explanation."

Dudley proceeded up the stairs, and presently a landing was reached.

Round to the right was another staircase, and this, after listening, and hearing no sounds, they also ascended.

They continued until a second landing was reached, and the distant sounds of the jingling glasses and shouts of laughter told the pair that the midnight revellers were still bent on pleasure.

A short flight of stairs brought them to a door thickly studded with nails.

Here Jameson shut off the reflection of the lantern.

At once a streak of light was noticed streaming through the keyhole of the door.

Placing his eye to the keyhole, Dudley found that he was at one end of the Tapestry Chamber.

At the farther end, engaged in earnest conversation, sat Mary and Anna.

Dudley knocked upon the door.

The knock was at once heard, for both the ladies, with startled cries, leapt to their feet, and looked earnestly in the direction of the sound.

Again Dudley knocked, and this time Mary slowly advanced.

In another moment she gave proof that she was possessed of courage, for suddenly opening a drawer in one of the tables, she brought out a large pistol, and advanced towards the door.

"Mary," said Jameson, in low tones—"Mary, 'tis I. Don't be alarmed—it is Jameson."

Mary recognised the voice, and with a glad cry, came close against the door.

"In heaven's name," she said, "how came you here?"

"Along a secret passage, Mary."

"But is your friend with you?"

"Yes; but open the door, dear Mary. Can you open it?"

"Yes; 'tis barred and bolted on this side. Wait a moment."

Mary removed the bolts and bars, though not without considerable difficulty, and opened the door.

At once Dudley proceeded to tell them all that had occurred.

"You have indeed acted most wisely, Master Jonas," said Mary; "for had Darvill got to know what those boxes really contained, murder would certainly have been done. I—and I am sure Anna, too—agree to do as you ask."

"Yes!" exclaimed Anna, quickly; "most anxious am I to quit this dreadful place."

The ladies now secured what articles they required.

In quick time the chamber below was reached, and there the two girls for a time waited.

Jameson speedily secured a boat, which he disengaged from the stern of a vessel, and brought it to the steps.

Then the ladies were brought forward and placed in it.

The direction of Captain Hawser's vessel being ascertained, they pulled towards it.

When they reached it, there at the stern was Captain Hawser and his scapegrace nephew, Solomon; and astonished indeed were they to see the boat and its contents.

Dudley quickly climbed up the side of the vessel, and with great rapidity, but strict accuracy, related all that had occurred.

"The ladies are very welcome," said Captain Hawser; "though I shall be very sorry to part with Jameson; for I suppose he will quit a seafaring life as soon as he is married. Solomon, go below and rouse Lock and Pritchard. This mighty treasure must indeed be cleared at once. And if this Darvill should make inquiries of me, why I'll send him about his business."

The first lady handed up was Anna.

Great was the surprise of the captain.

He was absolutely speechless with amazement.

When Solomon beheld her, and had recovered from his surprise, he said to Dudley—

"You don't mean to say that this tiny lady is Quicksilver's sister?"

"Certainly not. I never hinted such a thing," replied Dudley. "But do not speak of little Quicksilver. I have an idea, Solomon, which for the present must be kept to myself."

The captain suggested that three boats should be lowered and manned, and then they could bring away the whole of the treasure at once.

This was agreed to, and so presently the three boats pushed off.

The men were not long in reaching the treasure chamber, and having placed the boxes in the boat, the men once more pulled away.

All was now so far right.

CHAPTER XVIII.

OF THE NUMEROUS VISITORS TO LOMEW, AND OF THE NEWS BROUGHT BY MASTER RODNEY.

SIX weeks have elapsed, and we now find ourselves once again at the Tower of London.

The queen had taken up her quarters there.

One evening, the headsman was seated in his chamber examining the contents of a black chest—a chest containing many a relic of bygone days—happy days, when he knew no troubles, and before his father had met with a shameful death, the remembrance of which hung about his heart like a black cloud.

The only light the chamber contained was a taper, and a sickly and most uncertain light it was.

It was, however, sufficient for the headsman.

Presently one of the warders knocked upon the door, and the headsman directed him to enter.

"Good Lomew," said the man, "Master Walter Raleigh and a lady wish communication with you."

"Lead them here, good Phillis. Is Barcally about?"

"He is within his chamber."

"Have you observed aught of a suspicious nature?"

"Nothing. Should I get to learn anything, I will not fail to let you know it."

"I thank you heartily, Phillis. Here, lad, look—here is a fine gold ring. Take it, and place it on your finger."

"No, Jerome! I want no pay for what I choose to do for you."

"I well know it, Phillis; but I give it you to wear for my sake."

"Well, then, I will take it. But, Jerome, you are not the man you were a short time agone. Bear up, man—bear up! Listen! The lady who is with Master Raleigh is the Lady Herbert."

"Ah!" cried Lomew, starting up; "away, Phillis, and conduct them here at once."

Another few seconds, and Raleigh entered the chamber.

On his arm leaned Lady Herbert.

Terrible sorrow had changed the colour of her hair to white.

Lomew was much affected.

"Weep not for me, good Jerome," said Lady Herbert, "weep not for me; weep not for the woman whom heaven has forsaken!"

"Madam," said Raleigh, "depend upon it, Providence never forsakes those who believe in Him."

"Raleigh," replied Lady Herbert, sadly, "my prayers, poured forth from the depths of a broken heart, have remained unanswered."

"Yet hope on, madam! The blackest cloud has its silver lining. Your impression, I know, is that your son has met with foul play."

"That, like his poor brother, he has been foully murdered. Yes, Raleigh—that is my belief. And it is the belief of my poor old friend here. Oh, Raleigh, what a task you set my son!"

"Not so!" said Lomew, hastily; "let us not accuse each other of having done aught that should not have been done. Raleigh made a proposition to Dudley, and Dudley accepted it."

"And nothing has since been heard of him?"

"Say not so, Lady Herbert!" said Raleigh. "He was last heard of at London Bridge."

"Yes, when he escaped from the barge and leapt into the river."

"Let us have yet a little more patience," said Jerome, though he could not disguise his uneasiness. "Be seated, my lady, and let us converse respecting the future."

"The future!" repeated Lady Herbert, slowly shaking her head. "The future can have no joys for me."

"Let us hope to the contrary," said Raleigh. "And now we will discuss the latest movements of Marcus Montague."

"On whom I wonder you have not long since served your warrant," observed Jerome.

Raleigh smiled as he said—

"There is plenty of time, Master Lomew. Montague is like the moth about the taper. He will keep dancing about it until he falls—never to rise again!

"Many times the coward has come under my notice—when I have been alone, mark you—and each time I have felt an irresistible impulse to fall upon and slay him."

"He is not worthy of the steel of so brave a man as Walter Raleigh," said Lady Herbert.

"Your ladyship indeed speaks rightly," said Jerome. "The weapon which will slay Marcus Montague is the axe. In a leathern case within this chamber is a new axe. As yet it has never stricken off the head of a human being. I am saving it for Montague."

Lady Herbert shuddered.

"I dare swear he will come to the block," said Raleigh; "and if that should be so—though I am no seer of horrible sights—I will be present at his execution, even if I have to travel day and night for a week! Something is wrong between Montague and Barcally, Lomew, for I heard them speaking together at a certain house in the Strand, and their words were high and angry; also, when Montague had departed, I heard Barcally mutter something about 'papers,' 'evidence,' and so forth."

"You can depend upon it that—Ha! a knock. Enter!"

Phillis once more entered.

He held forth a letter addressed to the headsman.

"Who brought it?" asked Lomew.

"The Dean of St. Bidulph's."

The headsman tore the letter open and read—

"FRIEND LOMEW,—A few words respecting thine and the Lady Herbert's business. Not long will I detain you. Pray ask for my admission."

"Where does the dean wait?" asked the headsman.

"At Tower Hill—the second gate."

"I will at once repair to the lieutenant. Come with me, Phillis, for the pass."

"We will retire for the present," said Raleigh.

"No," replied the headsman, hastily, "I entreat you not to depart. Does not the letter say Lady Herbert's business?"

"Yes," said Lady Herbert; "let us stay; the advice of so eminent a man as the Dean of St. Bidulph's is always acceptable."

Lomew departed to the lieutenant's apartment, taking Phillis with him.

The headsman showed the lieutenant the letter.

"No pass is necessary," replied the lieutenant. "Phillis, conduct the reverend gentleman to Lomew's chambers."

Phillis went off, while Lomew returned to his apartments.

In a short time Phillis reappeared, conducting the Dean of St. Bidulph's.

His religious garb was supplemented with a heavy gown, the hood of which was drawn closely about his features, though the white hair was not concealed.

Having ushered him in, Phillis closed the door.

"Welcome, your reverence," said Lomew.

The reverend gentleman looked at the occupants of the chamber, but without giving utterance to a word; and then he suddenly shot the bolt in the door and, springing forward, clasped Lady Herbert to his breast.

"Mother!" he cried.

"Great heaven!" gasped Lady Herbert, "can this be you, Dudley?"

"It is. Your wandering son has returned once more."

"Thank heaven!" cried Lady Herbert, bursting into a passionate flood of tears.

In a few minutes mother and son were seated side by side, Dudley's disguise having, for the present, been relinquished.

"I will not now tell you all my adventures," said our hero, "and I will at once come to the most important part. My search, Raleigh, has been entirely successful."

A cry of joy left Raleigh's lips, and the cry was echoed by Lomew.

"Yes," continued Dudley, "the whole of the money is in my possession. It is at London Bridge. I should have sought you out before, but I have been prevented by a serious illness."

"Oh, that you had sent to me, that I might have nursed you, my son," said Lady Herbert.

"It was impossible, for it might have meant detection and arrest. I suppose the scoundrel Barcally is still alive?"

"He is," said Lomew; "and even now he does not despair of getting you into his power."

"No doubt! I was nursed through my illness by two ladies, and as soon as I recovered, I went to London Bridge. A man who has proved himself a firm friend, and who assisted me in recovering the treasure—a young sailor of the name of Jameson—made arrangements for me to call at the house of a relative.

"This man is eccentric, but honest in all his transactions, and he can keep a secret like the grave. With his advice and aid we conveyed the treasure to his cellars, and there Jameson and I opened the boxes and counted the contents. Not a noble missing!"

"You may consider yourself pardoned, Dudley," said Raleigh. "More than once I hinted to the queen that the treasure might be recovered in some mysterious fashion. But she laughed. Yet once she said seriously, 'If a subject of mine recovered that money, received from the hands of dastardly traitors, he should receive one-fourth of it, or any favour he might ask. So I think that when I say you will be freely pardoned, I am not wrong. But, with all his cleverness, despite all his expenditure—and that, to my knowledge, has been very great—Montague gets nothing. Thank heaven for it, he is foiled in that!"

"Then he escaped, after all?" asked Dudley.

"How do you mean?"

"Did you not hear that, by mistake, he threw himself into the Thames?"

"We did hear something from Barcally's men, but could never get at the truth."

"I will tell you the whole of the strange story by-and-by."

"How came you to disguise yourself as the Dean of St. Bidulph's?" asked Lady Herbert.

"I rendered the dean a trifling service," replied Dudley, with a smile; "and being at his house, it struck me that with his costume, and the aid of a costumier, I could seek admission here as the dean himself. I knew that Lomew and the dean were old friends, and I told him the truth. He readily agreed to help me, and he will be glad to know that the result has been entirely successful. Of course, when I entered, I had no idea that my mother was here. And now let me proceed with other matters.

"I spoke of two ladies who have been nursing me. Both of them were at the house where this money was recovered—at Rotterdam—and both escaped with us. The name of the one is, or was, Mary Darvill, though that was not her real name; but she is now Mary Jameson, having married the young sailor of whom I spoke. The other is called Anna Venn, and she is the daughter of a diamond merchant who lately died at Rotterdam."

"Venn!" repeated the headsman. "I knew a Venn who was a diamond merchant. But that was many years gone by."

"This Anna," continued Dudley, "is the smallest woman I have ever seen. She is shorter than Quicksilver."

A cry of astonishment left the lips of the interested listeners.

"Impossible!" muttered Lomew.

"No," smiled Dudley, "it is a fact; and anon you shall satisfy yourself. Abroad with her father she has travelled all her life, and for years her father has been in search of a man he was not sure was alive!

"At his death he left a letter directed to this man—a very old friend—and his wish was that the search should be continued in London. For the last few days Jameson and I have been making inquiries, but with no result."

"What is the name of the man, my son?" asked Lady Herbert.

"Matthew Jordon."

"Holy Virgin!" cried Lomew; "is it possible?"

"What? Why this—"

"Lomew's real name is Matthew Jordon," said Lady Herbert.

"The Jordon sought for," observed Dudley, "was a diamond merchant."

"Which was mine and my father's occupation," said Lomew, in low, sad tones.

Dudley produced the letter, and handed it to the headsman.

For a moment the latter looked at the writing, and then from the black box we have spoken of, he picked out a letter yellow with time.

"Look at that," he said. "See the signature?"

"Yes," replied Dudley; "it is the same handwriting. There is no doubt about it—you are the one to whom the letter is addressed."

Stifling his emotions, Lomew tore off the cover and read—

"FRIEND JORDON,—When last I saw you—and that must be more than twenty years ago—you showed me the tiny child on whom you had taken compassion, and whom you were going to bring up as your own. You may remember that, after my great astonishment, I laughingly said that if ever I had a child, I hoped it would be as small.

"Soon after this I married, and, marvellous to relate, my wife, twelve months after, presented me with twins, both of which were very diminutive. One of these tiny children died, but the other, a girl, lived. Her mother died a few months after giving the children birth. This little child, Anna, has travelled with me over half the world, and, of course, has been a source of intense astonishment, crowds flocking to see her wherever we stayed.

"Now, friend Jordon, all these years I have had a wish—a wish that has grown, until it is the only thing I can think of. It is to marry my child to the child you adopted.

"Never once in my prayers did I forget to pray that my earnest wish might come true. I prayed, too, that I might see that marriage performed. But I now know that it is impossible, for even as I write I am dying.

"Remember this, friend Jordon—though my child knows that I am in search of a husband for her, she knows nothing of whom he is, nor what he is. If you live, and if this little fellow lives, you will bring them together, will you not? Remember, too, that she is not without a fortune. My hand fails me now. With a last farewell and my blessing on you, I sign myself,

"Your true friend,

"ERIC VENN."

"Astounding!" cried Raleigh.

"It is almost beyond the bounds of belief!" exclaimed Lady Herbert.

"Indeed it is," said Dudley. "But it is a fact that, although I had no idea of the contents of the letter, I have been thinking of a wedding between Quicksilver and this little lady ever since I saw her."

"Let nothing be said for the present," observed Lomew, much agitated, as he folded the letter and placed it in the box. "Let us not breathe a word, Dudley. Is the little lady pretty?"

"Wonderfully pretty, and a perfect little model in every way."

"Excellent!"

"Where is Quicksilver?" asked Dudley.

Lomew became grave, or pretended so to become.

"He has deserted me," he said.

"Ha! Ungrateful!"

"No, he's not so bad as that," laughed Raleigh; "but Quicksilver has now a most important post."

"Indeed! Under whom?"

"Elizabeth herself."

"Just as I thought. But what post is it?"

"He is the queen's minstrel."

"Well done."

"Her majesty happened one day to hear him trolling a love ballad, and she at once attached him to her person," said Lomew.

"And a proud little peacock he has become," laughed Raleigh; "though he never forgets old friends—of whom, I think, with the exception of Lomew, you, Dudley, are the principal."

"I shall be glad to see him again," said Dudley. "But now I must come to something serious. Raleigh, you kept your word respecting the two unfortunate prisoners we rescued from Hollow Ground. You know that the poor girl died, and after that Claude disappeared."

"Poor fellow—he did."

"We met, and he was of the greatest service to me. For many weeks we were together, but he gradually sank, and a week ago he died."

"Heaven rest his soul!"

"You have not yet asked aught with respect to Madeline," said Lady Herbert.

"I have learned all," replied Dudley. "And I know that she is now in this Tower."

"Your mysterious disappearance has acted terribly upon her," sighed Lady Herbert. "She has wasted sadly—very sadly."

"What of the farrier," asked Dudley—"he whom for so many years she considered her father?"

"The duke used his great influence in his behalf, and he was appointed Master of the Royal Farriers."

"And well does he deserve so great a post. And have you heard aught of those who for so many years were my parents?"

"Yes," replied Lady Herbert! "they are in London, distracted at your continued absence."

"To you, my dear mother, I will give the task of communicating to them the news of my safety."

"Will you not return home with me?"

"At present it is impossible. My work is far from finished. I have yet many wrongs to right and to avenge."

"I hope, Dudley, that we shall now work together again," said Raleigh.

"We shall," rejoined Dudley. "It is my object to bring Montague to justice, and rest I never will until I have fulfilled that object."

"Be sure, Dudley," said Raleigh, "I will do my best to aid you. I feel certain that Montague, if placed upon his trial, would be found guilty of the murder of his beautiful wife; but the block will claim him for his dealings against the Crown. Yet the block is too good for such a murderous wretch. The rope should be his portion."

"I have for years promised myself the pleasure of striking the villain's head from his shoulders," said Lomew, in low, cold tones, which made Lady Herbert start and shudder, "and I trust that I shall not lose that pleasure."

At this moment a knock came upon the door.

Dudley resumed his disguise, and then Lomew opened the door.

It was the warder Phillis.

"Yet another visitor, Master Lomew," he said.

"Indeed! Who this time?"

"Her majesty's great chemist, Alexander Rodney, who is particularly desirous of seeing you. I informed him that you were engaged; but nevertheless he persisted in saying that as soon as I announced his name, you would desire me to usher him in."

"So I do, good Phillis; for Master Rodney is well known to my friends here."

Phillis departed, and in a few moments he returned with the celebrated chemist.

Master Rodney was greatly pleased to behold Lady Herbert and Raleigh, and he was more than pleased and astonished when Dudley once more discarded his disguise and revealed himself.

"I am thankful beyond measure," he said, "to see you, Master Dudley, for what I have to say concerns you most intimately. But, first, what of the treasure? Seeking it was, of course, like searching for the invisible island."

"True," smiled Dudley; "but with this difference: that whereas the island was invisible, the treasure was visible—so visible that I took possession of it, and in my possession it is at this moment."

"Gracious powers! And is it intact?"

"Quite."

"What has become of the wretch who took it away?"

"He was shot dead."

"Ha! Did this take place in London, or where?"

"At Rotterdam."

"You are all aware of the fact that Montague, though he has lost his principal companion, Redmond Compton, who, I was told, was killed in some brawl, has never relinquished the search after this money; but he knows nothing as yet of what has become of Hockley. He, I am told, has had a number of men at work in trying to trace the man for a long time.

"But to come to the object of my journey hither. I came as much to find Raleigh as you, Lomew, and for this reason: You know that when my servant, Patrick, was murdered, I engaged a youth in his place."

"Yes, I know it," said Lomew. "It was the youth, Merlin, who took the box containing Quicksilver to Hollow Ground. His master was ruined by Montague, Dudley, and so Master Rodney engaged the youth."

"And I have had every reason to be thankful for so doing," said Master Rodney, "for he is sharp, quick-witted, and shrewd. Since Redmond's death, Montague has taken possession of his friend's house at St. James' Park, and there he has lorded it as if he were master of all he surveyed. He has given it out that it was Redmond's wish that if anything happened to him, Montague was to take possession of his property; and it is said that Montague holds deeds to that effect.

"I need scarcely suggest that if he does, those deeds are forgeries. Now it happens that Merlin has a cousin at Compton House—a young girl—and as soon as I learned that, I gave him certain instructions. The consequence of this was, that he became a frequent visitor to the place, and thus had many opportunities of becoming acquainted with what transpired there.

"He let his cousin into the secret that he wanted to learn as much as he could. Last night came a grand opportunity.

"Proof the most positive I have that Montague is again deep in a plot against her majesty, and with many of those who had been concerned in the previous plot, and who had been the cause of the treasure being supplied.

"Previous to the meeting, Merlin entered the house, and by his cousin was conducted to the grand dining-room and concealed. Thus he was enabled to hear all that passed, and though he could not see the faces of the persons assembled, he learned the names of two.

"Now comes the most important thing of all.

"To-morrow night Montague pays a visit to Barcally—not here, but at the house of the lawyer, Grimley."

"What!" cried Lomew; "on London Bridge?"

"Yes. From what Merlin told me I fancy that Barcally holds certain important papers which Montague is desirous of getting possession of at any price. He is about to purchase them, and no doubt Grimley is to see that all is fair, though I know well enough on whose side he will be—Montague's."

"Raleigh," said Lady Herbert, "your opportunity has arrived. As soon as Montague crosses the threshold of that house you can execute your warrant."

"No," smiled Raleigh, "the time for that has not yet arrived. That arrest shall take place at Compton House."

"Yes," said Dudley, "we must take the traitor with all his co-conspirators."

"And you say this visit is to take place to-morrow night," said Lomew.

"Yes, at the hour of eight."

"Good! Proceed, Master Rodney."

"On the following night, the final meeting of the conspirators, previous to putting things in order, is to be held."

"Do you mean that at this meeting every plotter will take his instructions?"

"Exactly."

"And," said Dudley, somewhat excitedly, for a brilliant idea had suddenly entered his head, "do all these conspirators enter and leave the house without disguise?"

"No! Montague and the dastardly plotters associated with him are too fearful of the block to venture across the threshold of that house undisguised. Every man is disguised with a black mask, and he is likewise closely muffled, so that even his very figure is concealed. More than that—each man has about his neck a gold chain, to which is attached a noble. Merlin's cousin saw one of these coins before they were given out."

"Then they were prepared by Montague?" said Raleigh.

"Precisely; and this cousin explained to Merlin what was marked upon them. It is like this."

And Master Rodney took up a cinder, and marked on the wall this sign—

T.

D. ┌ E.

"What does that mean?" asked Dudley.

"I have heard it said that you are skilled in the decipering of mysterious signs, Master Raleigh," said the chemist.

Raleigh made no reply.

He was completely lost in thought.

Suddenly he said—

"By heaven! I believe that I have hit it. This, you see, is half a square. Good. The square would mean that the kingdom is undivided, while the half-square must mean that the kingdom is taken away from the queen and divided among the plotters."

"A very reasonable explanation," cried Master Rodney.

The others agreed.

"And I think," said Dudley, "that I have made out the meaning of the letters."

"I think I have also," said Raleigh. "Let me whisper in your ear, and you will see whether what I think corresponds with your own solution."

He whispered something to our hero.

"Yes," replied Dudley, "it is exactly my own solution! 'D. T. E.' means, 'Death to Elizabeth.'"

"You said that Merlin learned the names of two of the noblemen," said Raleigh.

"Yes, that came out quite accidentally, and, Merlin tells me, was immediately and sternly corrected by a gentleman whose voice he fancied he had heard before. Those names were Lord Bushby and Lord Delasart."

Raleigh started, and stared hard at Lady Herbert.

She understood the look, for she said, in low tones—

"I well know them, but I never had the least suspicion of either."

"Neither had I," said Raleigh, gravely. "To all appearance they were most devoted servants to her majesty. In this matter, Dudley and I will act, and at present let no word of this be said to anyone."

Silence, it was agreed, was absolutely necessary.

"In the first place," said Dudley, "we must attend to Barcally; for it is of the utmost importance that these papers pass to us. By heaven! if all goes well, the whole country will be astonished."

"At the way the villains are crushed?" said Lomew, a glitter of satisfaction in his eyes.

"Yes. But let us draw up our plans in reference to Barcally at once. To-morrow night the visit takes place, therefore no time is to be lost," said Dudley. "My dear mother, I charge you to convey all the news, together with my undying love, to Madeline."

"That shall be done, Dudley; but will you not hasten to let the queen be informed respecting the recovered treasure?"

"All in good time, sweet mother—all in good time. I must first attend to matters of far greater importance, for upon the success of Raleigh's schemes and mine depend the life of a queen and the peace and welfare of a nation!"

CHAPTER XIX.

WHEREIN OUR READERS ARE ONCE AGAIN CONDUCTED TO OLD LONDON BRIDGE—OF WHAT TRANSPIRED IN THE LAWYER'S "OFFICE"—HOW BARCALLY LOSES HIS LIFE, AND HOW THE IMPORTANT PAPERS PASS INTO OUR HERO'S POSSESSION.

ON the City side of Old London Bridge, among half-a-dozen other houses, was the residence of Septimus Grimley, an old lawyer.

It was the night following the meetings at the Tower, and eight of the clock.

Old Grimley was at his desk in the little apartment where he transacted his business.

There was one window in this apartment, and it reached from the floor almost to the ceiling.

It opened in the centre, like folding doors.

This was over a balcony, and that balcony was exactly over the last arch, and consequently over the river.

The apartment was illuminated with a battered ship's lantern, which was suspended from one of the beams across the ceiling.

No sooner had eight o'clock struck than Grimley started up and commenced to pace the apartment with quick uneven strides.

He was evidently anxious.

"I am always punctual to the minute," he muttered, "but other people are not. Yet they are certain to be here."

Ten minutes after eight one low knock was heard below.

At once the lawyer descended the stairs, opened the street-door, and admitted Barcally, chief warder now, for he had "removed" Champion, and been appointed in his place.

He entered the apartment, and the lawyer motioned him to take a seat.

Barcally at once turned and looked fixedly into his face.

"Be careful," he said. "I am a man to order, not to be ordered. So, I say again, be careful, or maybe I will force one of those rolls of parchment down your throat."

"I am sure I have done nothing to deserve so gross an insult," murmured Grimley. "This comes of consenting to do a man a favour."

"What! did you consent to do the favour, as you call it, in my behalf?" demanded Barcally.

"Well, it is in your behalf as well as Montague's."

"For whom you have transacted business for many years."

"How do you know that I have?"

"I did not know it until this moment," grinned Barcally; "but you have now as much as acknowledged that you have done business with Montague for years. Well, he will prove as big a turncoat to you as he has to me—mark that!"

"He might—he might!" replied the lawyer, as he slowly rubbed his thin beardless face; "but if he does—"

"Well, what then?"

"I could crush him if I liked."

"Pooh! Many have said that, but he has not been crushed yet. That is, of course, in consequence of the money he has."

"And of which you hope to take a goodly share this night."

"Yes, and it's the last I shall have to do with Montague."

"You, of course, have the papers?"

"Yes. Has Montague sent you the money?"

For the first time Grimley smiled.

"You might as well ask whether St. Paul's has moved westward," he said. "No; the money he will bring with him. I trust he will not be long, for I have other business to attend to, and— Ha! a knock. I pray you open the door, Master Barcally."

"Open it yourself!" growled the warder.

The lawyer looked carefully round, as if to be sure there was nothing that Barcally was likely to take a fancy to, and then he descended the stairs; but long before he reached the door another thundering, impatient knock was heard.

On the door being opened, Montague strode in, giving vent as he did so to a volley of imprecations.

He was hastily followed up the stairs by the lawyer.

"Well," said Montague, as he strode into the apartment, his gilt spurs ringing loudly on the uncarpeted floor, "and so I behold you once again, Barcally?"

"You do," was the surly reply; "and I behold you."

"Is there much alteration in me, think you?"

"There is," replied Barcally, sarcastically.

"Ah! and what is the alteration?"

"You have aged ten years since you lost your treasure."

Montague frowned.

"And I don't think," added Barcally, "that the beautiful Lady Margaret would now think you were the handsome man you used to be."

"Hound! I have a mind to slash your face with a whip," roared Montague.

"Attempt it!" said Barcally, quietly, "and if I don't silence you for ever—"

"Gentlemen—gentlemen," pleaded the alarmed lawyer, "consider what you are here for. Surely a lawyer's office is no place to quarrel!"

"I should have thought it the very place," replied Montague. "However, it is not my intention to quarrel, but to make terms with the thief we see before us."

"Thief!" repeated Barcally.

"Yes, thief; for what else can a man be called who rifles a gentleman's bag? Don't attempt to deny that that is how you got possession of those papers."

"No, I will not attempt to deny it."

"Nor will you, I suppose, deny that you have read them?"

"Yes, I can deny that. I did read the signature, it is true, but that is all. The writing is of so peculiar a description that I was unable to decipher it."

"Let me look at it," said Grimley.

"I would see you quartered first," was Barcally's reply.

From beneath his cloak Montague brought a large bag of money.

This he placed before the lawyer, saying—

"Count it."

Grimley opened the bag and carefully counted the contents.

Looking up, he said—

"One thousand exactly."

"Yes; and now let this man hand you the papers."

"Get farther away first," said Barcally.

Montague fixed a fierce look upon the warder, but the look had no terrors for Barcally, who added—

"If you don't, I will not put them down."

Montague drew farther back, and then Barcally brought out the documents he had stolen from the bag, and placed them on the lawyer's table.

"Put the money beside that," he said, "and then take your hands away."

"But—but I'll hand the money over all right. You believe that, don't you?"

"No."

Grimley sighed, and placed his hands beneath the table.

Then Barcally picked up the bag of money, and thrust it beneath his cloak.

"Have you any more to say to this man?" asked the lawyer of Montague.

"No."

"You may go, friend Barcally," said Grimley, in bitter tones.

"Friend Barcally will stay as long as he thinks proper," replied the warder, as he reseated himself.

Grimley looked hard at him for a few moments, then his eyes wandered to Montague, as if in search of instructions.

"Let him stay by all means," laughed Montague. "No doubt he would like to learn what is about to pass between us. But he will not have the opportunity."

"No," replied Grimley; "two's company and three none."

"That is not my meaning," continued Montague. "My meaning is this—that my arrangement with you, Master Grimley, must fall through."

"What! do you not intend to go through the documents?"

"Not now. It was my intention to take them with me and peruse them—if I found I had not time to do so here; but as I have for the next few hours to mix in strange company, I shall leave the papers in your hands."

"Very good," replied Grimley, his heart beating with delight, for he longed to read these most important papers, about which he had heard so much.

If, as he had understood, the documents contained conclusive evidence against Montague, written by the hand of his—at one time—principal accomplice, what a power he would wield over the villain!

"Strange company, eh?" he said; "then I would not trust them about my person. One never knows," he added, looking straight at Barcally, "into whose hands these things might fall."

"They can fall into no worse hands than the hands of a knavish lawyer," snarled Barcally.

"I trust you entirely, Grimley," said Montague.

"You will have no cause to repent doing so. I have always acted honestly towards you."

"And," continued Montague, "I repeat I shall leave the documents in your hands. The safest way would be to burn them, and I should do so but that they contain several names which I intend to take down, my object being to permanently remove the owners of those names. Any individual," he added slowly, and with significant deliberation, "whom I consider dangerous, I remove from my path, by fair means or by foul."

"If by that you mean me to take the hint," said Barcally, "let me tell you that I care not that for you."

And he defiantly snapped his horny fingers.

"So many a man has said," smiled Montague, "and many a woman, too. But nevertheless, their hour of doom has come."

"Depend upon it, Master Montague," said Barcally, "you will be in my power long ere you can move to get me in yours. I shall be your gaoler one of these days, and you will then have bitter cause to regret what has passed. I never forgive an injury."

"What injury has Master Montague inflicted upon you?" queried the lawyer.

"He has slighted me, scorned me, and he has treated with disdain all the numerous favours he has received at my hands."

"You were always paid for what you did," hissed Montague, "and now you are even paid for robbing me. What more do you want?"

"No more at present."

"Grimley," said Montague, "forget not my instructions. I will visit you again in three days. In the meantime, I consider the documents as safe in your hands as if in my own house."

"Rely upon me," replied the lawyer, rising and placing the documents in a large iron box, which he locked, and the key of which he placed in his pocket.

"Farewell, then," said Montague. "I can let myself out."

"Farewell," snarled Barcally, "until you are conducted through Traitor's Gate!"

Montague turned swiftly, hesitated, and then, with a low laugh, strode out of the apartment and descended the stairs.

A few moments more, and the door had closed upon him with a bang.

Barcally rose, and made as if to leave the apartment.

But, a sudden thought striking him, he reseated himself, placed the bag of money on the floor, opened it, and proceeded to finger the contents.

His movements were watched with curiosity and no small amount of agitation by Grimley.

Suspicious at first, he got gradually more nervous as Barcally, without giving utterance to a word, bent over and let the gold fall from his hand in a shower, only to be picked up and let fall again.

It presently struck him that Barcally, for some reason, was doing this to gain time.

Five minutes passed, and then the warder tied up the bag, and replaced it beneath his cloak.

Then he walked straight to the door, the lawyer's keen eyes watching his movements as a cat watches a mouse.

The door reached, Barcally suddenly turned.

The lawyer was prepared for this, for at the same instant he started up, and Barcally saw that he held in his hand a long rusty dagger.

A low chuckle left Barcally's lips.

"What!" he said, "do you apprehend treachery?"

"I am prepared for it," was the reply.

"Lawyer Grimley, you are a fool!" hissed Barcally, and suddenly dropping the bag, he snatched a pair of pistols from his belt, where beneath his cloak he had hitherto managed to conceal them, and pointed them full at the lawyer.

"Of what use," he asked, "is that rusty blade, when these are in the way?"

The lawyer was instantly cowed.

"I had always suspected that you were a murderer," he said. "But what is the meaning of this?"

"The meaning! Have you not sense enough to understand that it is my intention to take with me, not only the money, but that roll of papers?"

"Never! I would die sooner than part with them!" screamed Grimley, turning ashy-pale.

"Die!" sneered Barcally; "what then? I have killed many a better man than you. Die! Yes, you will die, as sure as I stand here, if you do not unlock that box and hand me over those papers."

"No, no! Let us argue the matter."

"Let you gain time, you mean? No, the papers! Quick! or I send your soul to perdition!"

The lawyer hesitated.

He looked helplessly into the brutal face of the man before him, and there read "Murder."

Great drops of perspiration stood on the old man's face, while his attenuated limbs shook as with the ague.

"What will Montague think of me?" he groaned.

"A lot you care what he thinks of you," laughed Barcally. "Quick! I will give you no longer than one minute in which to decide."

"Heaven help me!" groaned the terrified old man. "I suppose I must comply with your demand."

"I am determined to have revenge on Montague," cried the warder, "and these papers will enable me to have a speedy one."

Grimley staggered rather than walked to the iron box, opened it, and brought out the papers, which he held towards Barcally, but the warder saw that he still had the dagger in his hand.

"Throw the papers over," he said, "for I would not trust you on any consideration."

Grimley threw the documents, which were dexterously caught by Barcally, who said—

"Now we can part, Master Grimley, and of course you will at once inform Montague of what has taken place. But you need not fancy that I shall return to the Tower. No, with this money I can afford to wait—to wait until I— Ha! what is this?"

The door was burst suddenly open, and Barcally found himself grasped by a hand of steel.

That hand was Dudley Herbert's, and behind him was Walter Raleigh!

The two had easily effected an entrance into the house.

At first they had thought of proceeding to the next house, and entering the lawyer's by way of the roof.

That, supposing the proprietor had consented to their using his premises, would have been highly dangerous.

It was while they were considering, that Raleigh pushed the lawyer's door.

To his astonishment it flew open.

"'WHAT DOES THAT MEAN?' ASKED DUDLEY."

The reason was that though Montague had pulled it after him with a crash, it had not closed.

So Dudley and Raleigh had crept up the stairs, and had overheard the latter part of the conversation between Grimley and the warder.

Barcally, exerting all his strength, and giving utterance to a wild yell, broke away from Dudley's grasp, and springing forward, turned and pointed a pistol at our hero's head.

But Raleigh was too quick.

Suddenly dashing forward, he snatched the pistol from his hand, and before he could prevent it, pulled the other from his belt.

"Master Raleigh!" gasped Barcally, thunder-stricken to behold the gallant young courtier and soldier.

The next instant he recognised Dudley.

But now he gave utterance to no word.

The look of savage hate which rested on his features was sufficient indication of what was passing in his mind.

And on this scene the old lawyer looked like one spellbound.

He knew not Dudley, but he recognised Raleigh, and a feeling of fear seized upon him.

What had brought those two there? he wondered.

Had they got to know that Montague would be there, and had Raleigh come to arrest him?

More than likely, he thought; and he thought also it was a good thing he was gone, as Raleigh might have been inclined to arrest him (Grimley) as an accessory.

He resolved to ask no questions, but to await the course of events.

"Again, then, Master Barcally," said Dudley, "we meet, and this time under very different circumstances. What am I here for? Have you not asked yourself? No doubt, but you cannot imagine. I will tell you. We are here, first of all, for those papers."

And he stepped forward as if he would snatch them from the villain's hand.

But like lightning, Barcally started back and plucked his sword from its sheath.

"If you value your life, stand back!" he cried. "By heaven! you take not these papers from me."

Dudley drew his blade.

"You had better pass those papers over," he said, sternly.

"Never!" replied Barcally, through his clenched teeth. "I will die rather."

"Raleigh," said Dudley, "I desire that you will not interfere in this. I once told this wretch—this monster, who gloated over my sufferings in the vaults of yon gloomy Tower, that a day of reckoning between us would come. It has come. And here I will reckon with him—though, heaven knows, it is against my grain to cross swords with such carrion!"

"I will not interfere," replied Raleigh, folding his arms across his breast.

"But, gentlemen — gentlemen," protested old Grimley, "you surely would not shed blood in the office of a lawyer?"

"Why, you wretched old villain!" replied Raleigh; "the lawyer would have shed blood in his own office, and quickly, too, had he had the chance. Be silent, sirrah!"

Barcally was in possession of a ponderous frame compared with our hero's, and he considered that his success was certain, because he determined to bring all his brute force into action.

It never struck him that this was of no use when dealing with one who had a thorough knowledge and command of the sword.

The fight was commenced, and the lawyer stood in a semi-crouching attitude, watching the play of the swords as the gleaming blades went hither and thither like flashes of lightning.

Suddenly Barcally uttered a short, sharp cry, and at the same instant he dropped the roll, upon which Dudley pounced with the rapidity of an eagle.

He snatched up the papers and threw them to Raleigh.

"Mine!" whispered Grimley, hastening forward. "Mine—mine!" and he stretched forth his bony hands.

"Away, lest a Tower dungeon crush out all your hopes in this world," cried Raleigh. "Come not near me, as you value your safety."

Thereupon, trembling like an aspen, Grimley slunk back.

Meanwhile the fight had been resumed with increased vigour.

But it was not for long.

Barcally had been sorely wounded.

From the wound the blood was swiftly flowing, and he felt himself momentarily becoming weaker and weaker.

But his fury knew no bounds.

He now resembled a raging beast more than a human being.

Dudley watched his opportunity.

It came presently.

Barcally raised his sword high over his head, his intention being to cut our hero down.

Thus unguarded, he rushed to his fate, for in another moment Dudley's blade passed through his chest.

Dropping his sword, and yet giving utterance to no cry, Barcally staggered back.

"Stop him—stop him," yelled the lawyer.

Raleigh rushed forward to do so, but it was too late.

Barcally went with a mighty crash through the window and staggered to the balcony.

The frail wooden structure—built more for ornament than use—gave way, and he fell into the black river.

The strong current hurled him out of sight as swiftly as if he had been but a straw.

Silence fell upon the three—a silence of some few moments, during which Raleigh and Dudley looked out of the window.

But they saw nothing more of Barcally.

Presently they turned.

There was old Grimley, still trembling, against the wall.

"He's dead, eh? He's dead!" he whispered.

"Yes, he's dead at last!" replied Dudley. "But for us, it would have been your life instead of his."

"True. But—but look at the great damage, gentlemen—look at the expense of restoring the balcony and the window!"

"Why, you wretched scarecrow," said Raleigh, snatching up the bag of money and almost hurling it at Grimley's head, "here is more than enough to pay for your broken panes. No doubt 'tis blood money. Take it, then."

"But the papers—the papers?"

"Are mine," replied Dudley.

"But what will Montague say?"

"He will say that you are a bigger knave than he thought you. He will vow that you have sold them to his enemies."

"Oh, heaven," groaned Grimley,

"I must disappear for a time, or I shall fall a victim to Montague's fury."

"Come, Raleigh," said Dudley, "let us depart."

Without another word both left the house.

Reaching the steps, they paused.

"I," said Raleigh, "as you well know, am bound for Whitehall, so as to make all arrangements for to-morrow night. You will resume the dean's disguise and go to the Tower, where I wish you every success in the daring project you have formed."

The friends shook hands and parted

CHAPTER XX.

TELLS OF THE PRIVATE INTERVIEW BETWEEN QUEEN ELIZABETH AND DUDLEY—OF THE PARDON—OF THE PLAN, AND OF THE ARREST OF LORDS DELASART AND BUSHBY.

It was just past ten of the clock when Dudley reached the Tower.

Phillis had been informed by Lomew that the dean would again visit him, and so when our hero arrived he was admitted without difficulty.

As Dudley passed in, the guard was being changed, and he heard Barcally's name being called in every direction.

He smiled grimly as he thought that the wretch would never again answer to his name in this world.

Reaching Lomew's apartments, he found there the headsman and Quicksilver.

The latter welcomed Dudley with great warmth, and protested that amid all the new splendours which surrounded him, he had never ceased to think of him.

"Nor I of you, my little friend," said Dudley. "Nor have I forgotten the present I once promised you, and which I will duly hand over. What the present is I will not now tell you, but I feel sure that it will give you unbounded delight."

"Whatever comes from you will certainly give me delight."

"But I will tell you this, Quicksilver—that your greatest enemy within this Tower is no more."

"What—Barcally! Is he dead?"

"Yes. He fought with me and I slew him."

"Thank heaven! he was my only enemy. The other men within this Tower understand me. They know that my tricks and pranks—which I have in vain tried to check myself of—"

So seriously did he say this, that both Dudley and Lomew burst into laughter.

"Yes," continued the minstrel courtier, "I have tried to break myself of them, but up to the present it has been impossible. But as I said, the men now understand me, and always greet me with kindly words. So the wretch is no more! I am thankful—not only for myself, but for Lomew."

"Yes," said Lomew, "the man was a greater bane to me than anyone really knows. But now, Dudley, let Quicksilver know what you require at his hands."

"Quicksilver," said Dudley, after

a few moments' consideration, "I want you to do me a favour."

"Command me."

"Lomew has told you all about the discovery of the treasure?"

"He has—and I am overjoyed. I have frequently heard the queen speak of it."

"Well, I want you to break the news to her."

"Ah!"

"But more than this, Quicksilver, I want you to get her majesty to grant me a strictly private interview."

Quicksilver fairly jumped off his stool.

"An interview!" he cried. "Strictly private! I dare not ask such a thing."

"You can, Quicksilver," Lomew said; "and if you do so in your own way you will be successful. Her majesty is too fond of you to be displeased; also, there is no time like the present, since not a single courtier is within the Tower."

"Well," said Quicksilver, "I will do as you ask, though— But I will not anticipate. I will plunge boldly into the matter at once. What shall I say?"

"You will first speak of the money, and say that it is all ready to be laid at her majesty's feet."

"All of it?"

"Every piece."

"Good."

"And then you will speak of me, Quicksilver, and say that I have something of the utmost importance to lay before her majesty—something which concerns not only herself, but her people and her kingdom."

"I will go at once," said Quicksilver. "When I say what you have told me, methinks her majesty will command your immediate attendance."

He departed without further delay, and we shall follow him to the queen's apartments.

To the principal apartment of the suite, Quicksilver made his way.

Before this chamber was a luxuriously appointed lobby, in which were the usher and several of the guard.

But it was never necessary to announce Quicksilver.

He enjoyed a privilege denied to even the principal officers of State, and that privilege was, the entering into the queen's presence unannounced.

Elizabeth was reclining on an elaborate ottoman, surrounded by her maids, one of the most beautiful of whom was the Lady Madeline.

Lovely indeed did the maiden look, bedecked with the splendid apparel and the bright gems to which her high birth entitled her.

But yet, despite her entrancing beauty, she was very pale.

Her eyes, too, told the tale of sleepless nights and of hours spent in weeping.

One voice, and one voice only, was heard in that chamber.

It was a fine sonorous voice, and every word was loud and distinct.

The owner was William Shakespeare, and he was engaged in the recital of one of his pieces.

Just behind him stood his bosom friend, Edward Alleyn.

So deeply interested were Elizabeth and her maids in the delivery of the lines, that they did not even look up as the massive curtains across the arched doorway were divided.

Quicksilver remained beside the door until Shakespeare had finished, and handed his roll of manuscript to Alleyn.

Elizabeth had been deeply touched

by some of the beautiful lines, and she had become lost in thought.

Thus, for some few moments, she sat, her eyes fixed upon the heavy rug at her feet.

But suddenly she started up.

"Ah," she said, with a light laugh, "why, in thought I was one of the very characters whom you have thus skilfully placed before us. Take this, Will Shakespeare, as some slight token of our high appreciation of your talents."

So saying, she took from her finger a beautiful diamond ring, and presented it to the poet.

After some little conversation with Shakespeare and his friend, the queen rose.

Then Quicksilver moved rapidly forward.

"Thou truant," said Elizabeth. "Is it thus you desert your queen?"

"I crave your majesty's pardon," said Quicksilver, "and I entreat of you to grant me one moment."

"What! a pardon and a favour at the same time."

"Your majesty, I pray you let me utter but a few words where they may not be overheard."

Elizabeth looked hard into the little face, laughed lightly, and said—

"My ladies, our minstrel wants to give us the latest piece of scandal he has picked up. I pray you to withdraw, that I may catch the spirit of the jest."

With a smile, the ladies went back several paces.

"Most gracious madam," whispered Quicksilver, "I am charged with a message to you."

"A message!"

"Yes, madam; and one of the highest importance."

"Indeed! And who is the daring individual who charges you to deliver a message to us?"

"A most deeply injured person."

"Humph! Is that your opinion, or whose?"

"It is my opinion, madam, as well as the opinion of others. But, I pray you, hear me out!"

"I never before saw you so earnest. But I will hear. Proceed."

"The person to whom I refer is within the Tower."

"Ah, a prisoner! I see. Your sympathy is ever with the prisoners."

"The person of whom I speak, your majesty, is not a prisoner."

"Then who is he? What is his name?"

"Dudley Herbert."

The queen half started from her seat.

A deep frown rested for a few moments upon her brow.

Quicksilver hastened to proceed—

"Gracious madam, Dudley Herbert, since his escape from this fortress, has been untiring in his efforts to recover the vast treasure that was gathered by Montague."

"Or his double?"

"No, madam, there is no double, as you may find ere long; and Dudley Herbert has been successful."

"Ah!" cried Elizabeth, her face flushed with joy. "Successful, say you? What! would you tell me that he has recovered the whole of the treasure?"

"Every crown."

"This is news indeed. And this treasure is within the Tower?"

"No, gracious queen. But it is not far away."

"I think I understand. Master Herbert wishes to purchase his pardon with this money?"

"No, gracious madam—no. The treasure is yours, and you have but to name the place where it is to be taken to, and it will be done."

"Proceed."

"Dudley Herbert entreats you to grant him an audience of a strictly private character."

"Quicksilver, you have abused our confidence. You have violated the patronage we extended to you."

"No," murmured Quicksilver, his little hands fidgeting nervously together, for the queen's eyes were now looking him through and through.

"Then why did you consent to carry this message to me?"

"Madam, Dudley Herbert is my dear friend. And you will not regret granting him this audience, for what he nas to tell you concerns not only yourself, but your people and your kingdom."

At these words the queen started, and turned somewhat pale.

Lapsing into thought for some few seconds, she presently said—

"I will see him, and alone. But listen, Quicksilver. It is not only your entreaties which have caused me to grant this interview—no, it is also the sufferings of yonder poor girl."

"The Lady Madeline?"

"Yes. It is in my power to cause an anxious heart to palpitate with joy, for I well know the love she has for Master Dudley. She shall see him first."

"Noble queen!" murmured Quicksilver, tears of gladness starting into his eyes.

"I will see Master Herbert in the conference-room," went on Elizabeth, "and thither you will conduct him by the private staircase. When you have done that, tell him to wait. But say nothing of the Lady Madeline."

Quicksilver bowed low, kissed the royal hand, and left the chamber.

* * * *

The joyful intelligence, that the queen had consented to the interview, was hurriedly conveyed to Dudley, who was so agitated that he could scarcely contain himself.

Lomew breathed a sigh of relief.

Either one of two things he had been waiting for.

Consent to the interview, or immediate arrest and a Tower dungeon.

"May heaven grant you fortune," he said, as he pressed our hero's hand.

Dudley was too full of emotion for words.

Quicksilver took him by the hand and led him onward.

The private staircase was quickly reached and ascended, and Dudley found himself in the conference-room.

"Wait here, Dudley," said Quicksilver. "Her majesty will be but a short time."

"Thank you, Quicksilver," faltered our hero.

Quicksilver now vanished, and Dudley was alone.

Presently a door was softly opened, and he caught sight of a female figure through the opening in the curtains.

These in another moment were drawn aside, and there entered—not, as he expected, the queen, but Madeline.

She had no more idea that Dudley was there than he had that she would enter the chamber; and therefore it is not to be wondered at that for some moments each stood spellbound.

At last Dudley started forward with outstretched arms.

"What is this?" he cried. "Not the Queen of England? No, it is my queen!"

"Dudley, Dudley!" sobbed Madeline, as, in a transport of joy, she threw herself into her lover's arms, "how has this come about?"

"I am as ignorant as you, dearest," replied our hero. "I came here by her majesty's commands."

"And so did I. I was told that her majesty would speak with me privately. Dudley, the queen has pardoned you—I feel sure of it. Tell me that I am correct."

"I would that I could; but I am as yet unable to say so."

"And yet, heaven knows, you are as loyal a subject as am I myself," sobbed Madeline.

"As loyal?" repeated Dudley, proudly. "Yes, in her majesty's service I am ready at any moment to lay down my life."

"Well said," exclaimed a well-known voice; "well said! I am glad I heard such words from you, Dudley Herbert. Your pardon is granted."

At the head of the private stairs stood Elizabeth.

Dudley at once sprang towards her, and falling on one knee, kissed the jewelled hand extended to him.

"Rise," said the queen, whose face was unusually pale—"rise; for anxious as I am to learn what I am led to expect is astounding news, yet I will not further interrupt the meeting of lovers who have so long been separated. At the expiration of ten minutes I shall return: and you, Madeline, by that time, will have joined the ladies."

So saying, she abruptly turned, and passed down the stairs.

The lovers determined to make the best use of the ten minutes granted to them. They had much to say to each other.

When Madeline passed from the conference-chamber, she joined her companions with a look of joy that they had never seen before.

Her lover was pardoned! More, it was likely that the task he was about to undertake—and respecting which he enjoined her to preserve the strictest silence—might be the means of restoring to him all those rights and privileges severed from the family by his father's dreadful death.

Immediately after Madeline's departure, Elizabeth once more made her appearance.

"Let no time be lost in ceremonies," she said, hastily, "but at once tell me all."

"With respect to the treasure, gracious madam—"

"Wait," interrupted Elizabeth; "the treasure is of no importance compared with what else you have to say to me. Tell me the head of it at once."

"Treason, your majesty."

"Treason!" repeated Elizabeth, slowly, and in hushed tones. "And who is the principal in this?"

"Montague, your majesty."

"Or his double?"

"Gracious madam, dispel that idea from your mind. There is no double."

"You are right; there is not. I am well aware of it. Montague, eh? By heaven! you and he are deadly enemies. Either Montague will destroy you, or you will destroy him."

"Your majesty, I will tell you the whole story, which was told me by Master Rodney."

"Master Rodney! Then why did not he come direct to me?"

"You shall hear, gracious madam! And when I have told you the story, I will submit my plans for the capture of the traitors."

"Proceed; for, by heaven! I can scarce contain myself."

Dudley went minutely through the story, Elizabeth slowly pacing the apartment, but uttering not a sentence until the whole tale had been told, and the plan Dudley had in his mind had been placed before her.

Then she said—

"Dudley Herbert, you are brave and shrewd, though at times over hasty. Your plan is daring and bold; but, nevertheless, it is an excellent one, which, if worked out well, must prove successful. Does Raleigh know aught of your scheme?"

"As yet, your majesty, nothing."

"Perhaps it is as well he did not, for assuredly he would have persuaded you against such a thing, and thus an excellent idea would have been lost. You will now, of course, tell him all. But, beware! See that it reaches no one else. And this piece of paper? What is the meaning of this half-square?"

Dudley gave her Raleigh's solution.

"He has hit it," replied Elizabeth. "And the letters?"

"Death to Elizabeth?"

The queen turned ashy pale, but she neither started nor trembled.

With the greatest deliberation she repeated the words—

"'Death to Elizabeth.' Death to the woman who, night and day, thinks of naught but of the welfare of her country. What is your opinion of it?"

"Your majesty," replied Dudley, "there are no words in the English tongue capable of expressing my loathing of such fiends."

"May heaven spare me until these traitors have been paid their due. And there is no telling how many noblemen are mixed up in this?"

"At present, no, your majesty."

"Ah, we shall soon learn. Dudley Herbert, you are a faithful servant, and I will not forget you. Wait here. Presently a sealed packet shall be handed to you. It will contain warrants for the arrest and detention in their own houses of the two lords you have named. And the whole of the men Raleigh selects must be from Whitehall. When he has selected them, he will take them to the chapel, and there they shall be sworn to secrecy. A false step, and the whole thing will fall to the ground."

So saying, the queen descended the staircase.

No one would have thought that in defiance of the smile with which she greeted her maids as she passed through them, she was repeating the words—

"Death to Elizabeth—death to Elizabeth!"

* * * *

Again has the scene changed.

This time we find ourselves in the neighbourhood of Bloomsbury.

It was about half-past eight, and Lord Delasart sat in an easy chair in the study of his town house, a very fine residence at the edge of Southampton Fields.

Apparently he was intent on the perusal of a learned work of some kind.

But such was not the case.

The book was a manuscript one, and it contained a list of every province in the kingdom, with the names, in cipher— to which Montague held the key—of the individuals who would take the command of certain numbers of men as soon as the call to arms was made.

Presently a servant knocked upon the door, and being told to enter, announced—

"Lord Bushby."

"Lord Bushby!" repeated Delasart. Then he thought, "What brings him here?"

Aloud he said—

"Admit him at once."

Presently Lord Bushby strode into the room.

There was a striking contrast between these men, for whereas Bushby was very young, Delasart was old.

Having saluted and shaken hands with each other, Delasart said—

"You mentioned that you were behind time. Thus it would appear as if we had made an appointment."

"And you did make an appointment."

"I? Never!"

Lord Bushby looked astounded.

"You made no appointment to see me here, my lord?" he said. "You astonish me!"

"I did not make any appointment, though you are very welcome. There is a mistake somewhere."

"I, this afternoon, received a letter, or rather, a note. Here it is. Behold. It says, 'Call and confer with Lord ——, at Bloomsbury, this evening.'"

"Humph! And the handwriting? Why, 'tis certainly Montague's."

"To be sure it is. Of that there can be no doubt."

"But hold, Lord Fitzstephen is staying at the inn."

"Indeed!"

"Yes, and it is a thousand chances to one that he was meant. As you are aware, not even the initials of our names are used. Yes, Lord Fitzstephen is unquestionably the one meant. But no matter, Bushby: now that you are here we will crack a bottle together."

Bushby bowed, saying—

"And I trust your lordship will do me the honour of allowing me one peep at your beautiful daughter, the peerless Jane?"

"Certainly! She will be very pleased, Bushby. You shall see her presently. But let us talk for a few moments respecting the all-important events to take place on the morrow. Never was a plot so well thought out."

"Never. Montague has the brains of a dozen clever men."

"I would wager my head, my lord," whispered Delasart, in exultant tones, "that success is certain."

"There cannot be a doubt of it. The only thing is, of course, the money."

"Yes—the money. But I am so sure of success—so certain of becoming a great man before long—that I am willing to place half my fortune in Montague's hands, feeling confident that not a crown will be used without we are all consulted. And I have no doubt the others will be inclined to do likewise."

"As you well know, I am not worth a large sum. But half what I have shall be placed to swell the total."

"Good! And now— But list! Another knock. Enter," he added.

The door was opened, the curtains were snatched aside, and there appeared—not the servant, but the well-known face of Walter Raleigh!

Yes, Raleigh, sword in hand.

"Great heaven!" gasped Delasart, "what means this?"

"It means," replied Raleigh, "that you are my prisoners. Lords Delasart and Bushby, you are both charged with high treason, and, in the name of the queen, I arrest you."

Snatching the warrant from his doublet, Raleigh threw it upon the table.

As he did so, he was joined by a handsome young man, attired, like himself, as an officer of the queen's guard.

That person was the hero of this romance—Dudley Herbert.

"I am sure," continued Raleigh, "that you are both possessed of too much sense to attempt resistance, though I may add that the house is filled with the queen's troops."

"All is lost!" faltered Delasart.

"May heaven forgive us—for the queen will not," added Bushby.

"They are the truest words you ever spoke," said Dudley, sternly.

"And the house is filled with the queen's troops," said Delasart. "You mean, I suppose, that the house is surrounded?"

"Not at all. The house is filled. For certain reasons not a man was left without the building."

"Whither shall we be taken?" asked Bushby.

"You will not be taken hence at present," replied Dudley; "you will be confined to this house."

"For what reason?"

"At present we cannot answer you."

"Then I shall be able to communicate with my daughter?" queried Delasart.

"No," replied Dudley. "All within the house, except your lordships, will be taken to another house, and there confined."

"A counterplot!" cried Delasart.

"Yes," said Raleigh, "a counterplot."

"What will be the result?"

"Who shall say? But no doubt the axe will answer the question."

"I am thinking only of my daughter," moaned Lord Delasart. "Raleigh, let me appeal to you."

"My lord," replied Raleigh, coldly, "I am compelled to obey the queen's instructions."

"That I should not be allowed to communicate with my daughter?"

"Her instructions were that you should not be allowed to communicate with any person."

Raleigh was interrupted by a series of wild, passionate cries in a woman's voice; there were also heard men's voices.

It was thus evident that the female was endeavouring to force her way through the soldiers.

"'Tis Jane!" cried Delasart; "'tis my daughter."

"Since she is here, Dudley," said Raleigh, "we will not thrust her back."

"No," replied Dudley. "But this interview must be the last."

"Let her pass," cried Raleigh.

Another instant, and the daughter, a beautiful girl of some seventeen summers, bounded into the chamber.

Rushing with outstretched arms to her father, she was clasped to his breast.

"Father! father!" she cried, "what means this? What have you done—what crime have you committed?"

"Hush! hush! Be silent, my child, lest they separate us at once."

"Separate us! For what? Heaven, what can this mean? The house is filled with armed men. I charge you, in my dead mother's name, to tell me—what means this?"

In spite of this entreaty, her father was silent.

Suddenly turning to Bushby, she said—

"My lord, will *you* tell me what is the meaning of this?"

Bushby hung his head, but spoke no word.

Then Jane suddenly broke away from her father's embrace, and approached the two officers.

For an instant she looked at the glittering blades, and then raised her eyes.

First, they fell upon Dudley's face,

and she read there an expression of pity.

Next they wandered to Raleigh's face.

Her eyes searched that countenance eagerly. Then she said—

"Sir, you will tell me your name?"

"My name, lady," replied the young officer, "is Walter Raleigh."

"Ah!" cried the girl, with a start, "then I now know what this means. You, my father, are arrested for high treason."

Delasart did not reply.

"And Bushby—are you also charged? You make no reply. Ah! both charged with treason! Both traitors to your queen! Oh, father, father!" she cried, wringing her hands in bitter anguish, "you have been loyal all your life; and now, when England would have blessed you for a long and faithful servant, you will pass through dread Traitor's Gate to a felon's doom.

"But I cannot forget that you are my father; I cannot forget that my duty is to remain by your side—and remain I will."

"I am sorry that we cannot allow you to remain with your father, sweet lady," said Raleigh. "Our orders are strict, and must be carried out to the letter. You must leave this house, with your servants, under an escort."

"Sir! you do not mean to say that you arrest me?"

"No! But for a day or two you will remain at a certain house under charge of the guard."

"And the reason of this?"

"Precautions against rumours."

"Then, my father, I must bid you farewell. But I will plead to the queen for you. I will remind her of your long and faithful service."

"'Twill be useless, my child. Elizabeth never forgives a traitor."

"You own yourself a traitor, then!"

"I do. I have plotted against my queen, and I must suffer for it."

The parting was a most heart-rending one, and glad indeed were Dudley and Raleigh when it was over.

Dudley led the maiden from the chamber, and handed her to her maid.

When he returned he brought with him a tall, thin, elderly man named Gray, an individual well known at Court as a first-class costumier and designer.

He was a skilful artist.

"Sit down and sketch these two gentlemen," said Dudley. "My lords," he added, "you will please don your masks, cloaks, and hats."

Bushby had his mask in his pocket, and his hat and cloak being supplied to him, he donned them.

Delasart followed suit.

Then Grayson, in a rapid and skilful fashion, sketched the pair.

The sketches were simple outlines, but they were almost as accurate as if executed by the modern process of photography.

"My lords, you will please hand over the coins you have about your necks," said Dudley, when the sketches had been taken.

The two lords started.

"In heaven's name," said Delasart, "how came you with this knowledge? Who has turned traitor?"

"Not one among you," replied Raleigh; "our information comes from quite another quarter. Having received the coins, my lords, we will require you to hand over all the clothes you are wearing."

"What can this be for?"

"You will hear anon. At present we are powerless to give information.

My Lord Delasart, you can give your footman instructions to provide you and Lord Bushby with other clothing. Your present attire shall be returned before you quit this house for the Tower."

"We are compelled to do all you ask," sighed Delasart. "I pray you send my footman."

Instructions were given to this individual, the change was effected, and the attire the noblemen had been wearing was placed in a bag by the costumier.

The coins and chains, of which Dudley took charge, were found to answer to the description and the sketch Master Rodney had given.

"Death to Elizabeth," was stamped across the representation of her own face.

"And now, my lords," said Raleigh, "I shall be compelled to separate you. Perhaps you, my Lord Delasart, would like to remain in this apartment. I see there is a couch here, and so you can make yourself fairly comfortable."

"Yes, I should like to remain here. My books will serve to while away the time."

"I am sure I wish I could allow them to remain."

"What! will you take away my books?"

"Such are our orders, my lord. All books and all papers are to be taken to the Tower. My Lord Bushby, I pray you follow me."

Bushby spoke not a word.

He at once quitted the room, and it was seen that he was ashy pale, even to the lips.

In less than another ten minutes, the unhappy daughter, with all her servants, left the house.

The two lords were placed under a strong guard, and Dudley and Raleigh, with the remainder of the men, quitted the house and the neighbourhood.

With them was the costumier.

"Shall you have any difficulty?" asked Dudley of him.

"Not the least," was the smiling reply. "I find that I have a remarkably easy task before me."

"I am very glad to hear it. A load is removed from my mind. Raleigh, that note to Lord Bushby was remarkably well done."

"Yes," smiled Raleigh, "it was a clever forgery. But I would not have done it if the queen herself had not commanded me. Dudley, the whole of the traitors are doomed!"

CHAPTER XXI.

OF THE GREAT MEETING OF THE CONSPIRATORS, AND OF THE EXTRAORDINARY DENOUEMENT.

THE all-important night at last.

It was a night for which the double-dyed traitor, Montague, had long waited.

Everything had been prepared for the reception of the conspirators, the grand dining-room having been made to look as imposing as was possible.

It was brilliantly illuminated, but not a streak of that light could be seen from the street.

Every window in the house had been completely darkened.

So, looking from the outside, the place appeared to be deserted.

Only one servant remained in the house, and that was Merlin's cousin, Mary, and she was retained only because she was perfectly familiar with every portion of the vast mansion.

Little did Montague, as he sat at the head of that table in the grand dining-hall, imagine that there was another person besides the servant and himself in the house.

But there was, and that person was Merlin, who was there by instructions from Master Rodney.

On the table in the dining-hall were splendid drinking vessels of gold and of silver, together with choice wines, while here, there, and everywhere were books and plans, as well as plenty of pens, ink, and parchments.

Also around the long table chairs were arranged to the number of twenty.

It was about nine of the clock when the first gentleman arrived.

The signal having been given, the door was opened swiftly by Mary, and closed with the same speed.

No word passed between servant and visitor, who at once went into the dining-hall, where Montague, who had now assumed his cloak, hat, and mask, greeted him with the words—

"How fares?"

"Excellent," was the reply. "I have received further promises of support from the provinces, and I have been successful in spreading disaffection even among the sturdy farmers of Chester. From the chief of them I have promises, not only of large numbers of men, but of money also.

"The whole affair, we may say, has at last come to a head. Montague, we have been friends for many years; would it be too much if I ask what is the line you intend to adopt in the event of the rising proving successful?"

"My lord, I will tell you, but I would tell no one else. It is my intention to claim the presidency."

"As I thought. And you would make a clever ruler, Montague. But what will you do for me?"

"At present I am not able to say. But you shall certainly have no mean post."

"I am satisfied."

"Hist! another arrival."

Another of the conspirators passed into the room, and went direct to his chair.

For a moment he stood beside it, then he placed his hand within his cloak, and brought out the coin attached to the chain, which he held high over his head.

Montague uttered a few words, and the conspirator replaced the coin and dropped into his seat.

The gentlemen now began rapidly to arrive.

One after the other they came, but never by twos or threes, and before an hour had elapsed, every chair was occupied.

Montague now proceeded to call the numbers.

Each gentleman, as his number was called, rose for an instant, and then resumed his seat.

At length, with a few preliminary words, Montague rose from his chair and proceeded to read the latest news from the provinces.

Then followed a discussion, but never once was the name of any conspirator — except Montague — mentioned.

That discussion lasted until the clock had struck the hour of midnight.

Then Montague proceeded to call upon the conspirators—by numbers —for the amounts they were prepared to put towards the fund for the arming of the men.

Fourteen numbers had been called, and then Montague exclaimed—

"Number Fifteen."

Number Fifteen accordingly rose.

"My lord," said Montague, "what are you prepared to place at our disposal?"

"The Tower of London!" was the ringing reply.

Astounded beyond measure, the conspirators leapt to their feet.

"What foolery is this?" Montague said. "Surely this is no time for jesting!"

"I do not jest," replied Number Fifteen. "Behold, traitor—for as such I denounce you."

And the speaker threw off hat and mask.

"Dudley Herbert!" thundered Montague, instantly unsheathing his blade. "Draw, my lords, draw, and cut him down!"

"Touch me who dares," replied Dudley, drawing his sword, and throwing back his cloak. "My costume shows that I am an officer of her majesty's guard. I am here to arrest you, Marcus Montague, and all your companions. Put up your swords, for the house is surrounded by the queen's troops, and Walter Raleigh is in command."

A loud yell of astonishment left the lips of the conspirators.

For a few seconds no one spoke, but at last Montague said—

"Do not alarm yourselves, gentlemen. Be not frightened by what this mad upstart says. Anyone can don the costume of an officer. This person has a grudge against me."

"How came he here in place of Lord D.?" cried several voices. "He was disguised as that gentleman."

"I am unable to say," replied Montague; "but wait—wait! I call upon the fool to produce his warrant. Ah! observe how that has cut him. Gentlemen, if he does not produce a warrant, we will hack him down. If the house is surrounded, as he says, it is by the miscreants in his pay."

This speech had the desired effect.

"The warrant—the warrant!" was howled on every side.

"I have no written warrant," was Dudley's reply, amid a savage yell; "but here is warrant enough," and he pointed to Number Sixteen.

"Warrant enough!" said one. "What do you mean, fool?"

"I am, indeed, warrant enough," said Number Sixteen; "and I am witness, too."

So saying, the speaker threw off hat and mask, and stood revealed.

It was Elizabeth—Queen of England!

No cry was uttered by any of the conspirators.

They were for some moments paralyzed.

And there stood the queen—fully attired as a man—erect, calm, and firm. Presently Elizabeth said—

"I have done a duty to my Crown and my people; for thus, unexpectedly, I have, as it were, swooped down on a nest of vultures, who considered that they had my kingdom before them, and were discussing how best to divide it. 'Death to Elizabeth,' my lords, eh? By the heaven above me, you shall have the full value for those words. Take off those masks, I command you!"

"'THE HOUSE IS FILLED WITH THE QUEEN'S TROOPS!' CRIED RALEIGH."

The command was at once obeyed.

"Come hither, Raleigh!" cried Elizabeth; "and you, Dudley Herbert, collect the weapons of these double-dyed traitors! Never again shall hilt be held within their grasp."

Raleigh was just without the hall.

He no sooner heard the expected command than he entered the room, which then became filled with soldiers.

"One moment," said the queen. "According to the plans here laid down, and also according to what Montague has said, there are thousands of my soldiers ready to break out into revolt, and to follow their leaders—these now present, many of whom I had considered my most faithful servants.

"Soldiers, is this true? Are there thousands of your comrades ready to revolt against me, their lawful queen?"

"No!" was the emphatic reply, and this was instantly followed by a loud ringing shout—

"Long live the queen!"

The vaulted roof rang again with it, and the cry was caught up by the other men, and again and again, to the utter confusion of the traitors, came the shout—

"Long live the queen!"

Elizabeth leapt from the chair.

"I feel satisfied," she said—"I feel assured that my army is as true as my people."

The weapons of the conspirators were now taken from them.

"I trust, gentlemen," said Raleigh, "that none of you will be so foolish as to attempt the least resistance. If I have your promises to this effect, it will not be necessary to bind you."

All declared that they would offer no resistance.

"The indignity of binding can be spared them," said Elizabeth, "with one exception—and that exception is Marcus Montague.

"Montague, you are indeed a villain of the deepest dye; and I for so long proved your best friend! Attempt not to kneel to me; you shall kneel to the block, sirrah! I will not spare you—nay, did my crown, my very life depend upon it, I would not spare you."

Turning to Dudley, she said—

"Master Herbert, you need not accompany me to the Tower. A few men are all I require. Ah, what means that?"

A sound as of hundreds of persons shouting was heard.

"The public have got to hear of what is transpiring," said Raleigh, to whom one of the captains had been whispering, "and have collected about the premises."

"Is it, then, now known that I am here?"

"One of the soldiers unfortunately whispered it, your majesty, and the news spread like wildfire."

"Unfortunately? No, let us hope not. Dudley Herbert, pass forth, and let us see the spirit of these people."

Dudley at once went forth, and in a few seconds the cry of "Long live the queen!" was once more heard; and this time it was repeated again and again, and with tremendous power.

Elizabeth's face flushed with triumph as she said—

"Is this a proof of the correctness of your statements, my lords? Raleigh, to your and Dudley's safe custody I commit these traitors."

Raleigh bowed low as Elizabeth, proudly erect, passed out of the room and made her way to the entrance of the house.

She was instantly recognised, and

loud and long were the cheers that greeted her.

The people seemed frantic with excitement.

As the queen, amid thunders of applause, stood on the threshold, an elderly gentleman stepped forward and took her hand.

It was Master Rodney.

At once recognising him, Elizabeth said—

"You have done well in this dreadful affair, Master Rodney. You shall not be forgotten."

"Gracious madam," said the old man, "I entreat of you to allow me to accompany you to the Tower."

"Thankful indeed will I be of your good companionship, Master Rodney. I accept your offer."

The wondrous news had indeed spread like wildfire, for the streets were lined with thousands of people.

The noise of those in the streets had attracted the attention of those in the houses, and the windows were full of eager faces.

As the queen passed along, the cheers were continuous, and they ceased not until the Tower was reached.

There the queen was met by the lieutenant, as well as by the whole of her maids, and the officers on duty.

"The messenger has arrived, your majesty," said the lieutenant.

"The messenger!"

"Yes, to say that the capture has been effected."

"Ah, good! Whose thoughtfulness was that?"

"Master Herbert's, may it please you."

"And you have made all preparations?"

"We have, your majesty."

"Who is at Traitor's Gate?"

"Lomew, your grace. Colvert, the usual custodian, is absent."

The queen started.

"The headsman!" she muttered. "Lomew! Ah, I remember. Well, well, he is a very fitting custodian."

* * * *

In the meantime, Dudley and Raleigh were active in their preparations; but since each conspirator was placed in charge of four soldiers, these preparations for departure occupied some considerable time.

The ears of the traitors were assailed by the shouts and yells of the people without.

The populace were becoming impatient for the appearance of the conspirators.

Many of the traitors fairly shivered, and it was only Raleigh's repeated assurances that the soldiers would see they were not roughly handled by the mob, which at all lessened their fears.

Montague, looking completely crushed, had been standing far back in a corner, his hands clenched before him and his head bent upon his breast.

Thus he had remained for some time, apparently oblivious of all that was passing around him.

At one sudden and unexpected stroke all his great ambitions had been rudely shattered; he was now a prisoner, soon to be placed upon his trial as chief of the conspirators, sentenced, and beheaded by his old enemy, and all his possessions would pass into the hands of his hated and detested relative, Dudley Herbert.

It was while he thus thought that a loud, sharp voice cried out—

"Stand erect, Marcus Montague."

Montague started, lifted his head, and fixed his eyes on the speaker.

It was the very person of whom he had been thinking—Dudley Herbert.

"Stand erect," repeated Dudley. "Stand erect, you king of plotters. Marcus Montague, the hour of vengeance has come. Long ago you could have been slain, but this hour was waited for. Traitor's Gate has claimed you at last."

"You thus speak to me," hissed Montague, "because you see that I am unarmed."

"You well know that you lie; but even were you armed, I would not cross swords with a prince of traitors.

"Bind his hands firmly behind his back," went on Dudley, addressing the soldiers; "and be careful that when the prisoners are taken hence, a link is held close to this traitor's face, so that the populace may the better see him."

Montague groaned.

What if the crowd should break through the guard, he thought, and precipitating themselves upon him, tear him to pieces?

He shivered violently.

For a moment he looked at Dudley's stern face, and seemed as if about to ask some favour.

But whatever it was he had thought of, it was quickly dispelled, for with a deep groan, he placed his hands in position behind his back.

In another few minutes all was ready for departure.

One of the prisoners asked Raleigh how they were about to go to the Tower, and the whole of them were thunderstruck to receive the reply—

"Your lordships are now about to proceed to Whitehall. At the steps two of the queen's barges are in waiting to convey you to the Tower."

Here was proof positive that a remarkably clever counterplot had been in progress.

As they filed out of the building, closely guarded by the troops, each was greeted with a tremendous yell.

But when Montague, who came last, made his appearance, a more terrific cry than ever left the lips of the excited people.

Try how they would, the people could not learn the names of those captured, with the exception of Montague.

His name was on everyone's lips, and it was howled out in every direction.

So threatening became the attitude of the now vast crowd, that even Dudley and Raleigh became fearful lest Montague should be torn to pieces.

Raleigh had to call a halt, and turning to the people, threatened that if they persisted in obstructing their progress, he should be compelled to order his men to fire.

Whitehall Steps were at length reached, and quickly the prisoners were placed in the barges.

The soldiers taking their places, the order was given, and amid a wilder and more determined yell than ever, accompanied by volleys of abuse, the boats moved off.

Ere they were out of sight, yet another shout awoke the echoes of the night.

Away it rolled from shore to shore, from vessel to vessel, and from house to house.

It was the joyous shout of—

"Long live the queen!"

* * * *

Traitor's Gate.

The gloomy arch was reached at last.

The journey occupied over an hour, and that hour seemed like six to every one of the wretched prisoners.

When the old bridge had been passed—and that was not without the greatest difficulty, so swollen was the river—every prisoner turned his eyes eagerly towards the dreaded gate.

The whole of the Tower was in darkness, but just before Traitor's Gate was reached, one of the soldiers blew a shrill call on a bugle, and instantly the fortress was illuminated.

The whole of the battlements, as if by magic, became filled with armed men, whose arms glistened and flashed in the rays of the flaming links.

Then was heard the voice of Sir Edward Warner, the lieutenant—

"With all the power of your voices, my men."

Again and again the soldiers shouted—

"God save the queen!"

It was indeed a moment of bitter humiliation to these prisoners, caught thus red-handed by the queen herself.

Presently was heard a harsh, grating sound.

It was the levers of the ponderous water-gate being turned by strong arms.

Slowly the folding-gates opened inward, and there, on the steps, was seen a crowd of officers, soldiers, and warders, while here and there was the face of a curious maid.

There was no escape for the traitors—their doom was sealed.

The most striking figure of all was that of a man standing at the water's edge.

It was a well-known figure—a figure clad in tight-fitting black—the figure of Lomew.

The first barge was emptied and taken back, and then the second was pulled up to the steps, and, amid a scene of indescribable excitement, the prisoners were landed.

But Lomew never moved.

His eyes were fixed upon a bowed figure in the stern of the barge—that of Marcus Montague.

Beside him stood Dudley and Raleigh.

"Rise!" said Dudley. "Rise, Marcus Montague; you have reached the spot where you caused my brother to be murdered!"

"Maybe he cannot move without aid," said Lomew, "and I am the one to aid him."

"Away!" yelled Montague, suddenly starting to his feet. "Away! Touch me not, you foul haunter of dungeons."

"Come forth," replied Lomew, dragging him out of the barge. "Traitor and murderer, I have an axe which has long waited for you."

"What dungeon is for Montague?" asked Raleigh of the lieutenant.

Sir Edward consulted a sheet of paper.

"The Stone Chamber below the moat," was the low reply.

Those who heard it shuddered, for that terrible place was but too well known.

Each prisoner was now rapidly conveyed to his cell, and the Tower was, so far as the exterior was concerned, once more in darkness.

Montague, on learning where he was to be confined, dropped like a log on to the stones, and he was allowed to remain there until the whole of the other prisoners had been thrust into their dungeons.

Then he was told to rise.

He tried to obey, but he found himself unable; terror had taken away his strength.

So three or four of the soldiers

dragged him up and carried him to his cell.

He was followed, not only by the lieutenant, but also by Dudley, Raleigh, Lomew, and Quicksilver.

"At last you are here, Marcus Montague," said the headsman; "and you will go hence but twice. The first time will be to your trial, and the second to the block; and I thank heaven that I have been spared to strike off the head of such a vile traitor as you. And mark it well, Montague—with your death, Dudley Herbert comes into his own. Villain, what has become of your boasting, and all your plotting? What are all worth now? Stay in this vile hole, and think of all this; and think, too, that the author of the counterplot is Dudley Herbert."

Montague made no reply.

He did not even look up.

Backward and forward he rocked himself, groaning dismally, nor did he stir until the door closed upon him with a heavy clang.

"Her majesty," said the lieutenant, "has summoned those of her statesmen who chance to be in London, and she directed me to tell you to meet her in the conference-chamber. I congratulate both of you, Dudley and Raleigh. You are worthy of the distinction which the queen will certainly confer upon you."

CHAPTER XXII.

IN WHICH THIS ROMANCE COMES TO A CONCLUSION.

THE trial of the "Compton House Conspirators" took place in Westminster Hall.

The chief witnesses were Dudley, Raleigh, Master Rodney, Merlin, and his cousin Mary.

Of the twenty-one prisoners, extenuating circumstances were seen in the cases of sixteen, and these included Delasart and Bushby.

The sixteen had their estates confiscated, and they were banished from the country for ever.

The five others were condemned to death, and Montague was one of the five.

The four noblemen received the sentence of death with calmness, and with dignity, but Montague received the announcement of his doom like a thorough coward.

The bitterest ordeal through which he passed, as he stood in that vast hall, the observed of all, was the reading of the documents penned by the hand of his late factotum, Barber.

In those documents was an account of Montague's chief doings for years, and of Barber's share in them.

The account of the horrible murder of the beautiful "Windsor Rose" called forth loud and bitter cries of execration—cries before which the brutal prisoner shrank as before the scathing lightning.

Barber had given the names and addresses in full of those who had had to do with the affairs of which he wrote. We do not mean that they were participators in the various plots, but that they unwittingly assisted. And these persons were brought forward.

What they said satisfied all that the documents, though full of false statements, were in the main true.

Still, Montague having been sentenced to death, the documents were of no use except to fill the public with a greater loathing of the villain than before.

A week after the trial, the conspirators suffered death on Tower Hill.

It was about eight of the clock in the morning that the execution took place.

On the pretty green stood the scaffold, with the block in the centre.

Around this was a troop of mounted soldiers.

There were three or four rows of beefeaters, and as far as the eye could reach, to the right and to the left, were thousands of sightseers.

Beside the scaffold stood Dudley and Raleigh, commanding a portion of the troops, while at the foot of the scaffold steps sat Quicksilver.

When eight o'clock struck the first prisoner was brought forward, amid, save for the solemn tolling of the chapel bell, the most profound silence.

The ceremony enacted on the fatal boards was very brief.

Each prisoner acknowledged the justness of the sentence passed upon him, and asked the pardon of his Heavenly Father and his queen.

One after the other their heads were stricken off by the masked headsman, Jerome Lomew.

At last Montague came forward, and he was instantly greeted with loud and prolonged yells.

It was with the greatest difficulty that he reached the block.

Indeed it was necessary for the warders to render him support.

The lieutenant having informed him that he had the privilege of addressing the vast crowd if he thought fit, Montague tottered to the rail.

But so furious were the people, so loud were the shouts, that any word he might have said was lost.

His starting eyes travelled slowly over the sea of faces, and finally they rested upon the face of Dudley Herbert, who stood beside the scaffold, and whose eyes were fixed upon him.

"I should be a coward to mock him in his last moments," said our hero to Raleigh, who stood beside him, as calm and as collected as though nothing out of the ordinary was proceeding.

"Yes, my friend," replied Raleigh. "However great a villain a man may have been, we should always respect his last moments on earth, especially in circumstances such as these.

"Your moments of grace have expired," said a deep voice in Montague's ear; "shall I bind your eyes?"

A heavy hand fell upon the traitor's shoulder, and Montague turned to find the headsman beside him.

"Bind my eyes!" he faltered, "Yes, bind them if you will. But ask not my forgiveness, for I will give you my malediction."

"The malediction of a traitor carries no weight," was the reply; "but do not think that I had intended to formally ask you for forgiveness."

In another minute the traitor-in-chief had laid his head on the block.

Many hundreds of persons now noticed that Lomew opened a leathern case, and brought out a brand-new axe.

It was a fine weapon, which flashed and glittered in the rays of the sun.

But none, except our characters, knew that the axe had for a long time past been reserved for Marcus Montague.

"It is in my power to make you suffer," whispered Lomew to the kneeling traitor, "but I shall prove more merciful than you ever proved in your life."

The word was given, the axe flashed for an instant in the sunshine, and then with one blow it severed Montague's head from his body.

The head was held aloft, amid a storm of hisses and groans, and then—the last act was over.

* * * *

Another month passed away, and we find ourselves once more at Richmond.

Garth Castle was *en fête*.

Never before, in the course of its long existence, had it presented so grand an appearance.

The reason was that two weddings were to take place: one between Dudley and Madeline, and the other between Raleigh and Margaretta.

Elizabeth herself had promised to be present, and the arrangements for her reception, and that of her lords and ladies whom she had selected to accompany her, had already been carried out.

Every one of those principals who have taken part in this romance was invited, and all came, with four exceptions, these being Jameson, his wife, and Captain Nutt, with his nephew Solomon.

The first two had been entirely satisfied by splendid presents received from the queen on account of the recovery of the treasure (now safely stored in the State coffers), and from Dudley.

The two latter had gone on another voyage.

Richmond looked splendid! At all the principal points triumphal arches were erected, while cannon had been mounted on the battlements of the castle.

It was about four o'clock in the afternoon when the queen's cavalcade was sighted, not only by hundreds of expectant eyes within the castle, but by thousands without, and cheer after cheer arose.

There was nothing to mar the splendour of the cavalcade, nor the magnificence of the reception, for the sun shone out most gloriously, while there was just breeze enough to gently sway the banners which were placed at every prominent point.

Master Rodney stood at the head of the party to receive the queen, and behind him were Dudley, Raleigh, Madeline, Margaretta, and the others.

Elizabeth was conducted to the pretty little chapel where the minister was in waiting.

The ceremonies were at once proceeded with and quietly carried out.

For the first time for many a year, Lady Herbert's face was wreathed in smiles.

"I have been looking all around me for some time," said Elizabeth, "and I miss one whom I fully expected would be here."

"And that person, your majesty?" asked Raleigh.

"Is little Quicksilver," replied the queen. "He left the Tower some day or two previous to our departure. Pray heaven nothing has happened to him."

"I can assure your majesty," said Lomew, who came up at the moment, "that he will be here very soon."

At this moment a mighty shout was heard, and all eyes were bent in the direction of the highway.

In the centre ot the road a little coach was approaching the castle.

Its gilt top glittered in the sunshine.

As also did the gilt and silver ornaments on the six small white ponies by which it was drawn.

On the backs of the first and second ponies rode two little boys, dressed as postillions.

"In the name of all that is wonderful," laughed Elizabeth, "who is this?"

"Quicksilver, your highness," replied Lomew.

"Quicksilver! I am surprised! And who, in heaven's name, provided him with this small, but costly equipage?"

"Dudley Herbert, your majesty," replied Raleigh. "It is the first portion of a present promised him long since."

"And the second part of the present—what will that be?"

"Your majesty will pardon me if I beg of you to wait a short time," said Dudley, with a smile.

In a few moments the little coach drove up the great drive, and a passage was at once made for the occupant to advance to the queen.

The little minstrel was most graciously received by her majesty, and then the whole party adjourned to the banqueting hall.

There was upon the table one article which commanded the attention of everyone present.

It looked like a large box, covered with a handsome rug.

Elizabeth asked no questions concerning this singular article for a banqueting table, but she cast many eager and curious glances towards it.

The bounteous repast having been partaken of, Dudley rose.

"Your majesty," he said, "may I crave a favour at your hands?"

"Certainly," was the reply.

"It is a singular one," went on Dudley. "I beg you will allow Quicksilver to mount the table."

The queen laughed merrily at this idea, and so did everyone else.

Quicksilver himself laughed not at all.

He was wondering what this could be for.

"Such a favour is at once granted," said Elizabeth.

Thereupon the cloth and other needless articles were removed, and Dudley lifted Quicksilver upon the table.

And very brave the little fellow looked in his magnificent costume and his diamond-buckled shoes.

He was greeted with perfect thunders of applause, and he bowed gracefully on all sides.

"The second part of the present, your majesty," said Dudley, "is now about to be given. It is contained in this box."

So saying, Dudley took off the rug and disclosed a very handsomely-mounted oak box, the top of which was well perforated.

Quicksilver became very grave as he looked at it.

What sort of present could be contained in this box? he wondered.

Amid a deep silence Dudley raised the lid.

But nothing for the moment was seen, except a mass of fleecy wool.

Slowly Dudley raised this, and then there arose the tiny figure of a lady.

It was Anne.

She was beautifully dressed in pale blue satin, while her hair blazed with magnificent diamonds, part of the contents of the box left by her father.

Dudley held out his hand and aided Anne from the box.

Gracefully bowing on all sides, she next looked at Dudley for instructions.

Quicksilver was petrified with astonishment.

And not he alone, for the queen and all those not in the secret were also astonished.

So amazed indeed was Elizabeth, that she uttered not a single word.

"Quicksilver," said Dudley, "I promised you a grand present; I said it would be one which would astonish and please you. Though you have never before seen each other, this little lady has seen a sketch of you; she has also received a very high character of you, and if you will have her she is ready to become your devoted wife."

At this speech all silence came to an end, and loud cheers rang out.

Quicksilver advanced in the most gallant fashion, bowed gracefully, and offered his tiny hand, which was taken in a still tinier one.

"Salute your future wife, Master Quicksilver," laughed Elizabeth, "or you incur our displeasure."

Quicksilver did not require to be twice told.

He kissed the little lady on both cheeks, and his caress was returned with an earnestness which had the effect of calling forth another loud burst of cheering."

"A prettier match was never made," exclaimed Elizabeth.

"Nor a smaller, your majesty," said Raleigh.

"Even so. But I will show you how we acknowledge this matter. Descend, Master Quicksilver. But stay; first let Lomew tell the story as to the little man. I am told that he is his adopted son."

Lomew thereupon told the story, and it was added to by that of Anne, all of which proved deeply interesting to everyone.

Then Quicksilver was lifted off the table.

"Kneel, Quicksilver," said Elizabeth. "Dudley Herbert, your sword."

Dudley drew his blade, and handed it to her majesty, who laid the glittering weapon on Quicksilver's shoulder, saying—

"In the name of heaven and St. George, we dub thee knight. Be faithful, brave, and fortunate. Arise, Sir Quicksilver; for thus will you be hereafter known."

Quicksilver arose amid loud cheers.

"We have not yet done," said Elizabeth. "Come hither, John Garth, and kneel."

The master of the castle at once went forward, and he was dubbed knight in like manner.

He also was greeted with ringing cheers.

"As to you, Dudley Herbert," said Elizabeth, "you will assume your father's title and property—that will be undisputed, since the traitor Montague is no more; and you, as well as Raleigh, shall have a high position in our councils. And now let the revels proceed."

* * * *

Elizabeth's promise was fulfilled.

Lord Dudley Herbert attained a very high position—a position shared by his beautiful wife.

Raleigh rose, too, but it is not necessary in this romance to relate his dreadful end.

Master Rodney became a far greater favourite than ever.

His successful experiments became known not only in England, but over all the civilised world; and when, full of honours, he died, he was succeeded by no less a person than Merlin, to whom he had taught his profession, and left an enormous sum of money.

Lomew did not relinquish his post.

So, honoured and respected by all, a frequent guest of Dudley, Raleigh, and many another important personage, he still remained the Headsman of the Tower, as well as the chief custodian of

Traitor's Gate.

www.ingramcontent.com/pod-product-compliance
Lightning Source LLC
LaVergne TN
LVHW061243100826
845148LV00008B/1012
* 9 7 8 1 5 3 5 8 1 5 4 8 2 *